Double Hit

Chicago Cats, Book 1

Katie Steele

For Angy.
This too is volleyball. All the good and all the bad along the way.
I couldn't have done it without you.

10 Years Ago

"What's the matter?"

Kai startled a little at the question, the fabric of the quilt he was leaning back against catching on his hoodie as he shifted uncomfortably. He paused his game, setting his controller down in front of his crossed legs before looking up at Nicholas.

"Nothing."

Nicholas smirked down at him, head tilted to the side, one hand on his hip while the other held tight to a volleyball. Kai squirmed under his friend's intent gaze.

He could never hide anything from Nicholas.

Kai huffed out a sigh. "It really is nothing," he muttered, eyes focusing on the screen in front of him, staring at the paused game as though he could find a way into it to escape this line of questioning.

"Kai." Nicholas' voice was sharp, but not unkind. Never unkind. Nicholas squatted down next to him, shifting to hold the volleyball between both hands. "Just tell me what's wrong. You've barely said anything to me all day."

A sideways glance showed a hint of hurt in his friend's expression. Shame filled Kai, twisted his gut and made his fingers clinch around the ends of his sleeves. They had planned to spend today together, playing video games just

1

like they always did.

Like they always *had*.

These days occurred less and less often with every passing month, every passing year. And even planning this one in advance, Nicholas still had to leave earlier than usual to go play the *new* game that had taken over his life. Over *their* lives.

It wasn't an official practice. If it were, Kai would be going as well, falling into his new role as setter more naturally than he'd expected to. No, this wasn't a true practice like the ones they'd both be starting soon for the summer league they'd joined. Nicholas was just dedicated. He spent time every day bettering himself when it came to volleyball. It wasn't for nothing, the results were clear in his play style, in the way he was becoming a force to be reckoned with on the court, one of the best emerging middle blockers in their league.

So Kai couldn't fault him. He didn't fault him.

He did miss him though. Some days more than others.

Nicholas was still staring, those sharp, hazel eyes piercing Kai, pinning him in place. Just like a cat with its prey. Kai let out a harsh sigh through his nose, rolling his eyes.

"It's silly." His voice betrayed him , more emotion slipping out than he wanted. Nicholas tilted his head forward, pushing Kai on.

"I've just been…" Kai paused to screw up his courage. Was he really about to admit it out loud? "I've been worried you're going to move on."

Nicholas' expression changed, slipping into something a little more questioning, confusion scrunching his eyes up.

"Move on?"

"Gah!" Kai curled in on himself, his long bangs curtaining his face as he hunched his shoulders forward. Nicholas was really going to make him say it. Why couldn't he just read between the lines?

"From me, Nicky." Kai's words were mumbled, and a part of him hoped that maybe Nicholas wouldn't even hear them, would just shrug it all off and move on with his day.

"You think I'll move on from you?"

Kai couldn't see his friend, not with the way he was curled up, hiding from this conversation and the realities it brought to the surface. A hand brushed his shoulder, sending a shiver through his entire body. Something else he would ignore for the time being, the way every touch from his friend had turned into something electric recently. Something new, something Kai didn't know what to do about.

That same hand brushed Kai's hair back, long fingers finding his chin and tilting it so their eyes could meet once again.

"Kai." Nicholas' smirk was gone, all teasing wiped away from his expression. He went through most of life unserious, and Kai knew that when his friend was being sincere... well, it meant a lot. It meant Nicholas cared about this.

"You're in my life," Nicholas continued, shaking his head. Kai couldn't help but notice the way his messy bangs shifted over one eye. He wanted to reach out, push that dark hair back so he could feel the full weight of the other boy's gaze on him, even if it felt like he was being held open and exposed to the world. "You're a part of me, of who I am. You're there in every decision I make. You're my best friend, just because we're together less doesn't mean I'll ever forget about you."

Kai could feel the weight of truth in the words, could see it reflected in those piercing hazel eyes. And he knew, deep down, he really knew that what they had wasn't something easily broken. They had been friends, twined in each other's lives for so long, tangled together in a way that couldn't simply unravel.

It wasn't really something Kai had worried about before.

Nicholas had been around for so long that it felt like he had always been there, like his presence had been embedded in Kai's life from the very beginning. It had only been recently, when volleyball had begun to become a bigger part of their lives, when new friendships were being founded and social calendars began to fill up, that Kai had felt fear at what he could lose.

Fear that Nicholas would move on to bigger and better things, leaving Kai stranded in his wake.

"Are you going to say anything?"

Nicholas' question pulled Kai out of his thoughts, away from the treacherous depths of his spinning mind. He knew he needed to respond, needed to voice some sort of reassurance. Even if the sentiment was false, even if he was still terrified of a life without his closest friend. A life without the boy he was probably falling a little in love with.

It was hard. Always so hard to find his voice, to find the right words to express his feelings whenever he was put on the spot like this. Hard to push past those feelings when they were choking him, welling up in his throat and making it nearly impossible to speak.

Kai finally shrugged.

"I think I'm just tired," he said, fighting back warring emotions that tried to slip into the words. Nicholas was still staring intently, brows furrowed. Kai wanted to reach out, brush all traces of concern away. Instead, he picked up his controller, readying himself to get back into his game. "You're going to be late meeting the other guys."

He kept his gaze trained on the screen, hyper-focused on the enemies he was plowing down, decidedly *not* looking at the boy still crouched next to him. Kai could feel Nicholas' stare, could pinpoint the exact places that gaze trailed over the skin of his face.

After what felt like an eternity, a shift next to him had Kai finally glancing over to see Nicholas rising to his full height. He was getting so tall, leaving Kai behind in that way as well. Not that he minded. It was just another thing about his friend that Kai now found himself fixating on, the way Nicholas could look down at him and set his heart racing. Just as he was doing in that very moment, his expression slipping back into one of mischief, that trademark cheshire grin overtaking his features. He reached out a hand, ruffling Kai's hair and earning himself a scowl as he turned to leave. Kai hit pause on his game one more time.

"Are we still on for Saturday?" He couldn't help but throw the question out, almost wincing at the slight desperation in his voice. Nicholas paused in the doorway before turning back. His smile was wide, true and happy and the most beautiful smile Kai had ever seen.

"Of course!" Excitement laced Nicholas' words. He leaned against the door frame, and Kai felt the air of the room still as he waited for his friend to continue. "I meant what I said, Kai. You've got me forever."

Kai only stared as Nicholas finally slipped into the hallway, the space he had exited holding Kai's focus long after he was left alone in the house. He waited for his pulse to settle, for his heartbeat to stop echoing in his ears, before turning back to his game. He couldn't help the small smile that played across his lips.

You've got me forever.

Kai hoped with everything he had that those words would prove true.

1

Present day

Atticus knew it was his own fault that everyone held a certain image of him. That didn't mean he had to be happy about it.

He could pretend, though. Just for the night. Sulking about a negative reputation he had earned for himself over the years while attending Orion Harper's surprise going away party wasn't good friend behavior.

Three comments already, and he'd only been at the party for fifteen minutes.

Got your eye on anyone tonight?

Didn't you hook up with him once?

Atticus Mills doesn't let anyone tie him down, isn't that right?

Atticus just smiled through it all, playing the part everyone expected of him. Slick grins and hungry eyes. That easy, fuckboy air he'd perfected years ago.

It didn't seem to matter that he hadn't slept with anyone in months. Hadn't left a party with someone on his arm, hadn't been spotted out and about with a new fling-of-the-week in ages.

It seemed as though the whole world had an image of Attie Mills in mind, carved into stone, and no amount of *good* behavior on his part could change that.

Atticus drifted toward the bar at the far end of the crowded room. Julian Tate, rival setter for the Los Angeles Comets, had rented out the event space, and Atticus was impressed with the planning that had gone into the surprise. As far as he knew, no-one had spoiled anything for the man of the hour. He wondered if Julian had threatened people. Atticus wouldn't put it past him.

The man in question was also at the bar, finally relaxing. Everything seemed in place as the last few invitees arrived. All that was left was for Ori to finally show up.

"I hate to admit it," Atticus said, sidling up next to Julian, leaning casually on the bar. "But you did good. He's gonna love all this."

Julian smirked, eyes sly as he gave Atticus a once-over. He would never say it out loud, but he'd always found Ori's friend to be a *little* intimidating. Julian was imposing, both on the court and off, with those broad shoulders and that piercing, brown-eyed stare that Atticus thought could maybe *actually* see into his mind and read his thoughts. So very different from Ori's sunny personality in so many ways.

"Thanks," Julian said, tipping his glass of wine against his lips.

"Think he figured it out?"

Julian shook his head. "He's weirdly easy to keep things from, never questioned anything. I'm more worried about Parker spilling something trying to get him here."

Atticus laughed, accepting a beer from the bartender and taking a long pull from it. It was cheap, and tasted truly awful. He made sure to snap a picture of the bottle, firing off a text to his twin that would have her eyes rolling for sure. Sammie, beer snob that she was, hated when he pretended to enjoy the domestic shit. "Theo will keep him in line, don't worry."

Silence fell between them as Julian went back to his wine, and Atticus took the opportunity to scan the growing crowd. Many familiar faces, as well as a few he only recognized from pictures Ori had shown him over the years they had played together for the Chicago Wildcats. The man had *a lot* of friends. And it seemed as though every single one of them had turned out to see him off to California, where he would soon be playing for the Los Angeles Comets.

It was still jarring, thinking about Ori playing for a rival team. Surreal that at the start of pre-season they had been practicing their favorite quick set together. Trades were never exactly a fun experience, but the one that had resulted in Ori being sent across the country felt like a particularly nasty deal.

"Does he even know you're here?" Atticus asked, eyes still scanning the crowd.

Julian chuckled. He'd flown in the night before from LA. "He doesn't."

"He'll love that surprise then." Atticus flicked his gaze from face to face, failing to find one in particular. He was glad Ori would have a familiar face among his new teammates.

"Looking for someone special?" A knowing smirk lit Julian's face, his brows raised in question.

"Nope," Atticus said, popping his lips around the word. "Don't know what you're talking about."

Julian nodded his head, pointing with his wine glass in the same direction. "He's right there."

Atticus couldn't help himself, his eyes following his heart instead of his mind, his gaze finally landing on the person he'd been searching for.

Kai Reid stood off toward the edge of the milling crowd, a clear drink in his hand paired with a bored stare on his face as those clever amber eyes took in everything around him. He wasn't a wallflower. No, Kai wasn't standing on the outskirts as someone shy, someone excluded and awkward. Atticus knew the only reason Kai was even at this party was because he loved his friend, and he would weather pretty much anything for Ori.

Even the tedium of social interaction.

Atticus felt something tighten in his chest. Kai looked *gorgeous*. Shoulder-length dark hair pulled back in a low bun, hiding most of the pink that tipped the ends, exposing the soft lines of his face and the slender tilt of his neck. He wore a black blazer over a simple gray shirt, tailored to perfection in a way that emphasized his slim waist. Atticus' mind chose that moment to provide a *vivid* recollection of how it had felt to grasp that waist. Soft skin under his hands as Kai writhed above him...

A sharp laugh pulled Atticus out of the memory. It was probably for the best.

"Ori told me you had it bad," Julian said, laughter still lacing his words. "I didn't realize it was this bad."

Atticus could feel a pout pulling at his lips as he finally tore his eyes away from Kai. "*Ori* is a little gossip."

Julian snorted at that. "More like he blurts things out before he thinks better of it."

Atticus grinned as Julian brought his glass back up for another sip. "Does that mean he told you about the time he and I hooked up on the floor of the practice gym court?"

Julian nearly spit out his wine, choking a bit and coughing loudly. Atticus laughed, patting him on the back, not failing to miss the flash in the other man's eyes. Something he would almost label as jealousy.

"You're as bad as he is," Julian said after he finally gained control of his breathing.

"Hey." Atticus let his expression slip into a mischievous

smirk. "Maybe the two of you could recreate the moment while you're here. He still has a key to the gym!" A pause as he let his grin turn a little more teasing. "Who knows, maybe for you it'll turn into more than a hook up."

Julian's face turned an adorable shade of pink. Atticus thought it looked good on him.

"Maybe you're right about him being a little gossip," Julian said, frowning into his wine before side-eyeing Atticus. There was that fire that always made Atticus squirm a little. And sure, maybe he'd earned it with that comment.

Julian looked as though he were about to say something when another voice yanked their attention away.

"Who's a little gossip?" Bowen Kelly, wing spiker for the Cats, beamed as he slung an arm around Atticus' shoulders. Julian narrowed his eyes at the question.

"If I remember correctly," he said, "you are."

"Me? No, never. I'm offended, Tate!"

Atticus shoved his teammate's face away. "This is another one that's missing the brain-to-mouth filter." Bowen only laughed, releasing his hold on Atticus and running a hand through dark hair that curled around his ears. His early grays streaked through and shone in the low light of the bar, glinting along with the ring pierced through one dark brow. A ring he always forgot to take out before practice, only remembering whenever Coach Rodriguez chewed him out for it. Bowen's laughter was infectious, it always was, and neither Atticus nor Julian could resist grinning along with him.

"When have I ever gossiped?" Bowen asked, feigning hurt as one hand pressed over his heart. Atticus pinned him with a bored stare.

"Oh." Bowen's expression turned sheepish. "I guess I did tell the entire bus that time you hooked up with those two models when we played that tournament in Paris."

Atticus continued to eye him as Julian snickered next to them.

"And there was the time I accidentally told coach about you and that one chick in his office."

Atticus raised a brow.

"And that other time that I tweeted about your walk of shame the morning after the Hawks shut us down." Bowen frowned and rubbed his chin as Atticus nodded. "Maybe I do gossip a lot."

Atticus patted his back. "It's okay, we love you despite your flaws."

"Not to victim blame here," Bowen said after a moment, eyes playful as he poked Atticus. "But you make it too easy. You give us too much to talk about!" Bowen turned to Julian, who raised a brow. "He's a menace. Especially abroad. We can't stop him, so we don't even try anymore."

Atticus knew his friend was teasing, knew that Bowen didn't mean any harm. But he struggled to laugh along, struggled to keep a frown from forming on his face.

Because it hurt. Maybe not a lot, but enough for Atticus to bring his cheap beer back to his lips to hide his dismay. Sure, his past was full of casual hook-ups and short-lived flings that he hadn't even attempted to hide. But he'd thought that his team, the people he spent more time with than anyone… he'd thought that *they* would have at least noticed a difference in his behavior by now.

Atticus could feel Julian's stare burning a hole in his cheek, could perfectly picture his narrowed eyes and knowing expression as Bowen continued. "Gotta go, coach looks like he's about to knock Carpenter on his ass again!" Eric Carpenter, their libero, had a tendency to let his mouth run just far enough to get him in trouble. Maybe it was a Cats thing. Not a single one of them knew when to shut the fuck up. Just as quickly as he'd arrived, Bowen zipped off, heading across the room toward their coach.

Taking another long pull from his beer, Atticus purposely avoided the stare of the man next to him.

"Why don't you say anything?"

Julian's question was sharp as a dagger, but the violence didn't seem directed at Atticus. It felt more like those words were fighting *for* him.

"People are gonna think what they think." Atticus shrugged. "I made my bed, now I've got to sleep in it."

"You know..." The sudden softness of Julian's words finally pulled Atticus' eyes back toward him. "I sort of get it. It's hard to change people's perceptions when they've already made up their minds."

"Exactly." Atticus tipped his nearly empty bottle toward the other man. "Too much trouble to fight a losing battle."

Julian quirked his lips, contemplation softening his features. "You could easily just prove them all wrong by finally making a move, you know."

Atticus couldn't help himself, his eyes betraying him yet again by snapping his focus across the room, landing back on Kai.

"You think I haven't been trying?" Atticus watched Kai get pulled into a conversation by the very man who had just left their sides. Bowen animatedly said something that had both Kai and Coach Rodriguez rolling their eyes.

"Have you told him exactly how you feel about him?"

Atticus huffed. "Well. No. But I can't just say it. He just wants to be friends, so friends we are."

Just friends. For what felt like so long now. At some point over the last six months, Atticus had resigned himself to living out the rest of his life planted firmly in the friend zone. It felt an awful lot like being stuck on the bench his freshman year of college, just waiting for his team to give him a chance on the court. If he could just get his hands on the ball, he knew he could always set it perfectly.

But no, Atticus was sure he wouldn't be getting that chance. Not again. Didn't matter that his feelings never seemed to dull, never seemed to fade with time. Not since the night they'd spent together. The single best night of his life.

Atticus had always had a thing for his favorite streamer, NotYourKitten. Had always made sure his notifications were turned on so that he would never miss a single alert that the cute gamer was going live. It had been a shock, to say the least, to find out that the small time celebrity he had a silly little crush on was the very same Kai that Ori happened to be best friends with. They'd grown up two towns apart, had bonded over volleyball. Had stayed friends long after Kai had left the sport to focused his efforts on gaming.

Cut to several months after Ori caught Atticus watching one of Kai's streams, and the pro-gamer had finally agreed to go out with him. One date, one night.

Atticus hadn't stopped thinking about Kai since then.

Months of pining, something Atticus hadn't even realized he was capable of.

They hadn't hooked up again after that first time, had instead settled into an easy friendship. Countless evenings of online gaming, a few meals out together here and there. It didn't matter that one night with Kai had changed something in Atticus, because it clearly hadn't affected him the same way. And while Kai had also remained single for the entire duration of their friendship, Atticus knew he wasn't available. Not really.

"I'm going up front," Julian said, pulling Atticus from his thoughts. The brunette looked at his phone before downing the last of his wine and placing the glass on the bar top. "Parker said they just pulled up." He began to walk away before turning his sharp gaze back on Atticus one last time.

"I'm telling you this in more of a 'do as I say, not as I do' kind of way," Julian said, smirking. "But I think you should just tell him how you feel."

Atticus nearly squirmed at Julian's words as he turned away, heading off to surprise the man of the hour. A part of him knew that Julian was right. But it was much easier said than done, something Atticus was acutely aware of.

His gaze drifted back to Kai again, his heart tripping as a small smile formed on the those rosebud lips at something Bowen said to the group.

It wasn't like Atticus hadn't considered just telling Kai everything. Telling him how he thought about him constantly, how he didn't see anyone else anymore because all he could see was Kai. How he always looked forward to the times when they would end their nights with an hour or two of playing some mindless shooter together online, how his pulse raced at hearing Kai's voice over his mic. With every thought, every decision he made, he always found a way to factor Kai in, all in the hopes that he would maybe, *maybe* be more than just a friend one day.

But because they *were* friends, because Atticus *knew* Kai... well, that was how he knew it was for the best to just keep the extent of his feelings to himself.

Because Kai simply was not available.

As though some cosmic entity were pulling their strings, Atticus watched as the man that saturated his every thought suddenly stiffened. Kai's tiny smile disappeared completely as his eyes widened. Atticus followed Kai's stare across the room, knowing what he would see.

Ori had just arrived, smile bright as daylight as he gaped at the surprise waiting for him. And right behind him stood the couple who'd brought him to the party. Theo Whittaker and Nicholas Parker.

Nicholas. Kai's ex.

Kai downed the rest of his drink as the entire room cheered for his friend. He forced himself to keep his eyes on Ori as he flung himself toward Julian, arms wrapping tight around his middle, copper hair glinting in the low lighting. Watching his friend's joy at seeing Julian, at having an entire room packed with people there just for him, it was a pretty good distraction.

But maybe not quite good enough.

Kai couldn't help himself. His chest tightened as his eyes fell back on the two men who had arrived with Ori.

Nicholas looked good. Really good. He smiled easily, laughing as Ori almost bowled Julian over. Dark hair just as messy as ever. Kai hated how much it suited him. How it didn't clash with the sharp suit he wore, black on black, a red tie the only pop of color. The tie was crooked, of course. Nicholas was always *just* a little bit of a mess. Kai remembered the countless times he'd had to fix a collar or help tuck in a shirt. His fingers tightened on his empty glass, aching to reach out and straighten the tie.

He was still staring when long, pale fingers slipped into view. Theo Whittaker adjusted the tie, earning a sly grin from Nicholas.

Theo, who had been Kai and Ori's friend through college after he had moved to Chicago from London. He'd been Nicholas' friend too. The friend that had swooped in just months after Kai had been dumped to snatch Nicholas up.

Kai hadn't spoken to Theo either, not since the day Nicholas had announced his move to St. Louis. Not since Kai had realized Theo was the reason Nicholas had found the new teaching job, the catalyst for the end of the life Kai had grown so comfortable in.

It was time for a refill.

Kai fought back the wave of annoyance, of *pain*, as he slipped away from the group chatting around him, heading toward the bar. He was *not* going to be angsty at Ori's going away party. It didn't matter if this was the first time he'd seen as his ex in over a year.

It felt a little like the room was closing in on him, and Kai wasn't sure if it was from the anxiety of seeing Nicholas again or from the alcohol he'd already consumed. It probably wasn't a *great* idea to have another drink, since he'd already had two and hadn't eaten a thing since lunch. But Kai was sure he couldn't stomach food, not with the way his gut had been twisting into knots since he'd walked through the doors knowing full well who else would be at this party.

He wouldn't have missed it for the world. Ori was leaving, flying off to the other side of the country, and Kai suddenly wouldn't have his friend around anymore. Ori had been there for the worst parts of Kai's life, had helped him find his way back into the light. Had *been* the light. The least Kai could do was show up for his going away party.

Arms wrapped around Kai shoulders from behind as familiar laughter burst out next to his ear.

"I'm going to miss you so much." It seemed that Kai's thoughts had the ability to summon his best friend. He didn't understand how Ori had moved across the room so quickly, but it didn't matter. A different pinch in his chest, one unrelated to his messy love life, loosened within Kai as he leaned back against his friend.

"I'll miss you, too." Kai extricated himself from Ori's tight grip, turning to face him. He searched Ori's smiling face, looking for any hint of the sadness he'd seen when they'd met up two weeks prior for lunch. When Ori had hastily blurted out that he'd been traded, and would be moving so far away.

"I'm okay," Ori said, shoving Kai's shoulder, his eyes

scrunching as his grin widened.

"You sure?" Kai had a hard time believing that Ori was suddenly fine with the trade. Not after he'd seen tears fill his friend's eyes as he'd told him about it. Not after Ori had spent the better part of their meal blaming himself and the shitty season he'd had the year before.

"I'll be fine," Ori said, his expression going soft. "I'm staying with Julian until I find an apartment. We'll get to play on the beach in our spare time. It'll be fun." Another push against Kai's shoulder. "You don't need to worry about me."

It was easy to forget the other side of Ori when he was like this, when he was all smiles and optimism, when his very presence put Kai and everyone else at ease. But Kai had had a front row seat the summer before, had watched his friend fall further and further into a dark hole that had sapped him of everything that made Ori *Ori*.

Kai knew depression, knew it well. He knew how easy it was to put on a mask for the rest of the world.

And apparently he wasn't the only one worried about Ori.

Julian stood nearby, wrapped in a conversation with some other players, but his eyes flicked toward Ori more than once. Watching, waiting for any sign that the party was too much.

A drink was shoved into Ori's hands by his now ex-teammate, Bowen, who whooped something unintelligible as he continued on by. Ori frowned, nose scrunching as he sniffed the clear liquid.

Kai chuckled, taking the drink from Ori. "I'll get you something else."

"Something fruity!" Ori said hastily, as he was pulled away by more of his old teammates. Kai nodded as he downed the vodka, relishing the burn in his throat as he turned toward the bar.

Maybe it would be fine. Maybe the party would be a good enough distraction. Kai could stay focused on Ori, and could pretend there was no one else there. No one that made his chest ache and his stomach churn.

Except that his eyes found Nicholas easily, against his will. Kai *definitely* needed another drink.

He felt a little wobbly as he leaned his forearms against the bar, waiting for the bartender to notice him so he could continue making poor decisions.

"You okay?"

Kai knew that voice. He'd know it anywhere. Maybe if he'd been paying attention and hadn't been lost in his internal panic, he would have noticed who else was at the bar. Maybe he wouldn't have come over for another drink.

Or maybe he would have come over sooner.

"I'm fine." Kai turned, leveling a dry stare at Atticus' saccharine smile. Always so charming, always a hint of flirtation in those handsome features, but Kai could see sincerity in his eyes. Atticus might play dumb half the time, but he paid attention. He remembered things. He knew exactly why Kai might not want to be completely sober for this event. Atticus didn't say anything else, only raised his brows with a smirk as he looked back out at the crowd surrounding the newcomers.

Kai took a moment to study his profile. Atticus looked good; Atticus *always* looked good. It was a wonderful and frustrating fact about the man that Kai had a hard time ignoring. Leaning back against the bar, Atticus pressed his beer bottle to his lips, and Kai felt a flutter in his stomach that he blamed on the vodka. It was difficult though, denying that tug of attraction, especially when his eyes were drawn from that full bottom lip, pressed softly to the glass, down along a strong arm. Atticus wore a navy blue dress shirt, sleeves rolled up to his elbows, showing off the tattoos on his right arm, the top two shirt buttons undone casually to display the sharp lines of his collarbone. Kai's mind betrayed him, pulling up a tucked away memory of pressing his own lips to that very spot as he'd perched in the other man's lap, writhing above him in a way that had Atticus squirming and crying out…

"They're sweet, aren't they?"

The words pulled Kai out of his treacherous thoughts. He glanced back up, but Atticus' stare was still fixed across the room. Kai followed his gaze, his own landing on Ori and Julian once again. The latter was laughing, a hand resting on Ori's shoulder, lingering and gentle. Ori was beaming, because Ori was almost *always* beaming, but when he focused that look on Julian he seemed to burn just a bit brighter.

"Jealous?" Kai asked, leaning back against the bar next to Atticus, a fresh drink in hand. Atticus' brow furrowed, lips pressing into a line. "In another universe, that's you standing there with Ori."

Atticus' frown disappeared completely as he barked out a laugh.

"In no universe do Ori and me end up together."

A year ago Kai wouldn't have believed him. Atticus and Ori had been messing around together, hooking up casually, when he and Atticus had first connected. In fact, the only reason Atticus had ended up with Kai's number was because Ori had caught the other man watching his stream before one of those hookups. Had found out that Atticus had a little crush on NotYourKitten.

There had even been a time when Kai didn't understand *why* Ori never felt more for Atticus. After they had gone out and Kai had spent the night at Atticus' apartment. After he'd realized that Atticus was a lot more than just a silly himbo or shallow fuckboy.

But maybe Ori had only ever had eyes for one person, even if he still hadn't realized it. Kai sort of understood that.

"I meant you and Julian," Kai finally replied. Atticus

choked on his drink and Kai grinned into his glass.

The grin was short-lived, falling from his lips as his eyes locked on another pair across the room. Hazel irises, heavy-lidded, gaze sometimes a little mischievous. The way those eyes went wide as they focused on Kai had his stomach roiling. This time he truly couldn't tell if it was the alcohol or the anxiety.

"You sure you're okay?" Atticus had finally recovered enough to speak, had immediately picked up on the tension rolling off of Kai in waves.

Nicholas began to move, breaking away from his conversation, making his way across the room.

Kai couldn't help but be honest.

"No." The word fell from his lips softly, a barely-there whisper hidden in the cacophony of the party. He wasn't even sure if Atticus heard him.

Atticus must have, because a moment later a steady arm wrapped around Kai's back, a strong hand pressing firmly into his arm as Atticus pulled him a little closer. Warmth spread in Kai's chest as he was firmly tucked against Atticus' side.

Kai wasn't sure what the goal was there. Atticus had never seemed like the possessive type, and it wouldn't matter anyway. An arm around Kai's shoulders wasn't going to make Nicholas jealous. Nothing was going to make Nicholas jealous. Kai's gut churned again at the thought, but a light squeeze to his arm had him looking up at the man next to him.

"It'll be fine," Atticus said softly. Kai thought he could see concern there, hidden behind the charming grin and playful eyes.

Maybe the gesture wasn't to make Kai's ex jealous. Maybe it was just to prop him up, to lend him a little of that ever-sure strength that Atticus always seemed to possess.

Steeling himself, Kai downed the rest of his fourth drink before wrapping both hands around the glass, fingers aching as his grip tightened.

Nicholas stopped in front of them, taking in Atticus for only a moment, offering a nod and a bright smile, before his focus rested solely on Kai. The low lights of the room cast shadows that sharpened his features. Cutting cheekbones, a slicing jawline. Kai remembered what it had been like to tilt that face toward him, to press his lips along those harsh lines.

"Hey."

The single word threatened to send Kai to his knees. All of the hurt and pain and anger and despair he had worked so hard to bury over the last year and a half threatened to rise up alongside the contents of his stomach. A thousand wounds, reopened all at once, cuts dealt by the man before him. The one person Kai had thought could never, *would* never, hurt him.

"It's good to see you!" Atticus broke the tension, holding out the hand that wasn't wrapped around Kai toward Nicholas. They'd known each other for a few years, through Ori and Theo, through Nicholas' work with local youth volleyball programs. Had always been friendly, long before anything had passed between Kai and Atticus. "You did good getting Ori here without spoiling the surprise."

Nicholas laughed, and the sound of it rang through Kai in the worst and best way. A sound he had loved so much, had missed for so long. A sound he used to take pride in pulling from the other man. Nicholas shook Atticus' outstretched hand, grinning wide.

"He's easy to distract," he said, voice still laced with laughter and mischief. "Get him and Theo arguing and they can go on like that for hours."

The mention of Nicholas' partner was like a bucket of icy water pouring over Kai. His eyes flicked toward the group

Nicholas had just left, landing on Theo. He was still chatting with some friends, frowning at Ori, who was laughing loudly. So tall and sure of himself, but his eyes kept flicking toward their group, something like worry coloring his features as he adjusted his glasses absent-mindedly.

Kai hated that a part of him missed hearing Ori and Theo argue all the time. The alcohol was drowning his barriers, the ones he'd built up around the shattered remnants of their old friend group.

Even Ori would be gone soon.

"How've you been lately?"

Kai knew the question was for him. He realized he had yet to speak, to say anything. Pulling his gaze back, focusing on the man before him, it was nearly impossible. His movements felt weighed down, an anchor dragging him lower and lower into the pit he had just barely escaped from. His mind felt sluggish, fuzzy from the vodka. From the dread.

"Fine." One word was all he could force out. Kai couldn't even bring himself to meet Nicholas' eyes. He could feel that hazel stare boring into him, could feel Nicholas willing him to look up, to meet his gaze.

That's what hurt the worst. The fact that Kai couldn't even look at his oldest friend anymore. The fact that they *weren't* friends anymore.

They hadn't been for so long now.

The silence between them was terrible, a growing chasm that Kai would have fallen into if a hand hadn't still been wrapped around his arm, tethering him in place and holding him steady.

"Listen," Nicholas finally said. Kai looked up, still not meeting his gaze. Watched as he ran a hand through already messy hair. Kai remembered the exact texture of it, soft and a little frizzy. Nicholas dropped his hand down, letting it rest on his hip, that same easy stance he so often took, before he continued to speak. "I don't know if this is the best place for us to talk. Would you want to grab something to eat after? Or maybe get coffee?"

The hope is what finally did it. Kai could hear it clearly, the yearning in Nicholas' voice. Kai looked him in the eye, saw a semblance of his own pain reflected.

It only made him feel worse. Knowing that Nicholas hurt in a similar way to him. Similar, but not the same. Because while they both mourned the loss of their friendship, only Kai mourned the loss of what more they'd had.

"Mills, if you want to come too, the more the merrier!" Nicholas was scrambling now, a smile that didn't quite ring true, falling a little more with every second that Kai remained silent. "Theo said he knows a good place close to here. It's quiet, we can all catch up."

The mention of Theo felt like running face first into a brick wall. Kai was sure he really was going to be sick.

There was no way he could sit there and watch Nicholas be in love with someone else.

"I'm going back to Attie's place tonight." Kai didn't think before the words slipped out. He couldn't think, not with the alcohol blurring the lines he shouldn't cross and his nerves threatening to explode like firecrackers throughout his entire body. "We were actually getting ready to leave."

He purposely avoided thinking about the pain that flashed across Nicholas' features. Kai looked up at Atticus, saw momentary confusion cross his expression before he grinned in a way that was a little devastating. A grin that always twisted something inside of Kai's chest.

"Maybe we can take a raincheck, yeah?" Atticus asked, words cheerful and bright, such a contrast to the atmosphere surrounding the three of them. He stepped away from the bar, taking Kai's empty glass from his vice-like grip, setting it on the counter. Kai let himself be pulled away, thankful for the attention, thankful for the stable hands to guide him.

"Sure," Nicholas said, voice a little softer. A little sad. "Maybe next time. See you around, Atticus. Kai." A nod toward them both, but his gaze lingered on Kai. There was no real longing there, no reflection of what Kai felt, what he so desperately wanted to see.

"Bye, Nicky."

The nickname slipped out before he could stop himself, and Kai instantly wished he could take it back. Wished he could wipe away the flash of something bright and hopeful that flickered in Nicholas' expression.

They wouldn't be seeing each other again soon. Not if Kai had anything to say about it. There would be no 'next time.' He felt as though he'd barely survived *this* terrible interaction, pulse racing, stomach threatening to rebel, a persistent itching under his skin that made him want to tear into himself. He couldn't do it. He would never be able to act like things were normal between them, like he hadn't lost everything the day that Nicholas left.

Atticus led Kai away toward the exit, leaving Nicholas behind.

"We should probably get you out of here." Atticus was being gentle with him, voice soft as he leaned close, his words meant only for Kai.

"I need to say bye to Ori." Kai intentionally ignored the slight slur that came through in his words. Regret tasted an awful lot like cheap vodka.

"We can call him later." Atticus steered Kai toward the outskirts of the party. Kai let himself be led, too tired and drunk and sad to fight it. Once they were out the door, in a quiet, empty hall, Atticus turned to face Kai fully, a hand still steady on his arm.

"Want me to take you home?"

He looked so earnest, so sweet and concerned, and it

tugged at Kai, made a little spark that only ever lit for Atticus flash within him, pushing past his drunken haze. Or maybe adding to it.

"Or," Kai said, voice low as he stepped closer. He placed a hand against Atticus' chest, could feel the way his breath caught as he let his fingers trail along the silky fabric. "I really could go back to your place."

Kai looked up to see heat in Atticus' gaze. A part of him was screaming, railing against this flirtation. The part that knew that his words could mean more to Atticus, could push them in a direction that Kai wasn't ready to move toward. But it was hard to think straight, hard to not want to let go completely when he felt like his whole life had just crashed down around him again. Hard to ignore the way his body always responded to Atticus' touch, the way everything always felt a little lighter whenever Atticus looked at him.

Atticus blew out a long breath, looking away, a hand rubbing at the back of his neck. "I don't think that's such a good idea…"

He trailed off, looking away. Kai's hand gripped at his shirt, fingers tightening in the fabric as a wave of nausea threatened him.

"I can't be alone tonight." The blatant honesty was unusual for him, and Kai felt a creeping anxiety at laying himself bare in that way. But something about Atticus had always made him feel safe, made him feel like he could be vulnerable in a way he rarely allowed himself. And with Ori leaving the next day, Kai had no one else to turn to. "Please, Attie."

Atticus looked back down at him, brow furrowed, concern written across his face. He nodded, the movement small and quick.

"Okay." One word and relief immediately washed over Kai. Atticus pulled him toward the building's exit, slipping his hand into Kai's, twining their fingers together. Kai allowed himself to be led, a little unsteady. He was feeling too much, his thoughts blurring as his insides churned. A spark burned along his skin where a strong hand wrapped around his own.

Kai let himself focus on that spark, on the one thing that felt good about this night. He didn't think about how he'd left his friend's party early, didn't think about how his first interaction with his ex in over a year had been a complete train wreck. He simply allowed himself to feel Atticus' hand in his, leaning in close as they walked out into the night.

Atticus had to pull over, ten minutes from home.

Kai leaned out of the passenger seat, emptying the meager contents of his stomach onto the road. After a few moments, he pulled himself back up into the car, flopping back against the seat. His eyes were closed, chest rising and falling heavily as he caught his breath.

"You good?" Atticus kept his voice gentle. Kai nodded.

"For now," he said, voice weak.

They made it back to Atticus' place without any further mishaps, but the moment they were through the door he had to lead Kai to his single bathroom. Atticus went to get a glass of water for each of them as Kai heaved into the toilet bowl.

"Thanks," Kai mumbled, leaning back against the wall as he took the water Atticus offered him. He looked like a wreck, face pale and clammy, hair slipping from the tie he'd pulled it back with, the rose gold ends sticking to the skin of his neck. Eyes closed tight in discomfort.

"Here," Atticus said softly, holding out the other items he'd grabbed. "You might feel better if you're more comfortable."

Kai cracked one eye open, staring at the clothes Atticus held out. "I think I'll throw up again if I move."

Atticus chuckled, leaning forward. "I'll help you. Come on."

Kai let himself be undressed, limp as a doll. Atticus pulled off Kai's jacket before moving to unbutton the shirt that was damp with sweat. He desperately tried not to focus on what undressing the other man was doing to his own body, the persistent heat trailing up his neck, setting his cheeks on fire. Now was *really* not the time.

He quickly slipped Kai's shirt off, pushing his old Wildcats hoodie over his head. It was massive on Kai's smaller frame, engulfing him in a way that had Atticus gritting his teeth at the cuteness of it all. Kai roused himself enough to also change into a pair of athletic shorts, but the movement had him heaving into the toilet once again.

Atticus did what he could for him, a gentle touch along his back, a hand to hold back his hair. It was nearly impossible to keep himself from playing with the soft pink ends. The last time they'd hung out, playing a new JRPG that Kai had early access to, the ends of his dark hair had been a fading teal. Atticus thought the subtle pink suited him better.

Tears leaked from the corners of Kai's eyes as his body rejected the little water he'd tried to get down. It felt like hours later before they both leaned back against the wall. Atticus pulled the smaller man close, holding him back against his chest as Kai's breathing began to even out. He'd finally managed to get down the entire glass of water, his body heavy with exhaustion as he leaned back into Atticus.

It was hard, the closeness, the familiarity. It had taken Atticus months to get used to it, to understand how casual touch was for Kai. How it didn't mean anything, that it was just how he was with all of his friends. Atticus had gotten used to it.

Mostly.

"I'm sorry," Kai murmured, and Atticus couldn't help but

smile at the sleepiness in the words.

"It's fine," he said softly, his words close to Kai's ear. "We've all done it."

Kai relaxed at that, his head falling back against Atticus' shoulder as he curled in on himself slightly. Atticus held onto him, let his own mind wander as the other man drifted off with a mumbled, "Thanks, Attie."

Atticus wanted to laugh about it, he really did. He'd longed to have Kai in his arms like this again, had wanted it for months. Under different circumstances, obviously. But even this felt amazing, to have him curled up like a cat, pressed tight against Atticus, close enough that he could feel every slight movement and every steady breath.

When Kai had asked to come home with him, had called him *Attie* with so much unspoken in his request, Atticus had nearly come out of his own skin. Because it hadn't been like previous times, when they'd agreed to go out as friends, when they'd made plans to stay in for a night of gaming. No, this time there had been something more in Kai's gaze that ignited Atticus' entire being, something that sent fire racing along his veins.

If Kai had been sober, Atticus would have pressed him up against the wall right then and there and kissed him senseless.

He'd known immediately that *wasn't* an option, that he would be in this exact position by the end of the night. That they wouldn't be having a repeat of their first night together.

Atticus had also been very aware of how his exit from the party would look to others. How it would play into the image that he'd been trying to break away from. Playboy Atticus Mills, leaving early for another hookup. He ignored the way those thoughts felt like rocks settling in his stomach, weighing him down, ignored the way it hurt to imagine people would think he would use Kai like that.

Kai was fast asleep, still nestled into Atticus' broad chest. Color had returned to his face, his soft cheeks tinted pink, his lips parted slightly. Atticus brushed a few stray strands of long hair away from Kai's face. He could feel sleep tugging at him as well, his eyelids growing heavier with each passing moment. He knew he should move, should take Kai to his spare bedroom so he could sleep more comfortably.

But he had wanted this for so long, to hold Kai, to be close to him again. Just a few more minutes. Atticus would pick him up, carry him to the other room, but only after a few more minutes of enjoying this. Of feeling like maybe they could be more, pretending that they weren't just friends that had hooked up one time.

Atticus drifted off to sleep with his arms still wrapped tightly around Kai, curled into each other on the bathroom floor.

8 Years Ago

"Have you ever kissed anyone?"

The question took Kai by surprise. He shifted in Nicholas' bed, turning to face the other boy more fully. He could feel the tips of his ears burning, could feel his cheeks heating, and was glad for the darkness of night.

"No," he said, voice low but steadier than he expected, given the way his heart had begun to race. Kai could just make out Nicholas' profile in the dark. His friend lay on his back, almost close enough that they were pressed together, face pointed toward the ceiling. Kai thought he could make out Nicholas' brows furrowing.

"I haven't either," Nicholas finally said, seemingly unaffected by their conversation. Kai tried to ignore the relief that washed over him at hearing those words. At knowing that Nicholas hadn't kissed anyone else. They were sixteen now, so it wouldn't have come as a surprise to find out that Nicholas was ahead of him in the kissing department. The relief at finding out it was something they still had in common was like warm arms wrapping around Kai, heating him from the inside out.

Kai continued to stare as his friend shifted, turning onto his side so that they were facing one another fully. Their shared blanket was pulled up, hiding the bottom halves of their faces, making Kai feel as though they were in a world of their own. He was suddenly hot all over, too aware of the other boy's presence next to him. *Ridiculous*, he thought. He and Nicholas slept next to one another like this all the time, often waking up with their limbs tangled together and their heads on the same pillow. Why was now different? Why was he so painfully conscious of the way Nicholas' leg was pressed to his own, the way their noses were only a few centimeters apart?

"Do you want to try it?" The question fell from Nicholas' lips like any other words, but it slammed into Kai like a wave, drowning him in hope and fear.

Of course he wanted to kiss Nicholas. He'd wanted to kiss him for so long now. Months of figuring out why he suddenly couldn't stop thinking about his friend in ways both new and different. Months of longing for the heat of the other boy's skin against his own, a slight brush of hands or a hug after a good rally.

Kai thought he might throw up from his nerves.

He thought he might die from his excitement.

"Sure," was all he finally managed to squeak out, keeping his voice low, shrugging with feigned nonchalance. His eyes had adjusted to the dark, and with Nicholas so close Kai could see a smile light up his features, spreading across his face in a way that made Kai's blood fizz under his skin.

"Okay!" Nicholas said, a little too loud. He scooted closer, tugging the blanket over their faces, as if to hide from the dark and quiet room. To keep this moment just between them, something special, something precious. "You'll tell me if you change your mind, right Kai?"

Kai held his breath, nodding as his friend moved in closer, as Nicholas carefully pressed in. Their lips brushed together, soft and gentle and unmoving. Kai felt as though the moment lasted a lifetime and ended in a heartbeat. They didn't touch anywhere else, other than the leg that Nicholas still had pressed to Kai's.

Reality crashed back into place as Nicholas finally pulled away, just a little. Just enough that their lips were no longer pressed together. The other boy hummed softly.

"What?" Kai asked. His voice was a barely-there whisper, incapable of being more. When Nicholas took too long to respond, Kai gripped the covers tightly, his heart in his throat. "Nicky?"

"It was kind of nice."

Nice was an understatement. What they'd done most likely only *just* qualified as a kiss, but it was enough to set Kai on fire. He could feel every brush of fabric intensely on his skin, his pajamas, the blanket, Nicholas' sock against his bare calf. Every sound seemed magnified, their soft breaths turned up to maximum volume in his ears. He knew his face was burning red, knew that if the light were on then his secret would be laid bare and his feelings would finally be out there for anyone to see.

For Nicholas to see.

"It was really nice," Kai whispered, his brain screaming at him for the words. Too much, too much, he had said too much and Nicholas would *know-*

"Really?" Nicholas' voice dropped back to a whisper, holding something softer, something filled with excitement. "You liked it?"

Kai hesitated, gaining control of himself before more unintended words spilled out past his lips. But... Nicholas was still smiling, shifting closer again. He looked so happy, so cheerful, none of his usual mischievousness present. Only sincerity. Only a bright smile, just for Kai.

Maybe it wouldn't be so bad to say the things he wanted so desperately to give voice to. The things he had kept to himself for the last year.

"I liked it." Kai kept his voice low as he scooted closer to his friend. Closer to the boy he never stopped thinking about. Closer to the boy he wanted very much to kiss again.

"You want to try it again?" Nicholas punctuated the question by reaching out, pushing Kai's now shoulder-length hair back from his face, tucking the strands behind his ear.

Kai answered by closing the distance between them, sharing his second kiss with his best friend, the boy he was now sure he was in love with.

2

Present day

Julian: good morning loser :)

Atticus: What do you want fuckface?

Julian: just wanted to check on kai. saw you two leave together, ori was asking what happened

Atticus: Just between us?
Atticus: Wait you're with ori this morning? Details pls

Julian: just between us :)

Atticus: Thanks
Atticus: I guess I'm not getting details since it's been 5 mins and you're still ignoring my question
Atticus: ANYWAYS

Atticus: I don't think the party was a great idea for Kai
Atticus: Seeing his ex again like that

Julian: did nicholas do something??

Atticus: Nah, nothing that bad. I just don't think he was ready for any sort of conversation yet

Julian: man
Julian: it's been a while now
Julian: over a year

Atticus: Yeah
Atticus: I know
Atticus: Can you just tell Ori that he got sick?

Julian: yep :)

Atticus: Thanks, shitstain

Julian: anytime, chode cheeks

Kai woke to a pounding headache and the smell of breakfast. It took several long, agonizing moments for him to gain his bearings. To remember where he was.

Where he had spent the night.

He groaned, rolling onto his side and curling into a ball as he pulled the heavy comforter close to his face. His head throbbed, edging too close to a migraine, as he tried to remember details from the previous night.

Ori's party.

Nicholas.

He had talked to Nicholas for the first time in over a year.

Kai squeezed his eyes shut, trying to ignore the pain in his head and the embarrassment that coursed through him. He supposed *he* hadn't really done that much talking. Nicholas had, or had tried to. And Atticus had filled in the blank spaces. All Kai had done was act like a drunken mess before stumbling out of his best friend's party early.

Guilt gnawed at him, making his gut churn. Kai sat up, letting the blanket pool around his waist. He was still wearing Atticus' old maroon and gold Cats hoodie, and his cheeks warmed at the hazy memory of the other man helping him change clothes on the bathroom floor. He reached for his phone, which Atticus had apparently plugged in to charge and left on the nightstand.

He pulled up his message thread with Ori only to see an unread text already waiting for him.

Ori: Julian said you got sick last night :(:(:(hope you're better today!

Kai's guilt only grew. So Julian felt the need to cover for him? Fantastic. Kai cringed at how pathetic he must have seemed to everyone the night before.

Kai: Sorry Ori, it was my own fault. Had a little too much to drink on an empty stomach. Promise I'll make it up to you.

Ori: Ohhhhhh
Ori: Was it nicky?

His friend knew him too well. Kai sighed, the pain in his

head increasing to a persistent throb. He needed to get up and find his wallet, take his medicine before it was too late and he was down for the rest of the day.

Kai: It was me being stupid.

Ori: Oops :D:D julian also said you left with atticus…
Ori: …………
Ori: …………………..

Kai: UGH
Kai: YES
Kai: But not like that.

Ori: Boooooo

Kai: Just friends. I puked all over his bathroom

Ori: Gross man. That's not how you woo someone

Kai: What the fuck, did you just say "woo someone"?

Ori: Yeah, like you getting atticus to fall in love with you
Ori: Although I'm pretty sure you already did that
Ori: So maybe you don't need to worry about the puking stuff

Kai: I'm too hungover for this
Kai: I'm not trying to woo Attie

Ori: Hehe attie

Ori: You should be though :D:D:D

Kai smirked as he rolled his eyes and swiped out of their conversation, only to freeze at the sight of another text waiting for him.

Nicholas: I'm so sorry, I shouldn't have been so presumptuous last night, cornering you in front of everyone like that. I know it made you uncomfortable and that's the last thing I wanted to do, I'm really sorry Kai. But if you would be willing to sit down and talk while I'm in town, I'd really like that. I miss you, I've missed you so much. Just one conversation, that's all I ask.

He felt as though he really was going to throw up again. Grief and anger warred within him, turning his insides into a sickening battlefield. Kai deleted the message, wiping it from reality in the hopes it would be wiped from his brain as well. He couldn't do this today. Couldn't even begin to figure out a response to something like that. He didn't even know how Nicholas had gotten his current number, and he thought he might stab whoever had given it to him.

He would just ignore it, and Nicholas would go back to St. Louis with Theo in tow in a few days, and life could go on just the way it had for the last year.

Kai rose from the bed, a little shaky. He wasn't sure whether it was from his hangover or the message that seemed to be tattooing itself on his mind. He distracted himself by finally taking in the room around him. This was his first time in Atticus' new place. He knew the other man had recently moved outside of the city, renting a small countryside house not far from his own home actually, but this was Kai's first time visiting.

The room, what he assumed was the guest room, was cozy, if a little sparse. A bed, a nightstand, and a dresser, atop which were a few picture frames. Kai moved across the room, head pounding with each step, to look at them more closely.

Pictures of Atticus' volleyball teams over the years, going all the way back to his middle school days, littered the space. Kai took them in, one by one. He paused on the one of what he assumed was Atticus' high school team the year they'd won the national tournament. The whole team was crowded together, some players beaming at the camera while others had tears in their eyes. Even Sammie, Atticus' twin, had made her way into the photo. Kai had only met Sammie a few times, but he could imagine her running onto the court the moment the final buzzer sounded, throwing her arms tight around her brother. Their younger faces looked more alike, round and smiling, their eyes scrunched up in exactly the same way. Atticus had already been bleaching his hair, even back then, going from a dusty brown to a bright blonde. A small laugh bubbled in Kai at how yellow it looked. Clearly, Atticus hadn't discovered toner yet.

Kai's stomach flip-flopped a little, in a way that was different from the nausea he'd been dealing with, so he moved on.

His eyes scanned over the more recent photographs, Atticus with the other Chicago players. Kai couldn't help himself, smiling softly at one that showed Ori leaping into the air behind Atticus, hands on his shoulders and a bright smile pointed at the camera while Atticus scowled up at him.

It would be strange, seeing the team roster without Ori on it for the new season. His friend was taking the trade to the Comets in stride, but Kai had a sneaking suspicion that had more to do with *who* was on the new team than anything else.

The sound of a television turning on crept into Kai's room, and he noticed that the door was cracked open. He looked around for the clothes he'd worn the night before, giving up quickly when they were nowhere to be seen, realizing he needed to stop stalling and just get it over with.

Kai followed the smells of breakfast down a short hallway, smoothing his hair down in an attempt to look like less of a total mess. He turned into the kitchen, pausing at the sight before him.

Atticus stood over the stove, face relaxed and happy, smiling softly as he focused on whatever it was that he was cooking. He was also shirtless.

Sure, maybe Kai wasn't interested *like that*, but, well. He had eyes.

Atticus leaned forward, and Kai couldn't keep from staring as the muscles of his stomach tightened a bit, as his broad chest and shoulders blocked the view of the stovetop. One arm was covered in tattoos, a full sleeve of black line art that Kai hadn't seen in full since the one night they had spent together. He let his gaze trail lower, face warming at Atticus' low-slung sweatpants. The slight swell of the top of his ass, the sharp v of his waist that slipped below the band of his pants…

"Smells good," Kai said, a fruitless attempt at distracting himself. Atticus jumped, whirling toward him with wide eyes.

"Fuck!" The word flew from Atticus' lips as he accidentally bumped the handle of the pan he was using and knocked it off the burner. He whirled back toward the food. "Shit!"

Kai chuckled as he moved out of the doorway, taking a seat at the counter that separated the kitchen from the living room.

"Are you always this jumpy?" Kai watched from behind as Atticus fixed the mess he'd sort of made. This view wasn't so bad either. His back was just so *broad*. And those tattoos, every single one of them anime-related, spread across his right shoulder blade. Kai wiped a hand down his face.

"Ah," Atticus said, plating what looked like fried eggs before turning around. "No. I'm just not used to having anyone else here." He smiled at Kai, a too-charming flash of teeth, standing just a little above him on the other side of the high counter. A plate was placed before him, steamed rice and vegetables, a fried egg on top.

"I figured you'd be hungry, but don't feel bad if you don't want to eat it all," Atticus said, grinning as he began to dig into his own meal.

"Thanks." Kai returned the look with a small smile of his own, even as he eyed the food before him with distrust.

"You feel okay?"

Kai shook his head. "Not great."

Atticus grimaced, pointing his fork toward Kai's plate. "Eat. This is what Sammie always used to make for me if I had a hangover. Soaks up the alcohol or something." A pause as he shoved a forkful of food into his mouth. "I washed your clothes from last night, they're in the dryer now. Should be done soon."

"Thanks." How many times was he going to need to thank Atticus today? Memories washed over him, of his friend helping him into the car, of Atticus holding Kai's hair back as he heaved over the toilet bowl. A more blurry memory of falling asleep with strong arms holding him tight, making him feel safe and secure. That one he might have dreamed up. "I'm sorry about last night."

Atticus waved a hand, mouth full of food. "S'fine. I've been way worse off than that before, it happens. Happy to help." Their eyes met, and Kai saw a flash of tenderness there, a reflection of the care that the other man had shown the night before. It made his insides feel tight, and suddenly swallowing his mouthful of rice past the lump in his throat seemed nearly impossible. Kai looked away first, focusing his stare down on his food. They ate in silence for a few minutes before an extra-sharp throb in Kai's head made him remember what he needed to ask.

"Do you have my wallet?"

Atticus nodded, shoveling in another mouthful before he walked to the other side of the kitchen. He tossed the wallet toward Kai, who caught it against his chest with another mumbled thanks. Digging into a specific pocket, Kai pulled out a single blister-pack. Popping it open, he took the pill, swallowing it dry. Atticus watched carefully, setting a glass of water in front of him.

"Sure you're okay?"

Kai nodded. "If I don't take it now I'll be down with a migraine for the rest of the day."

Atticus frowned. "Do you get them often?"

"Often enough." Kai shrugged. "I've kind of learned to live with them. I know my triggers. Know better than to dive headfirst into a hangover like that." That pulled a laugh from Atticus, full and bright. Kai liked that he laughed about it, that he saw the humor there instead of showing pity or offering useless suggestions and remedies.

"Done?" Atticus gestured toward Kai's mostly empty plate that he'd pushed away. He nodded.

"It was good," Kai said.

"I'd hope so." Atticus chuckled as he emptied their food remnants into the trash and rinsed the plates. "Sammie and I spent enough time filling in at grandma's place, I should be able to handle a light breakfast at this point." Another grin pointed in Kai's direction, and *fuck*, it made Kai's pulse speed up. His body always reacted to Atticus, was always aware of the other man, always aware of how god damn attractive he was.

"Do you miss it?"

Atticus talked about his grandmother a lot. She'd raised

the twins by herself after their single mother had died of lung cancer. They'd only been three years old at the time, couldn't really remember her. But the memories of their grandmother were plentiful, and Kai loved to hear Atticus go on about her. Loved seeing the way his face lit up whenever he got to talk about Greta and the restaurant she'd opened and had kept alive for decades on her own.

"Sometimes, yeah." Atticus leaned casually against the counter, arms crossed over his chest. "Not as much as I miss her. Seems silly to miss a place, a business, but me and Sammie spent almost as much time there as we did at home."

Kai downed the rest of his water. "Sammie has her brewery now, you could hang out there."

"First off," Atticus said, pointing a finger. "It's not her's. And secondly, beer isn't food. Third, every time I try to hang out there, I get put to work. Which is the only thing about it that's the same as the restaurant."

Kai laughed softly. "If you say so." A silence filled the space between them, setting off an itch under Kai's skin as Atticus watched him intently. It made him feel too warm, made it hard to ignore the way the muscles on Atticus' chest looked *big* with his arms crossed that way.

Just as Atticus opened his mouth to respond, a chime sounded from another room, drawing Kai's thoughts away from dangerous territory.

"That's the dryer," Atticus said quickly, pointing toward the hallway. "It's in there if you wanna change. That hoodie looks good on you, though."

Kai flushed at the flirting. He should have been used to it by now. Flirting came as naturally to Atticus as breathing. But every now and then, it hit just a little different. A little deeper, a little more sincere. He knew that Atticus still had some semblance of feelings for him, but they'd also agreed long ago to just be friends.

And they were just friends. They worked well as just friends. Atticus flirted with all of his friends, hell, Kai was pretty sure he'd even been flirting with Julian the evening before.

But there was always something there, something in his eyes when he focused his efforts solely on Kai. Something sincere and soft, something that Kai didn't really like to think about. He left the kitchen, cheeks still warm, unwilling to confront the reason why his pulse was ticking just a little bit faster.

Atticus braced himself on the counter, blowing out a slow, quiet breath. He double checked to make sure Kai wasn't quietly hovering in the doorway again before dropping his head into his hands and groaning.

He could do this. He could be normal. Kai was his friend, they'd been friends for a decently long time now. Atticus could definitely handle seeing him in that old Cats hoodie, hair down and a little mussed from sleep, eyes tired and heavy lidded.

Atticus couldn't fucking do this.

He had to, though. The only other option was to just *not* have Kai in his life anymore, and well, that wasn't an option. Not one that Atticus was willing to consider.

It was getting more and more difficult, though. Every time they were together, Atticus could feel himself falling a little more. He'd thought that after a few months it would have faded, but no. Apparently his heart was just as stubborn as he was.

He turned, padding across the kitchen to snatch up the television remote, turning the volume up in an attempt to drown out his horny thoughts. He wasn't really paying attention to what was playing, some new battle shonen anime he'd randomly clicked on. Atticus just liked to have something on in the background, something to drown out the silence and make the space feel less empty. His grandma had always, *always* had music playing, and Atticus had often thought that it helped to make their home feel... well, more homey. Putting on whatever anime he was currently watching had turned into his way of carrying on the tradition, ever since she had passed peacefully in her sleep three years earlier. His way of trying to make his new house feel more like the home he'd grown up in.

It worked, sometimes. Atticus dropped down onto the couch, half-heartedly watching the newest episode while scrolling on his phone.

It had been harder than he'd expected, moving out of the city. He liked having more space to himself than he'd had sharing an apartment with two of his old teammates. And he did actually like the quiet of the countryside, the way it reminded him a little of the good aspects of growing up in rural Illinois. But every now and then... it was *too* quiet. Every now and then Atticus felt too alone with his own thoughts, found himself missing the sounds of the city, the lifestyle he'd finally nailed into a coffin by moving away from it all. Thus the constant need for background noise in the form of anime.

It was nice being closer to Kai's place, though.

"I like this one." Kai's soft voice pulled Atticus out of his thoughts. He sat down carefully at the other end of the couch as he nodded toward the tv, pulling his feet up to tuck himself into a ball, moving as though he was still in some amount of pain. Atticus fought every urge to pull him close, to hold onto him the same way he had in the bathroom the night before, to provide comfort in even a small way. That desire was made worse by the fact that Kai had chosen to keep the Cats hoodie on. The deep maroon looked good against his pale skin, the gold lettering bringing out the gold flecks in his amber eyes. Paired with his dark jeans from the night before…

"Never seen it," Atticus said, flicking his eyes away from Kai and toward the television. He watched for a few seconds, unseeing, uncaring about who was about to demolish whom on the screen, all too aware of the man at the other end of the couch.

He couldn't hold out for long, his gaze drawn back to Kai like the pull of gravity.

"You have plans today?"

Kai frowned, a common enough expression for him but not the one Atticus was expecting to see with that question.

"Yeah." An exaggerated sigh fell from his lips, his cheeks puffing out. "I need to get home and pack."

"Pack?" Atticus knew Kai took a lot of work trips. He was always attending some big shot industry event or another. Some kept him away for weeks at a time. A weight settled in his stomach at the idea of Kai being gone for that long once again.

"I had a bad leak in my bathroom," Kai answered, his whiskey eyes finally shifting to pierce Atticus. Eyes that were so wide and innocent and utterly deceptive. Atticus knew what went on in the thoughts behind them, the constantly turning gears and a decided *lack* of innocence. "Got under the flooring and everything. I was planning to remodel that portion of the house eventually anyway, so I decided to just go ahead with it. The contractor has people coming in tomorrow and said they should be able to finish in about a week. I'm staying at a hotel to keep out of their way."

"Oh," Atticus said. His mind was already racing ahead, closing in on an idea before he'd even had a chance to fully grasp it. "Stay here instead."

Kai blinked at him.

Stay with me instead. It was definitely a terrible idea, maybe the worst idea Atticus had ever given voice to. Just having Kai in his home for *one morning* had so far been nearly enough to send him into a fit. A couple more days of this and he would probably be walking around sporting a constant boner.

But as Kai's eyes narrowed a little, head tilting ever so slightly, the hornier thoughts subsided, giving way to the ones he tried a lot harder to ignore, to push down.

He wanted Kai here with him. He wanted Kai here with him *always*. He wanted something that was so very unattainable, but what if he could have it for just a week? A taste of a life he didn't let himself picture, not since it had become clear that their one hookup was never going to turn into anything more.

It wasn't a good idea to think about that night. The one time they'd had sex. It was never a good idea to think about that, about the way it had shifted something for Atticus, made him feel something new and terrifying and wonderful, something he would never get enough of but would probably never get again. Atticus' grip on his phone tightened as he pushed the memories down, the images of Kai in his lap, the phantom feeling of lips pressed to his own.

"I'd have to do a stream in a couple days," Kai said slowly. "It's already planned. I don't want to be in your way."

"Not a problem," Atticus said, trying desperately to keep his voice even, to keep the excitement from bleeding into his words. "The guest room is all yours, wouldn't be in my way at all!"

"You're sure?"

"Absolutely." Atticus held Kai's stare, felt as though he were being dissected a little more with every passing second. Could Kai see it, written clearly across his face? Could he see the way everything hinged on his answer? Atticus suddenly wished he'd been feeling a little less flirtatious earlier and had put a shirt on. He was pretty sure that if another few moments slipped by with Kai looking at him that intensely then his entire body was going to turn red from the heat building in him.

"Okay," Kai finally said, and Atticus barely held himself back from releasing a sigh of relief. "Would you mind taking me to get my car? Did you have plans today?"

"Nope!" Atticus failed at keeping the cheer from his voice, failed at holding back the smile that was spreading across his face. He hopped up from the couch. "Well, yes. Practice in a couple hours. And I was going to touch up my roots." He ran a hand through his hair, shifting the blonde strands away from his forehead. "Sammie usually helps me out because I'm shit at getting the bleach on even, but she's been too busy to come over. Lemme go put some more clothes on, we can go in just a few."

He hurried out of the room, not waiting for another response. Once in the safety of his own bedroom, Atticus pumped his fist in front of his chest, biting his lip to hold back a laugh. He knew he was a dork, knew that Kai would roll his eyes if he saw Atticus this excited at the prospect of what was essentially a sleepover. He hurried to put on a shirt, pushing down any and all negative thoughts as he pulled the fabric over his head.

Sure, it was risky. Sure, Atticus felt some sort of way toward Kai that was definitely not reciprocated. Which had been made *quite* evident the evening before, when the fact that Kai was clearly still hung up on his ex had been on full display for everyone to see. A display that Atticus got to witness firsthand.

But how much could go wrong in a week? It wasn't like Atticus wouldn't be able to control himself, as if being around

Kai all day every day would be more than he could handle.

It would be fine. It would be no different than the other times they'd hung out together over the last six months. Play some games, watch a movie or two. Just two dudes being buddies.

For seven days straight.

Atticus walked back into the living room, keys dangling from his hand. He grinned when Kai looked up at the sound, eyes wide, expression one of surprise. It made Atticus' heart trip a little. Especially when Kai smiled softly back at him.

"Let's go!"

3

"You're never late, man!"

Bowen's ever-loud voice assaulted Atticus as he burst into the locker room. He tossed his bag onto a bench. The very bag that was the reason he was late. He'd left it at home when he and Kai had gone back out to the party venue to get Kai's car.

Atticus figured he was the only one to blame, his giddy excitement at having his crush spend the night again pushing all other thoughts out of his head like he was back in high school. He'd hurried back home after dropping Kai off, snatching up his practice gear before rushing to the gym.

"Not late yet," Atticus replied, tapping on his phone's screen before chucking it into his locker. "A minute to spare."

"Bo's right though," Eric, their libero, sang as he damn near bounced across the locker room. Too much energy in one person. "You're always fifteen minutes early. Must have been something special that kept you away if you're just now getting here."

Atticus ignored him, changing quickly. He tugged his maroon practice jersey over his head, and damn his traitorous mind, he couldn't help but picture Kai in the same color. Kai, wearing his jersey, with the name 'Mills' stamped across his back.

"Ohoho," Bowen cheered, coming up behind Atticus and slapping him on the back so hard Atticus nearly banged his head into the open locker door. He glared at his wing spiker. Bowen only grinned back, his smile wide and all too knowing.

"He has a *very* special reason for being late."

"Shut the fuck up, Bo." There wasn't any true heat in Atticus' response, even if his gut did suddenly feel too heavy. He knew what was coming next.

"Aw, c'mon man, don't be like that!" A thick arm slung around his shoulder as Bowen aimed his words toward the rest of the team filing out the door. "I saw you leave the party last night, and you were very much *not* alone. Let us live vicariously through you, none of us have the luck you do when it comes to getting laid!"

Heat rose to his cheeks, despite Atticus' best efforts. Most of the team ignored them as they left the locker room, with only Eric stopping to reach out a hand for a high five as he passed. A few chuckles that echoed off the metal lockers, ringing through Atticus.

"You don't know what you're talking about." Atticus ducked his head, slipping out of Bowen's grip.

"Sure I do," Bowen sang, trailing behind him. "I saw you leave with Kai last night. Saw how close you two looked before that." Another slap on Atticus' back, one that packed a sting that shot through him. "Been a while since you hooked up with somebody a second time."

"Bowen."

The sharp voice, tinted with a southern drawl, rang out from behind them, right as Atticus was about to open the door. He turned to see Kieran McCullough, their team captain and starting middle blocker, standing impatiently behind them.

"Out," Kieran ordered, pointing at the door before planting his hands on the backs of Atticus and Bowen's heads and shoving them forward. "Now. We're late."

The three of them burst into the gym, the sounds of their teammates running drills already echoing throughout the space, shouts for the ball, the squeak of shoes on the shiny wood flooring, the sharp trill of Coach Rodriguez's whistle. Bowen jogged off, Kieran stepping up beside Atticus to take his place as they walked toward the court.

"Thanks man," Atticus said, voice low.

Kieran only shrugged. "Bo doesn't know what the fuck he's talking about eighty-percent of the time."

"What about the other twenty?"

A chuckle escaped Kieran. "All golden retriever energy, no thoughts at all. That's why you love him."

Atticus huffed, but he couldn't deny it. "When did you get back?"

"About an hour ago." Kieran sighed, running a hand over his scruffy face before reaching up to tie his chin-length tawny waves into a loose bun.

"Your dad okay?"

"He's fine. Just overdid it in the sun yesterday morning."

The whole team had received a text the morning prior letting them know that their captain might miss a couple practices. His father had collapsed in a field on the family farm, and Kieran had needed to rush home, a two and a half hour drive from the city. Tension had been high in the group chat, considering the fact that these were their last practices before the start of the season that coming weekend. Kieran was always a steady presence on their team, gentle- if firm- and he always knew how to wrangle their rowdy bunch into something special on the court. He'd only been with the Cats for a single season, having accepted a deal the year before and leaving the St. Louis Hawks. All so he could be closer to home, closer to the farm that had begun to take up more and more of his time.

"Glad he's okay," Atticus said, slinging an arm around Kieran's shoulder. They'd grown up two towns apart, had played together in middle and high school. Kieran had always been around, and both Atticus and Sammie had felt the loss of their friend when he'd left to play for the Hawks right out of high school. It was good to have him back, even if Atticus did worry about the bags under his friend's eyes and the way he seemed more and more stretched thin.

"Sammie sent him an edible arrangement." Kieran chuckled. "He loved it. Ate the whole thing and bragged to the doctor about her like she's one of his own kids."

Atticus held back a wince. Sammie would *not* like the idea of being considered a sister to Kieran. Considering the fact that she'd been pretty solidly in love with him since middle school.

"She said you're bringing her some grain this week?" They'd reached the court, and Atticus fell into his warm up stretches with ease, Kieran mirroring the motions.

"I'm going back to the farm in a couple days to check in on dad again." He stretched one arm across his broad chest, breathing out slowly before switching to the other arm. "I'll bring her pallets back with me."

Atticus only nodded, biting his lip to keep from saying anything more. Sammie would murder him slowly and viciously if he made any comment about how much she looked forward to the days when Kieran dropped off her grain shipment at the brewery.

Their conversation trailed off and Atticus went through the rest of his warm-up in silence. There was still a nagging at the back of his mind, an annoying stab like a splinter that had lodged into place when Bowen had been ragging on him for taking Kai home.

It hadn't been like *that*. Atticus hated the idea that his team, that his friends, might have gotten the wrong idea about why Kai had left with Atticus. Even Julian had jumped to the conclusion that it was another hookup when he'd texted Atticus that morning.

Atticus moved into position as they began to play in earnest, taking his place to serve. A deep breath in. Hold. He met Bowen's eyes across the net, his teammate glowing with excitement to get this practice match going. *Hold*.

A flick of his wrists had the ball soaring into the air. Atticus stepped forward, once, twice, launching himself up. He put all of his frustration, all of his annoyance at how people perceived him, how his *friends* perceived him, into the serve, slamming his hand into the ball to send it crashing across the net.

Bowen executed a perfect dig, sending the ball toward Aaron Jacobs, their second-string setter. Aaron's set was a little wobbly, sweat already beading on his dark brown skin. He'd gone too hard in the warm up, and his stance was just a little off. Atticus made a mental note to set aside some time to work with the rookie later in the week.

When Bowen leapt up for the spike he was blocked by Kieran. After a quick scramble, they finally got the ball to sail back over the net.

Eric crashed to his knees, but bumped the ball just right. "Second touch!"

Atticus was ready, eyes trailing the ball. This was his moment, a second touch meant for the setter. He was blinded by the bright lights above for the span of a single breath, but it didn't matter. He knew *exactly* where to be, arms up and ready, back arching as he pushed off the floor. He might be a fuck up in life, unable to break past the reputation he'd built for himself. Unable to win over the only heart he'd ever truly been interested in.

But he was a *damn* good setter.

The second touch landed perfectly against his fingers. Atticus locked eyes with Kieran at the same moment. His captain was already in motion, had known from the second that Atticus leapt for the ball where he would be needed.

A flawless set, the ball arching toward Kieran, who was already flying toward it, arm swinging forward and down. The players on the other side weren't ready, a heartbeat behind as two of them launched themselves up. A moment too late as Kieran slammed a cut shot past them.

Atticus felt it, the crash of the volleyball against the wooden floor. Felt the vibration in the soles of his feet, echoing up into his chest, through his body. This was what he loved about volleyball. The way he felt connected to it all. To the ball, to the court, to his teammates. They were all one organism, working in tandem, complementing, supporting. It didn't matter if they ragged on each other, didn't matter if Bowen drove Atticus up a wall with his teasing comments that didn't land quite right.

That feeling of making it all work, making it all come together. The way Atticus was at the core of it all, the whole team relying on him to set the ball *just so*. There was nothing like it.

As their teams reset, Atticus taking his place behind the line to ready for another serve, he couldn't help but wish that everything else was as easy for him as volleyball. Couldn't help but wish he could find the perfect set in everything else, as whiskey-colored eyes flashed in his mind.

"Is the lighting gonna be okay in here?"

Kai looked up at the question, before looking around the

guest bedroom he'd woken in that morning. He glanced back at Atticus, who was watching him with a soft, open smile and a question in his blue eyes.

"It'll be fine," Kai responded, letting the bag he carried slip off his shoulder to land on the bed. "I brought a light just in case."

It was Atticus' turn to glance around the room. "Not really anywhere to set up your stuff, though…"

Kai shrugged. "I can figure it out. I don't want to be in your way out there." He waved toward the common area.

"More like I don't want to be in the way of your streams," Atticus said. He paused, expression turning thoughtful. "Hang on, I think I've got something."

Atticus moved to leave the room, slipping past Kai as he did, a hand gently brushing across Kai's lower back as he passed by, sending a shiver up his spine at the contact. He could feel the heat of Atticus' skin, even through the thick fabric of the hoodie he still wore.

It had been like that all day. Atticus had never been shy about contact, had demonstrated a level of touch that had always felt comfortable to Kai. And since they'd left to get Kai's car earlier that morning, it had been more of the same. A shoulder bumping his own alongside a joke told, a hand lingering at the small of his back when they'd arrived back at Atticus' place at the same time, gently pushing Kai into the house. Every time, every single touch set Kai on fire.

He'd long since reconciled the fact that he was *very* attracted to Atticus. Physically. Who wouldn't be? But despite the way his blood fizzed every time the other man's skin brushed his own… that's all it was. Physical attraction. That's all Kai could allow it to be. Even if Atticus was good to him, even if Kai knew that the initial crush on NotYourKitten had transformed into something more since they'd gotten to know one another. Since the night they'd slept together.

Kai began unpacking his things, carefully placing his clothes into the drawers Atticus had said he could use. He tried to focus on the task at hand, tried to keep his mind from wandering back to that night.

He didn't tend to let himself think about the one time he and Atticus had slept together. Not often, anyway. But maybe it was the small touches that had been building up all day, or maybe it was the fact that he was in the other man's home, surrounded by things and scents that were distinctly *Atticus*. Because his mind did wander back to that night, just a bit. A memory of hands gripping his waist, harsh breaths against his neck, broad shoulders caging him in. A rush of something he hadn't felt in a long time as their bodies had moved together.

Kai huffed out a breath, scrunching his eyes shut as if he could block it all out that way. He shoved his socks into the drawer and pushed it closed too harshly. Turning back to the bed, he began to unpack some of his equipment, scowling at the way his hands were a little unsteady in their movements.

Another memory popped into his mind, unbidden and unwanted. A night, several months earlier, when he'd been sitting alone on his couch, feeling shitty and angry with the world. It had been months since his relationship with Nicholas had ended, all of the feelings of heartbreak and anger still sharp as razors under his skin, slicing with every movement, with every breath he took. He was angry with Nicholas, angry at the world. Angry at himself for sitting and wallowing in it all on yet another Friday night, after so much time had passed. What was so wrong with him, that he couldn't move on? Couldn't find a new way to be happy, a new way to exist that didn't hurt quite so much?

Kai had felt tears pricking his eyes, a lump in his throat and a tightness in his chest as he fought it all back. He'd been determined not to cry about it again, not to give his heartache any more of his tears.

He'd been so close to failing when his phone had chimed with a message.

Atticus: I loev you.

Kai had stared at his phone screen, blinking until his eyes were clear. It was the middle of the night, and he knew that the Cats had gone out drinking as a final celebration before more rigorous training for the end of season tournament.

Kai: Are you drunk?
Kai: Attie?

It hadn't really been what Kai had wanted to ask. *Do you mean it?* An affirmative answer came through next, followed by a slightly less drunk Ori taking Atticus' phone away. He'd asked Kai to be nice to Atticus the next day, not to embarrass him. It stung a little, the idea that Ori worried that he would be cruel to Atticus. They were friends at that point. Kai would never intentionally hurt him.

In the end, the messages had been deleted, and Kai had never brought them up. If Atticus remembered sending them, he'd never mentioned it.

Thinking about that night softened something in Kai, enough to brush the scowl from his face as he unzipped another of his travel bags.

He knew that Atticus felt some sort of way for him. Knew that the other man put their friendship first, pushed down whatever it was he felt so that they could comfortably stay in each other's lives. Kai's gut sank when he thought about his actions the night before, about the hazy memory he had of drunkenly asking Atticus to bring him here. About the implication in his words and actions.

It wasn't fair to Atticus for him to act like that. To say things like that, to imply that their relationship could turn into something more, even if it was just physical. Kai was too fucked up in the head, too unsteady even being on his own, despite the amount of time that had passed. Despite the fact that the person he was hung up on would never be in his life again. Not in the way he wanted.

Movement in the doorway pulled Kai's attention away from the microphone in his hands. He set it gently on the bed before turning to see Atticus lugging a small fold-up table into the room.

"Will this work?" Atticus asked, unfolding the legs and setting it up in a corner of the room. "You can use one of the chairs from the kitchen, I'll bring one in here for you."

"It'll be fine," Kai said, picking up a few things from the bed, moving to place them on the table. He turned to Atticus, staring until he had his attention. "I'm sorry about last night."

Atticus waved a hand. "I already told you, you have nothing to be…"

"No," Kai said, voice low. He forced himself to hold Atticus' gaze, to not look away from what he saw there, what it lit within him. "Not that I got drunk and you had to drag me home. I'm sorry that I acted like something was going to happen. That I used you like that in front of…"

His throat closed, refusing to let him finish the thought. Atticus shrugged his broad shoulders, that same charming grin still shining bright. "Nah, I get it," he said, turning to look at everything Kai had placed on the table. Kai didn't fail to notice the slightly pink tint on his cheeks. "You needed an out, I was happy to help. It's fine." Atticus leaned forward, snatching something up from the table.

"Cute," he said, his grin slipping into something a bit more teasing. He held a pair of Kai's headphones. They were a soft pink, nearly the same shade as the ends of his hair, and sported a pair of cat ears. Atticus put them on. "How do they look on me?"

Kai smirked, playing at nonchalance as he inwardly breathed a sigh of relief that the conversation had been diverted. Maybe it wasn't a good thing, maybe they needed to talk about it more. But Atticus always had a knack for knowing when Kai could handle talking about the hard stuff, and when he couldn't. It made Kai's heart beat a little faster, knowing that Atticus was trying to make him feel better.

Kai couldn't help but smirk. "Your big head is going to stretch them out."

Atticus narrowed his eyes, but his smile grew even wider, even brighter. He reached out, tucking a strand of Kai's hair behind his ear. The brush of his fingers sent sparks across Kai's cheek, lit up his skin from within. It dawned on him suddenly just how close they were standing to one another. He could feel Atticus' breath against his face as he leaned forward, pulling the headphones off his own head before placing them over Kai's ears.

"They look better on you anyway," Atticus said, that stupid, charming, *fucking* grin still there. His hand lingered, fingers brushing along Kai's jaw as he slowly pulled them away.

They were close, so close, and Kai couldn't help but think about how easy it would be to close the distance between them, to feel the press of soft lips against his one more time. It would be wrong, so wrong, but every now and then Kai couldn't help but want to toss all caution to the wind, consequences be damned. His heart might be shattered and caged away, but what was stopping him from simply enjoying himself, from letting his body take the lead?

Kai stood frozen in place, his breath hitching as Atticus moved his hand to cup the back of Kai's neck. He knew Atticus could feel it too, was sure that he wanted to act on whatever was happening between them even more than Kai did.

It could hurt them. Both of them. Kai didn't want to lead Atticus on, didn't want to lose their friendship. But with the other man towering over him, making him feel so small and so *safe*, blonde hair falling over his forehead- still a little sweaty from practice- as he looked down at Kai, all thoughts of the risks started to slip away.

Kai was going to lean in, he was going to close the distance between them. Capture those soft lips with his own and say fuck it to the consequences.

A squeak sounded, just outside the bedroom window.

They turned their heads at the same time, and the moment shattered. Another squeak, slightly louder, a little more recognizable. Kai looked back at Atticus, who had shifted back, putting space between them. As though he too realized what they'd been about to do, realized that maybe it wasn't such a good idea.

Another sound from outside the window.

Mrrrow.

Atticus finally turned back to face Kai.

"Is that a cat?"

The kitten sat on the kitchen counter, staring at Atticus for a long moment before going back to licking her paw. He bumped Kai's shoulder.

"Her eyes look just like yours," he said. He watched Kai squint, his expression thoughtful. He only hummed at the observation.

Her eyes did look like Kai's though, wide and amber, almost flecked with gold when the lighting hit just right, something behind them that was potentially life-threatening.

She was probably really pretty, too. Underneath all of the dirt. Hints of stark black markings, tabby coloring, peeked through. Atticus winced a little as she flopped onto her side, stretching languidly next to her empty food plate and spreading mud across his previously clean countertop. Sammie would murder him if she found out that a filthy animal was readying herself to take a nap in the same place Atticus typically prepared food.

"Should we give her a bath?"

Kai hadn't said much as they'd gone outside to investigate the meows that had interrupted whatever it was they'd been about to do. His question now was the first full sentence he'd spoken, in fact.

Atticus shifted, painfully aware of how close they were standing, how all he had to do was lean the slightest bit and their arms would be pressed together. "Yeah, a bath is probably a good idea." The words came out automatically, his mind distracted by the knowledge that he'd almost kissed Kai just fifteen minutes earlier. The knowledge that Kai had almost kissed *him*.

Well, *maybe* Kai had almost kissed him. Hard to say.

There was clearly an attraction between the two of them, that much had been obvious from the first time they'd met. But ever since that first night, they'd never acted on it again. Kai had very clearly not wanted to act on it again. But Atticus knew he wasn't crazy. He'd recognized the look in the other man's eyes, the heat and desire held there as they'd stood so close.

Would it have been a mistake? Probably. Still, Atticus couldn't help but mentally curse the kitten on his counter for interrupting them.

They'd found her outside, squawking as though she were hungry, a little skittish until Kai had knelt down next to her. Atticus had watched in awe as Kai's calm voice and gentle presence had lured her in, had watched as he'd scooped her up into his arms and she had melted against him.

"What?" Kai had asked, tilting his head as Atticus stared, a little amazed at the turn of events. He finally shrugged.

"Like calls to like, I guess," he had said teasingly, motioning from Kai to the cat. Kai had only scowled at him, moving past to take their new friend inside.

She was skinny, and was clearly hungry, so Atticus had pulled out some pre-cooked, frozen chicken he'd prepped a few days ago, thawing it quickly. The kitten had devoured it, begging for more before finally giving up and lazily sprawling across the counter. Atticus watched her cleaning a paw, saw the claws there.

"You ever give a cat a bath before?"

Kai shook his head. Atticus smirked. "Wear long sleeves."

An hour later, they had both managed to avoid those razor-sharp claws, but Atticus was pretty sure his ears were still ringing from the yowls the kitten had let out as they'd worked together to wash the dirt from her. Luckily, no fleas or other pests had been found in her fur. One of her ears was dirtier though, and it looked red and irritated inside.

Atticus placed her on his bed, still wrapped in the towel he'd been drying her off with. "Sammie knows a local vet, I'm gonna see if I can get her in tomorrow." He sat down on the bed as the kitten scrambled her way out of the towel, whirling around with her paws spread as though she could ward off another trip to the bath.

"You're going to keep her?" Kai asked, hesitating before he also sat down on the bed, pulling his legs up and wrapping his arms around his knees. His shirt was soaked from the water that had been splashed all over the bathroom, the ends of his hair wet as well, turning them a darker shade of pink. Atticus fought the urge to reach over, to push the hair away from his face again. Just like he'd done earlier in the guest room.

He felt as though he was constantly fighting the urge to touch Kai, in even the smallest of ways.

"Don't know yet," Atticus said. "Have to see if she's chipped, she might already have a home." He paused, watching as the small animal flailed around on his bed, damp spots appearing on his blanket wherever she rolled around. "She's kinda funny though, isn't she?"

Kai gave him a small smile, those brilliant eyes lighting up and making Atticus' heart feel like it might beat out of his chest. "She is."

Atticus needed a distraction, or else he might leap across the bed and pin the other man beneath him. That small smile, directed at him? Atticus could feel his entire body heating up at the sight, just the way it always did whenever Kai looked at him like that. He pulled his gaze away, reaching over to his nightstand to grab the remote there. He turned on the small tv that hung on the wall across from his bed, flicking through the options until he got to what he was looking for.

"This isn't the one you were watching earlier," Kai said, a hint of question in his voice. Atticus tossed the remote aside.

"I just like having something on in the background," he responded. "Doesn't matter what. I just click whatever pops up first. 'Sides, I've seen this one before."

He watched as Kai's eyes stayed focused on the anime for a few more moments. The light from the single window in the room was growing dim, the glow of the tv becoming their only source of illumination. Kai finally turned back to him.

"What are you going to name her?" Kai asked, reaching out to scratch his nails on the blanket. The kitten lost her mind at the motion, throwing herself toward him frantically, biting softly on the pad of his thumb. Kai's small smile turned into a bigger one, eyes scrunching, a soft laugh escaping him. Atticus felt as though he would lose his mind as well. He looked at the characters on the screen to distract himself.

"What about Kyo?"

Kai snorted. "Kyo's a boy."

"So what?" Atticus said, grinning. "Pet names transcend gender."

Kai laughed. "I guess," he said, and Atticus watched as he continued to play with the kitten. She was in his lap now, batting at the still damp ends of his hair that fell around his face. "Doesn't really suit her, though."

"Well," Atticus said, "we can keep trying then."

Kai looked up at that, and Atticus realized what he'd said. The implication that they'd be naming this cat together, that this was something they were taking on *together*. He felt his cheeks heat. He needed another distraction, anything to get out from under the serious gaze Kai was pinning him with.

"You hungry?" he asked. Kai blinked.

"A little."

Atticus rose from the bed. "You keep her company, I'm going to shower real quick and then I'll make us a pizza." He hurried from the room, decidedly *not* thinking about the fact that he and Kai may have just become pet parents together.

He hurried to get the frozen pizza in the oven- his grandma probably rolled in her grave as he did- before hopping into the shower, letting the cold water soak into him, soothing the burn in his muscles from practice, as well as the flush on his skin that had built a little more every time Kai looked at him. It wasn't long before he returned to his bedroom carrying two plates, pausing in the doorway.

"She fell asleep," Kai said softly. The kitten was curled up in his lap, a tiny ball of fur. He looked up, wide-eyed. "I can't move."

Atticus laughed softly, moving to sit cross-legged on the bed next to the other man, passing him a plate. They ate the pizza in silence, watching an anime they'd both seen before.

Atticus felt like he wasn't actually taking any of it in, his mind wholly focused on what was happening next to him.

This was what he wanted. It wasn't about the sex, the incredible, life-altering, one-time only sex. It was this. The quiet, the existing next to one another so comfortably. The eating in bed while they watched tv. The closeness, the unspoken solace they found in one another's presence.

Atticus wanted this. He wanted it with Kai more than almost anything. It made his heart ache a little, knowing he was alone in that desire. Knowing that he was the only one sitting there wishing the moment could last a lifetime. Knowing that Kai was right there, right next to him, but still so far out of reach.

But maybe he could have a week of this. A week of everything he wished for, everything he'd spent the last year desperately aching for.

Atticus took their empty plates to the kitchen, taking his time to wash and dry them, putting them away as if in slow motion. Soaking up the domesticity of it all.

When he returned to his room once again, Kai had shifted positions. The kitten was sprawled out on the bed, still asleep and content, pressed into Kai's chest where he lay on his side. His head was propped up by an arm, eyes heavy-lidded and sleepy as his other hand rubbed the kitten's fur.

"She's sweet," he whispered as Atticus propped a pillow up against his headboard. He sank back onto the bed, letting himself relax a little more than he had so far.

"Yeah," Atticus said softly, reaching out to run a finger across her forehead. She pushed into the touch without opening her eyes. "I wasn't planning on a pet right now, but I sort of hope she doesn't already belong to someone else."

Kai smiled. The small one again, the one that Atticus loved best. The smile that barely reached his eyes, the one that seemed to *just* break through any attempts to hold it back.

"Me too."

Kai woke with a start. The room was dark, the television stuck on a black screen that simply asked if they were still watching.

He didn't remember falling asleep. Didn't remember moving, didn't remember pressing up against the other body in the bed. He lifted his head, eyes barely adjusted to the dark.

The kitten was curled into a ball on Atticus' pillow, right up against the back of his head. Atticus was asleep as well, breaths even and deep. He lay so close that Kai could feel each exhale against his own hair as he let his head fall back to the pillow.

At some point he had moved, pressed himself close to Atticus' chest. A strong arm was wrapped around his shoulder, holding him tight, their legs tangled together.

It stirred something in Kai, something he couldn't sort out. Something he was unwilling to sort out.

His traitorous mind took him back, forced him to remember what it had been like to sleep this close to someone every night. Forced him to remember how it had felt to wake up with someone else, to not be alone in his bed. But instead of thinking about how he could have that again, how he could reach for that with Atticus, his mind brought up a different face.

Sly eyes that looked so soft in the mornings. Raven-dark hair that was always even messier after sleep. Waking up to a soft grin, an even softer press of lips to his own.

Kai hated himself a little, for thinking about Nicholas while he was wrapped in Atticus' arms. While he was so comfortable in Atticus' bed, their bodies pressed so close. He hated himself for the constant reminders, for not being able to look past them, for not being able to just forget and move on.

He felt so broken. Like something within him had shattered a year prior, and the pieces had fallen in a way that wedged the hole inside of him wide open. A gaping wound that refused to close.

His jaw began to ache from how hard he was clenching his teeth, a manifestation of the frustration he lived with daily. A part of him wanted to close his eyes, try to just go back to sleep, let them wake up together in the morning and see where things went.

A bigger part of him knew he couldn't do that. Knew that he couldn't let Atticus think that something more was happening, not when Kai couldn't give that part of himself to the other man.

Kai slowly, carefully untangled himself from Atticus' hold. Neither he nor the kitten woke. Atticus only shifted a little, his arm moving as though he were reaching out. It made Kai burn with resentment. At himself, at Nicholas. Maybe even a little bit at Atticus, for being so good. For being everything that Kai needed, and everything that his mind and heart refused to let him have.

He made sure to close the door on his way out of the room. Best to keep the kitten in there where she couldn't get into anything. He figured they would spend a portion of the next day cat-proofing the house. The thought normally would have brought a smile to his lips, but he was too wrapped up in the spiral his brain had him trapped in.

Kai slipped into his own bed. He knew it would hurt, but he pulled out his phone anyway. Pulled up the message Nicholas had sent him that morning.

I've missed you so much.

Fuck him. Fuck Nicholas for thinking that saying something like that was okay. That it in any way compared to what Kai had been through in the last year. They'd both lost a friendship, a friendship that ran so deep it had felt ingrained in their souls. But Kai had lost more. So much more. Because in the end, when it all had come to a crashing halt, it had become glaringly clear that Kai's feelings had been so much more. That what he'd felt had pulsed deeper in his veins, had sung louder with every beat of his heart. And Nicholas had taken it all away. Had ripped the rug out from under the entire life Kai had seen spread out before them.

How do you ever move on from that loss? Kai hadn't just lost a lover, he'd lost everything they had planned together. He'd lost the only person he'd ever let in like that, the only person he'd ever let see him in a way that laid him bare completely.

He'd lost his future.

Kai tossed his phone onto the other side of the bed. The empty side.

He fell asleep wishing he still felt an arm wrapped around him, holding him and keeping him safe, even from himself.

4 Years Ago

"Where does this one go?" Nicholas asked, head barely peeking out from behind the massive box. "I can't see what's written on the top!"

Kai stretched onto the tips of his toes as his boyfriend leaned forward.

"Bedroom," he said. Nicholas moved in the direction of their room, grinning as he walked past.

"Ohoho," he said with a wink. "Is this the box with all the sex stuff?"

"Jesus *fuck*, Nicholas!" Kai hissed, shoving the other man out of the main room. "Someone will hear you!"

Nicholas laughed as they made their way to the bedroom. "I love when you're mad enough to use my full name!" Kai rolled his eyes.

"I don't really need Ori asking me what you meant by 'sex stuff,' he'll start searching all the boxes so he can tease me about it all later," he said plainly, watching as Nicholas sat the box next to their bed. "Besides, I think that one's all of your shoes."

Nicholas stared down at the box. "I don't have that many shoes."

"You definitely have that many shoes," Kai said. He tried-and failed- to keep a stern look on his face as he moved across the room.

"Well," Nicholas said, reaching out and pulling Kai toward him. Even after so much time had passed, four years since they'd finally gotten together, it still made Kai's pulse tick up a notch whenever his boyfriend wanted him close. "Even if I *do* have that many shoes, it's fine because we have a big closet now."

Nicholas looked around the room as his arms tightened around Kai's waist. Kai followed his gaze, taking in the space. *Their* space.

The room was empty save the bed and the box. Nicholas had insisted on setting the bed up first.

"Just in case," he'd said with a wink as they were unloading boxes with their friends. Ori had snickered like an actual child, while Theo had only rolled his eyes as Kai's cheeks had heated. He hadn't actually minded, though. No longer having to deal with sneaking around each other's family homes sounded wonderful.

"It doesn't feel real," Kai said, voice low as he pulled himself back to the present, let himself soak in the feeling of Nicholas' arms wrapped around him. Nicholas glanced back down, his sly grin shifting into something softer, something just for Kai.

"Sure it does," he said, lifting a hand to brush Kai's hair back from his face. "It's everything we've talked about finally happening."

The words rang through Kai. They'd been together for so long now, had talked for years about getting a place together, about what it would be like to not have to leave at the end of the night, about how they would spend all their extra time with one another. Nicholas had a *lot* of suggestions for that.

Kai had started streaming his gaming as just a fun hobby. If he was going to be playing the games anyway, he might as well try it. He'd never expected to gain so many followers so quickly. The last year had been a struggle to find the right balance with his classes, his boyfriend, his part-time job at the arcade, and the streams that had quickly become more profitable than his job. He'd quit the arcade six months earlier, had moved that energy into his gaming, upgrading his equipment and turning the whole thing into a more professional venture.

And it had worked. It had worked so well that he and Nicholas had finally been able to afford renting a small apartment together. It wasn't in the nicest part of the city, and Kai really would have preferred to move to a more rural location, but it was still *theirs*. A place for them to be together, fully together.

"I'm glad it's finally happening, Nicky," he said, letting a smile slip through at last. Nicholas beamed at him.

"Me too," Nicholas said, leaning down to press their lips together. Kai could feel him still smiling.

They broke apart after a few seconds, when the sound of footsteps echoed through the empty main room and Ori's excited voice rang out, asking where to put the box he was carrying. Theo barked something at him, his clipped south London accent making him sound more stern. Their friends might be dysfunctional, but they'd jumped at the opportunity to help Kai and Nicholas get settled in their new place.

Ori had always been around, since their school days. They'd adopted Theo in shortly after he'd moved to the states and started taking classes at the University of Chicago. He was a teaching major, just like Nicholas, sharing many of the same classes. Ori had latched on to Theo as well, the only other openly gay man on the volleyball team. The four of them had been a little unit ever since.

"Come on," Nicholas said, grinning as he grabbed Kai's hand and pulled him out of the room. "Let's go find the box with all the sex stuff!"

Kai only glared as Nicholas' laughter echoed through the apartment.

4

Atticus felt like someone had punched him in the gut. His breath huffed out in a whoosh as his eyes flew open. He came fully awake to the sight of the kitten using his abs as a springboard. She flung herself off of him, continuing her mad dash around the room.

"Girlie, I don't think that's necessary," he wheezed, still reeling from getting the breath knocked out of him. The kitten continued to scramble around the room, her nails scraping against the hardwood floor in a way that made him wince. He grabbed his phone, blinking at the sudden light. Six in the morning. A little earlier than he liked to get up normally, but he was fully awake now so no sense in trying to go back to sleep.

Atticus rolled out of bed, flicking the light on, finally noticing a little bit of a smell permeating his room. He sniffed himself before glancing around.

There was cat shit in the corner.

He sighed. At least she hadn't done it on the bed. Atticus

mentally made note of making sure to get a litter box first.

The kitten flew out of his room the moment the door was opened. Atticus followed, watching as she ran through the house while he gathered stuff to clean up her mess. It didn't take him long, but by the time he was done and back in his living room, she had managed to knock every throw pillow off his couch, scatter some Wildcats forms he'd left out, and was perched on one of the end tables.

Right next to a glass of water he'd forgotten to put away.

The kitten stared at him, faint light from the sunrise glinting off her golden eyes, body stiff and completely still.

"Don't you dare," Atticus whispered, voice low so as not to wake his house guest. They watched each other for a long moment. A stand off.

The kitten moved, body jerking to the side as her paw snapped out and smacked the glass. Atticus watched it fall in slow motion before it hit the hardwood floor and shattered. The crash broke the complete silence that had engulfed the house. Atticus cringed as the kitten hopped off the end table, calmly walking over to one of the pillows she'd knocked to the floor and curling into a ball on top of it.

He was still sweeping up the shards of glass when he felt another presence enter the room. He turned, his body going still at the sight of a *very* sleepy Kai entering the kitchen.

"What happened?"

Kai's voice was huskier than normal, his words thick with sleep. His hair was mussed up and a bit tangled, eyelids heavy, shoulders slumped as he made his way to one of the barstools and perched there. He kept his gaze trained on Atticus.

"She knocked over a glass," Atticus said, waving toward the sleeping creature. He realized he was staring and pulled his attention back to the broom in his hands. "Sorry we woke you up."

Kai huffed out a small laugh. "I can't remember the last time I was up this early."

Atticus grinned. "Gimme a minute and I'll get some coffee going."

He could feel Kai's gaze on him as he moved through the kitchen, first tossing out the broken glass before moving to the coffee pot. Once he had that going, he turned, meeting Kai's steady stare.

"I don't usually do anything fancy for breakfast," he said. "There's still some rice and leftover veggies from yesterday. Oatmeal. Some fruit too."

Kai smirked. "You're not going to cook every meal for me while I'm here?"

"No," Atticus said, smiling as he leaned on the counter, closing some of the distance between them. "Not every meal. But a bunch of 'em."

"I was kidding." Kai looked a little flustered, and Atticus felt his grin widen. "You don't need to cook for me, it's enough that you're letting me stay here."

"I don't mind. It's kind of nice, actually," Atticus said. "Feels a little sad just cooking for one person all the time, ya know?"

"Not really." Kai laughed softly, and Atticus thought that hearing that laugh first thing in the morning was the best possible way to start his day. "Cooking isn't really my thing."

"Yeah," Atticus teased, "I've seen all the takeout boxes."

"We can't all be good at everything."

"Are you saying I'm good at everything?"

Kai rolled his eyes, pulling a full laugh from Atticus.

"Well, I'm not cooking for you this morning, so help yourself to whatever," Atticus said, grabbing an orange from a bowl on the counter. "I'm going for a run soon, you in?"

Kai gave him a bored stare. "Attie. It's way too early to be running."

"Nah!" Atticus moved around to the other side of the counter, bumping Kai's shoulder, his insides buzzing at the nickname. Only his family had ever called him Attie. Hearing it from Kai, it filled him with a sense of comfort. A sense of something that felt a little like home. "Come on, it'll be good for you!"

Kai flopped forward, head falling onto his arms, messy hair fanning out. It took everything in Atticus to keep his hands to himself, to not reach out and run his fingers through the soft strands. Kai released a hearty groan.

"Give me twenty minutes," he finally mumbled, his voice muffled. Atticus chuckled. He glanced toward the kitten, still napping on her pillow, before glancing back at the dishes he'd left drying on the rack the night before. Best to put those away before she caused another incident.

Twenty minutes later the kitchen counters were cleared and Atticus was waiting just outside the front door. He stretched, relishing the cool morning air on his skin. It was a pretty day, the sky giving way to a bright, cloudless blue. He turned as the door swung inward.

Kai had changed into athletic wear, shorts that showed off his slim, toned legs, a long-sleeved shirt that hugged his skin and left nothing to Atticus' imagination. He could feel his eyes being drawn to that soft, slender waist, forced himself not to stare, pulling his gaze up toward Kai's face. Wasn't much better.

A braid. Kai had braided his hair back, and all Atticus could think about when he saw it was how much he wanted to tug on it. A few strands of hair had already escaped, pink ends falling around Kai's face, framing his wide stare. He looked a little more awake as he began working through some stretches as well.

Atticus wasn't going to make it. Why had he invited Kai to run with him? He knew his own weaknesses. A hot guy in polyester? Done. He was done. And now he had that braid to contend with as well, a new discovery. He couldn't stop thinking about wrapping his hand around it, pulling just enough to expose Kai's throat, leaning in and…

"Ready?"

Kai's voice yanked Atticus out of his thoughts, which had been headed toward dangerous territory that the thin fabric of his own shorts wouldn't have been able to disguise.

Atticus shook himself, bouncing in place, focusing on anything besides how good Kai looked.

"Let's go!"

He took off, Kai right behind him.

Kai and Atticus stood side-by-side in the aisle, staring at the vibrant display of color before them.

"There are so many," Atticus whispered, a little awed.

"How do we know which ones she'll like?" Kai turned to look at him. Atticus was already reaching out, snatching toys off the shelves.

"Guess we just have to get one of everything," he said, shrugging. Kai looked back at the display, eyes searching.

They'd been in the pet supply store for half an hour already, had arrived right as one of the employees was flipping the sign from 'closed' to 'open'. Their cart was already pretty full- a litter box, a couple of small beds, a pet carrier, some food that Atticus had spoken with the vet about. He'd called earlier that morning, right after their run, setting up an appointment for later in the day and asking a few questions. Kai had watched and listened, still out of breath from the exercise.

Atticus' face had lit up when the vet mentioned that the chances of their kitten already belonging to someone else were slim. Kai could see the excitement there in his eyes, in the way they crinkled at the corners as he smiled brightly. It had made his insides flip-flop in a very noticeable way.

He looked over to see Atticus smiling in that exact way now, and his body reacted just the same. It was probably best to ignore his flopping insides for the time being.

As soon as it became clear that he would most likely be able to keep the kitten, Atticus had been full send on the idea, insisting they immediately go pick up some supplies. It was cute, the way he was so enamored by the tiny creature, even if Kai's mind, his heart, rejected the way it made him feel.

He kind of got it, though. The excitement. She was a pretty cute little cat.

Kai reached out, grabbing a toy hanging from one of the pegs.

"I think she'll like this one."

Atticus glanced over, pausing with an arm full of glittery, fuzzy balls and stuffed mice. Kai held up his find- a long stick with a string hanging down, a bell and a feather attached to the end.

"Yep," Atticus said matter-of-factly. "Put it in the cart."

Kai's phone pinged right as he placed the toy into their basket. He casually checked the screen, turning away from Atticus as soon as he saw who the text was from.

Nicholas: I just wanted to make sure you got my message yesterday. Maybe you've blocked my number already, I hope not. I hope that we can just sit down and talk while I'm still in town, I hope that you'll let that happen. I'm so afraid that too much time has passed, that it's too late to fix things now. But we were friends first Kai, we were friends for so long. I have to believe that we can get back to that place. Please just talk to me.

Kai felt an immediate gnawing sensation, deep in his gut, a pain that only ever surfaced when he thought about Nicholas. No, no, not today, not right now. He clicked his phone off harshly, shoving it into the pocket of his hoodie. Atticus was laughing to himself as he messed with a toy that lit up and whirled around at the press of a button. He looked so happy, and watching him relaxed something in Kai. He couldn't deal with Nicholas right now, didn't *want* to deal with Nicholas or the way thinking about his ex always turned him into such a mood killer.

"Get that one too," he said, voice soft as he stepped closer. He hoped Atticus didn't hear the hint of anxiety hidden in the words.

They continued on like that, adding more and more cat toys to their little collection, before finally moving on to the end of the aisle. There was one last thing they needed.

"Hmmm." Atticus put a hand to his chin, tapping his full lower lip, indecision coating his features. "I don't like these options."

Kai stared at him. "What do you *mean*? There are literally dozens to choose from." He waved a hand toward all of the collars displayed on the wall. Atticus narrowed his eyes.

"But none of them feel like *her*."

Kai glanced back toward the selection, eyes searching. Surely they could settle on one of the collars. He reached out, snatching up a solid black one. The material felt cheap in his hands. Kai put it back, studying the sparkly pink one next to it. No, that wasn't right either…

He sighed. "I hate that you're right."

Atticus grinned, bumping against Kai's side. "But I *am* right, eh?"

Kai scowled. "I'll look at the online options later."

"Great!" Atticus clapped his hands together before

grabbing their cart and pushing it toward the registers. "Let's go, I've gotta get her to her appointment. And you've got a stream, right?"

"Yeah." Kai followed close at the other man's side as they moved through the store. As the last of their items were rung up, he pulled out his card, swiping it before Atticus could catch on.

"No!" Atticus pushed Kai away from the card terminal, but it was too late. Kai slipped his wallet back into his pocket with a smirk.

"You're paying for the vet appointment," he said. The cashier glanced back and forth between them, a bored stare on her face. "It's only fair."

"But she's my cat," Atticus said, looking away to snatch up some of their bags. Kai felt something sink inside himself at the words. He turned away, picking up the pet carrier and beds, schooling his features into something close to neutral.

"I found her with you," he said, voice steadier than he felt. "I helped get her cleaned up. I feel a little responsible for her."

He could feel Atticus' eyes boring a hole into the side of his head as they exited the store. They were silent until they reached the car. Atticus popped the trunk and began loading stuff in, a small smile on his face.

"What?" Kai finally broke, his insides twisting at that little smirk now focused on him.

"Okay." Atticus nodded. "She can be your cat too."

It was silly, the way Kai's spirits lifted at the words. Of course she couldn't be his cat too. They didn't live together. This wasn't a co-parenting situation. She was Atticus' cat, and Kai was just Atticus' friend. But still, something about the idea of them doing this together made Kai's pulse speed up.

"Maybe just for the week," he mumbled, earning a laugh from the other man as he slammed the trunk closed. Atticus still wore that smug little smile as they pulled out of the parking lot and headed home.

Atticus had just set the pet carrier down on his porch to dig for his keys when the front door opened.

"Hey, thanks!" He grinned at Kai, feeling a little flustered as he picked up the carrier and entered his own home. It was still strange, having someone else there. Not to mention the fact that Kai looked kind of adorable as he helped Atticus with the items he'd acquired from the vet.

"How'd it go?" Kai asked as Atticus set the carrier on the living room floor. The moment he opened it, the kitten flew out, dashing across the room and skidding on the hardwood floor as she tried to keep from smacking into the wall. She failed, crashing in a mess of limbs and fur, only to bounce back up and disappear down the hallway.

"No chip!" Atticus couldn't keep the excitement out of his voice. Kai offered up a smile of his own, genuine cheer lighting up his amber eyes.

"She has an ear infection." Atticus placed some paperwork and a small prescription bag on the kitchen counter. "Everything else looked good though. Still waiting on the results from some bloodwork, but the vet said not to worry."

"Did you give them a name for her?" Kai smirked as he asked the question, leaning back casually against the counter as Atticus studied the antibiotic the vet had prescribed. Not that he could focus on the instructions. Not when Kai looked like *that*.

He'd clearly made an effort to look nice for his stream that he'd done while Atticus had been gone. Hair pulled back into a bun that was artfully messy, showing off the many piercings that studded his left ear, the gold jewelry glinting under the kitchen lights. A few strands of pink-tipped hair framed his face, screaming for Atticus to reach out and run his fingers through them. The white t-shirt Kai wore was several sizes too big, showing off his sharp collarbones. The long lines of his neck were emphasized by the plain black choker he wore.

Atticus was staring, and Kai was still waiting for an answer to his question. He looked away, his face burning. "I told them she doesn't have a name yet, so they just put mine down for now."

"We have to name her, Attie!" Laughter colored Kai's words, sending sparks down Atticus' spine. It took everything in him not to reach out, not to pull Kai close and feel that laughter rumble against his own chest.

"Well," Atticus finally said, turning away to put the medicine in the refrigerator. "Put on another show and see if any of the names fit her."

"Does she have to be named after an anime character?" Kai's voice came from further away. Atticus turned to see he'd moved to the couch, was sitting down, curling his legs up under himself.

"Yep," Atticus said. "That's how me and Sammie always picked pet names when we were kids. Had a dog named Luffy and a hamster named Goku."

Atticus almost tripped over the kitten as she ran back into the room. Kai snorted a small laugh at him again, eyes trailing the tattoos along his arm, gaze searing along Atticus' skin, before turning his attention to his phone. Atticus plopped down at the other end of the couch, watching as his new pet finally began to chill out. She padded around the room softly, rubbing against the furniture, sniffing at the new bed he'd placed in the corner. Her wide, golden eyes turned toward them often, as though she were making sure they were both still there.

"How'd your stream go?" Atticus asked. Kai chuckled, still

focused on his phone.

"It went great." His words came across as playful, and Atticus' heart beat harder when Kai's eyes crinkled at the corners. "They're all speculating about whose house I'm at. The fan server is going wild right now."

Atticus' brow furrowed as he made himself more comfortable, pulling his legs up onto the couch and stretching out. Kai glared as Atticus tried to plop his feet into his lap, pushing them away as Atticus cackled.

"They can tell you're not at home?" he asked. Kai nodded.

"They notice everything," he said. "The shippers are having a field day right now."

Kai's grin as he scrolled through comments on his phone was somewhat evil, and Atticus loved it.

"They talk about stuff like that? Your personal life?"

"Yeah," Kai said as he typed something. Atticus scrunched his nose up.

"That's a little weird, right?"

Kai shrugged. "I think it's funny. The ones rooting for me and Ori are losing their minds right now because someone brought up the mysterious, voice-only guy from a stream a couple months ago." He finally looked up from his phone, brows raised as he glanced at Atticus.

That had been him. Atticus had played on a few of Kai's streams a couple months prior, when they'd both been heavily invested in a new fantasy MMO. Dozens of hours spent playing together, until Atticus had started picking up more bartending shifts at Sammie's brewery to pad his wallet during the off season. He'd been voice only on the streams, identity kept anonymous because Kai had thought it would be fun to see people speculate. Atticus' pulse quickened as Kai looked at him.

"What are they saying about me?"

The kitten jumped into Kai's lap, startling him. The

mischievous look on his face softened into something sweeter as she curled up on his thighs.

"Some people think I had the best chemistry with the mysterious voice, so I must be at his place."

Kai was too distracted by the ball of fur begging for his attention. He didn't see Atticus look away at the words, didn't see the flash of something smug on his face.

Because he agreed. He and Kai *did* have chemistry. Why was Kai the only person who couldn't seem to see that?

He kicked Kai in the hip softly, a lopsided grin tilting his lips up. "Are you going to tell them it's me?"

Kai leveled a dry stare at him. "No. The chat would go nuts and it would only feed your ego."

"Aw, come on!" Atticus begged. "It'll be like a Cinderella story! I was one of them, once upon a time. A lowly viewer who only knew you through a screen. And look at me now! It'll give them hope!"

Kai chuckled, looking back at his phone as he mindlessly ran a hand through the kitten's fur. "Hope for what?"

"That they can have *the* Kai Reid, the famous NotYourKitten, puking in their bathroom one day!"

It was Kai's turn to launch a kick. His foot smacked into Atticus' thigh, and Atticus resolutely ignored the fire the contact sent through him.

They fell into silence, Kai still scrolling through his server. Atticus pulled out his own phone, opening up the camera and waiting for the right moment. Kai smiled at something on his screen, and Atticus stealthily snapped a picture. He opened his message app, typing quickly before hitting send.

Kai's phone pinged.

Atticus: *Attachment*
Atticus: How cute :D

A pink blush flooded Kai's cheeks. Atticus grinned as he looked at the picture again on his own phone. Kai, his face so relaxed and gentle, lit by the glow of his phone. A soft smile as his hand scratched at the kitten's head and she leaned up into the touch.

"Why are you texting me when we're in the same room?" Kai's words were bored and unamused, but the flush on his cheeks spoke to something else. Something more. Atticus felt his heart swell a bit inside his chest. He shrugged.

"Just wanted to." That was partially true. What he didn't say was that sometimes it was easier, saying things with a screen to hide behind. Even with the other person right there in the room. Because saying it out loud felt too real, and he knew Kai. Knew how skittish he was.

But Kai stared at screens all day, reading comments from others with a blank face or an eye roll. Maybe Atticus could be a little truthful, hidden behind a screen. Being together so much made him feel more bold, made him want to take chances.

Kai looked at him, gaze quizzical, cheeks still slightly pink. Atticus felt the weight of his stare fully. It made him feel like he was falling apart, like he couldn't hold his too big feelings inside much longer.

The doorbell rang, breaking the staring contest they'd been having. Atticus frowned in confusion as Kai got up. The kitten flopped out of his lap, still sleepy as she curled up in the spot he'd just left behind.

"I don't cook," Kai said sheepishly. "So I ordered us something." He left the room, left Atticus sitting on the couch, still a little lost in his own thoughts.

He knew Kai thought he was a flirt. Everyone thought he was a flirt, because, well, he *was*. So that made it safe, right? Safe to do things like send the text he'd just sent. He was just being his normal self, no harm no foul. He could be flirty while they were together for the week. Maybe it would get some of it out of his system, make it a little easier to just be Kai's friend.

Conversation was easy as they ate. They talked a little more about Kai's stream, about Atticus' upcoming game, the season opener. He threw out a few more names for the kitten, each one of them shot down by Kai for one reason or another, none of them quite fitting her personality.

It wasn't long after they ate and cleaned up before Atticus could feel sleep beckoning. They said their goodnights, going off to their separate rooms. Atticus was just slipping under his blanket when his phone chimed from where it sat on his nightstand. Sleep tugged at him, made his eyelids feel heavy as he grabbed the device and unlocked the screen.

Kai: *Attachment*
Kai: Cute

It was a picture of Atticus, apparently taken as he'd been washing their dishes. He was smiling, maybe even laughing at something Kai had said. His eyes were closed, expression cheerful as he leaned forward over the sink, the sleeves of his sweatshirt shoved up to his elbows. He looked happy.

Atticus smiled, focusing more on the message Kai had sent after with the picture. He knew it was just the other man teasing him for the text he'd sent earlier. Atticus couldn't help it, though, couldn't stop the spark it lit in his chest. Couldn't stop the smallest sliver of hope that swelled as he nodded off to sleep.

3 Years Ago

"What do you mean you have to work?"

Kai's voice rose, anger finally seeping into his words. Nicholas flinched.

"I'm sorry," the other man said, setting his briefcase down heavily on their kitchen table. "With the new position and all the new projects, I can't be gone for a full weekend. Not right now."

"But…" Kai sputtered a little. "I thought this is what *you* wanted to do!"

Nicholas laughed, harsh and biting. "It should be fine then, right? It's not like you ever want to go out and do anything anyway?"

"That's not fair." The accusation knocked some anger out of Kai, made his words come out smaller, weaker.

He'd planned a whole weekend for them, a short trip away, full of sightseeing. It was their anniversary, of sorts. Five years from the day they'd first kissed, the day they had fallen into their relationship. Kai hadn't known what to get Nicholas this year. They'd been together for so long, and the other man always just bought the things he wanted.

Kai's mother has suggested maybe going somewhere instead of getting something. His parents had just done something similar, had both come back from their weekend away acting like they were freshly in love all over again. All of the romance stuff, the cutesy couple stuff, it always came so easy to those two, and Kai couldn't understand why it was so different for him.

Kai always felt like he and Nicholas had to work a lot harder for that stuff.

And Nicholas was right. Kai *didn't* like going places. If given the choice, he would always rather avoid social situations, would always prefer the comfort of his home, of peace and quiet and routine.

But he had planned this for Nicholas. It wasn't about what Kai did or didn't want to do. It was a gift.

"Not fair?" Nicholas repeated Kai's words, sneering. "What's not fair is that we've cancelled plans a thousand times because you didn't want to go out. Or I've had to hang out with our friends alone because you needed to stream. But the one time I *can't* do something, I'm suddenly the bad guy?"

Kai didn't know what to say. Shock coursed through him, hitting him like waves, battering him against the cliff of his boyfriend's anger.

"I-," Kai began, choking on the word, throat tight with his dissipating rage and growing despair. It was always in situations like this that he couldn't find his voice, that it became physically impossible to respond, to speak up, to say whatever he needed to say to fix things.

But why hadn't Nicholas ever said anything before, about all of the times Kai didn't want to go out, didn't want to do things? It felt like something was lodged in his throat, something he had to push so hard to get past so that he could finally respond. "It's our anniversary, Nicky. I thought that it was different."

His soft words, his use of the nickname, it all seemed to deflate something in the other man. Nicholas was across the room in a heartbeat, hands on Kai's shoulders, fingers holding him steady, and Kai finally, *finally* felt like he could breathe easier with their eyes locked on one another.

"It is different," Nicholas said. "And I did want to go, Kai. I really did. But I just can't take the time off right now. I'm sorry." He pulled Kai into a hug, wrapping long arms around thin shoulders, resting his chin atop Kai's head. Kai leaned into the embrace.

"I'm sorry I yelled," Kai mumbled, melting a little against Nicholas' chest.

"It's okay," Nicholas said, pulling back to look down at Kai again. He smiled, lips pressed tight, the expression not quite reaching his eyes. "We've both been stressed with work stuff. I'm sorry too."

Nicholas pulled away, heading off down the hall to change out of his suit. Kai felt his absence immediately, acutely. They had apologized, but something still felt wrong. Out of place, maybe a little cracked. Kai wasn't sure what to say, what to do, to make that feeling go away. He followed after his boyfriend, leaning against the doorframe when he reached their room. The only light came from a small bedside lamp that Nicholas had flicked on, the rest of the room encased in shadow.

"Want to get takeout from the place on the corner?" It was Nicholas' favorite. If he had his way, they would order food from the little hole-in-the-wall diner every other night.

"Sure," Nicholas said. He was turned away, searching through his dresser for a t-shirt. Kai still wasn't sure how he ever found anything with the way he shoved all of his clothes into the drawers haphazardly. Only his work clothes got properly hung in their closet, his button up shirts and nice slacks, and only because Kai usually hung them there.

Kai moved across the room. He suddenly felt like he needed desperately to fix whatever was broken, was suddenly worried that something had wedged into the crack between them and if he didn't dislodge it soon then they would be pushed even further apart.

"Nicky," Kai said, right as the other man slipped on a wrinkled old t-shirt with their high school mascot holding a volleyball on the back. "Look at me."

Nicholas finally did, and Kai could still see traces of hurt in his eyes, in the tightness around his mouth. Kai stepped in close.

"I really am sorry."

Nicholas turned his head to the side, face falling slightly into shadow. He sighed, as if defeated.

"I know you are," Nicholas finally said. "I'm just tired. It was a long day, I had three more projects dumped onto my desk before I left. Just..." Nicholas looked down as Kai reached out and grabbed his hand, pausing his words. He smiled again, a slight tilt of his lips, and the expression made Kai feel a little better. Like he'd managed to shift whatever it was that was wedged in between them. "Just give me a few more minutes to decompress, okay?"

Kai nodded, squeezing the hand he still held. "I'll go ahead and place our order. Same as always?"

Nicholas grinned, that same cocksure smile he'd always been known for. It made Kai's heart raced hard, just like it always had. "Same as always."

Pulling out his phone and searching for the restaurant's number, Kai paused as he was leaving their room. He turned back, picking up the suit Nicholas had shed onto the floor and hanging it carefully in the closet.

"You know," Kai said. He could hear Nicholas moving around behind him, probably still searching for a pair of shorts in his mess of a drawer. "You're right. I really would rather just spend the weekend here at home with you."

He smoothed out the suit jacket before shutting their closet and turning to face Nicholas, expecting to see a smile at the fact that he'd acknowledged that his boyfriend had been right about him.

Instead, Nicholas was watching him. His face was somewhat shadowed once again, and Kai couldn't quite make out the expression there. Something soft, but maybe a little sad. It was gone in an instant, Nicholas flashing another grin.

"Come on," he said. Kai moved to follow him out of the room. "I'm starving, let's order!"

The words were cheerful. They didn't seem forced. It was as though their argument really was already in the past, forgiven and forgotten.

Kai felt as though the wedge had slipped right back into place, and he couldn't figure out why.

5

Present Day

Kai knew it was too late the moment he came to.

Pain lanced through his skull, splitting him open from the inside. Behind his eyes, radiating from his temples like a spider web across his skull, down the back of his neck. He took several deep breaths. In slowly, hold, out. His mind cleared enough for him to think straight, to gather the steps he needed to take into a neat and manageable order.

Medicine. He needed to get out of bed and find his medicine. Or maybe…

Kai reached out for his wallet, sitting right there on the nightstand. The movement sent a new wave of agony and nausea through him. He pressed the left side of his face into the pillow, desperate to relieve the pain with any sort of pressure, knowing it was futile. After a few more moments, he held his wallet close to his face, flipping it open to search through it.

Empty. The pocket he was looking in was empty. He'd used the emergency migraine pill he kept there the other day.

After giving himself a hangover, like an idiot. Kai tossed the wallet away with a groan.

He knew his triggers well at this point. Too much alcohol, too much screen time, too much stress. But every once in a while, a migraine would just… happen. No rhyme or reason. The random ones occurred less and less as he worked with his doctor on preventative measures. But every so often, one would come on suddenly, with a fury he was never ready for.

Which was why he always kept the emergency medication on hand.

Kai pressed the heels of his palms against his eyes, searching again for pressure that would distract him from the pain. He needed to get up and find the box with the rest of his medicine.

Another groan as he pushed himself into a sitting position. Every motion felt sluggish and heavy, took too much effort. He got up slowly, shuffling across the room to his duffel bag. He could hear movement elsewhere in the house from where he'd left the door cracked open. Atticus must be up already, had probably been up for a while, judging by the amount of light slipping through the window blinds.

Kai dug through his bag, tossing clothes aside. Where had he put the box when he'd packed? He couldn't quite remember, and thinking was so hard when he felt as though his head were being torn wide open.

"No," he said aloud, voice cracking a little. "No no *no*."

It wasn't there. The medicine was nowhere to be found in his bag. Kai felt tears of frustration, tears half brought on by the pain, stinging his eyes before slipping down his cheeks. And then he suddenly remembered.

He'd been gathering items from his bathroom, snatching up toiletries and tossing them into his bag. He'd pulled the box of medicine out of the cabinet, had placed it on the sink counter. Had forgotten to pack it into his bag.

"Fuck," he hissed, curling in on himself, still crouched on the floor next to his duffel. A knock sounded at his door.

"Kai, you up?" Atticus' voice, just as bright and cheery as it was every morning. Kai couldn't will himself to move, couldn't even turn his head to look toward the door. "I was gonna go for a run, you want to…"

His voice trailed off, and Kai heard the soft swish of the door swinging open. Hands were suddenly on his back, the touch gentle and unsure.

"What's wrong?" Atticus asked softly. A current of worry buzzed off of him, and Kai could feel how close he was, kneeling next to him. He lifted his head from his arms.

"I, um…" It was hard to speak, still so hard to think straight, between the pain and the frustration and the tears still stinging his eyes. "I forgot to pack my medicine."

"You have a migraine?"

Kai nodded, and the motion sent another throbbing ache through his head. He squeezed his eyes shut, felt a tear slip out to run down his face.

Arms wrapped around him, pulled him in close. A warm hand at the back of his neck, pressing at the tight muscles there, rubbing in a way that eased some of the tension. He could feel Atticus' breath against his hair as the other man held him close, speaking again more softly.

"You need it, right?"

Kai let himself melt a little into the embrace. "Or I'll be down all day."

Atticus seemed to think for a few moments.

"Do you know where you left it?"

Kai described where he'd placed the box, hoping desperately that it hadn't been tossed away in the ongoing construction. The contractor had called the evening before, letting Kai know they'd already begun to tear out the faulty pipes.

"Okay," Atticus said, pulling Kai up from the floor while still keeping a tight hold on him. He snatched Kai's set of keys off the nightstand. "I'm gonna get you some water, then I'll go get the medicine for you."

Kai nodded, letting Atticus help him to slip back under the covers. He immediately curled into a ball, earning a small chuckle from the other man.

"I'll be back soon, 'kay?" Atticus reached down, pushing Kai's hair back from his face. "Need anything else?"

"No," Kai replied, voice a little stronger. He felt marginally better knowing relief was on the way. He met Atticus' gentle, blue-eyed stare. "Thank you."

Atticus only smiled, a little lopsided, before turning away to leave. Kai's heart beat a touch faster as that image stayed in his mind, clear as day even after he closed his eyes and tried to fall back asleep.

He dozed off and on, unsure if minutes or hours passed. The pain in his head refused to recede on its own, no matter what position he lay in or how much water he drank. At long last, a ding sounded from close by.

Kai reached out, nearly dropping his phone to the floor in his attempt to grab it. He swiped the screen open, flinching a little at the brightness that sent another stab through his head.

Atticus: Omw back, be home soon

Just a little while longer. He'd survived countless migraines before, he would make it through this one too, even if the pain felt like it was breaking him. The end was in sight.

Kai was about to toss his phone aside when he noticed another unread message.

Nicholas: Please Kai. Please just respond to me.

Maybe it was the pain, or maybe it was the frustration that had welled at not having his medicine on hand. Maybe it was annoyance that Nicholas was reminding him of all of the hurt and loss when Kai already felt like complete shit. Kai had had enough.

Kai: Leave me alone. Stop contacting me. You can't fix this, there is nothing left to fix.

Somehow, typing the words out felt a little more harsh. He'd wanted to scream similar sentiments in the past, had wanted to rail against Nicholas for breaking his heart and shattering what they had. But typing it out, one letter at a time, it made it feel a bit more final. So emotionless, so uncaring. Because Kai couldn't bring himself to care, not today. Not when his mind could hardly form thoughts, could hardly even acknowledge the desperation in Nicholas' text.

He wanted to be done with it. He wanted to stop hurting, to stop being reminded of that pain. Kai wanted to move on.

That same image of Atticus smiling softly down at him popped into his head as he set his phone aside. It stayed there, at the forefront of his mind, pushing past all of the pain, as he dozed off once again.

Atticus wondered if he should go check on Kai again. He fidgeted on the couch, biting at the inside of his cheek as he stared unseeing at the television screen.

He didn't want to pester. Didn't want to do anything that would make Kai feel worse. But he was *worried*.

The still-unnamed kitten stretched out next to him on the couch, exposing her soft belly. Atticus reached out, scratching under her chin. She seemed to love it, pressing into his touch as the volume of her purring ticked up a notch.

It had been about an hour since he'd gotten back home and delivered Kai's medicine to him. He'd barely been conscious as Atticus had handed him the pill, flopping back to the bed as soon as he'd taken it and pulling the covers over his head.

Atticus had thought about going on a run, needing to expel his nervous energy. But he hadn't wanted to leave Kai alone again. Just in case.

So he had cleaned. He'd scrubbed his kitchen counters, cleaned the litter box, wiped down the bathroom, made his bed, and folded the laundry he'd left in the dryer the night before. It had helped, a little, had gotten rid of some of the restlessness he felt. Kept him from checking on Kai every five minutes.

He *had* poked his head in a couple times. Just to make sure Kai was okay. The first time he told himself it was to make sure he didn't need more water. The glass had still been half full, so he hadn't said anything. The second time it was to deliver the old Cats hoodie that Kai had worn that first day he'd spent at Atticus' place.

Atticus had washed the hoodie after Kai had given it back, but it felt wrong to put it away with his other clothes. It wasn't like he would ever wear it again. Not when just thinking about the way Kai had looked in it had his mind heading off in a *very* dangerous direction. So, instead of slipping it into his own dresser, Atticus had folded it neatly, carried it down the hall, and carefully opened Kai's door just enough to place the hoodie on his dresser.

Maybe he would wear it again. Atticus smiled a little at the thought.

He'd been sitting on the couch, watching an old episode of *Naruto*. The episode was nearly over, and he hadn't paid attention to more than thirty seconds of it. Maybe he should go check on Kai one more time. Just in case he needed something.

Atticus was about to stand up, having convinced himself that Kai probably needed a refill on that water by now, when the sound of soft footfalls reached him. He whipped his head toward the hallway, his movement disturbing the ball of fur next to him. She got up and moved to the other end of the couch, immediately curling up to go back to sleep

The first thing Atticus noticed was that Kai's face was no longer screwed up in pain. He looked tired, exhausted even, but his features had finally softened.

The second thing Atticus noticed was that Kai was, indeed, wearing the hoodie.

It took everything in him not to pump his fist in the air. His plan had succeeded. However, Kai was sick, so it was definitely not the right time to think about how fucking attractive it was that he was once again wearing something with Atticus' name plastered across the back.

"Feeling better?" Atticus worked to keep a normal expression, but struggled with holding back a grin. Kai nodded, rubbing a hand down his face as he made his way across the room. He hesitated for a moment when he reached the couch, staring at his usual spot, which was currently occupied by the kitten. A moment of hesitation passed before he flopped down next to Atticus.

"Mostly," Kai finally responded. His voice was still low and thick from sleep. Between that, the hoodie, and his close proximity, Atticus sort of felt like he was going to come out of his skin. "Head still hurts a little, and I'm always really tired after the medicine kicks in."

Atticus hummed in understanding. "You hungry?" He shifted in his seat, trying to make more room. He only managed to make it so that they were pressed closer together. Atticus willed his cheeks not to heat with everything he had in him.

Kai brought his legs up onto the couch, curling into a ball not dissimilar to the creature on his other side.

"Not yet," he said, leaning back into the cushions, settling fully into place. "Don't know if I could stomach anything right now."

Atticus nodded. "The tv going to bother you?"

"No, it's fine."

Just in case, Atticus turned the volume down a little. These characters did tend to yell a lot.

They watched in silence for several long minutes.

"We could name her Lee!"

Kai slowly turned his head, pinning Atticus with a bored stare.

"What?" Atticus grinned, pointing toward the screen. "She's kinda wild like he is!"

As if on cue, the kitten jumped off the couch, padding across the room to flop onto a patch of sunlight shining on the wood flooring.

"Why do you keep trying to give her boy names?" Kai's voice was as bored as his stare, but Atticus could see the hint of a smile at the corner of his mouth.

"It's not about boy or girl," Atticus said with a huff. "It's about her personality. You're the one who keeps insisting the name has to fit her."

"Then we might as well just keep her name as Atticus, like on her vet paperwork, since you're both so chaotic."

Atticus shoved Kai lightly, earning a true grin from the other man that set his heart racing.

"I'm not chaotic," Atticus said. Kai settled back into his seat, still pressed close, despite the fact that the other end of the couch was now open. Atticus didn't think too hard about that.

"You watch a different anime every day," Kai said, snorting a small laugh. "You don't finish any of them. That's a little chaotic."

"I finish some of them!"

"Oh yeah?" Kai asked, one brow raised in question. "What's the last one you finished?"

"It was…" Well. Huh. Atticus couldn't remember. His face pinched as he thought hard, earning a chuckle..

"Don't hurt yourself," Kai said, settling back against the cushion, making himself somehow even smaller. Atticus' arm had found its way to rest along the back of the couch, and he fought back a flush as Kai leaned into it.

Atticus' phone vibrated. He pulled it out of his pocket, his smile dimming slightly as he read the message.

"What's wrong?" Kai's voice was softer, still a little sleepy as he continued to lean against Atticus.

"Nothing's wrong," Atticus said, typing out a quick reply with one hand before setting the device aside. "Some of the guys from the team want to go out for food after practice."

"Is that a bad thing?"

"Nope," Atticus responded, popping the p. He paused, thinking a moment before continuing. "They're trying to set me up with someone. Carpenter has a cousin or somebody in town visiting. He wants me to meet her. And the PR team always loves when I go out with a woman. It's easier for them to spin it than it is if I'm seen out with a guy."

Atticus feigned nonchalance, pretended that he didn't care how Kai would react to the idea of him going out and meeting new people.

"Oh."

He watched as Kai fidgeted with the ends of his sleeves, pulling his hands inside of the too-large hoodie. He seemed to be thinking, so Atticus let him. Forced himself to breathe normally, hoped that his heart wasn't beating too loud.

"Do they try to set you up with people a lot?"

Atticus hummed. "Yeah, kind of. I used to go out a lot

more…" He paused, giving Kai a sly look. "Used to be a lot more *chaotic* in my dating life. I think they don't know what to do with me now that I'm not hooking up with somebody new every other week."

Kai frowned, eyes still focused on the hands hidden in his hoodie. "You haven't done that in a long time though."

"Reputations are hard to break," Atticus said with a shrug, jostling Kai and finally drawing his gaze.

"Everybody changes."

Atticus felt as though Kai's whiskey-bright eyes were holding him in place. He didn't want to read into the words, didn't want to let himself latch onto them. Didn't want to glean any hope, only to be let down once again.

He used the arm that was wrapped around Kai's shoulders to reach out, to ruffle his hair, earning a scowl that distracted both of them from the slight tension in the air.

"It's fine," Atticus said. He gave Kai a grin before turning back toward the television. "I really just wanted to come back home after practice anyway."

"Does it bother you that the PR team cares about your personal life?"

Atticus kept his eyes trained on the screen. "Not as much as it used to. Don't know if it's a good thing that I've gotten used to it. It helped that Ori was on the team, and he's been out publicly for years. But it's like I said, they don't really know what to do with me. The slutty bi who reinforced all their long-held stereotypes."

"Other players sleep around just as much."

It was true. A fact that Atticus was acutely aware of. "Doesn't matter as long as they're only sleeping with women. Nobody bats an eye." He turned to see a deep frown on Kai's face.

"It's not so bad," he continued. "My team's great, for the most part. At least they've accepted me, and Ori too. Could be worse." Atticus shifted, nudging Kai with his shoulder. "What about you? Your online community seems to be pretty accepting, what with how bad they want you and Ori to smooch."

Kai huffed out a soft laugh. "Yeah, they're great. I never really kept being queer a secret, because I just started out as a nobody streaming in my dorm. It was always just sort of a given for my viewers, even as more and more people started watching. I never had a big coming out moment, but they've always known. A few incels show up occasionally, because it's the internet. But it's a good community, for the most part."

They fell back into a comfortable silence. It wasn't long before Atticus felt the body pressed against his side grow a little heavier. He looked down to see that Kai had dozed off. Atticus shifted slightly to better accommodate him. Kai squirmed in his sleep, uncurling himself a bit. His head came to rest against Atticus' chest, arms tucked tight in between them.

Atticus froze, afraid that any more movement from him would wake Kai, would cause him to pull away. A quick glance at his phone told him that he needed to get up and get ready for practice soon. He was tempted to just skip, if it meant they could stay like this a while longer.

But he couldn't, not with the first game of the season coming up that weekend. He needed to be at practice, and his team needed *him*.

One more episode. Atticus let the autoplay continue, daring a careful movement to wrap his arm more comfortably around Kai. He could let himself enjoy the moment for a little while longer.

6

"Straighten the fuck up, Bo, I'm tired of tellin' ya!"

Atticus watched Bowen flinch at the booming voice of their athletic trainer. How someone so small could always manage to be so loud was a mystery to Atticus, but he was used to Ivy's training style after two years of working with her.

Ivy walked past, punctuating her order to Bowen by chopping a hand against his spine. He went ramrod straight before continuing with his stretches, and Atticus swore there were hearts shining in his teammate's eyes as Ivy picked up a clipboard to jot something down.

"Give it up, man." Aaron dropped to the ground between Atticus and Bowen. He leaned into a stretch, a knowing expression tilting his lips into a smile. "She yells at all of us, you're not special."

Bowen frowned, and Atticus couldn't hold back a chuckle. "You're not really her type, anyway."

That frown deepened as Bowen's shoulders slumped. "I know that," he mumbled, "but let me dream, alright?"

"Bowen, I swear to whatever gods exist..." Ivy was standing in front of them again in a heartbeat, all five feet of her towering over them. She was glaring, green eyes bright, dark waves spilling out of the messy ponytail she always wore, hands planted firmly on her hips. "If you're going to do the stretches wrong, you might as well just not do them at all."

As though he'd been shocked, Bowen straightened up once again. Aaron let out a small laugh, only to cut off as Ivy's attention turned to him.

"And you." She pointed a finger. "If I see you push yourself too hard again today, I'll make sure coach doesn't let you see any time in the first half of the season."

Atticus wasn't sure that she could actually boss their coach around with the same vigor she did all of them, but he thought maybe Aaron shouldn't tempt fate. He liked having Aaron as his backup, liked knowing the other man would be ready to step up if Atticus, if the team, needed him.

"Atticus." Ivy's stare finally landed on him, sending a chill down his spine. "Come on, I'll help you with your tape." He could sort of understand why half the team fancied themselves in love with her. Something about being bossed around...

Atticus rose from the floor to follow her, pulling off his shirt as he sat backward in a folding chair. Ivy grabbed some kinesiology tape from her bag.

"Coach said it looked like you were favoring your left shoulder last practice." Cold fingers against the skin of his back almost made Atticus shiver. Ivy's Kentucky accent was almost gone now that she'd lowered her voice.

"Didn't feel like I was." Atticus frowned. "Nothing felt wrong."

"I'll watch you today. Make sure to keep your head in the game, no more mind wandering or you're going to end up hurt."

Atticus scoffed, glancing over his shoulder. "My mind

doesn't wander!"

A smirk tilted the corner of Ivy's lips. "So when you were checking your phone earlier instead of warming up with everyone else, that wasn't your mind wandering?"

Atticus flushed. He *had* been waiting for a response from Kai, after he'd checked to see if his new housemate needed him to pick up anything on his way home from practice.

"Bowen said the guy you've been lusting after is staying at your place."

"Bowen needs to learn how to mind his own business." Atticus couldn't keep the sharpness out of his voice.

It made something twist in his gut, the idea that his team, his *friends*, were gossiping about him and Kai. Atticus shifted in his seat, a failed attempt to dislodge the discomfort that idea brought him.

"The timing isn't great, Atticus." Ivy's voice had gone gentle, cautious, which was unusual for her. Atticus thought maybe she had a soft spot for him, if only because she was friends with his sister. He fought the urge to squirm as she continued.

"Your first game is this weekend. Everyone needs you at the top of your game. This isn't a good time to let your love life drama get in the way of you playing your best."

"I don't know if this sort of advice is in your job description," Atticus grumbled, pushing his hair back from his forehead with a huff. Ivy poked him in the back of the head, stepping in front of him after she finished applying his tape.

"Put your shirt back on," she said, crossing her arms firmly. "I don't know this guy. But I know you. And you've been pining over him for a long time now while he's never given you the time of day."

"That's not true..." Atticus trailed off as she waved a dismissive hand at him.

"Just get past this week," Ivy said. "Don't let another hookup make you have a rocky start to the season. Now go tell Kieran I'm going to kick his ass if I don't see him stretching in the next thirty seconds."

Ivy smacked him on the back as she walked away. Atticus chewed on his bottom lip, thinking over her words. A part of him knew she was right, knew that he needed to focus on the upcoming game. That had never been an issue for him in the past. But things were different with Kai.

Maybe she was right about his mind wandering. Since the moment he'd left his house earlier, it had been as though his thoughts were spinning in the same circle, always landing back on Kai. Kai in his home. Kai wearing his sweatshirt. Kai curled up against him on the couch. Kai smiling at him.

Atticus didn't want to get his hopes up. He didn't want to be distracted from the other things in life that were important to him. He didn't want to let his little crush affect his game like he was back in middle school.

As Atticus walked across the gym to deliver Ivy's message to Kieran, who had only just arrived late to practice, something else she'd said pricked at his mind. Ivy had called Kai another hookup. But nothing had happened between them. Atticus didn't know which rankled more, the idea that his relationship with Kai was stuck solidly in the friend zone, or the fact that his team was discussing his sex life so much.

"Kieran isn't going out with us after practice either." Eric bumped against Atticus' shoulder as he joined their group. "You sure you don't want to come? My cousin looked you up and she wasn't disappointed. She's only going to be in town for a couple more days."

Annoyance had Atticus tensing up, his shoulders rigid and his jaw tight. "Not in the mood, Carpenter."

"Come on, man." Eric grabbed a volleyball out of the cart, bumping it casually as he continued. "You used to be more fun."

"It's because he used to get laid more," Bowen chimed in.

Atticus felt a muscle in his jaw twitch. So they had noticed that he wasn't sleeping around anymore. They had noticed, but it still hadn't changed how they saw him.

A shrill whistle echoed through the gym, pulling everyone's attention toward Coach Rodriguez. The conversation dropped off as everyone jogged over to where their coach waited. Kieran pushed Atticus forward with a whispered, "Ignore them and focus on your game," leaving Atticus alone with his thoughts.

It was hard to focus, though, as Coach Rodriguez went over their game plan, detailing what he wanted to see from them over the next two practices before the season officially started. Atticus couldn't keep himself from thinking about what Ivy and Bowen had alluded to.

Kai wasn't just some hookup. And Atticus didn't need sex to help him keep his head in the game. It made something in him pinch with guilt, because he *had* been thinking about Kai in that way more and more over the last few days.

But it wasn't because he just wanted sex. What he wanted from Kai felt so much bigger than that, even if sex *was* a part of it all.

Atticus had to pull himself back into the moment, his attention returning fully to his coach when he noticed Ivy glaring daggers at him.

Focus. He needed to focus, because she was right. Atticus couldn't afford to let his messy love life get in the way of things. Not now, not when so many people were relying on him.

Those thoughts stayed with him though, all through the rest of practice, a constant, nagging whisper at the back of his mind.

Kai scrubbed his hands down his face. Answering emails for two hours straight probably hadn't been a great idea after a migraine, but he hated to let them pile up.

He pushed away from his laptop, noticing for the first time just how dark the room had gotten. Light no longer streamed in through the window. He could hear crickets sounding off outside as evening set in.

Shutting off his computer, Kai sighed. He hated days like today. Days when he lost so much time to being sick. He'd fallen back asleep on Atticus' couch, exhaustion from the aftermath of his migraine pulling him under while they'd watched tv together.

He left the guest bedroom, checking the messages on his phone.

Atticus: Staying late with kieran to work on a new set we're trying

The message had been sent an hour earlier. Kai must have missed the notification as he'd buried himself in catching up on some of his work. That meant Atticus would probably be home soon. Kai wondered why the other man felt the need to let him know that practice was running long.

He didn't mind though, not really. It was comforting, knowing that Atticus worried enough to keep him informed. Not that he needed to.

Kai huffed out a breath at the circular and useless train of thought. Whatever reason there was for Atticus to feel the need to keep Kai informed, it didn't matter. They were friends. Kai was staying at his house. Atticus just probably didn't want him to worry. Because they were friends.

Another sigh escaped him as he heaved himself up onto

one of the kitchen barstools. The kitten appeared out of nowhere, batting her small paws at his socked feet.

It had been nice, having a friend around that morning. Having Atticus around to help when Kai had felt so awful. Kai groaned as he let his head fall onto his folded arms. The kitten continued to bounce around his feet.

Friends. Sure. Kai scoffed, the warmth of his breath trapped in the enclosure of his arms, fogging the countertop. It was getting more and more difficult to ignore the way Atticus treated him, the way he always acted toward Kai. Friends cared for each other, of course they did. But with Atticus, it felt like more than just caring. There had been fear in his eyes, as he'd helped Kai back into the bed. And then there had been something else there, something gentle and kind and safe, when Kai had been seated next to him on the couch.

Not to mention the conversation they'd had, and the fact that Atticus hadn't been with anyone else since they'd slept together.

It wasn't news to Kai. It wasn't a surprise. But it had hit different today, as they'd talked about Atticus' friends trying to hook him up with someone new. Kai had felt something wash over him, something he didn't want to admit even to himself.

He'd been jealous. In those few moments, when he thought that maybe Atticus would take his teammate up on the offer of an introduction.

Kai had been really fucking jealous.

Another groan escaped him as he clenched his hands in his hair.

It wasn't fair. It wasn't fair for Kai to be jealous of anyone else in Atticus' life. Kai had always been clear about there being nothing more between them. He'd always told himself he wasn't ready to give Atticus, or anyone else, a chance.

He'd thought he still felt that way.

But while they'd sat there, pressed so close together on Atticus' couch, a strong arm wrapped around his shoulders, Kai hadn't once thought about Nicholas. Hadn't once thought about the hurt or the sad or the anger. All he'd thought about was how it was nice, how he felt so comfortable, and how the thought of anyone else sharing a moment like that with Atticus made him want to claw their eyes out.

Kai's phone lit up on the counter next to him. Vibrations shook through his arms as a silent call came through. He picked it up, frowning as he was knocked out of his spiraling thoughts.

A number he didn't recognize. Kai squinted at the screen as he accepted the call.

"Hello?"

"What the fuck is your problem?"

The words were steady and harsh, a clipped British accent. Not yelling, but clearly full of rage. Kai knew that voice, but he had to ask anyway.

"Who is this?"

"Nicholas has been so patient with you, he's tried so hard, and you can't send him a single text that isn't steeped in your vitriol?"

Ah.

"Theo, I don't know why you're calling," Kai began. A barking laugh sounded through his speaker.

"Sure you don't. Because it's never you that's the problem between the two of you, between *us*, is it?"

"I'm not doing this with you," Kai said, voice grating. He could feel tension beginning to line his shoulders. He clenched his jaw hard before continuing. "I told Nicholas I don't want to talk to him."

Kai was about to hang up, about to maybe even throw his phone down the garbage disposal, when Theo continued.

"Are you just never going to talk to him? Never going to acknowledge that the two of you were friends? That we were all friends?"

"Nicholas and I were more than friends!" Kai was seeing red, his voice shaking with vehemence. The nails of his free hand dug into his palm sharply as he clenched his fist tight.

"But you were friends first! You were friends more than anything!"

The words slammed into Kai like a wall. His vision blurred as tears suddenly filled his eyes.

"No. Not to me we weren't." He didn't know why he said it. Didn't know why he didn't just hang up, why he was giving Theo the opportunity to hurt him even more.

Except a part of him did know. Theo was right about one thing, they had all been friends. Kai, Nicky, Ori, Theo. A unit, a little family. One that had been shattered when Nicholas dumped Kai, only to end up with Theo a few months later. Kai hadn't spoken to either of them since then.

There was a long pause, and Kai began to wonder if Theo had been the one to hang up, until a rough sigh sounded from the other end of the line.

"Nicholas knows he hurt you. Don't you understand that? He's known for the last year. Your absence in his life guarantees he could never forget how much he hurt you. How long are you going to keep punishing him for ending a relationship that was always going to end anyway?"

It was like a knife, slowly pressing in, turning the whole while. Kai closed his eyes, felt the tears slip past his lashes to fall down his cheeks.

It was always going to end anyway.

"I don't want to talk to him."

The other man let out a sharp *tsk*.

"Yeah," Theo said, some of the venom seeping back into his voice. "You made that clear the other night. And with the text you sent this morning. He's been a wreck all day, you know? The worst part is that I can't do anything to help him. You're the only person who can. You're the friend that was always supposed to be there for him. But you refuse to, just like how you refused to ever talk to him about your breakup. No closure for anyone. You're the one who is holding his head under water right now. Every time you refuse to let him up for air, you break him a little more. And I get to watch it happen, helpless to do anything, because you aren't my friend anymore either."

Kai screwed his face up, fighting to keep from sniffling, to keep from letting Theo know just how much those words hurt him. Because they did hurt, just in a different way.

There was a part of Kai, a small part that he'd always refused to acknowledge, that had always felt a small amount of shame at how much he was hurting Nicholas- and sure, Theo as well- through all of this. How much he was hurting his friends.

It was the same as it always was for Kai. He couldn't find his voice, couldn't force his words out. Just the same way he'd been unable to speak on the night that all of it had come to a crashing halt.

"This was something I thought I could try." Some of the bitterness had left Theo's voice. He almost sounded defeated. "If you ever decide you've had enough of hurting him, he'll accept you back into his life with open arms. I don't think you deserve it, but it's not up to me, is it?"

Another wave of grief washed over Kai as the line went dead. Theo had ended the call with those final biting words.

Kai tossed his phone away as though it were burning his hand. It crashed across the counter, startling the kitten from where she was drinking from her water bowl all the way across the room.

He pressed his palms against his eyes, a small sob breaking

past his defenses. All of it threatened to crash back down on him. All of the hurt, all of the pain. Mostly the anger. The anger that he held to the tightest. The anger that had kept him tethered for so long. Anchored him in place.

He felt that anger once again as his mind replayed everything Theo had said to him. Theo. The man Nicholas had moved on to after destroying the life he'd built with Kai. The man Kai had considered a friend, someone he'd never thought could hurt him like this.

You were friends more than anything.

A relationship that was always going to end anyway.

Kai wanted to scream, he wanted to beat his fists against the hard surface of the counter until he couldn't feel anymore. Until he couldn't feel any of it.

Every time he thought he'd escaped, something dragged him back down. That anchor, there again, but this time pulling him under and refusing to set him free. His chest felt tight as he swiped at his cheeks.

He didn't want Atticus to see him like this. Didn't want to show just how broken he truly was. How he was so full of shattered glass, of angry, sharp edges that would shred and tear anyone who got close. Edges that ripped him open from the inside, never letting him fully heal.

Kai worked to slow his breathing as he made his way to the bathroom. He let cold water run from the tap for several long moments, staring at his reddened eyes and blotchy cheeks.

Fuck. He looked awful.

He splashed the water on his face, barely aware of the stinging chill against his flushed skin.

Keys jangled at the front door.

"Shit. *Shit.*" Kai braced himself on the sink, letting the cold water drip from his chin. This would be the second time that day that Atticus had found him a wreck.

"Kai," Atticus' voice rang out as the front door clicked shut. "You still working?"

"No." His voice sounded unsteady even to his own ears. Kai hoped it wasn't noticeable. Footsteps echoed as Atticus made his way through the house.

"Hey," he said, stepping into the doorway of the bathroom. "What's wrong? Are you sick again?"

Kai squeezed his eyes shut. "No," he said, voice soft. "It's not my head."

"Did something happen?" He couldn't see Atticus' face, but he could picture it. The wide-eyed concern that was sure to be written across his features.

"Um," Kai tried. He couldn't talk about it with Atticus. He didn't *want* to talk about it with Atticus.

"Was it Nicholas?"

Of course he knew. What else could turn Kai into such a shell of himself? Of course Atticus could take one look at him and suss out the reason he was a mess.

Kai nodded, eyes still squeezed shut, hands still bracing himself up on the counter.

"Hey, look at me." Atticus' voice had turned gentle, as though he were talking to a cornered animal. Kai opened his eyes, met the soft blue ones that were watching him carefully.

"Wanna talk about it?"

They held each other's stare for what felt to Kai like an age. No, he didn't want to talk to Atticus about Nicholas. About how he, Kai, was still pathetically clinging to a dream that he'd never truly had hold of in the first place.

He shook his head, finally finding his voice. "Not really."

Atticus watched him for several more long moments. Kai worried that he was going to push, that his friend was going to demand an explanation. That Atticus would scoff at him, would finally be done with whatever it was that was going on between them.

"Mmkay." Atticus turned away. "Come on, I picked up some takeout for us. I'm starving!"

And that was that. The other man's words sounded almost cheerful as he walked away. Kai listened to the sound of containers being pulled from a bag, listened to the clicking noises Atticus liked to make when trying to get the kitten's attention.

Could they really just... not talk about it? Kai had been told for so long now that he needed to talk through things, needed to get it all off of his chest or he would never feel better. But he had talked. To Ori. To a therapist. He'd talked and he'd talked and he'd talked until he was sick of hearing himself. Sick of his own grief and rage.

Atticus wasn't pushing him. He had acknowledged that Kai wasn't okay, and was going to let him deal with it in his own way.

It was kind of nice, actually. A weight off his shoulders, knowing he wasn't about to go through some horrible, awful conversation that he didn't feel like having. Knowing that instead they could go on with their night, maybe go back to the easy way they'd shared each other's company earlier in the day.

Knowing that Atticus was there, if Kai did ever decide he wanted to talk about it.

Kai looked at himself once more in the mirror. He seemed a little better off, his eyes less red, his expression less strained. He sighed, leaving the bathroom to join Atticus in the kitchen.

Atticus chatted amiably while they ate. He talked about practice, although Kai noted something strained in his expression, noticed the way he didn't go into as much detail as usual. When Kai prodded, Atticus waved it away. And, well, if he was willing to give Kai space to work through things for himself, then Kai figured he needed to do the same.

They moved on to other topics. Atticus asked about the work Kai had done while he'd been gone. He didn't once push, didn't once poke at Kai to tell him what had happened. Didn't treat him any different, as though Kai were a porcelain doll that would break at the slightest provocation.

It was as if Atticus saw something in Kai, a strength there that Kai failed to even see in himself.

That thought hit Kai hard, as they sat together after dinner. They were back on the couch, and Kai had opted to sit close to Atticus again. There was no reason to, no ball of fur stealing his seat this time. He'd just wanted to sit close, because it had been nice earlier in the day. They were watching *Naruto* once more, finishing an episode that they'd started earlier.

The realization that Atticus didn't see Kai as all of those broken, jagged edges washed over him. Kai could no longer focus on the show, his mind fully preoccupied by the notion of how Atticus viewed him in light of all his pain and struggles to move on with his life. Atticus saw him as more than his broken parts. As someone who could exist despite them, as someone who was more than just his flaws, big and loud and consuming as they were.

Kai didn't even see himself that way. He hadn't for so long. Anytime he looked at himself, all he saw were the remnants of who he used to be, the pieces that had been left behind when Nicholas had stepped out of his life. Out of the life they had been building together.

The colors on the television screen blurred together. Kai felt his eyes begin to prickle, felt his nose begin to sting. He sniffled.

He hadn't meant to, really. Hadn't meant to lose it again.

But he was *sad*. He was sad, and he had been sad for so long about the life he didn't get to have with the person he had loved more than anyone. Sad about the phone call he'd received earlier, and Theo's terrible words that were ringing through his head over and over. Sad about the fact that he didn't see himself as a strong person. Not anymore.

Atticus didn't say anything, and Kai hoped for a moment that his tears had escaped notice. He had no such luck. Atticus moved his arm, shifting it from the back of the couch to rest more fully around Kai's shoulders. His eyes never left the tv as he pulled Kai closer, holding him tight.

Kai curled into his side, no longer paying any attention to the show. He let himself cry silent tears. Let himself feel whatever it was that he needed to feel. It didn't last long. Maybe it was because he wasn't fighting it, wasn't railing against his own emotions, wasn't hating himself for feeling too much. Just a few minutes, Atticus' warmth seeping into him, and Kai felt better. Not miraculously healed, but... better.

The kitten flopped around on the floor in front of them, batting a felt ball around, rising awkwardly onto her toes whenever it would move in an unexpected direction, before shooting off across the room. Moments later she would be back, facing off against the toy once again, over and over.

Kai laughed. It was a small, tear-soaked sound that escaped him, one even he hadn't been expecting. But it seemed to lift something, a blanket that had been hanging over the room. Atticus chuckled along with him as they watched the kitten's antics play out for a few more moments.

"One more?" Kai asked, nodding at the screen that had changed to an *are you still watching* message.

"Sure," Atticus said, clicking a button on the remote. "I'm beat though, gonna knock out after this." Kai only nodded in response, but couldn't keep a small smile from forming on his lips.

He wasn't ready to move away yet, wasn't ready to say goodnight and lose the comfortable warmth resting around his shoulders. Kai watched Atticus. He did look sleepy, eyelids heavy, expression soft. Kai didn't look away when their eyes met. He felt like he should say something, but didn't know what.

Atticus' grin was crooked and charming as ever, softened a little by his exhaustion. Kai felt his stomach flip, felt his blood go fizzy in his veins. He turned away, facing back toward the television before he did something stupid.

Because he had almost just leaned into Atticus and kissed him.

About halfway through the episode, Kai could feel his own eyelids beginning to droop. He was about to say something, to suggest they call it a night early, when he felt a pleasant sensation against his scalp. Kai held his breath as Atticus lazily ran long fingers through his hair, playing with the ends a bit before moving back to his scalp.

Sparks lit along Kai's spine at every touch, every brush of Atticus' hand. He couldn't help but lean into the contact, silently asking for more.

Kai *loved* having his hair played with. It was something he had missed, something that turned him into a puddle every time.

Atticus seemed to take a hint, growing a little more bold with his movements. Kai let his eyes fall shut, melting into every touch, resting his head against Atticus' chest.

He wasn't going to get up *now*. Not when Atticus' fingers ran through his hair, pulling gently through a few tangles in a way that was turning Kai into actual putty.

The gentle caress of Atticus' hand quickly lulled Kai to sleep.

The first thing Atticus noticed when he woke up was that it

was still dark. He had no idea how long he'd been asleep, but with no light shining in through the windows he figured it had been just a few hours, tops.

The second thing Atticus noticed when he woke up was that he had his arms wrapped around another person. It seemed as though he and Kai had passed out together on the couch. Kai shifted in his sleep, his back pressing more firmly into Atticus' chest, soft hair tickling Atticus' nose as their bodies melded together.

Which led Atticus to his third discovery after waking up.

He had a full-on boner.

Fuck. Atticus inhaled harshly as Kai shifted again, the friction nearly pulling a gasp out of him. If Kai woke to Atticus jabbing him in the ass, he was a little afraid the other man might throttle him.

Shit shit shit. What was he going to do? If he tried to move, to get up and go… take care of himself, he might wake Kai up. Might reveal himself with his traitorous dick.

There was also the fact that he had the man of his dreams in his arms, pressed tight against him, making his thoughts feel a bit jumbled.

Maybe if he just ignored it, maybe it would go away.

Atticus held his breath, which only helped to make him feel like he was going to pass out. It wasn't going to work, his situation wasn't going to resolve itself. Atticus shifted his arm, pulling it away from Kai to leverage himself up from where he was squeezed between a warm body and the back of the couch.

Fingers wrapped around his wrist. Atticus froze.

Well. It seemed Kai was already awake.

Kai pulled Atticus' arm back around him, pressing his hand to his chest. The movement jostled them both again, and this time Atticus did let out a small gasp. Kai's fingers laced in his, his grip tight.

Kai rocked his hips back, a shallow, slow push. Atticus jerked a little as the small, round ass he remembered so fondly pressed against his cock.

"*Fuck.*" He whispered the word against Kai's neck, pressing his face there as his eyes squeezed shut unbidden. Kai moved his hips again, and Atticus' arms tightened around him.

They probably shouldn't be doing this. They were probably both too groggy, and apparently too horny, to be thinking straight. But when Kai moved back against him a third time, Atticus couldn't help the way his own hips jerked forward. And when he heard a sharp breath leave Kai's lips?

Every coherent thought left Atticus' brain.

His hand moved, pulling out of Kai's vice-like grip. He trailed it down Kai's chest, along his side, until his fingers could slip under that goddamn Cats hoodie.

Oh. Kai was still wearing Atticus' hoodie, a realization that only served to turn Atticus on even more.

He splayed his hand against Kai's stomach, relishing the warmth radiating off of him and the way he twitched a little at the contact. A small sound escaped Kai as Atticus pressed them closer together, as his hips ground against the other man's backside.

Atticus felt fingers tangle in his hair. He leaned his head back into the touch and nearly growled at the feeling of Kai's nails against his scalp.

Kai took the opportunity to turn in his arms, to shift so that they were facing one another. One of his legs slipped between Atticus' own, giving him something to continue to rut against. Hands pushed at Atticus' shirt until it was up over his head, and then Kai's mouth was on his chest, kissing along his collarbone.

It seemed Kai remembered just how sensitive he was there. Atticus nearly whimpered as the Kai's mouth found his nipple, as teeth teased him. He was so hard, so overwhelmed that he thought he might simply die from the sensations overloading his brain.

Atticus suddenly realized how very one-sided their situation was.

He reached up, tangled his fingers in Kai's long hair, and *pulled*.

Kai moaned, the sound low and unsteady as it left him. Atticus tugged his head back, just enough so that he could reach him. Just enough so that he could kiss him.

Their mouths crashed together, and Atticus nearly came from just the knowledge that he was finally tasting Kai again after so long. Months of missing this.

It was every bit as good as he remembered.

Kai bit at his bottom lip. Always so feral, all teeth and claws, even like this. Atticus gasped, and Kai surged forward, deepening their kiss. Atticus pressed his tongue in, drinking him in as much as he could. As much as Kai would allow him.

Atticus reached down between them, let his hand press along Kai's hip. When he met no resistance, when the other man only continued to kiss him with a fervor Atticus half-thought he was dreaming up, he moved his hand to palm Kai through his sweatpants. Kai breathed harshly, his breath hot against Atticus' lips. Nails dug into his bare shoulders as Kai rocked into his hand, the length of his erection hot against Atticus' palm even through the fabric.

The sounds of their heavy breathing echoed through the room. Atticus could feel himself getting more and more worked up as they moved against one another, a heat growing in his core, burning brighter as Kai's hands roved across his body. One came to rest at the back of his neck, yanking Atticus into another searing kiss, while the other trailed lower.

Fingers teased across his abdomen, ran along the waistband of his shorts before dipping underneath. Atticus groaned as Kai's hand wrapped around him, as it stroked him once, then again. Atticus couldn't help it as his hips bucked into the touch. A finger teased along his tip, pressing at the wetness beading there. Atticus had to pull away from the kiss, gasping for air. Kai stroked him again as Atticus held him tight.

"Kai, I'm-"

It was too late. Atticus came hard. He pressed his face into soft hair as Kai worked him through it, as clever fingers drew out his pleasure. It took him several long moments to regulate his breathing, to clear his head enough to pull back, to loosen the death grip he had on Kai.

Atticus tried to look into Kai's face, tried to gauge any sort of expression there, but it was too dark. He could just make out the lines where their bodies were still tangled together. Kai pulled his hand out of Atticus' shorts, wiping it off on the already-soiled fabric. Heat warmed Atticus' cheeks.

When Kai didn't immediately pull away, Atticus leaned in, capturing his lips again. Kai let out a small whimper as Atticus' hand found its way back to his still-hard cock.

Atticus broke away from the kiss, fingers tugging at Kai's sweatpants. "Can I-"

A resounding crash interrupted him. He sat up immediately, yanking Kai up with him.

"What the fuck?" Kai sounded breathless, voice low and more than a little wrecked.

"Cat," Atticus said, sighing. He scooted out from under where Kai was halfway sitting in his lap. "I think I left a glass on my nightstand."

He moved toward the closest light switch, pointedly ignoring the wetness on the front of his shorts. Flicking the switch, Atticus didn't let himself look at the man he'd left on the couch for too long. A moment was enough for him to see Kai's mussed hair, his flushed cheeks and heaving chest.

Nope. Atticus needed to go check on his cat. What if she'd hurt herself?

She was, in fact, fine. The kitten sat perched on his nightstand, striped tail flicking back and forth, head cocked to the side as she stared at him with those wide eyes.

He'd been right. On the ground below her were shards of glass sparkling in a puddle of water.

"Girlie," he said, puffing his cheeks out with a long breath. "I'm not gonna have any glasses left if you keep at this."

"Is she okay?" Kai's voice sounded out from just down the hall. Atticus popped his head back out the door, saw him standing outside the guest bedroom.

"She's fine," he said.

"Need help cleaning it up?"

"Nah." Atticus grinned a little. "I got it."

Kai nodded at him, looking away. His cheeks were still somewhat flushed, and Atticus couldn't help but think about why, about what they'd been doing before the goddamn cat had interrupted them.

"I'm going to get ready for bed then," Kai said, still not quite meeting Atticus' gaze.

"Right, yeah." Fuck. *Fuck.* Was he upset? He wasn't exactly giving off the sort of vibes that said *let's keep going, you were about to stick your hand down my pants!* Had they just fucked everything up?

"Hey," Atticus said as Kai began to turn away. He probably sounded desperate. He probably didn't care. "You good?"

Kai turned back. His cheeks were a slightly brighter shade of pink, but he was smiling just a bit, and it set Atticus' heart racing in a less horrible way.

"I'm good," Kai responded softly. "Night, Attie."

He couldn't help but flash another grin. "Night, Kai."

It was the work of just a few minutes to clean up the kitten's mess, but by the time he was walking back to his room after throwing away the broken glass, Atticus' eyes were growing heavy. He yawned as he pushed his door shut, leaving it open just enough for the creature to come and go as she pleased.

He was about to slip into bed when he remembered. Atticus looked down at himself.

He had cum in his shorts. Kai had touched him for what, thirty seconds? And he'd blown his load. Right there in his shorts.

Atticus couldn't even find it in himself to be ashamed. Well, maybe he was a *little* ashamed, considering the fact he'd sort of left Kai hanging while he had to go take care of the demon he'd let into his house. He wondered, if after Kai had closed the door to his room, if maybe he had...

No. *No.* It was late, Atticus was tired. He definitely didn't need to think about Kai finishing himself off on the other side of the wall.

He couldn't seem to wipe the stupid grin off his face as he changed his shorts and crawled into his bed. Atticus knew that the less tired version of himself that woke up tomorrow would probably be more anxious about it all.

About what it might mean, what they had just done.

But for now? For now, Atticus was just going to let himself be happy. Dumb, stupid, wonderful happy.

1 Year & 6 Months Ago

Kai had been staring at his handheld console's screen for a solid five minutes. His game was paused, his mind racing as he lay in bed, propped up against his pillow, his boyfriend asleep next to him.

How long had it been since he and Nicholas had last had sex?

The question had barreled into his mind as he'd been playing his game, the bright screen the only thing lighting their room. It had been... a while. At least a couple of months, maybe? Possibly longer. Kai couldn't even really remember the last time.

Why hadn't he noticed sooner?

He glanced over to the other side of the bed. Nicholas, as usual, had shifted so that his head was stuck between their pillows. It always sort of seemed like he might suffocate himself sleeping that way, but Kai was used to it. He had also kicked off the blanket. Nicholas always ran a little hot when he slept, a warmth that Kai loved to burrow into, curling against him throughout the night.

Except he didn't really do that anymore, did he? No, these days they tended to fall asleep on their separate sides of the bed, Kai hogging the covers to himself.

When had that changed as well?

Kai felt a knot growing in his chest, a strange sense of dread rising as these realizations washed over him. He was never really one to feel touch starved, but Nicholas was. Nicholas had always been the more tactile of the two of them, always reaching out to make contact in small ways. He'd also always been more likely to start anything that would lead to them having sex.

Kai felt a heat spreading through his chest and arms. Not a comfortable, exciting warmth. One that hurt, one that scared him.

Why had Nicholas stopped touching him?

A wave of guilt washed over Kai. He hadn't even *noticed* that anything had changed between them. Hadn't even noticed they hadn't had sex in longer than he could remember. Hadn't even noticed that the extent of their physical contact had dwindled to nothing more than a peck on the lips for a goodbye and sitting against one another on the couch as they watched tv.

A massive part of their relationship was seemingly missing, and Kai had gone on with his daily life completely oblivious.

It could be fixed though. Kai set his game aside, mind racing toward a new train of thought.

Maybe it was his fault. Maybe Nicholas wanted Kai to step up, to initiate things more. Thoughts of why something like that wouldn't have been communicated were pushed aside as Kai shifted in the bed.

He leaned in close, pressing up against Nicholas' bare back, the skin there so hot to the touch.

"Nicky," Kai whispered, his mouth close to his boyfriend's ear.

Nicholas hummed a questioning sound, slowly lifting his head from between their pillows.

"Hey," Kai said, running a hand down his side, his fingers

settling on Nicholas' hip. Kai teased along the waistband of his boxer briefs.

"Hey," Nicholas finally echoed, voice still so thick with sleep. Kai leaned forward, pressing their lips together. Nicholas shifted so that he was on his back, gently kissing Kai back before pulling away.

"What's up?"

Kai moved so that he was half on top of him, soaking in that ever-present warmth through the oversized t-shirt he wore. It was one of Nicholas' old ones. A few holes in the neckline, a frayed hem at the bottom. It made Kai feel silly every time he put it on, but he couldn't bring himself to throw it out, no matter how ratty it was.

"Nothing," he said, leaning to press his lips against Nicholas' jaw. Large hands found their way to his slim waist, gripping him softly. Nicholas made no other movement, and Kai didn't let himself think about it.

He snaked a hand up into Nicholas' hair, tugging gently to tilt the his head, exposing his throat. The motion pulled a small gasp from Nicholas. Kai didn't know if it was a good or a bad thing

Kai had always been so *soft* during sex, from the very beginning. It was all he had ever known.

Maybe it was time to try something different.

Kai used his other hand to grab Nicholas' wrist, yanking it above his head and holding it tight against the pillow. If Nicholas didn't want to use his hands then maybe Kai could help with that.

He continued to trail a line of kisses down Nicholas' neck. The other man wriggled a little at the contact, pushing up against Kai's grip. He let out a sound as Kai's teeth sank into the skin right above his collarbone.

Kai paused.

Was he *laughing*?

"What are you doing?" Nicholas asked, his voice lighter than before as he chuckled through the words.

Kai sat up, immediately releasing his grip on Nicholas, disentangling his fingers from sleep-mussed hair.

"What do you mean?"

Nicholas laughed again, and Kai felt that knot in his chest grow. Felt his stomach sink, felt that same sense of dread that he still didn't quite understand.

"You're never like this," Nicholas said, reaching up to push some of Kai's hair back from his face. It was so much longer now, and he loved when Nicholas played with it. When they would sit together on a weekend night, catching up on the shows they watched, Nicholas' long fingers trailing through Kai's hair over and over until they both inevitably passed out.

That hadn't happened in a while.

"I...," Kai began, unsure of what to say. He felt embarrassed, something he hadn't felt with Nicholas since the early, childhood days of their relationship. Kai looked away, focusing on the still bright screen of his game sitting on the nightstand. The faint light it cast throughout their room wasn't nearly enough to see by clearly. It lent an almost eerie glow to the space. As if anything could be hiding in the corners, just waiting for the right moment to jump out.

"I just thought maybe we could try something different," Kai finally said. He still couldn't quite bring himself to meet Nicholas' gaze.

Nicholas laughed again, but this time it held something sweeter, something softer. He placed a hand against Kai's cheek, rubbing his thumb gently below his ear.

"Not that I don't like where your mind is headed," Nicholas said, voice soft. "But I have to be up in a few hours for work. Can we hit pause on this one?"

Kai nodded. He was still sprawled across Nicholas' chest. He shifted, moving back to his side of the bed. Nicholas' hesitated, hand still pressed to Kai's face.

"I love you, Kai," Nicholas whispered. "You know that, right?"

There was something there in the words. Something heavy, something unspoken that Kai couldn't parse out. He nodded again.

"I know," he whispered back. "I love you, too."

He meant it, with everything he had in him. Something between them had shifted recently, something that Kai had failed to notice. But it didn't matter, it would never matter, because the one thing that would never change would be how he felt about Nicholas. That love would always be there, ever-present.

They drifted off to sleep together, Nicholas with one arm wrapped around Kai, curled into his warmth. A warmth that, for the very first time, failed to sink in all the way.

7

Present Day

Atticus: Theoretically

Julian: adverb, meaning according to theory rather than experience or practice

Atticus: Theoretically
Atticus: If I were to have made out with Kai last night, do you think it would be a bad thing?

Julian: awwww my second favorite himbo is finally making progress in his love life!

Atticus: Who's your first favorite himbo?
Atticus: Wait no I know don't answer that

Julian: the shortie pie who is passed out on my living room

floor after challenging his new teammates to a ten mile run. he looks so cute, like a little starfish on the rug, drool running out of the corner of his mouth, sweaty and stinky and very adorable, you could never compete with him for first place

Atticus: Wow
Atticus: You're worse off than me I think

Julian: so you kissed kai, the man you've been in love with for actual ages, i do not see the problem

Atticus: Well okay so
Atticus: It was a little more than kissing

Julian: still not seeing the problem

Atticus: There's been some flirting, more than usual
Atticus: And we fell asleep on the couch

Julian: how quaint

Atticus: And we woke up and started making out and then his hands were down my pants and ten seconds later it was all over and then my cat broke a glass and I sort of just left him hanging to go clean it up with a huge wet spot on my shorts and then he just went to bed and I'm a little worried that I might have fucked everything up

Julian: okay so here's the thing
Julian: i know we're friends or something now

Atticus: Took a screenshot of that

Julian: but i really don't need details about what you did or didn't do in your shorts
Julian: and i need you to know how hard i'm laughing at you right now :D

Atticus: I'm trying to build a scene
Atticus: So you can tell me if I messed up or not

Julian: kai was into it, right?

Atticus: I think so
Atticus: No he definitely was

Julian: was he upset when he went to bed?

Atticus: It didn't seem like it. He seemed fine. Maybe a little embarrassed

Julian: i know that this is wild advice, but you could just talk to him

Atticus: Yeah I know

Julian: better to just make sure everything is okay if you're worried about it
Julian: although maybe he doesn't want to talk to the dork who blew his load in his shorts

Atticus: Maybe I actually shouldn't tell you things

Julian: that's what i've been saying all along :)
Julian: and since when do you have a cat?

Kai lay in his bed, staring at the ceiling.

He had jerked Atticus off last night.

After six months of insisting to everyone, himself included, that there was nothing between the two of them, after resisting whatever physical chemistry that always seemed to be there, he'd finally given in.

And he couldn't stop thinking about it.

Kai groaned, rolling over onto his side and smashing his face into the pillow. Surprisingly, he wasn't spiraling. No, spiraling over what had transpired between himself and Atticus the night before would have been almost easier to deal with because it would have been familiar. Kai was kind of always in a state of spiraling, had been for the last year.

Instead, his mind insisted on replaying their interaction over and over, again and again, in *very* vivid detail.

The sensation of Atticus' hands on his waist, grip tight and burning. How his cock had felt in Kai's hand, thick and hard. The way his fingers had tangled in Kai's hair, pulling in just the right way...

Kai frowned into the pillow. He lifted his head, grabbing his phone to distract himself. Instead of a distraction, as though muscle memory had possessed him, he found himself pulling up his text chain with Ori, looking at the message he had sent last night before falling into a strangely peaceful sleep.

Kai: Attie and I just fooled around on his couch

Ori had responded at some point with a string of eyeball emojis. Kai chuckled as he typed out a response, immediately receiving another one from his friend.

Kai: I feel like I should be more worried about it.

Ori: Not being worried is good!!! It means you can finally BE HIS BOYFRIEND

Kai: Let's not get ahead of ourselves.

Ori: NO. LET'S

Kai: It doesn't necessarily mean anything. We were both half asleep and then suddenly all over each other.

Ori: I AM SO HAPPY FOR YOU

Kai: I have to talk to him about it though and I think I would rather rip my skin off.

Ori: TALK TO HIM ABOUT BEING BOYFRIENDS

Kai: ORION. FOCUS.

Ori: I'm just excited!!! Don't be nervous!
Ori: And don't call me that only my mom calls me that
Ori: I'm laying on the floor and julian thinks I'm still asleep so he hasn't noticed that I noticed he's texting someone and I'm pretty sure it's atticus because they're friends now so he's probably just as nervous as you but neither of you need to be

because instead you could just be boyfriends

Kai: Why were you sleeping on the floor?

Ori: Because I ran the fastest
Ori: Don't change the subject!
Ori: So was the fooling around good? :D:D:D

Kai: It wasn't not good...

Ori: :D:D:D:D:D:D:D:D:D:D

Kai: Got interrupted by his cat though.

Ori: Since when does atticus have a cat???

Kai huffed out another laugh as he flopped back onto his pillow, tossing his phone aside. Something about talking to Ori always made things feel a little more manageable. His friend had a way of whittling issues down to their simplest core, turning them into something less terrifying. Why did Kai need what happened the night prior to be a bad thing?

He knew, of course. Just hours before they'd 'fooled around,' Kai had been in the bathroom crying about Nicholas. Again. And that always insistent whisper in the back of his mind never stopped reminding him that Atticus *wasn't* Nicholas. Atticus wasn't the person he'd planned his entire life around.

But even if things had ended in chaos, last night had been... good. Good enough that Kai couldn't get it out of his head, had been replaying the scene over and over since the moment he woke up. Bringing up the fact that they'd been interrupted by the fucking cat only served to remind Kai of what he had done once he was alone in his room.

He yanked the pillow out from under his head, stuffing it over his face and groaning into it as he felt his body heat up. As he felt himself starting to grow hard.

Kai had said goodnight to Atticus, had barely closed the door to his room, before leaning back against it, a hand wrapped around himself in his sweatpants. He'd finished himself off, cumming to thoughts of what it would have been like to have Atticus' hand there instead of his own.

Lifting the pillow, Kai glanced down at the bulge in his sweatpants. He bit his lip, letting the pillow fall to the side as he reached down, pressing along his dick through the soft fabric before palming himself.

He could hear movement through the house, knew Atticus had been up for at least as long as he'd been awake. Knew he was going to have to take care of his *problem* before he could leave his room.

Kai rolled his eyes at himself, but all hesitation flew from his mind the moment he had a hand wrapped around his own cock.

Biting harder into his lip, Kai let his head fall back, eyes slipping closed as his mind filled with the same images that'd had him nearly crying out with pleasure the night before. Limbs tangled with Atticus', one strong hand fisted tight in Kai's hair as the other tugged at the waistband of his sweatpants. The way Atticus had been about to ask if he could touch him.

Kai stroked himself steadily, pushing his shirt up to his chest, abs clenching as he breathed hard through his nose, teeth still sunk into his lip to keep any sound from escaping him.

Footsteps in the hallway reached Kai despite the blood roaring in his ears. Atticus had a habit of just walking into his room, as though privacy were a foreign concept to him. Kai's eyes flicked to the door, pleasure building as he continued to stroke himself.

The thought of Atticus opening the door, popping his head in to say good morning the way he always did, of him seeing Kai splayed out on top of the covers, catching him flushed with one hand on his cock...

Kai spilled over his hand and onto his stomach, a gasp finally wrenching free from his lips. His chest heaved through the aftershocks, his limbs nearly trembling from the relief.

He'd now jerked off *twice*, in less than twelve hours, while thinking about Atticus. Awesome.

Kai lay flat, star-fished on the bed, once again staring at the ceiling. He needed to get up, needed to clean the mess he'd made on himself. Needed to figure out what he was going to say when he finally worked up the courage to leave his room.

What did he *want* to say to Atticus?

His heart was still pounding, echoing through his entire body. A steady, loud beat he could focus on and try to settle his thoughts.

Ori had made it all sound so simple. But it wasn't, was it? Kai knew, he *knew* that he wasn't in a place where he could handle any sort of real relationship. He didn't know if he would ever be in the right place for that. Just because Atticus accepted all of his broken pieces and sharp edges didn't mean they weren't still there. It didn't mean that Kai could just make them go away after some dry humping on a couch and a couple of good orgasms.

But the fact that he wasn't spiraling over all of this, the fact that Kai felt okay enough to even think about the possibility of more... that was new. That was something he couldn't help but recognize, couldn't help but let float inside of himself, a bit of hope shifting on gentle waves.

No, Kai didn't think he was ready for more. He knew that was what Atticus wanted, that his friend wanted so much more, and that stung. The idea that he might have made Atticus think that whatever this physical thing was that was happening between them would mean something more than it did. The idea of a new relationship, a new life, felt terrifying still. Felt so far out of his grasp that Kai wasn't sure he could even see it.

But what had happened between them had happened, and it couldn't be changed. And Kai was okay with it. He didn't feel worse off, and he didn't think Atticus would either.

Maybe it would be fine. Maybe they could both just acknowledge it and laugh it off. Kai was nervous, hard conversations about things like *feelings* always made him nervous. But he wasn't scared.

Atticus was his friend, and they'd done something that maybe they shouldn't have as friends, but it had happened and Kai didn't regret it.

They would be okay.

Kai sighed, finally rolling toward the nightstand to grab some tissues and clean himself up. Hearing footsteps in the hallway again spurred him to move a little faster. Post-nut clarity made the idea of Atticus catching him now *much* more embarrassing.

Changing into a fresh set of clothes quickly, Kai escaped down the hall to the bathroom. He moved through his morning routine with muscle memory, mind still stuck on the conversation waiting for him elsewhere in the house. Braiding his hair back loosely, Kai took in his appearance in the mirror. At least he looked somewhat chill on the outside, his face trained into a normal level of apathy that hid his inner turmoil well.

Kai tied his hair off and let his hands fall to his side. He inhaled deeply before opening the door, leaving the safety of the bathroom to find Atticus.

Atticus knew Kai had entered the kitchen. He was becoming more and more accustomed to having another person in his home. Despite the fact that Kai moved silently at all times, creeping into rooms and popping up out of nowhere like he was a creature in a horror movie, Atticus was getting a sense for how he moved and where he was, always. Like that kid who could see dead people in that one film, only for Atticus it was a Kai-specific power and it didn't fill him with dread.

Except that this time it did. Just a little.

Atticus knew he should turn around from where he was filling up the kitten's water bowl at the sink, knew he needed to acknowledge Kai, or else he might make things worse than they already were. But were they bad? Atticus didn't feel like it was bad on his end.

Sure, he'd woken up to some initial panic. Had messaged Julian of all people, because for some reason that asshole tended to give him good advice. Tended to understand some of the nuances of Atticus' situation better than most. Was it a setter thing?

But Atticus hadn't been filled with regret the way he'd thought he would be. Maybe it was the fact that Kai had smiled at him before saying goodnight. A small smile, tinted with a blush that had Atticus' pulse racing just thinking about it. Or maybe it was the fact that Kai was still there, that he hadn't left in the middle of the night or decided to hide in his room all day.

Whatever it was, Atticus knew that the worst case scenarios weren't happening. All that was left was for them to talk about it. Acknowledge it.

Even still, Atticus was nervous as fuck.

And now too many long seconds had passed, the water bowl was nearly overflowing, his Kai-sense told him that the

140

other man had moved across the room to sit at the same barstool he always sat at, and Atticus had lingered too long and had most likely made things awkward.

He turned around, ready to cringe and apologize for being such a fucking weirdo.

Atticus froze.

Kai was watching him, face impassive, nonchalantly peeling an orange he'd grabbed from the basket on the counter. His head tilted as their eyes met, and Atticus felt his nerves dissipate.

"Morning," Kai said, voice steady, the word falling off his tongue the same way it did every day.

Because Atticus knew Kai, knew him so well at this point, he knew that Kai was fine with the silences. Knew that Kai was fine with taking time to think. The man practically *lived* in his own head, the gears in his mind constantly churning. Atticus didn't need to worry, he didn't need to rush and over think. Kai would always let him take his time to figure things out.

The thought made his heart feel almost too full, just like the water bowl he was sloshing all over the kitchen floor as he made his way across the room to place it next to the matching food bowl.

Atticus walked back over, leaning casually on the counter across from Kai. The same position they'd found themselves in several times at this point.

"Morning," Atticus said. He might have sounded too cheerful, but he didn't really care. He was a morning person, and Kai needed to get used to it.

He watched as Kai placed a slice of orange on his tongue, couldn't help but stare at his lips, remembering what they'd felt like against his own the night before. Kai's bottom lip was red, redder than usual, and Atticus wondered if he'd been chewing it out of nervousness. If he were as anxious about this conversation as Atticus had been all morning.

"So," Atticus said as Kai continued to eat his orange in silence. "Um…"

His hesitation finally seemed to alert Kai, who paused to stare a little more intently. Atticus cleared his throat before going on.

"Are you okay?"

The question, to Atticus' surprise, brought a slight blush to Kai's cheeks. He nodded, looking down to focus on the pieces of orange peel he'd placed on a napkin.

"I'm okay," Kai said. Atticus let out a breath.

"Good!" he said, probably a bit too loud. "Good. I wasn't sure if I needed to apologize."

Kai cocked his head to the side. "I'm pretty sure we were both involved."

It was Atticus' turn to flush. He chuckled. "Yeah, uh, I noticed. I was just afraid I- no, *we* might have screwed things up." He paused, forcing himself to maintain eye contact. "Do you think it was a mistake?"

Kai watched him, waiting a long time before responding. Atticus could practically see those overworked gears turning in his head.

"I'm not sure," he said. "I don't regret it though."

"I don't either."

The words felt heavy on Atticus' tongue. Not a bad sort of heavy, but one filled with more emotion than he realized he'd be bringing to this conversation. Having Kai in his arms, pressed close, tangled together with him? No, he would never regret that. And before he really knew what he was doing, before his thoughts had thoroughly aligned, Atticus spoke again.

"What does it mean for us, though?"

He immediately felt as if the question were too much, as if he was putting something out there that he was afraid to find the answer to.

"I'm not sure," Kai repeated, his voice soft as he looked away. Atticus waited, giving him time to think it through, watching as Kai chewed at the inside of his cheek, hands pulling into the long sleeves of the oversized black t-shirt he wore.

Atticus really took him in, observing Kai more thoroughly than he had since he'd entered the room. His hair was pulled back into a loose braid, a few dark strands falling loose, the light pink ends brushing his jawline. Atticus remembered what it had felt like to have that hair held tight in his grip, remembered the sounds it had elicited from Kai, the sharp breaths and small whimpers. He remembered how natural it had felt for them to be pressed so close together. How *right* it had seemed.

He knew how he felt, what he wanted it all to mean. Maybe Julian was right.

Maybe Atticus just needed to say it.

"Kai," he said, forcing his tone to stay calm and even. "I don't think I've done a great job of keeping how I feel a secret. So if this all means something more from us, that's something I want."

Kai looked back at him, something like fear in his eyes, and it made Atticus' chest feel tight. He pushed aside the unease and continued.

"I want us to be okay, though. In whatever way we need to be. So if you still don't want something more, I can deal with that. I just need you to tell me."

He felt as though he were throwing some sort of lifeline out, desperate for Kai to pull him in. Atticus had meant the words. And maybe it was pathetic for him to be this hung up on someone, for him to be willing to push his feelings aside if it meant he could at least keep his friend. But he didn't really care. As long as he could have Kai in his life, Atticus would make it work.

Because the only other option was to lose him.

And that wasn't really an option at all, was it?

"I-" Kai began, cutting himself off as his lips pulled into a tight line. He was thinking, he was thinking so hard and Atticus felt just a bit of hope at the fact that an immediate no hadn't been spoken.

Kai looked at him, a little desperately. "Can I take some time to think about it?"

Atticus blinked. "Uh," he began, so eloquently. "Yeah, of course."

Kai was going to think about it. Atticus wasn't one hundred percent sure what all that *it* entailed. But it was something. It was more than Kai had given him in the last six months.

He couldn't help himself. Atticus grinned wide, slapping his palms down on the counter playfully.

"As long as we're okay," he said, "you can think about it as much as you need to."

Kai nodded, his mouth pulling into a small smile that he might have been trying to fight back. "Thanks."

Atticus pushed back from the counter. He felt lighter, so much lighter than he had felt all morning. Lighter than he had felt in a long time.

"You got plans today?"

Kai shook his head. "Not much. I need to record some stuff for a new game I was sent, but it's not pressing. You?'

"Yep," Atticus said. "Half of Sammie's bartenders are out with some kinda stomach bug. I'm going in this evening to help out with the closing shift. Have a couple things I need to get done first." He ran a hand through his hair, thinking about the fact that his roots were getting out of hand and how he needed to finally bite the bullet and pull his bleaching supplies out.

144

Kai nodded in acknowledgment. Atticus turned away, thinking about the laundry he needed to finish up and how he wanted to change the sheets on his bed.

"We *are* good." Kai's voice had him turning back before leaving the kitchen. He looked a little skittish still, a little uncomfortable. But he also held himself with a kind of determination Atticus wasn't used to seeing on him.

"We're good," Kai continued. "And I *am* going to think about it all."

A promise in those words. One that had Atticus grinning brilliantly as he nodded, that same silly smile plastered on his face as he left the room to get on with his chores.

Kai left his room, stretching as he did. It had been simple work to record a couple of promo videos. He wasn't ready to do a full review yet, still needed to put a few more hours into the game before he could form a full opinion on it. But unboxing videos were nothing anymore.

He made his way down the hall, wondering where Atticus was. When he reached the open bathroom, Kai drew to a full halt, eyes wide as he stared at what was happening inside.

Atticus stood before the sink, latex-gloved hands held before him helplessly. He was staring hard at a small bowl filled with a white substance. Kai recognized the smell.

"Is that bleach?"

Atticus turned, and Kai almost laughed at the pitiful look on his face.

"Yeah," he responded, letting out a huff with the word.

"What's wrong?" Kai stepped into the small room with the question, leaning against the doorway.

"Sammie usually helps me."

This time Kai did laugh. "Haven't you been bleaching your

hair since you were like fifteen?"

Atticus frowned. "I'm kind of terrible at it. It always comes out patchy if she doesn't help me."

Kai couldn't help but marvel at the fact that Atticus Mills, arguably one of the most confident people he'd ever known, had been toppled by the fact that he didn't know how to bleach his own hair. Kai picked up the bowl and the long-stemmed brush, stirring the mixture.

"You need to mix it more," he said, still chuckling. "Make sure there aren't any clumps of the powder left."

Atticus looked at him as though Kai had just saved his life.

"Can you help me?"

Desperation and hope filled his question. He looked so pathetic standing there, hands still held up awkwardly before him, eyes wide, shoulders slumped in defeat.

Kai fought back a grin. "Sure, I can help. Here." He set the mixture back on the counter, grabbing a white towel and draping it over Atticus' bare shoulders. He had to lean up onto his toes because of their height difference. Kai's mouth went dry as he was forced to take in the fact that Atticus was shirtless, his broad chest and shoulders right at eye level, black ink swirling across one shoulder to trail down the length of his arm. The designs were mesmerizing, and Kai had to make himself look away. It had his stomach doing things he decided to ignore for the moment, careful not to touch Atticus' skin as he pulled away.

"You're too tall," Kai said, keeping his words even, as though he weren't painfully aware of every inch of skin exposed before him. "I'll go get a stool for you."

"Thanks!" Atticus gave him one of *those* grins, one of the big, silly ones that Kai hated to admit he liked best.

Once they were settled into place, Atticus on the stool, Kai standing behind him, gloves on and bleach mixture in hand, Kai finally spoke again.

"Ready?"

"Yep!" All trepidation was gone from Atticus' countenance as he waited for Kai to get started.

A thought gave Kai pause, though. He looked down at the shirt he was wearing. He really liked this one.

"Just a second," he mumbled, setting the supplies down once again. He yanked his shirt over his head, tossing it into the corner, far away from the bleach. Atticus glanced over his shoulder, but made no comment. Kai didn't miss the hint of pink dusting his cheeks.

As Kai began to spread the mixture into floppy, soft hair, focusing on the roots, he was glad for the towel on Atticus' shoulders. If he'd had to deal with the sight of that broad back, the solid muscles there shifting with every tiny movement his friend made, he might not have been able to get through it.

"I didn't start messing with my hair until I was sixteen, thank you very much."

Kai snorted, meeting Atticus' stare in the mirror above the sink. "Why did you start?"

Atticus shrugged, and Kai poked his back to keep him still. "Because Sammie went through a blonde phase. People stopped thinking we were twins. Teenage me didn't know how to handle the fact that we were finally developing our own separate identities."

"So the solution was to bleach your hair?"

Atticus chuckled, looking down at his hands. "It was so bad back then. Yellow, fried to oblivion. Sammie's was just as awful, but she'll never admit it. She gave up on blonde after six months, but by then it had sort of grown on me. And I'd started to realize that just because we weren't just 'the twins' anymore, it didn't mean I was going to lose her."

A tug in Kai's chest had him focusing hard on the task at hand. The soft, fond smile that crinkled the corners of Atticus' eyes was too much as a current flickered through Kai's veins.

"That's kinda cute."

A brighter smile, one that wasn't steeped in memories, but was full of something only for Kai. It radiated with hope, and it made Kai feel too full of things he didn't want to think about.

They were silent for a while as Kai worked. Every so often he would use his hand instead of the brush to spread the mixture evenly. It was hard to ignore the way Atticus reacted to that, leaning in to every touch, breaths shuddering out as Kai's fingers ran along his scalp.

It wasn't long before the back and most of the sides of his hair were done. Kai pressed lightly on his shoulder, just above one curling tail of the nine-tailed fox inked along his arm.

"Need you to turn around." The words came out weaker than he'd intended. Something about the whole situation was affecting Kai in a way he hadn't been expecting. Maybe the fumes were getting to him.

Atticus shifted on the stool, turning his body so that he was facing Kai fully. His eyes were heavy lidded, cheeks still a little flushed. Kai's breath hitched at the sight. He paused, gathering himself before leaning in to continue.

Atticus' eyes fell closed the moment Kai's hand was back in his hair. Kai abandoned the brush fully, unable to stop himself from using his fingers alone to run the mixture along Atticus' roots. He could feel soft breaths against his chest, warm and uneven.

As Kai worked his way down the side of Atticus' face, following his hairline, his fingers grazed behind an ear. Atticus let out a sound, small and breathless. Kai felt a hand at his hip, fingers brushing lightly over the skin just above his pants. A trail of fire lit there, at every point where Atticus touched him.

Kai held his breath as he ran his fingers over the same spot, only breathing out when the hand at his waist tightened.

"I need you to tilt your head," Kai said. Atticus obeyed immediately, head leaning to the side as a thumb ran along Kai's hip. Kai let out an unsteady laugh.

"Good boy."

A harsh breath escaped Atticus at those two words, and he tugged Kai a little closer. Kai struggled to keep his hands steady, struggled to ignore how close Atticus' lips were to his skin. Just the slightest shift from either of them and those lips could be on Kai's neck, could run along his collarbone.

Kai swallowed, his mouth too dry. Focus. He needed to focus. He was helping his friend bleach his hair, that was all.

His friend that he'd jerked off the night before. His friend that he'd fantasized about earlier that day. His friend that he was potentially considering in not friend ways.

Moving along, Kai tugged a little at Atticus' hair to tilt his head in the right direction, no longer trusting his voice to give commands. Another sound left Atticus, a sound that was deeper and filled with more heat than before. Kai was breathing harder, his chest rising and falling in rhythm with his racing pulse.

It didn't take long to finish up, but Kai found himself not wanting to pull away. Both of Atticus' hands were on his waist now, holding tight and steady. They were each a little breathless, Kai still standing over Atticus. He sort of liked it, the way he was finally able to look down on the taller man.

It reminded him of the night they'd spent together, of what it had been like to be in Atticus' lap. Of the thrill it had given him, having the other man relinquish any power beneath him. The way Atticus had turned to putty as soon as Kai had taken charge.

The bleach was setting, Atticus' roots growing lighter by the second, and Kai had yet to pull away. One hand was still in Atticus' hair, still running through the damp strands. He moved the other, the one that had held the bowl and was therefore still clean, running his fingers along the tattoos that sprawled over pale skin, before trailing them up Atticus' neck. He pressed a gloved thumb along Atticus' jawline and thought that maybe he could feel his racing pulse. Thought that maybe it matched his own.

Kai settled his hand at the back of Atticus' neck, watched him lean back into the touch, and Kai couldn't resist. He tugged on Atticus' hair again, tilting his head further back.

Atticus' eyes flew open as he let out a small gasp. Kai stared down at him, their faces only inches apart. Atticus was flushed, breathing hard, each puff of air brushing Kai's lips. Kai looked down, focusing on that parted mouth, on that full bottom lip, on how easy it would be to lean down, just enough. How easy it would be to press their lips together, to taste Atticus again the way he'd longed to since the night before.

Maybe for much longer than that.

"Kai." His name on those same lips pulled Kai's eyes back up to meet the ones staring at him. They watched each other for a long moment. Kai shifted closer, his hips settling in between Atticus' legs.

"What?" Kai was going to make him say it.

"I want you to kiss me."

The longing in the words, the way Atticus was giving him the power, giving him the reins, it set something off inside of Kai. Unleashed a side of himself that he wasn't used to, a side that enjoyed taking control in these situations, a side that he'd denied himself for so long.

Kai pressed on the back of Atticus' neck as he leaned in, guiding him forward. Where their kiss last night had been full of fire, had been a crash of tongues and teeth, this one was more subdued, laced with intention. Kai was in control, and he drew it out, pressing into Atticus' mouth carefully, steadily. He breathed in the sounds coming escaping those soft lip as his hand tightened in bleach-damp hair.

Long fingers trailed up Kai's bare back, setting off sparks along the path of skin. Atticus' other hand stayed at his waist, grip nearly bruising as he kissed Kai back.

The smell of the bleach so close stung Kai's nose as he breathed heavily, made his eyes water. He didn't care. It was impossible to pull away, impossible to end what they had allowed to begin. Atticus tasted like toothpaste, with a hint of the banana he had eaten earlier, and Kai couldn't get enough. He pressed in deeper, letting his tongue explore as his stomach came flush against Atticus' chest.

Arms wrapped around his waist. Atticus held him close, tight in a way that told Kai that he too didn't want to let this moment go. Didn't want it to end.

A blaring alarm went off from the sink's counter.

Kai jumped back. He couldn't go far, still braced in by Atticus' arms. Atticus blinked several times, as though he were having trouble coming back to reality.

"You set an alarm," Kai breathed out, unsure if he was asking a question or stating a fact.

"Yeah," Atticus said, loosening his hold around Kai's waist. "Yeah, before we started. So I wouldn't leave the bleach in too long."

He still looked a little dazed. Honestly, Kai kind of felt the same. He forced himself to focused on the task at hand.

"Let me look," he said. "Tilt your head forward."

Atticus obeyed, and Kai checked the progress of the bleach on his roots.

"Not gonna call me a good boy again?" Atticus asked, a cheeky grin on his face as Kai motioned for him to get up. Kai rolled his eyes.

"You should be good to go ahead and rinse it out," Kai

said, removing his gloves and cleaning up the mess of supplies. His heart was still pounding, so loud he wondered if Atticus could hear it.

"You'll help me with the toner too, right?"

Kai looked back over his shoulder. There was sincerity in Atticus' expression, sure, but there was also a good amount of mischief there as well. Kai felt his cheeks heat, but he nodded.

"Yeah, I can." The words came out as a fucking squeak.

As Atticus began to disrobe, because apparently he was going to take an entire shower instead of just rinsing his hair, Kai exited the room hastily with the stuff that needed to be either cleaned or thrown away.

He stood over the kitchen sink, rinsing out the bowl they'd used for bleach and scrubbing away any remnants. The kitten sat on the counter, staring at him with wide, knowing eyes, as though she could read his mind. Atticus' voice could be heard from where he'd left the bathroom door wide open, off-key singing floating throughout the house.

Kai held the kitten's stare until he couldn't anymore. Atticus always said they had the same eyes. Was Kai that intense when he looked at people?

She continued to watch him cleaning up, until Atticus hollered that he was ready for Kai's help again. Kai sighed, still shaken by how flustered he'd become. By how much that whole scene with Atticus had affected him. By how natural and *right* it had felt.

The kitten jumped off the counter as he made his way out of the kitchen, settling into one of her beds and curling up. He'd lost her attention, as though she'd simply wanted to make him squirm and could now go on with her day.

Kai reentered the bathroom to Atticus blow drying his hair. And goddammit, he looked *cute*. Hair a mess, blown every which way, a little wiry from the bleach. He smiled as Kai came back into the room, a look so genuine and happy that

Kai couldn't help but return it.

He thought that maybe... maybe he was just a little bit in trouble. And maybe he was going to have to think a lot harder than he'd realized about what Atticus had asked him that morning.

8

Sammie set a bottle of bourbon down on the table as Atticus flopped back in his chair.

"That was fucking brutal," Atticus whined. His sister rolled her eyes as she filled both of their glasses.

"That's the service industry," Sammie replied. Her voice was laced with exhaustion that mirrored Atticus' own. "You've got your little pampered volleyball life while my people are over here actually working every day."

"Don't be an ass," Atticus said, sipping his bourbon. He really wasn't *supposed* to be drinking, his nutritionist would have a fit if she found out, and his coach would rip into him about staying sharp for the game in a few days. But damn, after bartending all night, he really wanted something to take the edge off. As a treat for all his hard work.

Sammie only smirked in response to his bitching. She looked tired though. More tired than Atticus had seen her in a long time. Shoulders slumped as she leaned forward in her seat, elbows braced on the table. Her heavy-lidded gaze seemed more weighted than usual, dark circles under her grayish blue eyes, her brow almost constantly creased.

"You okay?" Atticus asked after a long moment of silence. His sister let out a slow sigh.

"Yeah," she finally said, running a hand over her face as if she could wipe the exhaustion away, tucking her shoulder-length dark hair back behind an ear. "It's just been a long couple weeks. It'll get back to normal soon." Sammie paused, chewing on her words a bit before finally letting them out. "Thanks for coming to help tonight."

Atticus grinned wide. "I know I saved the day, you don't have to say it!"

Sammie rolled her eyes, *hard*, but there was the normalcy that Atticus was looking for. There was the twin he didn't feel like he needed to worry about.

Except that he did, a lot. He worried that Sammie overworked herself every day to keep the brewery running, worried that she never set aside enough time to have a *life* outside of her career.

"Do anything fun lately?" Atticus threw the question out and hoped for a positive answer. He didn't get one. Sammie waved an arm toward the mess left throughout the bar after their final rush before closing.

"What do you think?"

"'Same," Atticus said, his voice dipping toward something more serious. "You need to get laid."

He earned a hard, sharp look for that one.

"No," his sister said, "I don't."

Atticus flopped back dramatically in his seat. "Fine! But you need to do something to let out all that tension." He gestured vaguely toward Sammie. "It's radiating off of you so hard I'm afraid it's going to infect me or something."

"Like you don't have your own shit you're freaking out about."

Atticus sat back up, tried to keep from squirming. Sammie was too good at that. At getting right to the heart of whatever was banging around in Atticus' head at any given moment.

"At least I'm having fun," he replied with a wink. "Have you talked to Kieran lately?"

And suddenly the tables had turned.

"Couple days ago," she said, pointedly *not* making eye contact. Atticus smirked. "He had to make the grain delivery himself."

"He looked good, didn't he?" Atticus asked teasingly. "Got that good farmer's tan from helping out back home. And damn, those arms he has from volleyball *and* farming!"

"Please shut up."

"Imagine the two of you," Atticus continued. "He comes here for a delivery after hours, it's just you and him and a bunch of machinery. He says something cute about helping his ma and you just can't help yourself anymore, pushing him up against the counter to ravish hi-"

"No *fuck* no!" Sammie nearly screeched as she cut him off, slapping her hands over her ears. "Stop making it sound like porn!"

Atticus laughed hard, reaching out for the bottle to refill their cups. He didn't miss the smile that his sister was trying to hide.

"I think it could be good for you," he said, voice still teasing even if his words were more serious. "Get over this whole pining phase and just ask him out."

"Is that what you're doing?" Sammie crossed her arms, a sharp eyebrow raised at him.

Again, right to the heart of things.

"Touché." Atticus took a long drink, savoring the taste in an effort to stall. He chuckled as he set his glass down. "In my defense, things might finally be going somewhere."

Sammie only stared at him, a bored expression that told him she didn't believe him. Atticus took it as a sign to continue.

"There's been some," he began, "*things* that have happened this week."

"Do not go into detail," Sammie said. "I'll kill you."

Atticus frowned, pouting. "Why does everyone say that to me?"

"Because you're a menace and you probably need to be muzzled."

He thought for a moment. "I wonder if Kai would be into that?"

"Jesus christ," Sammie breathed out, leaning forward to let her head fall onto her arms on the table. Atticus decided not to tell her that some of her hair had landed in a puddle of spilled beer.

"Okay okay, I'm sorry," he laughed. "I'll be serious." Sammie lifted her head so that only her eyes were visible.

"I don't believe you."

"I will!" Atticus insisted. "I'm such a good brother, I'm even going to ask you for advice! My wise, sage, serious twin." He paused, raising his cup. "I need your help."

"With what?" Sammie asked, finally relenting and sitting back up.

"Well…" Atticus chewed on his lip. The lighthearted candor seemed to evaporate from within him. He felt a little nervous. "I'm not sure actually."

Sammie's eyes narrowed. "Tell me what's going on, just don't get weird about it."

Atticus pressed a hand over his heart. "Promise."

And so he did. He told his sister everything that had happened over the last several days, careful not to go into *too* much detail. It wasn't like he needed to. Sammie was always good at reading between his lines, at seeing the things that Atticus maybe wasn't quite ready to say out loud.

His sister sat back after Atticus finished, draining her glass as he did and waving a hand toward him.

"He did a good job," Sammie said.

Atticus stared at her. "What?"

Another hand wave. "On your hair."

"Oh," Atticus said, reaching up to mindlessly run his fingers through the freshly-bleached strands. "I guess he did, didn't he?"

"Do you love him?"

The question slammed into Atticus, caught him fully off guard. And he knew, *he knew*, that his sister had done it on purpose. Had distracted him with the first comment to get him to inadvertently spill the truth.

Atticus bit his tongue to keep from blurting out the answer, and Sammie only raised a knowing brow at him.

"I think you should probably tell him," she said.

Atticus couldn't keep his mouth shut any longer. "I said I'd give him time to think."

Sammie shrugged, tugging at her tight black shirt as she rose from her chair. "You did. But it sounds to me like all he does is think. Maybe you can give him that much so he doesn't have to think, doesn't have to wonder about it."

"Is that what you're going to do? Just tell Kieran exactly how you feel?"

Sammie frowned. "Get off your ass and help me clean this place up so we can leave. You staying at my place tonight?"

It was already late, later than Atticus had planned to be out. There was still so much to be done, and his drive home wouldn't be a short one. Normally, it would be a given, spending the night at his sister's apartment in the city. But after how he'd left things with Kai, after the moments they'd shared in his cramped little bathroom, Atticus sort of wanted to see where the night might take them.

A yawn broke through his train of thought.

"You should stay," Sammie said, walking away toward a closet full of cleaning supplies. "You'll see him tomorrow."

Atticus let out a sigh. She was right. And he had to admit, the idea of being in a nice fluffy bed soon instead of on the road with his eyes slipping shut from exhaustion sounded wonderful. He pulled his phone out, shooting Kai a quick text to let him know he wouldn't be home that night.

As Atticus rose from his seat, a spray bottle and wet rag were shoved into his hands.

"Wipe down the tables and chairs," his sister ordered.

"No need to be so bossy!"

"You'd never get anything done without someone telling you what to do," Sammie hollered from back behind the bar. "I hope Kai bosses you around all the time."

Atticus thought back to words Kai had breathed against his skin. *Good boy*.

"Actually," he yelled back, an obnoxious grin spreading across his face. "Earlier today…"

By the time Atticus finished his story, Sammie was once again begging for him to shut up.

Atticus: How's our girl doing

Kai clicked a quick picture. The kitten was currently curled up in his lap, and had been for the last hour while he'd been playing a game on his laptop.

Kai: *Attachment*

Atticus: Awwwwwwww

Kai: Had to fight with her to get the medicine down her throat.

Atticus: Just a couple more days of it

Kai: Ear isn't red anymore, so it's working.
Kai: You make it to Sammie's place?

He set his phone down, going back to his game while he waited for a response. Kai hated to admit, even to himself, that he'd felt a good amount of disappointment at finding out Atticus would be spending the night at his sister's place. But it was a good thing. Probably.

Kai frowned as he sniped another player from across the map. It *was* a good thing that he and Atticus were apart for the night. It gave him time to think, like he'd promised Atticus he would. If the other man had come back home, had walked in the door with that cheeky grin and those bright eyes...

After the last twenty-four hours they'd had, Kai wasn't sure he would have been able to keep his hands to himself.

That worried him. His body kept reacting to Atticus in ways that were hard for his mind to keep up with.

His phone dinged, but Kai forced himself to let the game timer finish its countdown before he backed out to the lobby and looked at Atticus' response.

Atticus: Yep, just got here

Kai: I'm online, you wanna play a round? Sammie has a pc doesn't she?

Atticus: She does, but I'm already in this nice fluffy bed and I'm not getting up :D

Another pang of disappointment. It was becoming more and more difficult to ignore the way that even just talking to Atticus like this, casual day-to-day nonsense, was something Kai looked forward to. If he were being honest with himself, it was something he'd looked forward to for a long time. His mood always lifted at seeing the other man's name on his screen. Atticus had that effect on everybody, and Kai wasn't immune.

But the last day had turned their steady friendship on its head. Kai had ripped away the physical boundaries he'd set so long ago, had given in to a side of himself that had wanted Atticus since the first night they'd spent together.

Now he was scared, once again. Scared of the way he couldn't stop thinking about Atticus and what they had done. Scared that he was giving too much, giving Atticus more than he, Kai, was ready for. Scared of the way he *had* been thinking about them, about what it all meant.

He'd been contemplating it all day, from the moment the door had shut behind Atticus and Kai had been left with the house to himself. Afternoon had faded to evening, and Kai had spent the entire goddamn time thinking about what all of it meant. About what he wanted. About where whatever it was they were doing was going to lead them.

Kai chewed at the inside of his cheek, staring blankly at his computer screen. A part of him, a part that grew louder with every bright smile Atticus gave him, *did* want to try for something more. But giving voice to that, even just in his head?

It made Kai feel as though a rug were being ripped out from under him once again. Because it would mean everything would change, just as much as things had changed a year ago.

Another ding from his phone pulled Kai out of his thoughts. The sound finally woke up the kitten, who stretched her long legs out before leaping down from his lap.

Atticus: Plans tomorrow?
Kai: A stream in the evening. You?

Kai swiped out of the string of messages, thinking maybe he would text Ori again for advice. His gaze landed on another message chain a little further down. Kai hesitated before pulling it up.

Nicholas: Please Kai. Please just respond to me.

Kai: Leave me alone. Stop contacting me. You can't fix this.

A swell of guilt rose in his chest. Theo's words from their argument the day before had also been replaying in his head, over and over and over until it seemed as though they were carved into his skull.

You were friends more than anything.

A relationship that was always going to end anyway.

What if Theo was right? What if Kai had thrown away a friendship he shouldn't have?

The thought brought those familiar feelings of grief and anger back to the surface. They were more muted than in the days and months passed. But they were still there. A lifeline that had tethered him for so long. Who would he be if he let those things go?

Because he would have to, wouldn't he? He would have to move on, at long last, if whatever was happening with Atticus were going to actually go anywhere. Kai couldn't bring all of that baggage, all of those ugly and hateful parts of himself, into another relationship. He couldn't let his darkness dampen Atticus' light.

And that was the part that scared him most. The idea of

figuring out who he was all over again, without those things. He'd already had to rewrite himself once, had already had to upend his entire life and try to find himself in the rubble. The pain and rage were a part of him now, the only things left tying him to the life he'd wanted with his whole heart.

Kai knew it had been so long. He knew that everyone thought it was ridiculous that he'd been stuck, that he'd been hung up on a breakup that had happened a whole year ago. He knew it wasn't right, wasn't healthy.

But he couldn't find a way to fully escape the rubble.

His phone vibrated in his hand, and Kai clicked back to the message from Atticus.

Atticus: No plans, unless you wanna bleach my hair again ;)

Kai couldn't help the small laugh that escaped him. Atticus' dumb way of flirting always did make things a little better. Like a hand stretched out, reaching down to help him up.

Kai: Only if you want your hair to fall out.

Atticus: That won't work
Atticus: Then you'll have nothing up there to tug on

A flush rose up Kai's neck, and there it was again. His body reacting and leaving his brain far behind. And as much as he didn't want Atticus to just be a distraction, didn't want his friend to think he was ready for something he wasn't, it was becoming more and more difficult to tell himself no.

Kai: You liked that?

Atticus: Not as much as you seem to, but yeah :D
Atticus: Might need you to try it a few more times before I decide for sure though

Memories flooded Kai's mind of how it had felt to have his hands in Atticus' damp hair, to tilt his face in just the right way so as to deepen their kisses. He could feel his dick stir in his sweatpants and shifted in his chair. Were they really doing this?

Kai thought for a moment, taking his time to reply. He'd been worried about what they would do, about how far they would go if Atticus had come home that night. But Atticus wasn't home. And with a screen between them, it did feel like some of the pressure was off. Kai bit his lip as he typed out a response.

Kai: I guess you'll have to make do with your own hands tonight

Was it too much? Had he read the conversation wrong? Sexting wasn't something Kai had done... ever. Other than a few random hookups and blind dates set up through friends since the breakup, he didn't have a whole lot of experience with any of this stuff, not really. His cheeks felt like they were on fire as he waited for Atticus to respond. The vibration of his phone nearly had him jumping out of his skin.

Atticus: Oh I am aware
Atticus: Believe me I am aware
Atticus: I should have just driven home
Atticus: Fuck
Atticus: Is this ok? I haven't stopped thinking about your hands in my hair like that all day

Kai let out a breath of relief.

Kai: It's ok. I've been thinking about it too

Atticus: Oh yeah? :D
Atticus: Be specific

Kai: You're shameless.

Atticus: Come onnnn!

Kai: The way I was able to look down at you.

Atticus: Kai
Atticus: I wanted to pull you into my lap so bad
Atticus: Have you above me telling me exactly what to do to make you feel good

   The race of his heartbeat grew louder in his ears as Kai clicked his laptop shut. He pushed his chair away from the desk. Atticus always, always just *said* things. How was it so easy for him? How was he so confident, so comfortable in his own skin?
   Kai didn't let himself think too hard before sending off another message.

Kai: You like me telling you what to do?

Atticus: Absolutely
Atticus: Yes
Atticus: 100%

Kai's dick was growing harder by the second, aching for any sort of touch.

Kai: Ok then.
Kai: Send me a picture.

Fuck *fuck* he was pretty sure he'd just asked Atticus for a dick pic. No, Kai had definitely just asked Atticus for a dick pic.

Logically, he knew that the reason he hadn't received an immediate response was probably because Atticus was taking said picture. Kai couldn't help but think that he'd gone too far, that he'd rushed because he didn't know what the fuck he was doing or where he wanted all of this to go. His thoughts from earlier started to crowd in again, telling him he was making a mistake and that he shouldn't be doing this, shouldn't be giving this much of himself away yet.

And then the picture came through and Kai's mind went completely blank.

On one hand, Atticus was a fucking troll.

The top half of the picture showed his best shit-eating expression, tongue out because he never could seem to be serious for pictures, eyes scrunched with mischief. One hand held his shirt up, exposing the broad expanse of his chest and his sculpted abs. Kai's eyes followed the exposed skin lower.

On the other hand, Kai really, really wanted to be split in half by Atticus' dick.

Kai pressed a hand against his rapidly hardening cock through his pants as he stared at the bottom half of the picture. Atticus had his fingers wrapped around himself, his cock long and hard in his hand. Kai knew that a hand around his own cock wasn't going to be enough tonight, not after seeing Atticus' again so clearly for the first time in six months.

Another message popped up on the screen.

Atticus: I did what you told me to :D
Atticus: Do I get something in return??
Atticus: Wait no, no pressure, you don't have to send
anything unless you want to
Atticus: Kaiiiii pls don't leave me hanging

Kai: Hang on.

Kai thought for a few seconds before rolling his chair across the room. He grabbed the small bottle of lube that always stayed in his travel bag, hands shaking a little at the thought of what he was about to do. Turning on his front-facing camera, he mounted his phone on his desk tripod.

He readied himself as the countdown for the picture began.

"Hang on?"

Atticus didn't mean to say the words out loud, cringing at himself. Only a thin wall separated him from his sister, so he needed to keep his mouth shut.

But what did *hang on* mean? Was Kai upset? Atticus had completely given up jerking himself off, too nervous that he'd messed up and crossed some line he hadn't seen.

He shouldn't have asked Kai for a picture. That was too much pressure.

He was still fretting when his phone finally buzzed. Atticus slapped a hand over his mouth to keep from making a sound.

Kai was leaned forward, braced against his makeshift desk with one arm. His pants were gone, or at least pushed down far enough to be out of the frame, leaving the hard length of his cock exposed, a bit shadowed by his upper body. He still wore his shirt, a dark grey one that was tighter than the clothes he normally wore. It did wonders to show off the lines of his upper body, which was arched from the way Kai was reaching behind himself.

Atticus bit back a whimper.

Kai was fingering himself.

Atticus finally read the message that had accompanied the picture.

Kai: How's this?

He couldn't tell if Kai was being coy or if the question was genuine, and honestly, either option had Atticus' cock aching with need.

Atticus: Perfect
Atticus: 10/10
Atticus: Tell me what you're thinking about

He knew he sounded corny as fuck, and he didn't want to push too far, still nervous from before, from the thought of messing this up. But goddammit, Atticus wanted to know what was going on in Kai's mind.

Kai: I'm thinking that my fingers aren't quite the same as what I'm imagining you feel like.

Atticus bit his hand. He was definitely hating himself a little for not going home that night. Then his mind snagged on something. He didn't let himself think, just typed out the words and hit send.

Atticus: I might have something you could use instead…

Kai: ?

Atticus: Top drawer of my nightstand

His phone went silent, and the lack of response had Atticus thinking about what he'd just done. *Oh god, what had he just done?*

Kai: Attie…
Kai: *Attachment*
Kai: Why is it so pink?

Atticus felt like electricity was running through his veins. Kai had sent a picture of the opened drawer, Atticus' bright pink dildo centered in the frame. He laughed softly, not letting his mind jump ahead to where this was going.

Atticus: Because I ordered the first one I found

No reply again for several long seconds. Atticus wanted to touch himself, wanted to wrap his hand around his cock once again and find his release. He was forcing himself to wait, forcing himself to see where Kai would go with all of this.

Time ticked by, slower than Atticus had ever felt it move.

Atticus: Kai?
Atticus: Are you still there?

Kai: Still here
Kai: Little distracted

No. No no, that wouldn't do. Atticus hit the call button. It rang twice before Kai picked up.

"Why did you call?"

His voice was soft, breathless, and very nearly wrecked. Atticus gave up neglecting himself and wrapped a hand around his cock.

"I wanted to hear you," he said, careful to keep his voice low. "Wanted to know how you'd sound thinking about me inside you."

A sharp exhale came through his phone. Atticus squeezed his eyes closed, moving his hand a bit faster. He was done waiting, heat coiling low in him.

"It's tight," Kai forced out, harsh breaths punctuating each word. "Feels good."

"It's not quite the same though, is it?" Atticus tried to keep his voice steady. He was pretty sure he failed, as warmth crept up his chest, as his breathing became more and more ragged. Kai didn't answer, but Atticus could still hear him. Every gasp for air, every small moan.

"I can never get the angle right by myself, can never hit quite as deep," Atticus continued. "If I were there though, you wouldn't have to worry about that. If I had you in my lap, I'd make sure I hit just the right spot."

Kai let out a choked sound that sent a shiver down Atticus' spine. His chest heaved with the effort to keep himself quiet as he continued to work his dick, his hand beginning to lose its rhythm.

"You don't have to be quiet, baby." Atticus kept his voice a low whisper. "You have that whole house to yourself. I'm the only one that'll hear you."

Kai moaned into the phone, the sound loud and obscene, conjuring an image for Atticus to latch onto. Kai, arched on Atticus' bed in nothing but that tight shirt, hair falling loose around his face, expression screwed up with pleasure as he filled himself with Atticus' bright pink dildo.

Atticus bucked into his hand. He came hard, ropes of white streaking up to his chest.

"Kai," he groaned, mind hazy as his whole body went limp in the aftermath. "I just made a mess all over myself thinking about what you look like right now."

Another cry sounded out from his phone, and Atticus knew Kai was finding his release as well.

They spent the next thirty seconds or so in near-silence, only the sound of their winded breathing echoing through the room.

Atticus' thoughts straightened out as his pulse finally began to slow.

"Kai?" His whisper came out ragged. He hadn't moved, was still lying prone on his sister's guest bed.

"Yeah?" Kai's voice was just as low, just as tentative.

"You good?"

A long pause. "I'm good." He sounded hesitant, but it was hard for Atticus to make it out over the phone. "I've never done that before."

"Used a dildo?" The question flew out of his mouth before he'd thought it through. But apparently it was the right thing to say, judging by the soft laughter that came across the line.

"No," Kai said. "What we just did. Over the phone."

"Oh," Atticus responded, thinking for a moment. "I don't think I have either. At least, not sober I haven't."

Another light chuckle. Atticus loved when he could do this, when he could pull Kai out of his head, could bring a moment of levity to times when Kai might not find that on his own.

"You'll be back in the morning?" Kai asked after another beat of silence.

"Bright and early." Atticus knew the silly grin on his face colored his voice.

"I should let you go to sleep," Kai said, the words broken up by a yawn.

Atticus didn't want to hang up, didn't want the gentle sound of Kai's breathing to be cut off. He wanted to keep talking until they both drifted to sleep. Wanted to ask Kai more about what he was thinking. Not the sort of thoughts he'd been having while they'd been on the phone, but the ones he'd promised earlier that day. Atticus wanted to ask if Kai had given any more thought to *them*. Whatever that meant.

He didn't though. It hadn't even been a full day since they'd had that conversation in the kitchen, since Atticus had thought he would once again be shut down only to be shocked when he wasn't. He would do what Kai had asked for, would give him more time to think. Wouldn't pressure him for an answer, even if that became more and more difficult every time they let themselves have moments like the ones they'd just shared over the phone.

"Yeah, probably should," he finally said. "I'll see you in the morning."

"Goodnight, Attie."

"'Night, Kai."

Atticus ended the call, surprised to see a message from his sister had come through.

Sammie: I can HEAR YOU you asshole, if you make a mess on my bed I will murder you, find you in the next life, and murder you then too

Atticus chuckled. He thought about her question from earlier that evening.

Do you love him?

He let that question roll around in his head a bit before shooting off a response to Sammie.

Atticus: Ew quit listening

He ignored the slew of angry texts that came in after that, focusing instead on cleaning his mess before curling up under the blanket. A part of Atticus was glad he hadn't gone home that night. It gave him something to look forward to as he drifted off to sleep.

1 Year & 1 Month Ago

Kai sipped his drink- a rum and cola that was probably a little too heavy on the rum- as he hovered in the corner of the room.

The party was in full swing, as loud and raucous as the pre-season parties always tended to be. People milled about the main room, conversations overlapping with music playing in the background, filling Kai's head in a way that made him want to curl in on himself.

He really didn't want to be there.

Why had he let Ori talk him into coming?

He loved his friend, would take a bullet for him in an instant. But the rest of his new team, the Wildcats, they were... well, wild. And this sort of thing? The constant need to put on a less-than-bored expression, being drawn into small talk over and over again? Kai could feel his pulse start to throb at his temple.

Kai couldn't really begrudge them this last hoorah, though. Even Ori was starting to get nervous about practices starting for the upcoming season. He'd needed to let off a little steam, so Kai had given in to his pestering for a night out.

And, well... staying home hadn't been an option. Kai shifted, side stepping someone he didn't recognize as they barreled past him in search of a restroom, sloshing the drink they held in a firm grip. Kai frowned as the liquid barely missed splattering across his shirt. He let his eyes scan the crowd. It wasn't long before his gaze settled on a small group in the opposite corner of the room.

No, staying home hadn't been an option. He felt a little of the tension leave his body as he watched Nicholas from across the crowded space. His boyfriend was smiling, frame relaxed as he laughed at something one of Ori's new teammates said. Nicholas had been looking forward to this night with his friends, after weeks and weeks of overtime. Late nights spent curled over his laptop at their small dining table, eyes straining as he typed up a proposal for a non-profit youth volleyball program aimed at underserved communities. Unending emails looking for backers and funding. Kai had been watching Nicholas give so much of himself to a job he loved, and a dream he wanted desperately and that he felt he *needed* to succeed at.

When Ori had told them about the party, had nearly *begged* them to come, some of the exhaustion had slipped from Nicholas' frame, and his eyes had lit up with an excitement Kai hadn't seen in longer than he wanted to admit.

So of course Kai wasn't going to mess up this night out. This opportunity for Nicholas to relax, to goof off with his friends, to not have to think too hard about anything.

Nicholas had seemed more than a little surprised when Kai had agreed to tag along. Despite the fact that Kai really had been trying to make more of an effort to be social, to be a part of the sort of things Nicholas enjoyed best, it was still always assumed that he would rather just stay home. Especially for these sorts of loud, uproarious parties that Ori and Nicholas had always enjoyed.

His eyes snagged on someone else who seemed equally out of place. Kai watched as Theo Whittaker approached Nicholas' group. The look on his face was serious, unbothered but out of place amid the loud music and dim lighting. The tall blonde hovered just outside of the laughing group of friends, hands in his pockets. His dark green sweater emphasized the long lines of his arms and torso as he leaned in closer, Ori pulling him into the conversation. Kai watched as Nicholas noticed the final member of their old college quartet, saying something that set off another round of laughter as he slapped a hand on Theo's shoulder. The touch didn't linger, Nicholas' attention immediately pulled away by another friend, but Kai didn't miss the way Theo's posture straightened, the way his eyes flicked to the place Nicholas had rested his hand. The way he leaned a little, as though his body were seeking out just a bit more of Nicholas' warmth.

Kai had noticed before. Since their final months together in college, Kai had noticed the glances that lingered a beat longer, the hint of longing in Theo's bright eyes whenever they fell on Nicholas. Kai had even brought it up before, earning a chuckle and an eye roll from his boyfriend.

"Nah," Nicholas would always say, "there's no way Theo has a thing for me." A kiss pressed to Kai's head, warm breath against his hair. "Wouldn't matter even if he did."

Kai knew he meant it. He didn't doubt Nicholas' loyalty, not when he'd never given Kai a reason to. But Nicholas was wrong. Because watching from across the room, Kai could see it clear as a full moon on a cloudless night.

The look in Theo's eyes, the small smile that formed as he watched Nicholas charm everyone with his sly grin and endless wit... Kai knew that look. He'd given it so many times himself, for years and years. And Kai knew that Theo had always been there, just off to the side, watching Nicholas.

Wanting Nicholas.

Kai's stomach churned as he forced himself to look away, forced himself to ignore his spiraling thoughts. He frowned down at his drink. The rum had lost its appeal, souring inside him. Kai watched as Nicholas and Ori broke away from their group, watched as Theo's gaze followed them until the moment they were out of sight.

He should probably go talk to Theo. They were friends too, even if Kai had never grown as close to Theo as Ori and Nicholas had. Sure, they'd grown apart after Theo had been picked up by St. Louis a year earlier. But they *had* been friends. For so long it had been Kai and Nicholas and Ori and Theo. The four of them against the world.

Kai tried to force himself to move, to take a step toward his friend. But all he could see was the look on Theo's face as Nicholas had walked away, the longing that mirrored something deep inside of Kai that he had been ignoring for far, far too long.

A sudden need to follow after Nicholas filled him. An ache, spreading from his chest, something possessive and harsh. The part of Kai that had been clawing for any reassurance that he and Nicholas were okay reared its ugly head. He finally moved, emerging from his corner of the room. Every line of his body felt tense, his movements jerky and unsettled.

Kai was halfway across the room when he bumped into someone. His drink sloshed a little, splashing a few drops onto the person's shirt. Hands gripped his shoulders, steadying him.

"Sorry about that!" A sunny voice, too bright for the dimly lit room. Kai looked up to see a wide smile and brilliant blue eyes that crinkled at the corners.

"Your shirt," Kai said, pointing at the place where his drink had now soaked into the fabric. The stranger released his grip, eyes flicking away from Kai, clearly distracted as he searched the room.

"It'll wash," he said, waving the spill off before running that same hand through his bleached-blonde hair.

"Mills!" A voice shouted out from elsewhere in the room. Kai watched the man before him wave, his smile somehow growing even brighter.

"Sorry again," he said, starting to move away before he paused, doing a double-take. Kai saw a flash of recognition on his face. The stranger froze, eyes going wide as he pointed a finger at the middle of Kai's chest. "You're-"

"Atticus! Get the fuck over here, man!"

Kai watched him flinch, watched his cheeks go a little red. "Ah," he began, shaking his head, a knowing smile quirking up the corner of his mouth. "Don't worry about the shirt." A wink, and then he was gone.

The whole interaction left Kai flustered, left his mind racing to catch up to where it had been headed before he'd been distracted. He sighed, pushing his long hair back from his face.

Nicholas. He needed to get to Nicholas. Kai's pulse ticked up at the thought, that same urgent need filling him once again. He moved in the same direction the other men had gone. The light of the kitchen shone bright at the end of a dim hallway, and Kai could barely make out Ori's voice as he approached.

"St. Louis?"

Nicholas and Ori froze when Kai entered the room. They were huddled close together, voices low enough that Kai couldn't make out anything else were saying. The three of them stood silent in the otherwise empty room.

"I wanted to pour this out," Kai mumbled, heart in his throat pressing to choke off the words. He raised his plastic cup helplessly. Nicholas smiled, moving to grab the cup out of his hand, tossing the drink away. He seemed fine, everything about him seemed as light and cheerful as earlier.

Ori though… he never could keep his emotions off his face.

"Kai!" His voice was bright. Too bright. It rang false, and

Kai nearly flinched as those big brown eyes filled with some unknown sadness trained on him.

What had they been talking about? Why was Ori upset? *What was in St. Louis?*

"You want something else? I'll get it for you!" Nicholas' voice pulled Kai's mind away from the revolving questions.

"I'm good," Kai responded, forcing himself to look away from his friend and meet his boyfriend's stare.

There was something there. Something in Nicholas' gaze that felt heavier than usual. A wavering confidence that Kai wasn't used to seeing.

Something was wrong. Something was wrong enough that Nicholas needed to talk to one of his closest friends *and not Kai*.

"Are you okay?"

A small, nearly manic part of Kai's brain wanted him to laugh at the question. Shouldn't he be the one asking? Shouldn't he be the one reaching out to steady Nicholas with gentle reassurance? Because something was wrong. Something was so clearly wrong, and Kai felt utterly lost.

"I'm good," he repeated, continuing before he could think better of it. "My head's starting to hurt, though. I think I'm going to get a car home." Kai pulled his phone out of his back pocket, waving it in front of himself as though he could wave away the guilt of lying.

"Oh." Nicholas didn't sound surprised. Ori still stood off to the side, eyes flicking between his two friends, all pretense at hiding his worry falling away. Kai pretended he couldn't see the way his friend's shoulders drooped, the way he slumped back against the counter.

"Do you want me to come with you?" Nicholas asked.

Kai watched him for a moment. What if he said yes? What if he told Nicholas that he wanted him to go home with him? What if he asked what was wrong, what it was that had Ori looking at Kai like he'd just received a terminal diagnosis?

"Stay," Kai finally said. "You're having fun."

And there it was again. Another flash of something sad, something pained, there and gone on Nicholas' face.

Kai knew he was making a mistake. Part of him was sure of it, as sure of it as he'd ever been about anything. But the louder, more insistent part of him dug in its heels. He didn't want to be at this party anyway. Nicholas clearly wanted to talk to their friend in private. Kai could always ask him about it later.

He could feel himself shutting down, going silent as the panic within him refused to recede. Kai knew that even if he changed his mind, even if he did decide to stay and ask, he *knew* that his voice would be gone, that the words would be too heavy to make it out of him.

Strong arms pulled him in as he concentrated on his phone screen, paying for his ride home. A warm breath ruffled his hair as Nicholas pressed a kiss to the top of his head, holding Kai tight to his chest.

"Let me know when you get home," Nicholas said softly. He didn't let go for several long moments. Kai leaned into the embrace, one hand tangling into his boyfriend's shirt as though it were a lifeline he couldn't afford to let go of.

Kai nodded as Nicholas finally let go of him. He felt the absence of that familiar warmth around him acutely.

"Car's almost here," he managed, forcing the words out, hesitating only a moment before heading for the door. A voice in his head was screaming for him to stop, desperate for him to turn around and demand a conversation, demand that they finally fix whatever it was that had been cracking between them for so long now. That voice drew him up short. Kai paused on the threshold, glancing back to see Nicholas watching him intently. Ori was trying to look at anything but the two of them.

"Nicky," Kai said, voice soft but steadier than it had been throughout their short conversation. Because this part had always been easy for him to say. "I love you."

Nicholas smiled, small and soft. It didn't quite reach his eyes, but some of that sadness dissipated. Not all of it, but some. Enough that the voice in Kai quieted. Whatever it was they needed to talk about, it would keep. Nicholas needed this night out, and Kai wasn't going to ruin it for him.

"I know," Nicholas said after a moment. "I love you too."

Kai left the party without turning back. His ride home was blessedly silent, no forced conversation from the driver. By the time he reached their shared apartment, Kai's head really was starting to throb a little. He blamed the stress.

He was still awake, lying still in their bed, sleep seemingly unattainable, when Nicholas got home a few hours later. Kai pretended to be asleep, aware of the exact moment Nicholas entered their room. He could feel a weighted gaze land on him.

He was still pretending to be asleep when Nicholas slipped under the covers that he would inevitably kick off. He was still pretending to be asleep when Nicholas' breath evened out and he shifted so that his head fell between their pillows.

Kai lay awake for most of the night, replaying the moments in that kitchen again and again, dreading what it all might mean.

9

Present Day

Kai squeezed water from his hair, ringing as much out as he could. He stepped out of the shower, dripping onto the soft floor mat as he toweled himself off.

The hot shower had helped to wake him up, as getting out of bed early had been an ordeal. He still felt groggy, but not too bad considering how late he'd been up.

Kai hadn't gone to sleep after his call with Atticus the night before. No, he'd lain on his friend's bed, replaying the interaction again and again. His heart had raced a bit every time he thought about what they'd done, about the things Atticus had said.

You don't have to be quiet, baby.

Remembering those words now sent a shiver across his skin. Kai finished drying himself, wrapping the towel around his waist.

He'd been up late, playing a game in an attempt to distract himself from the phone sex, but he had still wanted to rise early. He wanted to be awake when Atticus got home, just in case they needed to talk about it. Even if talking about things had never been Kai's strong suit.

Kai looked at himself in the fogged up mirror. His cheeks were a little pink. It was definitely because of the hot water he'd just been under and *not* because he'd been remembering Atticus' voice whispering through his phone. The voice that had sounded wrecked as Kai had cried out on Atticus' bed. The bed he had *eventually* fallen asleep in, surrounded by Atticus' familiar scent.

They were pushing things further and further. Kai tucked his wet hair behind an ear, the long, damp strands brushing at his shoulders. His pulse thumped harder as he thought about how far the two of them might have gone had Atticus been home last night.

Kai touched the ends of his hair. He would need to touch up the color soon, maybe try something other than pink. The idea of asking Atticus to help him, despite the fact that he was perfectly capable of doing it himself, flickered in his mind. Kai tamped out that thought before it could catch fire. He wouldn't need to do that for another week or so.

He'd be back home by then.

The thought of returning to his home, returning to the way life had been before this week twisted his insides. His stomach felt funny, and a wave of something like homesickness washed over him. Not for his own home, with its freshly remodeled bathroom. Kai thought that maybe it wasn't even homesickness for a place.

Maybe it was for a person.

He let out a deep sigh and attempted to wipe away the furrowed brow and small frown that were reflecting back at him. He didn't want Atticus to get home and think he was upset.

Because he wasn't upset. Kai was enjoying everything he and Atticus were doing. But still... that undercurrent of anxiety was always there. A whisper at the back of his mind that it was all too sudden, that he was going to hurt his friend.

Kai ignored that whisper, opening the bathroom door to head back to his room and put some clothes on.

He smacked into another body right as he stepped into the hallway.

"Oof!" Atticus let out a huff as his hands reached out, steadying Kai. The feeling of those hands pressed to the bare skin of his shoulders set sparks off along his skin, sent light racing through his veins. Kai inhaled sharply, his own hands instinctively coming up between them and resting on the soft fabric of Atticus' brewery t-shirt.

"Sorry! Didn't mean to scare you," Atticus said, grinning down at him. Kai took in the man standing before him, so close he could feel his warmth. The tight black t-shirt that emphasized his broad chest, rising up from where Kai gripped the fabric, showing off a strip of skin at his waist. Kai looked up to see Atticus watching him, eyes sparkling, hair still messy from sleep, smile still just as bright as always. But there was something else there.

Something a bit feral.

And then Kai remembered what he was wearing. More precisely, what he *wasn't* wearing. Suddenly, the towel around his waist felt too loose, like it could come untucked at any moment and leave him standing there completely bare. Kai felt his skin heat up, felt warmth crawling across his chest and up his neck, heating his face.

"Morning," Kai mumbled, barely able to get the word out as Atticus continued to look at him. His gaze was fiery, like he wanted to devour every inch of Kai's exposed skin.

Atticus was looking at Kai... well, the way people usually looked at Atticus. The way others would stare, taking note the moment he entered any room. Eyes trailing along his sculpted body, lingering on his wide thighs or broad back. Kai wasn't sure he had ever been on the receiving end of a look quite like *that*.

"Morning," Atticus echoed, trailing his eyes down Kai's body. His hands still held tight to Kai's upper arms. Kai suddenly felt self conscious, something he hadn't felt about how he looked in a long time.

He wasn't a volleyball player anymore. All of the hard muscle of his high school days had faded, softened over the years. He exercised semi-regularly, but lacked the definition he'd had in the past, and what muscle he did still have was hidden under a layer of soft padding. Kai didn't have the sort of body that Atticus' past partners typically had.

It didn't seem to matter, though. Not with the way Atticus was drinking him in, eyes burning a trail over every part of Kai. A thumb caressed his bicep as Atticus' other hand moved, sparking along Kai's skin and coming to rest at the back of his neck. Fingers tangled lightly in his wet hair.

Kai held his breath as Atticus' eyes finally settled back on his face. He didn't think about anything. Not the night before and what they had done. Not what they had been doing all week or what it could be leading to. Not the fear he still held, that held him, grip unrelenting.

The only thing Kai could think as he and Atticus watched one another was that he *really* wanted to be kissed.

Atticus leaned down, and Kai felt as though his heart were close to bursting through his skin with how hard it was beating.

Lips came to rest on his forehead, and Kai could feel the shape of a smile still there, pressed softly to his skin.

Atticus pulled away, squeezing Kai's arm before letting go and stepping past him.

"Got us some breakfast," he said cheerfully, as though the air around them wasn't charged with tension. As if he hadn't just looked at Kai like he wanted to taste him, as if Kai hadn't just turned to putty in his grip. "Let me change into fresh clothes and then we can eat. You still don't have plans this morning, right?"

Kai could only nod, sure that his face was as bright red as his old high school jersey.

"Good," Atticus said with a grin. "I've got plans for us. Wear comfy shoes."

He left Kai standing in the hallway, head spinning from their interaction. And all Kai could think about as he entered his room and leaned back against the closed door was that he still *really* wanted Atticus to kiss him.

"Windows down?"

The slight grin on Atticus' face made Kai's lungs feel too full. He only nodded, squinting as the morning sun shone bright through the windshield. The cool morning air was a relief against his skin that had felt overly warm since he'd smacked into Atticus outside of the bathroom.

"Here," Atticus said, one hand on the wheel as he leaned close to Kai, popping open the glove compartment and snatching a pair of sunglasses. He held them up, that same sweet as candy grin aimed right at Kai even as he kept his eyes on the road.

"Thanks." Kai slipped the sunglasses on, thankful for the sense of false privacy they afforded him, as though he could hide the mix of emotions swirling in him behind their dark lenses.

Spring was in full swing, trees blooming alongside the country roads. Kai's hair whipped against his face, but before he could move to tie it back, Atticus' hand was there once more. Kai froze as fingers brushed along his cheek, pushing his hair back behind an ear. An internal battle took place in Kai's mind over the span of a single breath.

It all felt like too much, but not nearly enough. He glanced over, meeting Atticus' gaze for a brief moment.

"I've always liked these," Atticus said, eyes flicking back to the road as his fingers brushed along the piercings in Kai's ear. A shiver ran down the length of his spine as heat crept up his neck. The moment Atticus' touch disappeared, his arm falling to rest on the console between them, Kai missed it acutely. He wanted those fingers in his hair again, wanting to feel that warm touch against his skin, even if he still didn't know what it meant. Where it was going.

"Are you nervous for the game Saturday?" An attempt at distraction, though Kai wasn't sure if it was a distraction for Atticus or himself.

Atticus shrugged. "A little. The team's doing great, but we definitely feel the loss of Ori. Still trying to fill that gap."

Kai shifted, bumping Atticus' arm with his own. "You'll get there."

A charged silence settled between them. Kai lost himself in the passing scenery, soaking in the warmth of the morning sun. This felt right, it felt good. Their arms pressed together on the console, an easy camaraderie between them that didn't require constant chatter. It was several minutes before a thought hit Kai like a volleyball to the face.

He spoke before thinking much on it. "Can I come?"

Atticus glanced at him, confusion etched across his features. One heartbeat, then another, before Kai watched realization dawn in his eyes.

"To the game?"

Kai nodded. His skin felt tingly, his stomach tied into knots as Atticus beamed at him.

"Yes!" Atticus looked radiant, excitement lining his posture. The hand that sat so close to Kai's own moved to grip his forearm. Kai could feel the heat of Atticus' palm even through the thick fabric of his hoodie.

Atticus continued. "I would have asked… you've had so much going on, with the streams and your bathroom and everything. I wanted you to come. Of course I wanted you to come. I'll call coach and get your name down for a ticket."

The exuberance in Atticus' words, the way his eyes shone with happiness as he glanced once, twice, looking for confirmation from Kai… it was almost too much. Kai hadn't realized just how much it would mean to Atticus.

"I'll be there then," Kai said, hoping Atticus didn't pick up on how the words felt too big as Kai said them, filling the space in the car with everything that seemed to lay unspoken between them.

The grip around Kai's arm loosened, and as Atticus' arm returned to where it had rested before, long fingers brushed the back of Kai's hand.

His breath caught in his lungs as Atticus didn't make any moves to put more space between them, as a fire continued to burn along the places where their skin touched.

It couldn't be this easy. Not after everything, not after Kai hadn't felt anything like this in so, so long. The subtle touches that made his heart race and his blood fizz. The looks that tied his stomach into knots and set his skin aflame.

Had it been like this before? It had been so many years since Kai had experienced dawning attraction, since he'd had to deal with new feelings that he still didn't understand.

But Atticus made it seem so easy. He made Kai feel as though this was what was most important. Not the sex, not the aching needs that continued to pull them together again and again. No, it was this. The everyday moments, the little ways that Kai brought a smile to his face, his eyes lighting in a way that only seemed to shine so brightly for Kai.

A small movement. The slightest shift. Kai brushed a finger

across Atticus' knuckles. He knew that he shouldn't do it, shouldn't let things keep going like this until he'd sorted out his own feelings, his own mess. But it was too tempting, and the flutter of butterflies in his stomach that even the slightest contact brought was addicting, a high that Kai couldn't seem to let go of.

Kai sucked in a sharp breath through his nose as Atticus' hand shifted, as he carefully wound their fingers together. His grip was strong, steady, his hand larger than Kai's own. Atticus' warmth soaked into Kai, sending flames dancing through his veins.

And somehow, despite the constant worries and doubts that haunted Kai, the ghosts of his past that lived in the darkest places within him... somehow it all seemed to fade. To fall away for the length of a single car ride. As Kai held on to Atticus, he felt more at peace than he had in ages.

Atticus and Kai stood side by side at the entrance to the farmer's market.

"I don't know what I was expecting," Kai began, eyes narrowing slightly. "But I don't think it was this." Atticus chuckled, bumping against his shoulder.

"Here, city boy," he said, holding out a large canvas tote bag, one of two that he'd grabbed from the trunk of his car. "You might need this."

Kai took the offered bag, slinging it onto his shoulder. Their fingers brushed together, and Atticus fought back a shiver at the contact. A reminder of what it had felt like to have Kai's hand in his own.

It had taken every ounce of willpower he possessed not to pick Kai up and toss him onto his bed when he'd found him nearly naked in the hallway that morning. Seeing him like that, fresh out of the shower, hair still damp and clinging to his skin, cheeks tinged pink with embarrassment... honestly, Atticus was proud of the self-control he had displayed. He thought that maybe he deserved a medal or something.

And then he'd left Kai standing there, teased him in a way that had been quite thrilling, only to walk into his bedroom and see the bed unmade. Kai had slept in his bed, and Atticus didn't know why but his caveman brain was delighted by it. Although, if it were going to become a habit, they'd have to have a talk about making the bed.

People brushed past as the two of them continued to hesitate by the entrance to market, the crowd growing thicker by the minute.

"Come on." Atticus didn't think, he just reached out, acting on instinct. He wrapped his hand around Kai's, tugging him forward. Tension laced Kai's posture, but only for a moment. Atticus smiled to himself, eyes trained ahead toward their destination as he felt soft fingers intertwine with his own.

"Are we here for something specific?"

Atticus felt Kai move closer. He glanced sideways, watching as amber eyes roved over the many stalls and vendors.

"I need a few things," Atticus said. "Figured we could pick up some fruits and veggies to make lunch later."

Coming to the market had become a habit for Atticus in the short time he'd been in his new home. It reminded him of the times he and Sammie had accompanied their grandma to their local farmer's market as children. And now that things seemed to be going somewhere for him and Kai, well, Atticus had thought that maybe it would be nice to show Kai a normal day in his life.

It wasn't long before Kai's curiosity began to get the better of him. He gently tugged Atticus toward stall after stall, taking in the many crafts and baubles quietly while Atticus chatted with the vendors. A few had begun to recognize him, calling out his name cheerfully, asking about his friend. Atticus' face heated every time he introduced Kai, and he hoped his blush wasn't *too* noticeable. But the introductions also filled him with something warm and cozy. Something he didn't mind at all.

Atticus filled his bag with fresh produce as they made their way along the rows of booths. Kai, on the other hand, seemed to be collecting trinkets like some sort of gremlin. Watching him survey the many options, only to light up when his eyes fell on one he wanted, it had Atticus grinning like a fool nearly the entire time.

A handmade notebook, the pages sewn in with care. A lavender scented bar of soap that sent Atticus' mind heading in a dangerous direction. A pot of cat grass for the kitten. Two ceramic mugs, one for each of them. Kai's face lit up the moment he saw them. He snatched up a pink one first, eyes searching before settling on a maroon one that matched.

"For our coffee in the morning," he said, smiling at Atticus as the lady behind the booth wrapped both mugs carefully. Atticus felt as though the air in his lungs were stuck, his chest too full.

Kai so rarely smiled like that, so open and wide. So unbothered, as though nothing at all weighed on him. It crinkled the corners of his eyes. His cheeks were rosy from the sun beating down on them. Atticus wanted nothing more than to reach out, to tug him close, wrap his arms tight around his shoulders and never let him go.

He had the sudden urge, as they walked away from the ceramics booth, Kai still smiling softly, to blurt out the words he'd been keeping to himself for so long now. His sister's question from the night before flashed through his mind.

Do you love him?

Atticus fought against his impulsive nature, chewing on

his bottom lip so he'd keep his big mouth shut. They continued along, nearing the end of the line of vendors. He couldn't just spit out a declaration like that, not here in the middle of the local farmer's market. Not when he knew that saying it out loud, admitting it to someone besides himself, admitting it to *Kai*, would probably make that sweet smile disappear.

That thought hurt. Atticus didn't let himself dwell on why, on how he wished he could tell Kai exactly how he felt and make that smile shine brighter.

Kai's voice pulled him out of his thoughts.

"This was fun," he said. The fingers entwined with Atticus' squeezed slightly, sending sparks up his arm. "I'm glad you brought me here." He bumped his shoulder against Atticus, staying close as they began to walk back toward the exit.

"Glad you liked it," Atticus said, all negative thoughts disappearing as he focused on just how easy it all felt. "Should have told you to put sunscreen on, though." He reached over, poking a slightly reddened cheek. Kai scrunched his face up, and Atticus couldn't help but think that it was very, very cute.

Kai glanced up. "Yeah," he said, rubbing at his nose. "No clouds today." Atticus looked up as well, taking in the bright expanse of unending blue sky. It really was a beautiful day.

"Good!" The excitement in Atticus' voice pulled Kai's attention back. He pointed back toward the vendor stalls. "The guy back there selling artichokes said there's some big meteor shower tonight, we should be able to see it!"

Kai cocked his head to the side, bright eyes focused solely on Atticus. It felt a bit like he could see into Atticus' head, could read all of his unspoken thoughts. Atticus wanted to squirm under the attention, but forced himself to continue walking steadily. They were already almost back at the entrance, and he felt a slight pang at the fact that this little adventure was already almost over.

"Hang on," Kai said, suddenly releasing his grip on Atticus' hand. "Wait here."

He scurried off, back into the crowd, leaving Atticus stunned at the market entrance. It left Atticus with too much time to think, too much space for his impulsive thoughts to start pushing forward again.

Would it be so bad if he just blurted out the words he wanted to say? The last few days had proved to him, to both of them, that there was more between them than they'd been willing to admit. And it wasn't just physical. Atticus wanted the life he had in this moment. He wanted the regular bits, the moments with Kai that piled together and built up to all the other exciting stuff. He wanted to walk the farmer's market every weekend, hand in hand, sharing soft grins and boring conversation. He wanted to curl up on the couch together, to fall asleep with the television still playing. He wanted to make coffee in the morning, to watch as Kai stumbled into the room with messy hair and a grumpy expression.

He wanted a life with Kai.

Atticus had thought that he would be okay with just getting a taste of it. A week together where he could drink his fill and then go back to how things had been before. But he'd been wrong. Because all of this? It only served to make him want more. And he wasn't sure he could go back to just ignoring it.

Atticus leaned back against a fence post. He let himself focus on the light breeze, on the way it cooled his heated skin and blew through his hair. He waited, watching the crowd, searching for the face he most wanted to see above all others.

Kai popped out of the throngs of people as suddenly as he'd disappeared. He was carrying something large, fabric of some sort folded in his arms.

"I saw this earlier," he said, coming to a halt in front of Atticus. He fumbled with the bundle for a moment before raising his arms high and shaking it out.

It was probably the ugliest blanket Atticus had ever seen.

The woven colors were a hodgepodge of muted neutrals, browns and grays and tans. A green in the background that was decidedly off-putting. But the best part was the fact that the entire thing was covered in cats. Misshapen, hideous, wonderful cats.

Kai lowered his arms as Atticus burst into laughter, peeking out from behind the blanket.

"Why?" Atticus asked between his giggles. Kai glanced down at the blanket briefly before grinning back at Atticus.

"For the meteor shower," he said, his words matter-of-fact. "So we don't have to lay on the grass."

"I have extra blankets," Atticus said, reaching out to grab onto the material so he could examine it closer. It was well made, obvious care put into it. But it was really fucking hideous.

"I like this one," Kai said with a shrug as he started folding it back up. They began to make their way back toward the car.

"I guess that's all that matters," Atticus said, earning a nod from Kai. As they loaded their purchases into the trunk, he couldn't help but wonder if Kai would continue to fill his house with hideous things.

Atticus sort of thought that he wouldn't mind it, not at all.

They made lunch together, fancy salads filled with the fresh produce Atticus had picked out that morning. They moved around the kitchen together seamlessly, Kai washing the vegetables, handing them off for Atticus to prep them.

It was so easy. Comfortable. Even when they weren't talking, Atticus couldn't help but think that it all felt so right.

They ate mostly in silence. The kitten danced around the pot of cat grass Kai had gotten her, unsure at first what it meant and what she was supposed to do. Atticus jumped up the moment she began to push at the pot, attempting to knock it from the end table he'd placed it on. Kai snickered as he sat the plant on the floor.

"Still not used to her destructive ways," Atticus grumbled as he sat back down. Kai only nodded, smiling softly at his nearly empty bowl before speaking.

"What are you doing this afternoon?"

Atticus shrugged. "Don't know. Coach gave us the day off to rest up. Kind of feels like a good day to be lazy. When's your stream?"

"This evening. It'll be a long one but I should be done before the meteor shower is supposed to start."

Tightness gripped Atticus' chest, knowing that Kai was planning to spend that time with him, that it was important to him at least a little bit.

"Let's be lazy then! I'll open the windows, get some fresh air in here, and we can sit on the couch and not move until we have to."

Kai nodded again as he chewed his bottom lip. Atticus could tell he was fighting back a full grin. "Okay," he finally said, and Atticus clapped his hands together.

Kai washed their dishes while Atticus made good on his word, opening all the windows in the main room. Crisp, spring air began to flow through the house. Atticus watched as Kai pushed hair out of his face, a few pieces having escaped the bun at the nape of his neck, only for the slight breeze to blow them right back into his face. He sighed, face pinched with exasperation, cheeks and nose just a bit red from the morning sun, gaze intent on the dish in his hands as he scrubbed it clean.

Atticus pictured himself walking up behind Kai, wrapping his arms around his small waist, pressing his chest to the other man's back. Leaning in to brush a faint kiss against sunburned skin.

It felt too intimate. Too big. It felt like the sort of thing that meant more, more than anything they'd done together in the past few days. Phone sex? Easy, exciting, harmless. It was the small things, the slight touches, the thoughtless kisses, the things that piled together to mean something more, those were the things that were hard, that were scary.

Those were the things Atticus wanted most.

It felt like they were still just out of reach. Like Kai was still *just* out of reach.

"Want to watch something?" Atticus asked as they settled onto the couch. The kitten jumped up immediately, settling herself into his lap, turning into a ball of vibrating fluff as her purring grew loud with contentment.

Kai grabbed the remote out of Atticus' hand, immediately flicking through their options. He stopped on one, turning to face Atticus. His knees brushed Atticus' thigh.

"You didn't finish *Trigun*?"

Atticus shrugged, glancing at the television. He'd apparently stopped on episode seventeen.

"I don't finish anything."

Kai looked at him, long and hard, those amber eyes piercing deep. Atticus hadn't meant anything more with his answer. He *didn't* finish watching most shows anymore, usually too distracted to pay attention properly. Too ready to move on to something else, something different. But the way Kai was watching him, the slight furrow to his brow, the way his lips pulled into a line, Atticus could tell that Kai was thinking hard about what he'd said.

Atticus could see it too. Could see the reflection there in his own life. The way he had never taken any of his past relationships seriously. The way he had moved from one hook-up to the next, always looking for something more exciting.

But he didn't do that anymore. He hadn't in a long time.

"Let's finish it," he said, snatching the remote back. "It's a classic right? You've watched it?"

Kai nodded, turning away from Atticus and settling back into the couch. They were sitting close, not quite touching. Atticus fought back the urge to reach out and pull the other man to him. He was giving Kai space to think about what they were, and this time there wasn't a phone screen and dozens of miles separating them. Atticus wanted to let Kai come to him now. Not just for Kai's sake, but because sometimes it was nice to be reached out to. Atticus had been reaching out for so long, and he desperately wanted to be the one on the receiving end for a change.

They were half an episode in when he got his wish. Kai leaned over, resting gently against Atticus' side. He lifted his arm so the they could be closer, settling it carefully around Kai's shoulders. It made him feel warm inside, made it feel like things really could fall into place.

The afternoon slipped by, the sun slowly sinking, coming in through the open windows, setting a golden glow off across the room. They stayed there together, cuddled up on the couch, watching the show. At one point, Kai wordlessly leaned forward, grabbing the box of tissues so Atticus wouldn't have to move and dislodge their furry companion from his lap. He blew his nose loud, sniffling as tears stung his eyes.

"You could have warned me it was gonna make me cry," he whispered. Kai swiped at his own cheek, brushing away a tear.

"It's better if you don't know when the sad parts are

coming," he replied, voice soft.

It wasn't much longer before they finished the final episode, sitting in silence for a moment as the credits rolled.

"I liked it," Atticus finally said, tilting his head as a thought came to mind. "We could call her Milly." He poked the kitten, who was now sprawled across both of them. Her tail flicked toward his hand.

Kai made a face of distaste. "No."

Atticus shoved him a little. "Why not!"

"It doesn't fit her personality."

Atticus laughed. "First you said she can't have a boy name, so I pick a girl name, but you don't like that either. I think I'm giving up."

Kai frowned, side-eyeing Atticus. "We'll think of something."

We. Atticus tugged Kai closer, noting his drooping eyelids and sleepy expression. He shifted so that his legs were on the couch as well, pulling Kai back against his chest, their limbs tangling together.

"Nap time," he said. Maybe it was too much, maybe it was too normal, maybe he didn't care after they'd just cried together over an anime. But Kai didn't resist, settling against Atticus' chest, tucking in and closing his eyes. Dissatisfied with all of the movement, the kitten rose, stretching for several long seconds before moving to settle at their feet.

Atticus kept his arms around Kai, holding him close. Holding on to whatever he could, praying it wouldn't slip away as he finally drifted off to sleep.

10

Kai leaned against the kitchen counter, watching out the window of the back door.

His stream had ended early, but it was already after midnight. The sky had gone dark long before he'd come out of his room. Several minutes had passed as he stood there, arms tucked into the sleeves of the Cats hoodie that he'd slipped into once again. Just watching.

Atticus lay sprawled out in his backyard on top of the ugly cat blanket that Kai had purchased, knees bent and arms tucked at his sides as he stared up at the sky. The meteor shower was starting. Even from inside, Kai had already seen several lights streak across the sky.

Movement to his right pulled his attention away. The kitten had jumped onto the counter next to him, padding over to sit by his elbow. She watched him carefully, striped tail flicking back and forth. Kai reached out, scratching under her chin and earning a soft purr.

Only a few seconds passed before his attention was drawn back to the yard. It was becoming more and more difficult to ignore how something in his chest seemed to swell every time he even so much as looked at Atticus. He'd been paying it no mind all day long, but the feeling had been there, from their encounter in the hallway to their trip to the market to waking up from a nap wrapped in strong, steady arms.

Kai had a pretty good idea of where the night was going. Where he wanted it to go. It was as though his body had been reaching out all day, longing for more than the small touches and soft brushes of skin that were all Atticus had been willing to give him. Kai wanted Atticus. Wanted him in a way he never had, yet somehow in a way he maybe had for a very long time.

It was different from that first night they'd spent together, six months prior. Kai had gone into that night looking for a hookup, and that's what he'd gotten. He felt so far removed from the person he'd been then.

It terrified him.

It terrified him that he was doing things he'd told himself he'd never do again, never feel again. He felt like he was at war with himself. The Kai of five days ago was still there. He still felt a sharp pain when he thought about where life had taken him, when he thought about the texts he'd received from Nicholas, the call from Theo. Those things still hurt enough to take his breath away.

But the moments when Atticus looked at him, when he made Kai laugh or roll his eyes or level him with a glare, those simple moments made it feel like he was finally at peace. That, at long last, he didn't have to hurt all of the time.

It was like a drug, and Kai craved the distraction. Craved the way Atticus' hands on his body made him feel so much like who he wanted to be, someone he'd thought was out of reach.

But it wasn't fair to treat Atticus as a distraction, was it? Kai was going back home the next day. He'd received a text from his contractor during his stream saying the work was done and his home was ready for him.

Thinking about it made Kai's stomach churn. He pulled his hands into the sleeves of the hoodie, fingers tangling in the golden cuffs of the fabric.

Atticus had done so much for him. Not just this past week, but for as long as they'd known each other. Atticus had been a friend, someone new, someone who wasn't there for Kai's messy past, who only saw him as someone worthy of that friendship without anything else to color his judgement.

And Kai was leaving the next day. He hadn't thought it would be something hard when he'd agreed to stay. Hadn't thought that he would feel any amount of guilt. He hadn't even told Atticus yet, dreading the disappointment he knew he would see in his soft blue eyes.

But life had to move on, didn't it? Kai knew, he *knew*, that he wasn't ready for more. That he still needed to work through some things for himself. He still had so many broken and shattered pieces lying on the floor, and no one could pick them up but him. Atticus had done enough by making him feel like that was even possible. For the first time in so long, Kai felt like maybe the future had more for him than an ever-broken heart.

Movement outside caught Kai's eye, pulling him out of his thoughts. Atticus was sitting up, head cocked to the side as he stared back. The moment their eyes met, a wide, shit-eating grin spread across his face, and he waved an arm to beckon Kai out. He looked so welcoming, so happy and warm. Hair a bit of a mess, shirt hiked up as he scratched at his chest. His smile dimmed a little when Kai didn't immediately respond.

It wouldn't be so bad, would it? To enjoy one more night together? Kai let himself smile, holding up a hand, signaling that he just needed another minute. Atticus' expression softened, eyes lighting up, grin slipping into something more sincere.

Kai walked out of the kitchen, ignoring the parts of himself that were rising up in protest. The reminders that he was leaving tomorrow, that he wasn't ready for more. The memory of a drunken text from months prior, confessing that Atticus probably felt more than Kai knew what to do with.

They'd been messing around for days now, and everything had been fine. Atticus had said he would give Kai time to think about where it all was going, about what they were. Kai dug through his duffle bag, finding what he was looking for quickly and slipping the packet into his hoodie pocket. He grabbed the small bottle off his nightstand as well, heart beating faster as he made his way back into the kitchen.

Kai gave himself one more minute to change his mind. One more minute to figure out if he was making a mistake or not. But watching Atticus, sprawled back on the blanket with one arm tucked under the back of his head, Kai couldn't really remember all the reasons why he should slow down. All he could think about was how the entire day had seemed to be building to this. The entire week.

"Am I making a mistake?" The kitten only stared at him, unblinking and unbothered, until she moved forward, rubbing her head against his arm and leaving a trail of fur on the maroon material.

Kai bit his bottom lip, chewing at it as he moved toward the back door. He breathed deeply before he opened it and walked outside.

The sky was beginning to brighten with more and more streaks of light across the black expanse. Not a cloud in sight, and the night air had cooled comfortably.

Atticus forced himself to stay still when he heard the back

door swing open. He didn't sit up, didn't tilt his head to see Kai approaching. His heart did start to beat a little faster though.

Kai crouched down on the blanket, lowering himself to sit at Atticus' side. He pulled his knees close to his chest, curling himself into a little ball, head tilted skyward.

He was wearing the damned hoodie again. Atticus nearly let out a groan. What was wrong with him? Why did Kai wearing his too-big clothes turn him into such a donkey? Atticus wanted nothing more than to have the other man in his lap, hoodie *on*, letting his hands rove up under it.

Stop.

He needed to stop. They were outside to watch the meteor shower, not for Atticus to get a hard-on because Kai looked cute.

"It's supposed to pick up more in the next half hour or so," Atticus said, trying to distract himself with small talk.

Kai looked down at him and nodded. There was something there in his gaze, something heavy that set off a spark low in Atticus' belly. A blush tinting those soft cheeks, so faint that he almost missed it.

"How was your stream?" Atticus asked.

Kai shrugged. "It was good," he said quietly. Hair fell around his face as he looked down at Atticus. "Views have been up all week, people are still trying to figure out where I am."

"Did you wear that?" Atticus tugged on the sleeve of Kai's hoodie. *His* hoodie.

"No," Kai answered with a snort. "Maybe I should next time. Really give them all something to talk about."

The words were meaningless, but they pierced something Atticus hadn't been ready for. If Kai wore the hoodie, if people began to speculate that he was with a Chicago player, of course they would think it was Atticus. Regardless of the fact that their friendship wasn't public, people would immediately jump to the conclusion that Atticus was at it again. One more tally to add to his endless string of hookups and meaningless flings. People would talk, they would speculate. They would laugh about the fact that it would be over in no time, that Atticus would be seen with someone else the next week.

The thought that people would think that about him, would think that he would treat Kai that way, it made Atticus feel a little sick.

Kai was still watching him, brow creased. He must have been able to see something there, something on Atticus' face that showed more than he wanted it to.

"You can keep it," Atticus blurted. Kai's eyes narrowed in question, and Atticus thought that maybe the distraction was successful.

"The hoodie," he continued. "I never wear it anymore. And it looks better on you anyway."

That brought the slight flush back to those round cheeks. Kai pulled his hands into the sleeves, looking down for a moment before focusing his gaze back on the sky, curling in on himself. Atticus could just make out his own last name emblazoned across the back. His name, written across Kai's shoulders.

Fire flared in Atticus' gut.

"Thanks," Kai mumbled, and Atticus didn't miss the hint of a smile coloring the word.

They were silent for several long minutes, their attention captured by the show above them. More and more lights began to flick across the sky like sparks. Kai scooted closer, until his hip was pressed against Atticus' side. Atticus raised his hand from where it had been resting on his chest, reaching up tentatively to rub small circles into Kai's back, brushing his fingers over his own name, a satisfied smirk tilting his lips when Kai leaned back into the touch.

"It's really beautiful," Kai said, eyes still trained upward. Atticus chuckled.

"Is this where I'm supposed to agree while I'm looking at you instead of the sky?"

Kai made a face, scrunching his nose up. "Ew."

Atticus laughed fully. He moved his hand, slipping it under the hem of Kai's hoodie, letting his fingers trail the same circles across warm skin. He could feel the way the muscles under his hand tensed at the contact. Atticus paused, hand freezing out of fear that he'd pushed too far.

"Attie?"

Kai's voice was small, but not scared in the way Atticus had heard it so many times before.

"Hmm?"

Atticus' hand was still frozen in place. Kai turned to look at him again. His amber eyes were lit with something that mirrored the brilliance of the lights crashing across the sky.

"I want to kiss you."

Not a question, but it felt like Kai was asking him something. Something more than the simple words he'd spoken.

"Okay." Atticus' voice sounded weak to his own ears, tremulous and soft. He began to sit up, but was pushed back down by a hand on his chest. Kai held him in place, shifting so that he could swing a leg over Atticus' hips. He sat there for a long moment, looking down at Atticus with both hands pressing steady on his chest. Atticus stared into the wide eyes that were watching him so carefully.

"Sky sure is beautiful," he finally said, grinning brightly as Kai rolled his eyes.

"Shut up," Kai responded. Atticus was readying a retort when Kai leaned down, shutting him up with a press of their lips together.

The loose strands of long hair that had fallen from his half bun caged their faces, tickled at Atticus' cheeks and neck. Kai's hands were still braced against his chest as Atticus pushed against them, leaning up into the kiss.

It started out soft, nothing more than a press of lips together. A fire raged in Atticus' belly, flames licking at his chest, down his limbs, as he silently asked for more. Kai's lips parted as Atticus pulled him closer. Atticus pressed his tongue in deeper, tasting him as if he would never get enough.

Kai breathed harshly against his mouth as they parted, hot breath fanning across Atticus' skin. Atticus leaned in, nipping at his lower lip, earning a small sound from him that had Atticus' cock stirring. Kai shifted, pressing a kiss to Atticus' jaw. His breath hitched as Kai sucked hard at the skin just below his ear.

Atticus squirmed as Kai continued to kiss down his neck, surely leaving bruises in his wake. He tried to move, to tug Kai's face back to his so he could capture his lips once more. But Kai was stronger than he looked, and he held Atticus down. Hands moved to pin his shoulders. Hips pressed down against Atticus' own, kept him from moving more than the slightest shift. Everywhere they were pressed together felt overheated.

Kai sat up suddenly.

"Take off your shirt."

Atticus rushed to do as he was told, yanking the white shirt over his head the moment Kai released his grip. Amber eyes raked over his exposed torso, snagging on his tattoos, sending shivers across his skin.

He had never really been one to shy from attention paid to his body. Atticus knew he looked good. He'd worked hard to look good, and he didn't mind people appreciating him in that way. Partners had complimented him countless times, to the point where it had sort of become meaningless.

But right then, with Kai looking down at him? Atticus could feel himself flushing, could feel his chest and neck growing warmer under that gaze. Kai's eyes dragged across Atticus' body in a way that felt vicious, like he was prey about to be devoured. Fingers trailed across his skin, and Atticus found himself wishing they were claws that scraped and gouged to match the untamed gleam in Kai's eyes.

Kai leaned down again, picking up where he'd left off, pressing a kiss to Atticus' chest. He was more careful this time, lips and tongue gentle against Atticus' flushed skin as he moved lower. He teased around a nipple until Atticus was squirming beneath him once more. Kai's hands found Atticus' hips, holding him still. He longed for any sort of friction, desperate to move his hips, to grind up against the other man.

Kai sucked on his nipple, *hard*, and Atticus let out a moan low in his throat, the tendons in his neck pulling tight.

"Shh," Kai said softly, rising up slightly. His thumb ran over Atticus' tender skin, pulling another half-choked sound from him. "The neighbors will hear."

Atticus huffed out a laugh, breathless. He was nearly panting. "Let 'em. I don't give a f-"

He was cut off as Kai's mouth crashed back against his own. Kai pressed into him hard, finally rocking his hips against Atticus'. Hands tangled in hair, tore at clothes, gripped at skin with bruising strength until both of them were hot to the touch and gasping for hair.

They paused for only a moment, just long enough for Kai to look around, eyes narrowed at the privacy fence as though it might betray them, before he shimmied out of his pants. Atticus' own were long gone already, tossed halfway across the yard the moment he pulled them off.

It was dark, with only the light of the moon to show

Atticus the man above him. His eyes had adjusted enough, and Atticus watched as Kai pulled something out of his hoodie pocket. He recognized the crinkly sound of the packet that Kai dropped onto the blanket next to them.

"Are you sure?" Atticus had finally lowered his voice, asking the question as though he were afraid Kai would change his mind with it voiced aloud. But he had to know, had to be certain this was okay before they went any further.

Kai nodded, the motion sharp, more certain than Atticus had expected. He grabbed the lube Kai had dropped next to the condom, unlatching the top of the bottle.

"It's been a while," Atticus said with a chuckle. "You might need to go easy on me." Bright eyes looked down at him, seeming to almost glow in the darkness. Kai took Atticus' hand, tugging him up into a sitting position. He squirted a generous amount of lube onto Atticus' fingers. Their faces were close together, and Atticus could hear Kai's breaths turning unsteady.

"I don't want to do it like last time," Kai said, guiding Atticus' hand down between his legs.

Last time. Six months ago. "Oh." Atticus had thought that Kai preferred...

"Just go slow," Kai whispered. "It's been a while for me too." It felt like there was a lot more behind those words.

Atticus' mouth went a little dry. He sucked in a shaky breath as his fingers pressed at Kai's hole. Kai latched onto his shoulders, pressing down against Atticus' hand. He gasped as a finger breached him, as Atticus began to work him open slowly and carefully. Atticus captured those panting lips with his own, licked into Kai's mouth as he slowly worked to add a second finger.

It wasn't long before Kai was writhing in his lap, face pressed into the crook of Atticus' neck. His dick was aching for attention, and every rock of Kai's ass had him desperate to thrust upward, to find a way toward his release. He could feel Kai's own hard cock against his stomach, dripping against his skin.

Hands pressed at Atticus' chest. "Okay," Kai breathed. He sounded wrecked, the word hoarsely escaping him. He pushed harder, groaning as Atticus' hand left him empty. Atticus lay back as Kai grabbed the condom, tearing the wrapper open, gasping at the contact as Kai rolled it onto him.

Atticus watched as Kai grabbed the hem of the hoodie. The sky behind him was lit up, more shining streaks flashing across the dark with every passing moment. Kai lifted the bottom of the hoodie, pulling it up.

Atticus had thought Kai wearing his clothes was probably the best thing ever. But watching him take them *off*? He was pretty sure he just might die from the sight.

Kai tossed the hoodie aside. So much of his hair had come loose of his bun, framing his face as he looked down at Atticus. Gentle fingers played along Atticus' skin, tracing his tattoos, trailing up his neck. A thumb rubbed softly across his bottom lip. Atticus made to lean up, to get closer, to capture Kai with another kiss. A hand pushed on his chest.

"Stay down."

Bossy Kai was back.

Atticus did as he was told. But that didn't mean he was going to keep his hands to himself. He ran them up Kai's thighs as he moved, positioning himself over Atticus' straining cock.

Kai lowered himself slowly, carefully, breathing harshly. Atticus used every bit of restraint he had to hold himself back, to keep from rocking his hips up. He had fantasized probably too many times about what it would feel like to be inside Kai. That single night they'd been together, Kai had been adamant about not bottoming.

When the other man was fully seated on him, ass flush against hips, both of them stilled for several long moments. Kai still had a hand pressed to Atticus' chest, and Atticus' hands had turned to vices, fingers digging into the soft flesh of Kai's thighs as tight heat enveloped his length. Kai began to move, slowly, his own cock bobbing with the motion.

Atticus watched as Kai moved above him, the night an exploding backlight as the meteor shower continued. He could just barely make out the flush on Kai's cheeks, could just barely see his parted mouth and the way his eyes would squeeze shut tight with every thrust downward of his hips. Atticus could hardly think straight. It was all he could do to keep from cumming immediately at just the sight spread out before him. He released his grip on one thigh, moving a hand to wrap it around Kai's cock.

Kai grabbed his wrist. "Not yet," he panted. He began to move faster, bouncing his hips downward again and again. Atticus wove their fingers together, held tight as Kai continued to move.

His instincts wanted him to sit up, to press closer and move against Kai, to give just as much as he was getting. But something about Kai making him just watch, about Kai putting on this show just for him, it had heat coiling low in Atticus in a way that felt new. Thrilling.

Atticus was getting close, and could no longer keep himself quiet. Kai was wringing gasps and small moans from him with every movement, and soon Atticus could no longer hold still. He thrust upward with his hips, meeting Kai harshly. Kai rocked forward, bracing himself on Atticus' chest, grip tightening to the point of pain.

"Do it again," Kai breathed out, free hand tugging on Atticus' waist.

Atticus thrust upward again, over and over, building a frantic rhythm between them. He fought to keep control of himself, fought to hold back. He knew he was getting close, could feel himself crashing toward his own release. But Kai...

"Touch me," Kai finally said. "Now."

Atticus didn't hesitate. He wrapped his hand around the other man's cock, moaning at the heat that met the skin of his palm. He matched his strokes with every thrust of his hips. Kai rocked into his touch, hips pressing down to meet Atticus over and over. He threw his head back, the lines of his neck bared. Atticus wanted to sink his teeth into the skin there, wanted to mark him up just how Kai had done to him.

"Kai, I'm close." Atticus' voice was shaky. He was barely holding on, and it took every ounce of focus to get the words out. He tried to sit up again, but Kai continued to hold him down.

"Don't stop." The words were punctuated by forceful thrusts, as Kai began to ride him even harder.

Atticus always had loved a challenge.

He didn't let up, and it only took a couple more long strokes of his hand before Kai let out a choked cry, spilling onto Atticus' stomach. He clenched, and that was all it took to send Atticus over the edge as well. Pleasure exploded within Atticus as he came, and he couldn't just lay there anymore.

He pushed upward, breaking past Kai's hold, pulling the other man into a tight embrace as he rocked through the aftershocks of his orgasm. Kai tucked his face against Atticus' shoulder, small gasps escaping him. Atticus tangled a hand in the other man's hair, holding him in place. Kai's arms were tucked between them, and after they both finally stilled one hand moved to Atticus' face, pressing gently against his cheek before pushing his hair back from his forehead.

Atticus looked into Kai's eyes as he leaned back, putting just enough space between them to see one another. There wasn't anything concerning there. No, the other man looked content. Eyelids drooping, face still flushed, sweat dampening his skin and making the hair around his face stick. Atticus could feel the mess between them growing sticky as it began to dry, knew he needed to move, needed to get them inside and cleaned up.

But having Kai in his lap, skin against hot skin, a small smile tilting up the corner of his lips as he watched Atticus intently... Atticus didn't want to let go. He wasn't ready for this moment to pass. He had wanted this, had wanted *more*, for so long, and it felt like he finally had it all in his grasp. Everything that he'd been wishing for.

The feelings building inside him, rising up in his chest... he couldn't keep fighting. He sat holding the man he'd fallen for over the course of a single night six months earlier, the sky above them lighting up to match the sparks in his veins. And in that moment, Atticus realized that he was never going to be able to go back to how things had been between them before. How they had been just days earlier. Close friends, nothing more. Atticus knew what he wanted, had known for so long, and he knew he wouldn't be able to go back to just wanting in silence.

It terrified him. He had told Kai he would give him time, give him however long he needed. But the problem was that Atticus didn't need any time. He had never needed time. And now the overflowing feelings in his chest were starting to hurt, starting to stab at him, demanding release.

Atticus' arms around Kai tightened. The other man squeaked a little as he was squeezed, and Atticus chuckled at the sound, hiding the sting in his eyes as burning emotions that threatened to escape him.

"We should go inside," Kai said, the words pressing into Atticus' skin. "Get cleaned up."

Atticus pulled back again, moved his hands to cup either side of Kai's face. He kissed him once more, softly. Hardly more than a whisper of their lips together. Kai moved his hips so that Atticus was no longer inside him. The loss of that contact sent a shiver dancing across Atticus' skin.

"Okay," Atticus finally said. He was careful with his words, careful to keep his brain from letting something escape too soon. "Let's go."

With that, he flung a fully naked Kai over his shoulder, rising suddenly.

Kai yelped. "What the fuck!"

Atticus could only laugh.

Kai had an excellent view of Atticus Mills' ass.

Unfortunately, he couldn't really enjoy it all that much because he had no fucking clue what was happening.

"Put me down." He beat a fist against Atticus' back half-heartedly, before opening his palm wide and smacking down hard on one of the round cheeks beneath him. Atticus let out a shocked cry.

"Hey now," he said, voice light and teasing as he flipped on a light in the kitchen and continued to pad softly through the house. "I don't know if I'll be up for another round so soon."

"Put. Me. Down."

"Just a second!"

Kai felt the arm holding him in place tighten around his midsection. He let himself flop against Atticus' back with a groan. Atticus continued to walk around the house, as though he were searching for something.

"What are you *doing*?" Kai grumbled.

Atticus paused, his torso turning from side to side as he gave the living room one more glance.

"I'm making sure we didn't leave any glasses out this time."

Kai snickered. He could see the kitten curled up in one of her beds, watching them with bright eyes.

Atticus began to move again. They entered his room, and suddenly Kai was flying through the air, eyes wide and limbs splayed. He landed with an *oomph* on the bed, half the wind knocked out of him. Atticus left the room, and Kai could hear him turn on the sink in the bathroom.

It was a little chilly. Kai tried to scurry under the blanket. He was still fully nude, and he longed for the hoodie he'd left outside on the blanket. A memory of the way Atticus had looked at him as he'd pulled it off, soft desire burning in his eyes, made his stomach flip-flop.

"Don't get under there yet!" Atticus whipped the blanket off of Kai.

"It's cold!"

A warm washcloth landed in Kai's lap.

"Clean yourself up first before you get my bed all messy."

Kai obeyed as Atticus crawled into the bed with him. He tossed the washcloth toward the hamper in the corner, fixed his eyes on the man next to him, before reaching out to poke at one of the bruises forming on Atticus' neck.

"Ow!" Atticus smacked his hand away. "What was that for?"

Kai could feel a smirk tugging at his lips. "They look good on you."

Atticus grinned, but Kai could see the faint blush there high on his cheeks. "It's not really fair," he said, voice slipping back into something low, something promising. A hand came up to caress Kai's neck, making his skin pebble. "Not a mark on you."

Kai held still as Atticus leaned in, pressing soft lips against the skin he'd just touched. It only lasted a moment before he pulled back, looking Kai in the eye, a gentle smile tilting his lips up.

"I love kissing you."

A tiny laugh escaped Kai, even as his mind snagged on the words. He pushed the slight unease aside. "You're cheesy."

"You like it," Atticus said. He poked Kai in the side. "Admit it." Kai shook his head, hair tickling his face as it whipped back and forth.

Atticus narrowed his eyes before tackling Kai back onto the bed. Kai couldn't hold back any longer, laughter escaping him as he was held down.

"You're the most stubborn person I know," Atticus said, looking down at Kai with a soft expression that didn't quite match his teasing words. Kai's laughter trailed off as they held each other's gaze. He lifted his head, one hand reaching up to gently tug Atticus down to him.

Their lips met, moving softly together. Kai let himself drink Atticus in, let himself get lost in the kiss. It wasn't heated, not like how things had been outside. There was no desperation in their movements, in the way their hands carefully explored. Atticus' fingers brushed down Kai's ribs, palm sliding along his thigh up to his bent knee, cupping his calf. Kai shivered at the contact.

They didn't escalate, didn't let things go any further. Kai could feel sleep beginning to tug at him. Atticus broke the kiss, pulling back as his thumb brushed across Kai's cheek before tucking some hair behind his ear.

And then Kai let himself be manhandled. Atticus adjusted them so that they were both tucked in under the covers, shifting to find just the right position, making sure to ask if Kai was comfortable *several* times, before he finally flicked off the bedside lamp. Kai was pulled tight against him, their legs tangled together. Every breath Atticus took pushed his chest against Kai's back, and the steady rhythm was lulling him closer and closer to sleep.

"You still awake?" Atticus' voice was soft, a mere whisper

in the dark. Kai let out a small, affirmative sound.

"I need to tell you something." That same voice had somehow grown even quieter, something so unusual that Kai was suddenly fully awake.

"You don't have to say anything," Atticus continued. Each time he breathed, it was a warm brush against Kai's neck. "I don't like keeping things in. I never have. But with you, I feel like I've been keeping this big secret for so long. Since the day I met you. Only, I don't think I'm doing all that good of a job at keeping it a secret. I think I've said it a million ways already except for the one that counts the most."

He paused, letting out a shaky breath. Kai had gone completely still, afraid to even breathe. He knew where this was headed, knew what Atticus was going to tell him. His mind screamed to stop him, to pull away, to make any excuse to keep him from saying more. But he couldn't. Kai couldn't bring himself to utter even a single word, and so Atticus continued.

"I wasn't going to say it out loud, even though I've been saying it in my head for so long. But tonight... tonight felt so different, Kai. And I feel like I'm betraying a part of myself if I keep quiet any longer."

A long pause fell over them. Kai prayed that Atticus wouldn't keep going, that maybe he had fallen asleep.

"I love you."

Kai fought to keep his breathing steady, to keep his body from revealing just how much he wanted to run, to crawl out of the bed and hide away. Every place that their skin touched felt like it burned, like he was being seared by the weight of the confession. The blanket was suddenly too heavy, too suffocating.

Atticus loved him. And Kai was not ready for that.

His thoughts raced as the seconds ticked away, as Atticus continued to hold him tight. Kai could feel the other man holding his breath, waiting for any indication of where Kai's mind was. But Kai didn't want to let him see into his shattered and dark places. Not tonight. Not after what they'd done outside, after everything Atticus had just said.

Kai wanted to give him one more night. One more night before he showed that his broken pieces couldn't be put back together.

"I know," Kai finally whispered. It was true. Kai had known for a long time, since that night, months prior, when he'd received a drunken text that Atticus didn't seem to remember sending. He'd maybe even known before then.

Atticus had loved him from the beginning, and Kai had always been too damaged to love him back.

His answer seemed to be enough for Atticus, who shifted to hold Kai closer, tucking his face against Kai's neck, pressing a light kiss there. Atticus' breaths evened out in a matter of seconds as sleep took him.

Kai lay awake as the hours crept by. He had told Atticus he would think about it all, think about where things were going with them. But the way the confession made him feel, the terror that filled him at the thought of Atticus wanting more than Kai was able to give, that was his answer, wasn't it?

Haunted by his past, by the life he had wanted with everything he had, only to have it ripped away. Full of jagged edges that stabbed through his skin, threatening now to slice the man next to him. Kai had only ever been meant to hurt Atticus, to hurt anyone who tried to love him. Because Kai was broken, too sad and angry and *scared* to ever do anything but cause pain.

He lay awake as the night slipped away, letting himself be held one last time.

1 Year Ago

As he sat on their couch, knees pulled tight to his chest, Kai thought back on that day when he and Nicholas were still just kids.

"I've been worried you're going to move on. From me."

"Kai, you're in my life. You're a part of me, of who I am. You're there in every decision I make. You're my best friend, just because we're together less doesn't mean I'll ever forget about you. You've got me forever."

Forever turned out to have had an expiration date.

Nicholas sat at the other end of the couch, so far away. He was visibly shaking, face ashen, eyes welling up. Kai wasn't really sure why Nicholas was the one who was so distraught, since he'd been the one to just drop the bomb on their entire life.

"Aren't you going to say anything?" Nicholas' voice came out strained, as though he had to work to push the question out. He'd never seemed so scared to talk to Kai before.

The room filled with an aching silence. Kai felt as though he were growing smaller and smaller in the space, as though the world around him were expanding, enlarging, leaving him far behind and too frozen to do anything about it. His hands were pulled into his sleeves, gripping the cuffs so hard his fingers began to throb.

"What am I supposed to say?" Kai finally responded. His voice sounded far off, even to his own ears. It was a struggle to get the words out, it was always a struggle when things became overwhelming. But besides that, what *was* he supposed to say? What did Nicholas want from him? In seven little words he had brought everything to a crashing halt, and Kai was powerless to change it.

I think we have to break up.

The words were still echoing in Kai's head, seeping into every part of him, pushing at his pieces, snapping them apart and leaving the bits shattered and broken on the floor.

"I-," Nicholas began, his voice choking on the word. He looked away, breaking Kai's unrelenting stare as though he couldn't handle that weight any longer. "I don't know. Anything. Please just talk to me."

"I can't change your mind, can I?" Kai knew the answer, even as he felt his throat growing tight, choking him off. He might have known it for a while now, that constant strain of worry that had played on loop in the back of his mind for months.

Nicholas shook his head, the movement small but steady. He still wouldn't look at Kai.

"Then I don't think there's anything for me to say."

The face of the man he had loved for so long crumpled at the words. Kai had rarely seen Nicholas cry. It satisfied something in him to know that he wasn't the only one hurting. That he could control one thing in this situation, could twist a single knife little by little.

"There's so much to say, Kai." Nicholas finally looked back up, tears spilling onto his cheeks. Kai's own eyes felt dry, as if when his emotional well had dried up it had taken all the moisture from his body too. His tongue felt heavy and sticky in his mouth, his skin felt paper thin. All of the physical sensations became his focus, because inside, where everything had been scared and hurting for so long? Inside he felt nothing.

"I don't want to lose you in my life," Nicholas kept going, voice turning frantic. He seemed to shrink under Kai's unending stare, his words turning shaky. "We've been friends for so long, we were friends before anything else. I think we can still have that! I just... I just think it's time to move on. For both of us."

Time to move on. Nicholas was finally moving on from him, just as Kai had always feared he would.

For a moment, Kai's memory of the boy he'd first befriended seemed to transpose over the man before him. That same messy hair. A small, smiling face, eyes set wider with childish glee and mischief. The image blurred atop the man crying before him, hair wilder than usual from the way he kept anxiously running his hands through it. Face crumpled, something broken in his eyes.

What right did Nicholas have to feel broken? He had done this. He had taken a hammer to the life they had built together, smashed it into a million pieces in a handful of words.

"Please just talk to me!"

Kai's attention focused back on the present, the image of that young boy fading away, disappearing forever. He chewed on the inside of his lip, his mouth sealed shut against his will. It didn't matter, though. Kai didn't *want* to say anything. He didn't want to talk about all the reasons why everything he'd wanted hadn't been enough to keep the man before him.

"Kai, we aren't happy! Not as happy as we should be," Nicholas said, his voice filling with panic. "Not as happy as we could be. We fell together when we were kids, and neither of us have ever known anything else. We were friends, we are friends, and I think we both deserve the chance to find something more than that."

Friends. If he could, if his body would let him, Kai almost wanted to laugh.

He loved Nicholas with everything he had. He may have felt unsteady sometimes, *they* may have felt unsteady, but Kai was sure of how much he loved him. Was sure that he would never feel more for anyone else. And Nicholas was whittling it down to what they'd been to each other as children.

"I think you need to leave."

The words were hardly a whisper, but Kai watched them land like a blow.

"You have nothing else to say?" Nicholas looked angry, finally. Kai only continued to stare at him, unblinking, masking the cracking pieces inside of himself.

Nicholas deflated, that tiny trace of anger disappearing completely. Fresh tears slipped past his long lashes. He wiped them away, breathing deeply. Nicholas always had been able to steady himself quickly. It was something Kai loved about him, something he could always depend on. Only he couldn't anymore, could he?

"I'll go stay with Ori," he finally said. He waited several more long, tortuous moments, watching Kai, willing a response to come. Kai moved his gaze away from Nicholas, his stare intently focused on a bit of paint chipping away from the wall across from him.

Nicholas left the room quietly, moving quickly throughout their home to gather a few things. Kai continued to stare at the wall. He imagined that small chip spreading, spider-webbing out from that central place. Cracks forming along the paint, crawling toward the floor, toward the ceiling. Pieces chipping away one by one, until the ugly surface beneath was fully exposed.

"I'll call you in a few days." Nicholas' voice snagged his attention, but Kai didn't pull his eyes away from the wall.

"We can talk then." His voice sounded so tired.

Footsteps receded across the room. The sound of their door unlatching froze Kai. He suddenly wanted to jump up, wanted to run to the other man, beg him for time to mend what was breaking between them. Was he making a mistake, sitting in silence, attempting to punish Nicholas for doing what he thought was right?

"I don't want to lose you in my life." Nicholas voice was soft, almost a whispered echo of his earlier sentiment. "You're my best friend, Kai."

Kai's walls crashed back down into place. He held perfectly still, not moving a muscle as Nicholas left, the door clicking shut behind him.

He was Nicholas' best friend, but Nicholas was the love of his life. Kai could never go back to less than that.

He continued to stare at that chip in the paint until the tears finally came. Kai curled into a ball on their couch, crying long into the night, aching for the touch of the person he'd just lost.

Nicholas had been true to his word. Kai let his phone ring through to voicemail several days later. He listened to the message, listened as Nicholas asked him to call back.

Kai didn't call back.

It became a new routine, Nicholas calling every couple of days, his messages turning more and more desperate, until something resigned replaced the urgency in his voice. Kai listened to them all, read every text.

He never responded to any of them.

Time healed all, isn't that what everyone always said? Kai let the time slip by, days and weeks and months. He was sure that if he waited long enough, if he pushed it all down, pushed past the anger and the agony, that eventually his cracks would begin to heal. That eventually his sharp edges and stabbing, broken shards would stop threatening to tear through his skin.

It did get easier over time. Easier to not cry through the night, to put on a fake smile and pretend that he was moving forward. Easier to hide it.

A handful of blind dates and hookups convinced all of his friends that he really was past it. They couldn't see the web of cracks spreading under his skin, chipping pieces of him away bit by bit.

Over time, the messages from Nicholas stopped coming. It hit Kai one day, like he'd walked into a brick wall. The seed of doubt that had been there since that terrible night, the seed that whispered of regret, it seemed to finally grow roots, to latch itself into place permanently. Nicholas had stopped trying, but Kai's grief and rage were still there. Still going strong. He couldn't bring himself to let go of them, because suddenly they were all he had left of the man he loved.

11

Present Day

Atticus wasn't sure why he felt nervous waking up. Like there was a weight on his chest, pressing into him, stealing his breath. He reached across the bed, searching for another presence.

Kai wasn't there.

He sat up slowly, letting the blanket pool around his hips. He was still naked from the night before. A rush of memories flooded his mind. Kai on top of him, light streaking the sky as they'd moved together. Kai's smile as Atticus had teased him in the bed, the way his eyes had gone soft and happy when Atticus leaned in to kiss him.

Atticus had fallen asleep with Kai in his arms, but he wasn't there now. The room felt cold, empty. The anxiety in Atticus' chest dug its claws in a little deeper.

His immediate instinct was to go check in. Just like how he'd done all week, every time they'd gotten physical. Call out, get up, rush to wherever Kai was, ask once again if he was good, if everything was okay.

Atticus knew that was the right thing to do, but this time it felt different. This time a lump formed in his throat. Because he sort of thought he knew why Kai wasn't in his bed.

I love you.

The words had felt like a weight lifted from Atticus' shoulders when he'd spoken them the night before. But now? Now they felt like his biggest mistake. Heavier than ever before, pushing him down.

The thing he'd been so afraid of had happened. He'd pushed Kai too far, had shown too much of what he had felt for so, so long. And Kai had run away.

Atticus got up, dressing slowly, every movement measured and careful. He didn't understand why he felt on the verge of breaking down. But for once, he wished he was the one getting checked on. Wished that he could hear the words *are you good* directed at himself. Just this once. Because he wasn't good.

No, this time he felt like things were about to spin out of control, and Atticus wasn't sure he'd be able to hold on.

He walked into the kitchen. It was another sunny day, a bright morning. Soft light filtered in through the blinds.

Kai sat in his usual spot, and Atticus' heart clenched. Kai had a spot now, right there at his kitchen counter. He sat there every morning, hair usually kind of a mess, eyes sleepy as he slowly sipped on coffee, drowning in a too big hoodie and sweatpants.

He looked different this morning. Kai's hair was pulled back into a ponytail, only a few strands escaping to frame his face. He wore jeans and a button up that hugged his frame, the sleeves rolled up to his elbows. No coffee steaming in a mug before him. Instead, his packed duffle bag was sitting there on the counter. His attention was focused on his phone, until Atticus finally stepped into the room.

Their eyes met, and Atticus felt as though he could see

walls behind Kai's gaze, shutting him out.

"Morning," Atticus said. Maybe it was all in his head. Maybe he was overreacting, worried over nothing. But he couldn't stop thinking about that packed duffle bag, about how Kai hadn't been there when he woke up.

"Morning." Kai's voice was soft, just more than a whisper. A long, awkward silence stretched between them. Atticus leaned back against the counter.

"Do you want coffee?"

Kai shook his head. "I, uh...," he began. Atticus knew what was coming. That lump in his throat expanded a little more before Kai continued. "I was waiting for you to wake up. My bathroom's done, they finished it yesterday." He paused before glancing down at his phone. "I can go back home now."

And that was it. Atticus' mind began to race in a way it rarely did. Words began to fall out of him, too big to be held back.

"You're just going to leave?" Atticus blurted. His voice came out louder than he intended, and Kai's attention snapped back to him, eyes wide.

"After what we did last night," he continued, "what I... what I *said*, you were just going to leave without talking to me?"

Kai stared at him, dumbfounded. Atticus knew he was losing control, knew that his thoughts were spinning toward the irrational. But he'd told Kai he loved him, and the fear that came with that declaration was blurring everything.

"You said I could take time to think about things," Kai said slowly, voice unsteady.

Atticus barked out a harsh laugh. He couldn't slow down, even though some part of him screamed to stop and think and find a way for things to be okay.

"So it's been enough time for you to decide to fuck me," he

said, the words like acid on his tongue. "But not enough time to figure out if there's something between us worth talking about?"

Kai sat up straight, his phone clattering to the counter, eyes narrowing to burning slits.

"That's not fair. You wanted it too. We didn't do anything that you weren't okay with."

It was true. Atticus knew it was true, and he *had* been okay with it all. But he wasn't okay now. He was so far from okay, because he had put everything on the line, had given all of himself, and there was no one there to make sure he was fine the next morning. His bed had been empty, and the person he wanted most, *needed* most, was leaving as though none of it had meant anything.

Atticus' thoughts continued to spiral as his hands clenched the edge of the counter behind him, fingers aching as he held on.

"Is it your ex?" The words were hard, harsh. Atticus didn't even know where it came from. They hadn't talked about Nicholas at all that week. The only time it had come up had been when he'd come home from practice to find Kai crying about something he hadn't been ready to talk about. So they *hadn't* talked about it. Atticus had wanted to give Kai space, give him time.

Time. He was always giving Kai time. Atticus had given him six months of his life, hours, days, weeks that piled up into so much time that he had spent hoping and waiting. And he knew the whole time that Kai had been thinking about someone else. Atticus had always known, but he had never pushed. Suddenly, it felt like he needed to. Like he needed to press into that bruise with all his strength, because if he was hurting then he wasn't going to be the only one.

"You're still so hung up on him, on someone who has been gone for so *fucking* long, that even me loving you isn't enough?"

Kai was silent. His lips had parted, his eyes growing even wider as a look of shock overtook his features. That voice in Atticus' head, the one screaming for him to stop stop *stop*… it told him he had fucked up. He had gone too far.

But it was only natural for a kicked dog to lash out.

"Isn't it a little ridiculous to be pining for so long over someone who doesn't want you back?"

Atticus felt a shiver run down his spine as his words hit Kai. He watched that lovely face contort, shock transforming into anger.

"Isn't that what you've been doing since the day we met?"

Time slowed to a crawl. The words sank into Atticus, seeped into his skin, invaded every part of him.

Kai didn't want him.

The whole time Atticus had been hoping that somehow Kai would see him as someone worthy of being loved… Kai hadn't wanted him. Suddenly, everything they had done over the last few days felt embarrassing. All of the small touches, the heated kisses. They'd had sex. All of it suddenly filled Atticus with shame, knowing it truly had meant more to him than it had to Kai.

Atticus didn't like to feel embarrassed. He couldn't stand to be the butt of the joke anymore. All of his defense mechanisms kicked into high gear, the facade he had thought he'd finally outgrown falling back into place seamlessly.

"Nah," he finally said. He released his grip on the counter, crossing his arms casually across his chest. Confusion mixed in with the anger coloring Kai's features. "Maybe I was just playing the long game." His mind screamed for him to stop talking, scraped and tore at his insides as he lied.

Kai clenched his jaw, his eyes turning hard and narrowing as Atticus continued.

"Maybe I just needed to get it all out of my system. Just

like all the times before, with the others. We did what we did," Atticus said, pausing, letting the tension between them overflow. He grinned, something mean and sharp escaping through the look he gave Kai. "Now I can move on."

Something in Kai's expression cracked. It was slow, the way the anger seemed to fall away bit by bit, replaced in increments by sorrow.

It snapped Atticus out of his rage, broke through the shield of harsh words he had raised around himself.

Kai's phone dinged from where it had fallen to the counter. They both looked at it.

"I have to go," Kai said. His voice shook with the words, and Atticus could see a tremor in his hands as he quickly snatched up his things, his car keys rattling as he stood quickly. Atticus' arms fell to his sides as he stood there, frozen with regret. Kai had already reached the front door when he finally broke out of his stupor.

"Wait!" Atticus cried, moving across the room as fast as he could. Every step felt weighed down, like he was being pushed back by some invisible force. Like all of the words the two of them had just spoken were too heavy to push through.

Kai paused at the door for only a moment. Atticus crashed to a halt in front of him. He wanted to reach out, wanted to wrap the other man in an unbreakable embrace.

"I didn't mean it," Atticus said. His voice shook, desperation leaking from his every pore. "I'm sorry, Kai. Please just stay and we can talk about it."

Kai watched him for what felt like an eternity. Atticus couldn't move, couldn't breathe under the weight of that shattered stare. It hurt more than anything, knowing that he was the one who had caused the pain he saw in those beautiful, bright eyes.

For several long, too long, moments, it seemed that Kai couldn't speak, his lips parting in silence. When words finally did fall from him, they seemed stilted, pained. As if he could hardly manage to speak to Atticus at all anymore.

"Bye, Atticus."

And that was it. Atticus remained frozen, locked in place as Kai stepped outside, shutting the front door softly behind him. A few seconds later, the sound of a car door closing reached him.

Kai was gone.

12

Kai entered his home. It was quiet, quieter than he'd expected. Quieter than he remembered.

He walked through the entryway, dropping his duffle bag next to the door. There was none of the background noise that he'd grown so used to over the last several days. No television playing in another room, no coffee pot going, no jingle of a cat toy being pushed across the hardwood floors. No Atticus singing off-key as he went about his day.

No Atticus at all.

Kai passed through his own home like a ghost. He didn't pause to look at his new bathroom, just walked slowly past, eyes unfocused as his mind raced. All he could feel, as he sat on his sofa, was the overwhelming way his mind was beginning to spin out of control. His limbs felt numb, all the way to his fingertips. The dull throbbing in his chest that had plagued him the entire car ride home had faded, leaving only an empty void in its place.

Curling in on himself, Kai wrapped his arms around his knees. The room was dark, his blinds closed and the light still off. It helped, masking the emptiness. If he couldn't see it then it just wasn't there. The silence though... it pressed in on him relentlessly, from all sides, a weight he felt acutely.

A choked sob finally broke past his defenses, the sound echoing through the room, reminding him just how alone he truly was. Tears stung his eyes, spilling past his lashes as he squeezed them shut.

A part of Kai had known what he was doing. From the moment he crept out of Atticus' bed, pulling away from the warmth of the of those steady arms and leaving him lying there peacefully, Kai had known what the end result would probably be.

He just hadn't expected it to be quite so bad.

The weight of Atticus' feelings, the pressure that came with knowing how much his friend felt for him, it had made Kai want to do what he did best. Pull away. It was something he'd perfected over time, grown so good at that he had thought he could get away with it.

He hadn't been prepared for Atticus to look so shattered the moment he'd walked into the kitchen. That normally vibrant, cheerful face had been anything but, and Kai had known right from the start that he had fucked up.

And when things escalated, when they had both flung hateful words at each other, Kai did the only other thing he knew how to do. He shut down. He ran away.

Isn't it a little ridiculous to be pining for so long over someone who doesn't want you back?

The words had been a spear through Kai's gut. Because, in truth, he hadn't been thinking about Nicholas at all. Not directly. But Atticus had brought him into the conversation, because he'd just seen Kai crying over his ex mere days earlier, and had only ever known a Kai that couldn't get over his past life.

Kai had never been able to move on, had never been able to break past his grief and his anger, and even Atticus didn't have faith that he would be able to.

Now I can move on.

It was as though fate was playing a trick on him. An endless game, a maze that only had false exits, leading Kai to those same words again and again.

He was someone that others moved on from. He was too shattered, too filled with razor-sharp edges, for anyone to be able to hold on to him forever.

Another sob broke past Kai's guard. He sucked in air, trying desperately to calm his breathing. He wanted to retreat, to hide away from even himself. His hands automatically looked for sleeves to pull into, cuffs to tangle his fingers in. But he wasn't wearing long sleeves. He wasn't wearing the hoodie Atticus had given him. He'd left it behind, along with the horrible things he'd said in that morning-bright kitchen.

Feeling returned to Kai's chest the moment he remembered what he'd said to Atticus. The words he'd spun around, only to spit them back in his face, calling him out for doing nothing more than loving Kai for so long. Pain rushed in to fill the void in his chest, squeezing so tight he feared he would implode.

Kai was so ashamed of what he had said. It didn't matter that Atticus had said horrible things right back. All he could see in his mind was the look of hurt on the face he'd grown so fond of. He'd never seen Atticus look that way before, eyes wide with betrayal, shiny with unspent tears. He'd looked defeated, and Kai had been the one to best him.

He hated himself for it.

But it didn't matter now, did it? Because regardless of the pain they had caused each other, Kai had left. He stared out blankly into the dark room. It was for the best, him leaving. Because everything he feared about himself had turned out to be true.

Kai was too sad, too angry and broken, and it was all too permanent. Too much a part of everything he was. Nicholas had moved on, and now Atticus would as well.

His phone chimed, and Kai pulled it out of his back pocket. The light of the bright screen burned his eyes as he swiped away the notification. He paused a moment, not really thinking when he pulled up Ori's contact and hit the call button.

The call immediately went to voicemail.

Kai deflated a little. He'd wanted to hear his friend's voice, wanted that sunny presence in whatever small capacity he could get it. Wanted to hear Ori tell him that it would all be okay, even if it wasn't true.

He was probably busy with practice, with settling in with his new team and new life. Kai felt as though Ori's going away party had been a lifetime ago, so much passing in the week since then. He knew Ori didn't have a place yet, was waiting for an apartment to open up in the same complex where Julian lived. He'd been crashing with his friend since flying out to Los Angeles earlier in the week, so maybe…

Kai chewed at his bottom lip as his phone rang against his ear. He didn't really know Julian all that well. If he was being honest, he hadn't always had the best impression of the guy, considering the way he and Ori seemed stuck in a perpetual dance around one another. But Julian was Ori's friend, first and foremost, and he had been a lifeline for Ori when his life had turned upside down with his unexpected trade to the Comets, so Kai couldn't really bring himself to stay wary of the man anymore.

"Kai!"

Julian's cheery, sing-song voice blared through the phone's speaker.

"Hey," Kai said, his voice still too thick with emotion. He hoped it would go unnoticed. "Is Ori with you?"

Julian laughed. "He is. Did you try to call him? He lost his phone yesterday."

That sounded about right. Ori never had been great about keeping track of his things.

"Is he around?"

"Well," Julian said, and Kai could hear him grinning as he spoke. "He is. Sort of. He's in the middle of something."

"Oh," Kai said. He winced at the disappointment that was clear in his voice. Julian didn't respond for a long moment.

"I'll go get him." His voice was suddenly serious. "It's not that important. We're at the gym, some guy made a comment about his height, and he took it as a challenge. You know how he gets."

"No," Kai said quickly. He suddenly felt ashamed of himself, ashamed that he was dragging his friend into the mess he had created. The mess he had become. "That's okay, I can call back tomorrow."

"Kai." Julian said his name slowly. "Something's wrong."

Kai didn't respond. His throat felt too tight, and he had to clench his jaw to keep whatever was building in him from spilling out.

"Did something happen with Atticus?"

Hearing Atticus' name brought it all raging back to the surface. A small sound slipped past his lips. Something ragged. Something defeated.

"Hey, hey," Julian said, his voice lowered, his words soothing. "I can go get Ori right now. Or you can just tell me what happened. Or we can talk about something completely unrelated. But don't hang up, okay?"

Kai nodded, a beat passing before he realized he needed to answer verbally. "Yeah, okay," he said, the words tight and aching as he pushed them out.

"Are you hurt?" Julian paused, and Kai could hear him suck in a shaky breath. "Did he hurt you?"

"No," Kai said, suddenly desperate to defend Atticus. "Not like that. We both just said some things."

"Do you want to tell me about it?"

"It doesn't matter." Kai's words were still thick, but his tears were drying up as his mind settled back on the pain he'd seen in Atticus' face earlier that morning. And there was something about the way Julian was handling it all, the patience he was showing for someone he hardly knew. It soothed some of the tightness in Kai that had so often kept him from finding his voice."It's for the best."

Julian hummed a little. "I don't know about that. I have some insider information, you know. He's head-over-heels for you."

Kai felt his chest squeeze tight again.

"He'll move past it." The words felt like blades slicing his tongue, shredding his lips. "It'll be better for him."

"What do you mean?"

"I just..." Kai began, unsure of how to put it into words. He'd never voiced it aloud to anyone, and he wasn't really sure why he was telling Julian Tate of all people. But the concern in Julian's words sounded so real, coming across the line in waves. Kai thought about the way he made Ori smile, so bright and soft. Something about that made Kai feel comfortable talking to him. He sucked in a breath to continue.

"I'm just too fucked up for any of this. I have too much baggage. I've never been able to move past being so sad and so angry and so broken by everything that happened. All of my edges are too sharp, I'll only hurt him if I stay too close. I already did hurt him. He's..."

Kai couldn't keep going as he choked on the last word. He cried silently, tears once again staining his cheeks.

"It's okay," Julian said softly. "Take your time."

Time. Atticus had given Kai so much time, had waited for so long, and Kai had brought it all to an end with a few thoughtless words.

"He's done," Kai said, nearly spitting the words out. "He's done waiting. He's going to move on."

Julian laughed.

He fucking *laughed*.

Kai was shocked out of his sniffling by the sound.

"I don't know what he said to make you think that," Julian began, still chuckling softly. "But I can confidently say that it's not true. Maybe he just needs some time, some space to get over whatever you two fought about. But I promise you, Atticus is not going to move on from you. Not after one hard day."

The words washed over Kai, going against everything he felt inside. Everything his mind had been screaming at him since the moment he'd gotten in the car and left Atticus standing in his doorway.

"And take it from someone who has always been royally fucked in the head," Julian continued, "you are not broken."

Kai couldn't help but scoff. Just because Julian had gone through some shit in the past, shit that Ori had only ever alluded to in the few conversations they'd had about it, didn't mean Kai's problems weren't real…

"You are allowed to be sad." Julian's words interrupted his thoughts. "You're allowed to be angry, you're allowed to be sharp. Be those things as much as you need to. They aren't bad things to feel, they don't mean that something in you is beyond repair. You can be all of those things and still be worth loving. You don't have to have one without the other."

Kai didn't know how to respond. He had always thought of the negative emotions he felt as exactly what he'd told Julian they were. Baggage. Something he needed to break free from but didn't know how.

"It's okay to have bad days. Or even weeks, or months. Maybe a part of every day will be bad, sometimes that's just how it is. But you can still exist with all of that. You can still have the things you want, the things you deserve *with all of that*."

Kai couldn't keep quiet any longer, a question pressing past his defenses.

"What if it's too late?"

The words came out as a whisper, made him feel so small in the dark room he sat in.

"Kai," Julian said, his voice solid and almost teasing. "Atticus has seen you sad. He's seen you living with the hard stuff. And he's stuck around through it all. I don't think he's going anywhere any time soon."

The pressure holding Kai's heart and lungs in a vice-like grip lessened. Just a bit. Just enough that he felt a little more at ease. He remembered the night Atticus had come home, had seen him breaking down over the call with Theo. Remembered the way Atticus had handled it all, had just let Kai sit with his overwhelming emotions. Had just been there, a steady presence, a shoulder to very literally cry on.

"Are you going to be okay?"

Kai didn't know if he would be okay, and said as much. Julian hummed once again.

"I think you will be," he said. "I would bet real money that Atticus is just as scared about all of this as you are. Just give it a day or so, let him lick his wounds and he'll be back to his normal, dumbass self."

Kai couldn't suppress a small laugh.

"Thanks, Julian."

"Of course," the other man said. "Unfortunately, I'm being summoned. Ori needs my assistance in this apparent pissing contest."

"Your sets do always make him shine a little brighter," Kai said. He could practically picture Julian smirking at his words, preening at the compliment.

"It's true," he sang. "You sure you don't want to talk to him right now?"

"No," Kai said. He did feel better, if only just a bit. "I'll text him later. You can fill him in on everything."

"We do love a good evening filled with gossip," Julian said, his voice laced with a teasing lilt. "It's going to be so *boring* once he moves into his place next week."

They said their goodbyes, and Kai set his phone on the cushion next to him. He felt lighter, like he could sit a little taller, no longer quite as weighed down by it all. Not just the things that had happened that morning, the words spoken in the heat of anger. But all of it, all of the things that normally tore at him, normally filled him with such piercing shards... it all felt a little less sharp. It was as though, as Julian's words sank into him, each of those shattered pieces were ground down a bit, just enough to keep them from tearing through his skin.

Kai rose, walking across the room to the window. The sunlight was harsh, searing his vision as he twisted the blinds open. His skin warmed immediately, tear tracks drying, pulling at the skin of his cheeks.

The room seemed less imposing as he turned back toward it, light reaching every corner, filling every empty space. The quiet was still there though. It still left something in Kai feeling empty and desperate.

But after his conversation with Julian, Kai felt like maybe the emptiness was something he could deal with. Even if it was only for today. Kai wanted to sit with the words he had offered him, wanted to parse them out and see if he could find it in himself to believe them.

For the first time in a year, Kai felt a little less broken.

The sound of the can cracking open echoed through the kitchen. Atticus looked around, searching for the kitten. Typically, any time he opened her wet food, she came running. Crashing into the room as though she hadn't eaten in days.

There was no sign of her.

Atticus decided to wait, to give her a couple more minutes before he went searching. He began to clean up the kitchen in the meantime. The trash needed to be taken out, a few dishes needed washed. He was putting away several glasses when his eyes snagged on something in the cabinet.

The two mugs that Kai had gotten them. One maroon, the other a pale pink.

A sickened feeling settled in Atticus' stomach. He pushed it down, along with all of the thoughts it brought to the forefront of his mind. Memories of the horrible things he had said earlier that day.

The kitten still hadn't turned up for her meal, so Atticus began to search the house for her. He checked her bed in the living room. Empty. But sometimes she preferred to sprawl on the couch and sleep, so he checked there as well.

The only thing he found on the couch was the blanket Kai had also gotten at the market. The hideous cat faces stared at him from where it had been folded neatly to drape over the couch's arm.

Atticus had noticed that his clothes from the night before, the ones he'd shucked off outside, had been placed in the laundry hamper. Kai must have gone out and gathered everything. He must have been the one to pick up the blanket, to fold it up and bring it in. Atticus couldn't help but remember what they'd done on that blanket, how he had felt in those moments.

He couldn't help but wonder if Kai had thought about it as well as he'd picked it up.

No. No, Atticus couldn't do it. He couldn't follow the train of those thoughts, couldn't let himself think about how he'd fucked everything up. It was too much, his fight or flight instincts kicking in, trying desperately to keep him from crumpling beneath the weight of it all. He returned to his search to distract himself.

He checked everywhere, room by room. Each one was empty. It weighed on him, the way he felt so alone in his own space. He'd gotten used to not being by himself.

Atticus knew he was procrastinating. He'd walked right past his guest room, despite the fact that the door was cracked open. He checked every single other room in his home. Twice.

Still no kitten.

He could feel it before he even entered the room. The tightness in his chest, the clenching in his gut. Atticus pushed open the guest room door.

She was there, curled up into a tiny ball, her side rising slowly with measured breaths as she slept soundly.

She was sleeping on top of the old Cats hoodie.

The one that Atticus had told Kai to keep. The one that Kai had been wearing all week. It was folded neatly, placed purposely on the corner of the bed. Kai hadn't thrown it in the hamper with the other clothes from outside, as though he had maybe, for just a moment, considered packing it up and taking it with him.

Atticus reached out, gently waking the kitten. She yawned, blinking slowly, stretching out languidly before jumping down from the bed and leaving the room. Atticus stayed behind, his gaze fixed on the hoodie, fingers brushing lightly across the worn fabric.

Tears stained his cheeks as he finally picked it up and clutched it to his chest. Atticus sat on the edge of the bed, his hands gripping the hoodie so tightly that his knuckles were beginning to burn.

A sob wrenched itself from his chest. Everything that Atticus had been fighting to hold back, everything that had been building in him since Kai had walked out the door, it all came spilling forth. Wave after wave battering him, leaving him reeling with pain.

Atticus curled up on the bed, still clutching the hoodie close, as though he could keep from truly losing it all by holding on tight enough. Tears soaked into the blanket, burning lines down his skin as they continued to fall. He could hardly think straight, everything he wished he could have done or said differently pushing forward in his mind, fighting for the spotlight, filling his aching chest to bursting.

Guilt weighed on him, pushing back all of the anger he had felt in a flash of stupidity that morning. Atticus had waited so long. He had never wanted to push too far, had never wanted to scare Kai away. And he had ruined it all in a single moment, had said things he would never be able to take back.

The worst part? Atticus hadn't meant a word of it. Telling Kai that he was nothing more than another of his infamous hookups, as if what had happened between them were nothing.

Now I can move on. Atticus fucking hated himself for the words. For the way he had tried to turn Kai's grief over the past into a weapon, as if he weren't just as guilty of being unwilling to let someone go.

He loved Kai. He had said as much aloud, had finally given voice to what he had desperately wanted his friend to know. Only to viciously act as though he hadn't meant it, as though his feelings for Kai were fleeting and disposable.

What kind of love was that? Atticus curled himself around the hoodie, knees pulling up to his stomach, squeezing his eyes shut against fresh tears. Kai deserved so much better. He deserved someone steady, someone who didn't fold so easily.

As much as Atticus wanted Kai to fight for him, he knew that he himself hadn't shown that sort of resolve. All he had done was lash out at the first sign of trouble. He had gone back on what he had told Kai, had pushed him into a corner because Atticus was tired of waiting and had felt a moment of fear. It had been unfair, and the other man had been well within his rights to be angry.

But still... it hurt. It hurt so much to know that Kai *hadn't* been willing to fight for whatever was between them. It had been like a knife to the chest as Atticus had watched Kai leave, unwilling to talk to him. Unwilling to try to fix what they had both broken together.

Atticus felt lost as he lay there on the bed that Kai had occupied all week. He thought that maybe he could smell the soft scent of the lavender soap he had bought at the market. Remembered how it had smelled on his skin as they'd held one another the night before.

The fear that Kai truly didn't want him was still there. Atticus' feelings were all so big, so overwhelming and loud, and it seemed clear that Kai's simply... weren't. That Atticus felt so much more, and Kai couldn't match him. Couldn't feel for Atticus what Atticus felt for him. Because otherwise he wouldn't have left, right?

Maybe there had been some insidious truth to Atticus' lie about moving on. Maybe it was all for the best, maybe Atticus truly did need to finally let go.

He was pretty sure he would never be able to.

His phone suddenly rang.

He sniffled as he pulled it out of his back pocket, the hoodie still held tight in his other hand. Julian's name was on the screen.

"Hi," he mumbled into the phone, making no attempt to hide the tears that turned his words thick.

"WHAT DID YOU DO."

The voice on the other end of the line was *not* Julian.

"Where's your boyfriend?" Atticus asked. He really needed to grab a tissue before he dripped snot onto the bed. "I want to talk to him, not you."

"Julian isn't my boyfriend," Ori blurted, his voice loud and obstinate in Atticus' ear. "And too bad. He's busy. Why did you tell Kai you're done with him?"

A fresh wave of sadness crashed over him upon hearing those awful words flung back at him. Atticus finally did grab a tissue from the nightstand, blowing his nose hard as tears blurred his vision once again.

"Wait," Ori said, his voice going a little softer. "Are you crying?"

"Ori." Atticus' voice cracked on his friend's name. "I fucked up. I ruined it all."

Ori hesitated before responding. "What happened?"

It took Atticus several deep, shaking breaths to settle himself enough to speak. But then he told Ori everything. Everything about the last week, about the argument that had happened that morning. Atticus was surprised to find out that Ori already knew some of what had transpired. Surprised to find out that Kai had been telling him about their time together.

"He talks about me?"

Atticus' question came out watery and pathetic. Ori laughed at him.

"Of course he does," the other man said, voice more cheerful than Atticus was ready for. He frowned at the phone. He was crying, and Ori was laughing. This wasn't exactly the pity party he had hoped for.

"He's just not as loud about things as you are," Ori continued. Atticus scoffed. "But you're wrong thinking that means you feel more than he does. Just because his feelings

244

are quiet doesn't mean they're not just as big." His voice turned a bit more contemplative. "Kai feels a lot, sometimes too much, so much that it traps him, in a way. That's why you're good for him. I've never seen anybody pull him out of himself quite the way you do."

Atticus let the words sink in. He guessed that Ori was probably right, that it was unfair of him to discount whatever Kai might have felt just because he didn't show it the same way Atticus did. Just because he had needed more time after hearing Atticus say the words I love you.

"It doesn't matter," he finally responded, rather petulantly. His tears were finally drying, and he was beginning to settle into the self-pitying part of his sadness-cycle. "I fucked it all up and he's never going to speak to me again."

Ori laughed. Again.

Atticus tossed his phone across the room.

He waited several seconds before getting up to retrieve it, Ori's tiny voice yelling from the floor.

"Did you *throw* your phone?" Ori was too loud, and Atticus held the phone away from his ear with a hiss. A part of him missed it though. He and Ori had gotten close over their time playing for Chicago. Practice wasn't the same without his friend's sunny, loud presence.

Atticus could hear another person, probably Ori's asshole not-boyfriend that had somehow weaseled his way into Atticus' good graces, laughing merrily in the background.

"Quit laughing at me," Atticus said, pouting.

"Quit being dumb," Ori said. He was definitely holding back more giggles. "You're giving up in the first set. So you had a bad toss, get the fuck up and try again."

"Julian told you to say that."

"Yep!"

"I don't know." Atticus sighed, some of his sulkiness fading away as he tried to face the situation clearly. "Ori, I said some awful stuff to him."

"And he said some mean things to you too."

Atticus could hear the words clearly, as if Kai were there in the room with him still.

Isn't that what you've been doing since the day we met?

Kai had twisted Atticus' anger back around, had flipped the knife so that it was aimed directly at his heart. Had taken the thing Atticus was sort of proud of, the fact that he'd finally found someone he wanted to stick around for, and made it sound like a fault.

But only because Atticus had done it first.

"What about Nicholas?" Atticus whispered. Strangely, he thought he could practically hear the smile leave Ori's face. His heart sank as his friend sighed into the phone.

"I've been trying to get Kai to move on from that mess for a year now." Ori's words felt like a choking grip on Atticus' hope, cutting it off to a dwindling flicker. But then he continued, his voice less resigned, tinted with a smile Atticus could still picture. "It's been hard for him, an uphill battle the whole way. But he's not the same person he was a year ago. He's better, so much better, even if he doesn't see it. And, well, *you* played a part in getting him this far. And he told Julian this morning-"

Ori cut off. It sounded as though he had been tackled, the phone knocked out of his hand.

"Julian talked to him?" Atticus' voice rose in a panic. "Ori, you little shit! Pick your phone up!"

He could hear the sounds of a scuffle on the other end of the line. What had Kai said to Julian?

"Atticus! So sorry," Julian sang into the phone, "Ori isn't so great at secrets. We're going to have to have a talk about that." He cut off, more sounds of a struggle coming through. Julian came back to the phone, slightly out of breath. Atticus could hear the smirk in his voice as Ori argued with him in the background. "Got to get back to practice. Bye!"

"Julian, don't you dare hang up on me you fucking-"

Atticus didn't finish the sentence. The line was already silent.

He dropped his phone next to him on the bed, flopping backwards. A long, slow sigh left him.

Kai had talked to Julian. About *him*. It had only been a handful of hours since their fight, and Kai had already reached out to someone about it.

It filled Atticus with a perverse sense of hope. Hope that maybe Kai had desperately reached out for the same reasons he had. Hope that maybe Ori was right, that it wasn't too late for Atticus to fix things.

The timing was all wrong though. Atticus had a game that night, and needed to head to the gym soon for a team meeting and warmups. The season was starting, and he needed to be focused, regardless of the fact that his love life was in shambles.

He had invited Kai to the game. Kai had *wanted* to come to the game. And despite the mess he'd made of whatever was between them, Atticus still wanted Kai there. He wanted Kai there more than anyone else. He'd imagined Kai watching him win, watching his team successfully kick off the season. Imagined Kai in his arms, celebrating with him afterwards.

Atticus ran a hand through his hair, tugging it in frustration as he chewed his lip, squinting up at the ceiling.

A part of him wanted to text Kai, to ask him, *beg* him to still come to the game. He opened and closed their text chain several times, before chucking his phone onto the other side of the bed.

It would be best to wait. Give Kai more time to think, something that Atticus should have given him anyway. And he *was* thinking, that much was evident from whatever conversation he'd had with Julian. Ori had been so sure that it would all turn out okay. That Kai would give Atticus another chance.

Atticus let himself believe it, just a little, as he got up and began to get ready for the first game of the season.

13

Kai paced his room, grip tight on his phone.

Atticus' game was set to start in a half hour, and Kai had yet to decide if he was going.

Honestly, it was probably too late. He'd checked an hour earlier for tickets online, and they were all sold out. A few had been listed with resellers, but Kai wasn't about to fork over that kind of money. Sure, he made a decent living as a streamer, but it rankled to pay scalpers that much.

And besides, he knew he had other options if he *really* wanted to get into the game. The first of which was to call Atticus himself and ask if he could get Kai in.

Kai chewed at the inside of his cheek. It wasn't that he didn't want to call Atticus... he was just so scared. So filled with fear that Atticus would tell him no, that he didn't want Kai at the game anymore. And Kai just wasn't sure he could handle that sort of rejection, even if a part of him was sure he deserved it after the things he had said that morning.

That left him with the only other option he'd come up with. The option that had set him pacing back and forth across his room, phone in hand, for the last twenty minutes.

There was someone else at the game that just might be able to get him in.

Kai frowned at his phone screen as he unlocked it, brows pinched as he pulled up his recent calls. He hesitated for a few moments more before pressing a number with no name attached to it.

The sound of the call ringing through seemed too loud as he held his phone to his ear, drowning out the pounding beat of his heart.

"Hello?"

The sharp question, laced with hesitance, all the more piercing because of his posh accent, made Kai's palms go sweaty as Theo answered the call.

"Theo," he began, his tongue nearly tripping over the name. "It's Kai."

"I know. What do you want? I have a game in half an hour."

Always to the point, something Kai had admired about Theo in the past, before their friendship had evaporated completely.

"I, ah…" Kai trailed off, his nerves getting the best of him. This was a mistake. Theo hated him, he'd made that much clear when he had called Kai days earlier. And Kai hated him back, didn't he? Except that now Kai wasn't sure that was entirely true, at least on his part. No, Theo had never given Kai much of a real reason to hate him. Sure, they had begun to drift apart when Theo had left Chicago to play in St. Louis. But Theo had always checked in, until Kai had cut off all contact.

Ori had always assured Kai that Nicholas hadn't cheated on him. That nothing had happened with Theo until months after Nicholas had also moved to St. Louis. That Theo had been the hesitant one, had waited longer than even Ori had expected, despite his longtime feelings for Nicholas.

Kai had *known* Theo, had known that he was abrasive, sharp, sarcastic. But he also knew that Theo was observant. That he was loyal and good.

"Kai." Theo interrupted Kai's too-long silence with a sigh. "I have to go, coach is going to start yelling soon."

Of all of the things Kai expected to hear in his old friend's voice when he'd pressed the call button, resignation and defeat hadn't been among them. Kai wondered if maybe Theo's decision to be with Nicholas hadn't been as easy as Kai had always thought it had been.

"Wait," he blurted. Silence met him, but the line didn't go dead. Kai screwed up his courage.

"Kai, I'm serious, if I don't go now-"

"Can you get me into the game?"

It was Theo's turn to fall silent. Kai's heart threatened to beat out of his chest as he waited for an answer.

"Can't you ask your friend on the Cats?"

Kai winced. "Attie doesn't... I can't, actually. Please, Theo. If you can get me in we'll call it even."

Theo sucked in a sharp breath. "I..." A long pause that had Kai nearly squirming. "Okay, yeah. I'll have coach put your name down. I really do have to go now."

"Thanks," Kai said, offering a quick goodbye before ending the call. He glanced at the time. The game was set to start in twenty-five minutes, and he was a half hour from the stadium. Probably closer to an hour with downtown traffic.

Was he even doing the right thing? Hesitance gripped Kai, threatening to choke him. What if Atticus didn't want him at the game? Sure, Julian said that Atticus wasn't going to be done with Kai, despite what had transpired between them. But what if it was too soon? What if Atticus was still too angry to see him?

Kai moved through his home mechanically as his mind whirled with indecision. He paused next to where he'd dumped his keys onto the kitchen counter earlier that day. All he could see was the defeated look on Atticus' face before Kai had left him standing in his doorway. There hadn't been any more anger there, no more of the vitriol that had colored the awful things Atticus had said to him. Only hurt, regret, and something pleading in those pretty blue eyes.

Making up his mind, Kai snatched his keys up and headed out the door.

"Huddle up!"

Coach Rodriguez's shout boomed through the locker room. Atticus moved in close, sandwiching himself between Kieran and Bowen. Where Kieran was the same rock-steady presence as always, calm and focused, dirty blonde hair tied back for the game, Bowen was nearly vibrating with energy, excitement lining his posture. Atticus normally would have been bouncing around just as much, under normal circumstances.

He shook off any reminders of the shitty way his day had started, leaning in as their coach gave them one final pep talk.

"We only get to start this season one time, and we're going to start it letting the rest of the league know that *we're* the ones they need to be afraid of this year."

Whoops echoed through the room as his teammates voiced their agreement. Atticus felt a familiar thrum start up under his skin, his pulse ticking up as anticipation rushed through his veins.

"You men have trained hard for this, and even if it felt like I was wrangling clowns half the time..." Coach shot a pointed look at Bowen and Eric. Both of them grinned broadly, not a hint of shame in their expressions, earning them a hearty eye roll. "You've made me proud to be a part of this team, regardless the outcome of this game. But that doesn't mean I don't want to see you all out there on the court giving me and your fans everything you've got. And if you lose tonight, I'm going to kick all your asses on Monday. Hands in!"

Each player reached toward the middle of the huddle, hands slapping atop one another.

"You ready?" Coach grinned at them, something feral and gleaming that Atticus saw reflected on the faces of the rest of the team. They all shouted in unison, breaking the huddle with more whoops and hollers.

Atticus followed, ready to file out of the locker room, ready to let the din of the cheering crowd fill him up and, hopefully, block out everything else, when a hand clamped around his forearm. Kieran pulled him to the side as the rest of the team made their way out into the gym.

"You good?"

Atticus should have known that if anyone could pick up on his less than stellar mood, it would be his oldest friend.

"I'm fine." He winced when Kieran only raised a brow at him, expression bored.

"Try again."

Atticus sighed, and worry quickly filled his captain's expression. "Is it Sammie? Is she okay?"

"It's not Sammie," Atticus mumbled. He sounded pathetic, even to his own ears. "She already let me know she's on the sidelines cheering for us."

Relief flickered across Kieran's face, before he tilted his head to the side in question. "Is it that streamer you've been hooking up with?"

Atticus flinched. "It's not like that. Me and Kai haven't been hooking up…"

"Attie boy here doesn't do more than one night!" Bowen's voice was too loud as he slapped Atticus on the back.

"Nah," Eric said, popping up out of nowhere. Liberos. "He made an exception this time. Must have been a good lay to rope Mills in for another round."

"Guys." Kieran's voice turned sharp, but Eric barreled on.

"Maybe this one's a good luck charm."

Atticus' hands tightened into fists, his nails biting into his palms. He was sick of it, so sick of the way his teammates talked about him, about his past, about the person they thought him to still be. And now Kai was being roped in, associated with Atticus' playboy reputation.

"No, you heard what he said," Bowen answered with a laugh that grated along Atticus' spine. "They aren't hooking up. Not even the great Kai Reid was good enough for our Atti-"

One moment, they were standing next to the door to the gym. The next, Atticus slammed Bowen back across the room, hands fisted in his spiker's shirt as he shoved him up against the wall of lockers. Fury filled Atticus, vibrating from his core, even as Kieran pounced on him in an instant, tearing him away from their teammate.

"What the fuck, Mills!"

Bowen was angry now too, face red as he pushed off the lockers and stepped toward Atticus. Eric jumped in between them, arms out to keep them separated.

Atticus pointed at Bowen, adrenaline pumping through him. "Keep his name out of it. Say whatever the fuck you want about me, gossip about my sex life as much as you want, but don't say another *fucking* word about Kai."

"Jesus christ, man," Bowen spat, brushing Eric off as he threw his hands up in surrender. "I didn't mean anything by it. Chill out." He left the locker room in a rush, Eric following two steps behind him.

Atticus pulled out of Kieran's grip, planting his arms against the cool concrete wall before leaning his head against them.

"What was that?"

Kieran sounded mad, madder than Atticus had heard him sound in years.

"Nothing," he said, struggling to calm his racing heart as his limbs tingled from the rush of emotion.

"Fuck that," Kieran said. "If it's affecting this team, it's something, and I'll have coach bench you if you don't figure this shit out in the next two minutes."

Atticus sighed, shoulders slumping in defeat.

"I didn't mean to go off on him," he mumbled. "It's been a long day."

"Doesn't give you the right to hit him."

"I wasn't going to hit him!" Atticus turned around, splaying his hands out to the sides. "At least, I don't think I was going to."

Kieran chuckled at that. "He might have deserved it, actually. I've talked to him about giving everybody shit all the time, not that it seems to have done any good. Now, why don't you tell me what's really going on."

Atticus hesitated. He and Kieran hadn't really talked about personal stuff, not for the last few years. Not since high school, really. They weren't as close as they'd been back then, not since Kieran had graduated first and left to pursue professional volleyball. Their friendship had rekindled when they'd begun playing on the same team, but still, Atticus had never talked much with Kieran about Kai.

"I might have screwed things up with somebody I really didn't want to screw things up with," Atticus finally said.

"The streamer?"

He nodded.

"You say something dumb to him?"

Atticus frowned. "You're an asshole."

A chuckle escaped Kieran as he shrugged. "Maybe. I'm

right, though, aren't I?"

Atticus frowned harder. Kieran moved, throwing an arm around his shoulders as he led him toward the door. "I'm right. The thing is, you've said dumb shit to everybody for as long as I've known you. And the rest of us stuck around, didn't we?"

"Sammie didn't have a choice."

That pulled a full laugh out of Kieran. "Sammie is just as much of a brat as you, and twice as stubborn. You're going to be fine, it's going to work out with the streamer. And if it doesn't, then that's his loss."

They pushed through the door, and the roar of the crowd crashed into Atticus. A hint of excitement, of anticipation, began to build in him.

"I hope you're right," he said to Kieran, his voice nearly a shout as they began to jog onto the court. Kieran winked at him.

"I usually am."

Kai was out of breath as he rushed up to the ticket taker.

"Kai Reid," he said, nearly wheezing. Maybe Atticus was onto something with the running every morning. "Theo Whittaker should have had my name down for a ticket."

The young woman at the stand looked at him with a brow raised. "Aren't you the streamer?"

Kai nodded, blushing at the recognition that lit her eyes. He'd never quite gotten used to the way random people would, on occasion, recognize him. He tucked his hair back behind his ears, needing it out of his face, as she looked down at a paper in front of her.

"Yeah," she finally said. "We have your name down. Wasn't Whittaker that put you on the list though."

"What?" Kai stared at her blankly.

"Wasn't Whittaker," she repeated, smiling at him brightly. "Atticus Mills called down a couple hours before the game, said to hold a seat for you."

Kai felt rooted in place, every racing thought in his mind suddenly going silent.

Atticus had saved him a ticket to the game. Even after everything, after their fight, after the terrible things Kai had said to him, Atticus had still wanted him there.

Kai wasn't sure what to do with that information. He didn't want to let himself trust that it meant anything. Didn't want to let his heart latch on to something that could still go wrong.

"Oh," he finally mumbled. "Sure. Yeah, that works."

"Here's your ticket," she said, handing him the small slip of paper. "Ushers inside can help you find the right section."

Kai took it from her, and felt as if he were floating outside of his body as he made his way through the stadium. He'd been before, knew exactly where he was going from the countless times he'd attended Ori's games. Screens in the hallways showed that the game was in the third set already, sets tied, with the Cats down eighteen to twenty.

The sounds of the cheering crowd pulled Kai toward the court. He blinked against the bright lights as he made his way down the stairs, heart pounding as he tried to focus on putting one foot in front of the other. He was almost afraid to look down at the court, to let his eyes land on the two teams battling it out below.

Another glance at his ticket showed him his seat number. Kai found the right row, scooting past several seats before he arrived at the one reserved for him. He was about to sit down, about to finally chance a look at the game happening in front of him, when the person in the next seat over spoke.

"Kai?"

He looked up, only to be met with blue eyes that looked so, so familiar.

"Sammie."

They stared at each other for a beat too long, and Kai wanted nothing more than to turn tail and retreat. What if Atticus had talked to his sister about what had happened between them that morning? Sammie was... intimidating, to say the least. Tall, strong, and just as imposing as her twin, with a sharper wit and a no-nonsense attitude. Kai had only met her a handful of times, but he liked her. Especially any time she made her brother squirm with a scathing retort.

Kai really didn't want her attention turned on him if she knew he had upset Atticus.

"Attie didn't tell me you were coming," Sammie said. Kai hesitated before taking the seat next to her. A raucous cheer rose from the crowd around them, and Kai had to almost yell to be heard.

"I don't think he knew I was," he responded, leaning in close so Sammie could hear him. They were on the front row, just behind the Chicago bench.

"Well," she said, smirking in a way that made Kai even more nervous. "He'll be glad you're here. Maybe it'll get his head out of his ass and he'll start making some good plays."

Another cheer went up around them, and Kai glanced at the score. Twenty to twenty-one. The Cats had closed the gap by a point, but they were still down.

He was stalling. Kai knew he was stalling, but he still had to force himself to finally search the court. His eyes found Theo first, watched as the middle blocker jumped up, hands rising above the net to shut down a spike from one of the Chicago players. The ball slammed against Theo's arms, bouncing back and forcing the other side into a dig.

Then, finally, his gaze landed on Atticus.

Kai watched as the Cats recovered from the block, as

258

Atticus set the ball for a wing spiker with the name Kelly on the back of his jersey. The set went a little long, but Kelly was still able to smash the ball past the blockers, earning their team another point and bringing the score to a tie.

"Not good," Sammie said, even as their side of the stadium screamed for the point. She looked at Kai. "Do you know what's going on with him?"

So Atticus hadn't told her yet. Kai swallowed thickly. "He had a bad day."

Sammie frowned, concern knitting her brow. She reached up to tie her dark hair back into a loose ponytail. "He's stressing me out. He'll be miserable to be around if they lose this game. Nobody sulks as hard as Attie does."

Her words were accompanied by an eye roll, but Kai could see real concern etched into her expression. Sammie was worried about her brother, and it made guilt gnaw at Kai.

St. Louis rallied to score again, and Kai felt his own anxiety over the game start to build. Atticus would be devastated if his team lost, and it would be partially Kai's fault.

Kai sank low into his seat, eyes glued on the court.

The constant din of the cheering crowd faded as Atticus focused on the ball in his hands. By the time he made it to the end line, turning back to ready for his serve, it was as if the whole room had gone silent.

His heart was racing, both from the last rally and from the knowledge that he needed to land this serve. They were tied with St. Louis at twenty-three points, and if Chicago couldn't take this set, they would need to win the next two. His team needed him.

Atticus let the sound of his own pounding heart focus him, let it tether him to the moment. He'd been sloppy with his last few sets, and it sent a wave of anxiety coursing through his veins, trailing under his skin in a way that itched.

Slow breaths, one after another. The ball felt heavy in his hands as he twirled it, the weight of what this serve meant to everyone in the room absorbed into it.

One heartbeat, then another.

Atticus glanced to the sideline, toward where he knew his sister would be. Looked for her the same way he had before every serve. Sammie was his tether, grounding him with her support, ever since the day they had watched their first volleyball match together at seven years old. Even if she didn't play anymore, even if she worked too much and never took time for herself, she always made sure she was at every one of Atticus' home games.

Sweat dripped into his eyes, blurring his vision. Atticus knew the clock was ticking, time dwindling. He needed to move, needed to make his play. But he had to see her. It was the only tradition he had, the only ritual he needed.

And there she was, leaned forward in her seat, hand fisted tightly on her thighs. Sammie had pulled her hair back, something she only did when she was nervous. The eyes that looked so much like his own met his gaze, and she gave Atticus a small nod, her lips tilting in a particular smirk that she always saved just for him. It settled Atticus, a calm unlike any other washing over him.

His gaze snagged on the person next to her. The man leaning in to say something in her ear.

Atticus felt his heart stop completely as his eyes landed on Kai.

Kai was there. Kai had come to his game. Atticus needed to move, he needed to move *right now*. It took every ounce of strength he had to turn his attention back to the game.

Kai was watching him.

Atticus did move, tossing the ball up, stepping into his

serve. He could feel the rush of power that always came with the motion, let it propel him forward as he leapt into the air. His hand hit the ball with a powerful *thwack*, sending it careening across the net.

It was over in a blink as the other team failed to get into position, setting up a nice little campfire as they watched the ball crash to the floor between them.

Twenty-four. The Cats were ahead.

Bowen let out a whooping yell, smacking his hand into Atticus', his grip unrelenting. Kieran shouted for all of them to get back into place, for Atticus to keep it going.

Making his way back to that same spot behind the end line, Atticus went through his ritual once more. He let the ball twirl between his palms before glancing at his sister, who was grinning wide, standing up out of her seat, shouting something he couldn't make out.

Atticus met Kai's stare, let those wide, amber eyes the only thing he could see as everything else in the room faded away.

Kai was there, and Atticus didn't know what it meant.

But when a small smile turned up one corner of Kai's lips, Atticus thought that it didn't really matter what it meant. Because Kai was there, he was there at a time when Atticus needed him.

And that was all Atticus had wanted, since the moment he'd found his bed empty that morning.

The ball soared into the air, leaving Atticus' hands just so. He could tell before he even began to rush forward that the serve was going to be *perfect*. There was a charge in the room, buzzing through him. Fear in the eyes of the St. Louis players as he sent the ball hurtling toward them. It smacked the floor once again, colliding against the wood with a crack that was audible even over the screaming crowd.

He'd done it. They had taken the third set, only needing one more for the win. The rest of his team rushed him, sweaty man bodies pinning him in place between them all.

Atticus only caught a glimpse of Sammie bouncing in place, gripping Kai's arm next to her, dragging him into the motion.

He felt lighter. Steadier. As the players moved into place for the fourth set, Atticus felt the familiar excitement and anticipation course through him, the same feeling that he lived for, that had kept him coming back to the game again and again his entire life.

Atticus fell into place in the lineup, ready for the next set.

14

The Cats lost the fourth set.

Kai winced as their captain, a player with McCullough written across his back, slammed to his knees, arm outstretched as he *barely* missed the dig. The ball bounced away as the St. Louis players broke into cheers.

Both sides had played hard through the entire set, and even though Kai could feel a palpable difference in how Atticus was playing, how he was nailing every set and racking up service aces, the other team rose to match the Cats beat for beat.

"God *dammit!*"

A short woman with a dark, messy ponytail moved behind the player's bench, tossing a clipboard to the ground as she walked over to them.

"They'll get it together, Ivy," Sammie said.

The woman, Ivy, looked up, and some of her tension evaporated as her gaze landed on them.

"I've already had to tape up Bowen's fingers, and Kieran nearly blew out his knee with that dig. He's gonna have one hell of a bruise in the morning. They're pushing too hard."

"They always do," Sammie said with a scoff, crossing her arms as she leaned back. "And you always manage to keep them in line. They just need one of your pep talks."

Ivy grinned, something sharp and wicked in her expression that sent a chill down Kai's spine. He'd never met an athletic trainer that was quite so... terrifying.

"You a friend of Atticus'?"

Kai reached out a hand, shaking the one Ivy offered. "Yeah, I'm Kai."

Recognition sparkled in her eyes. "Ah. You're the one he's been all messed up about."

Her words twisted something in Kai's gut.

"Don't be mean," Sammie said, reaching out to push the other woman's shoulder. Ivy chuckled.

"Don't worry about it," Ivy finally said. "Clearly, you being here finally got his fucking head in the game tonight. If only you could come to practices too."

"Trust me." Sammie rolled her eyes. Kai was struggling to keep up with the conversation, his cheeks warming at the attention. "You don't want my dumbass of a brother distracted like that. It's gross." She turned to Kai, bumping against his arm. "No offense."

"None taken," he said, unsure if he meant it. He thought maybe he did. It had been nice, fun even, watching the game with Sammie. Kai was sure she didn't know about the fallout between him and her brother, but regardless, she made Kai feel at ease. He liked watching her excitement, the highs and lows that washed over her with every rally. Watching her cheer on Atticus, it was something special to see.

"You going out with the team after this?" Ivy leaned in closer to Sammie, and Kai thought he could see something in her eyes, something soft and hopeful, different from how she had looked at him.

He didn't hear Sammie's answer, pulling his phone out as

it vibrated against his thigh. A text from Theo popped up on his screen.

Theo: Have you seen Nicholas?

Kai frowned, glancing up, searching the sideline across the court. Theo looked tense, eyes scanning the crowd anxiously, phone held in a tight grip. Kai sent back a quick message. He hadn't seen Nicholas. Hadn't even thought to look for him, a realization that surprised him. He hadn't considered that if Theo was playing, Nicholas was probably somewhere nearby.

Movement around the Chicago bench snagged Kai's attention. The players were jogging back onto the court, readying for their final set. Atticus lagged behind.

When their eyes met, Kai felt that same pulse of *something* that he'd felt when Atticus had first seen him at the end of the third set. A pounding thrill that radiated from his chest, enveloping him in a warmth that made his blood turn fizzy.

Atticus tilted his head as he watched Kai, a smile spreading across his face. It wasn't as big as the ones he normally offered. More tentative. As though he were asking Kai for permission.

For what? Kai didn't know. For permission to be happy that he was there? Kai wanted nothing more than to bring back the sort of smile that Atticus had been gifting him with for the last week. The smile that spread wide, filled with laughter and light and something more that Kai hadn't been ready to hear.

He thought that maybe he was finally ready.

Atticus broke the steady eye contact, turning to follow his team onto the court. Their brief moment left Kai reeling. His lungs felt too big, his heartbeat too fast. Before he could recover, the final set began.

The end of the game felt like a lifetime and a single

moment all wrapped into one. It was close, too close, the Cats only up by a single point as the clock ticked down. Both teams were running on fumes, sweat dripping from their faces, every movement filled with more effort than before.

St. Louis called a time out, and Kai watched as Theo was pulled aside by his coach. Their conversation was private, but the way Theo grew more agitated with every word was plain for anyone to see. Kai was surprised when his old friend suddenly turned away, rushing out of the gym.

As the players made their way back onto the court, Kai's phone rang. Even though he still didn't have the number saved, he recognized it.

"Hello?"

"Kai." Something close to terror threaded through Theo's voice.

"Something happened," he continued. His words were shaking, his voice thick with emotion. Kai's grip on his own phone turned painful. "Nicholas had a meeting with a local non-profit. After he left, when he was on his way here… there was an accident. They said his car was in bad shape but they couldn't tell coach anything about his condition."

Kai couldn't breathe. The entire world slammed to a halt around him, each second stretching into an eternity. His change in mood must have been visible, as Sammie leaned in close to ask if he was okay, a hand resting gently on his arm.

He could hear Theo suck in several harsh, broken breaths, could feel the fear and heartache radiating off him as if they were standing side by side.

"Kai," Theo repeated his name quietly. "Can you come to the hospital with me?"

They were still up by a point, and if Atticus could get his

hands on the ball just *once* more, he knew he could bring their fight to a close.

One more point, that was all they needed.

The rally began, Eric digging the serve, sending it flying back across the net. St. Louis scrambled for the receive. Their setter slipped, whether from sweat that had dripped to the floor or muscles that had been overexerted and were too tired to keep going, Atticus didn't know. But he was ready.

Bowen dug the ball, sending it in a high arch that gave Atticus time to settle, time to ready himself. Muscle memory took over as he fell into place, as he raised his hands and breathed deeply.

The ball landed in *just* the right place.

This was why he played, why he loved the game. When the outcome relied on a single moment, where he could make or break his team with a single touch. He trusted his guys, knew that as long as he could get the ball to them, they could make the play.

The volleyball seemed weightless as he pushed it back into the air, sending the quick set off toward the other side of the court. He felt just as light, hanging at the top of his jump as he watched Kieran crouch before pushing off the floor with everything he had.

Atticus' feet hit the ground with a crash, sending reverberations all the way up his spine. He didn't blink, didn't even breathe as the ball sailed toward Kieran's ready hand. His captain spiked it, *hard*, his arm whistling through the air, connecting with the ball for a perfect, glorious cut shot that whizzed past the blockers.

The ball hit the floor just on the right side of the line, and the stadium erupted.

Atticus clenched his fists, crouching down with a shout of victory as Kieran landed back on solid ground. The rest of the team rushed their captain, Eric leaping into the air to land on

Kieran's back, Aaron and the rest of the guys from the bench running onto the court to join the pile of bodies that were smothering Kieran. Atticus crossed the court in a heartbeat, jumping into the fray with a howling whoop.

Excitement made the air feel charged, static victory filling the room, rushing into his lungs with every breath he sucked in. The fans were spilling onto the floor as the team broke away from one another, crowding around them with shouts of congratulations.

Bowen appeared before him suddenly, face a mask of joy as he tugged Atticus into a bear hug.

"We did it," he said, voice too loud in Atticus' ear. He didn't care, because he was just as happy. "We did it, man!"

"You set us up with that dig," Atticus said, pulling back. "You gave me time to think."

Something shifted in Bowen's expression, and he leaned back in close, a hand on the back of Atticus' neck holding him in place while another gripped his bicep.

"I'm sorry," Bowen said, the words just for Atticus. "I shouldn't have fucked with you before the game. It's my fault you played like shit in the first two sets."

"Fuck you." Atticus couldn't keep the grin off his face. "I played just fine."

"Keep telling yourself that," Bowen said with a laugh, pushing dark hair away from his face. "I mean it, though. I was an ass, and you're my friend. I don't give a fuck who you do or don't sleep with, it doesn't matter. You're important to this team, to all of us, and I need to learn how to keep my mouth shut and my nose out of your business."

"Thanks," Atticus said, his smile going soft. He could see sincerity in his teammate's expression. "I mean it. Thank you."

Bowen smiled brightly at him. "Your sister is coming this way, you better go." And that was that. A weight lifted, one that Atticus hadn't even realized he was holding. Maybe his team did see him for who he was. Maybe it didn't matter if he'd slept around in the past, maybe they judged him for it less than he assumed.

Atticus felt as if he were floating, riding a high he might never come down from, as he turned to see his sister jogging toward him. Sammie slammed into him, her arms going around his neck as he squeezed her tight, lifting her off the ground to twirl her around.

"You had me worried," she said, voice muffled against his shoulder. "Your head was in your ass for the first two sets."

Atticus dropped her, and she landed with an *oof*.

"Why does everyone keep saying that?" He knew, though. Atticus knew exactly why he'd been half-distracted for the first half of the game. His eyes searched past Sammie, scanning the faces of the milling crowd.

"He left."

Stones settled in Atticus' stomach. Had Kai not wanted to see him after the game? The thought rang false. Kai had smiled at him. Kai had come to the game, even after Atticus had done his best to ruin everything between them.

"It's not like that," Sammie continued. "Fuck, you look like a kicked puppy right now."

Atticus frowned. "What's it like then?"

The celebratory gleam left his sister's eyes, her face falling. "He had to leave. Something happened with his ex. The guy on St. Louis called and asked Kai to go to the hospital with him."

A conflicting swirl of emotions twisted in his gut as Atticus listened. Something had happened to Nicholas? Atticus didn't really know the guy. Ori was the only friend they had in common, and Atticus had been asked once to participate in a day-long training event for kids, with Ori, in conjunction with Nicholas' organization.

Kai never really talked to him about Nicholas.

Atticus knew it was absurd to be jealous, knew that it probably meant he was a piece of shit. The guy was hurt, enough to warrant a hospital visit, and Atticus was fighting back jealousy that Kai had decided to go see him. Truly loser behavior.

"Kai came here to see you," Sammie said, gripping Atticus' hand, leaning in close as people began to leave the court. "He was here for you. He didn't say much, but I know you, and I know you must have done something that has you thinking you've screwed it all up. He was here though, Attie. He was here for you."

Atticus' jaw clenched as he fought back emotions that were too big, too overwhelming, too loud to let out in front of everyone. Sammie pulled him into another hug.

"You'll be fine," she said. "Give it a bit and then check on him. He looked pretty upset when he left."

"Thank you," Atticus whispered into her hair.

"That set was perfect." Kieran's voice had them pulling apart. Atticus felt his sister go stiff as she stepped away from him.

"Only because you were ready for it," Atticus said, pushing aside the turmoil churning inside to smile brightly at his teammate.

"Hey, Sammie." Kieran gave her a fond grin, leaning in to wrap an arm around her shoulders and pull her in for a side hug. Atticus nearly flinched at the sight of it. He might need to pass his friend-zone crown along to his sister, if he could work out the mess he'd made with Kai.

"Come on, you two," Kieran said, stepping away from Sammie, who had gone quiet and, Atticus thought, looked a little petulant. "Let's go celebrate."

They followed the rest of the team toward the locker room to change, Sammie making a hasty exit to ride to the bar with

Ivy, saying she'd meet them there. She left Atticus with a meaningful look, prompting him to pull out his phone as he snatched up his gym bag.

Kai had left the game to be with Nicholas. Atticus knew it was silly to be so scared, to think that he had missed his chance because of their fight that morning. But the more he thought about it, the more he began to realize that he wasn't scared about that, not really.

He was scared because, one way or another, things were going to change. They had reached a tipping point, one that was unavoidable, one that would lead them in a new direction regardless of anything Atticus did.

His phone felt heavy in his hand. Sammie was right. He needed to say something, anything to Kai. But what if it went wrong? Atticus hesitated before slipping his phone back into his bag. He would wait, just a bit. He would ride the high of their win, enjoy a night out with his friends, and then he would contact Kai.

Atticus wanted to hold on to his hope, to the memory of that small smile he had seen on the sidelines, for just a while longer.

15

Kai kept himself from stealing another glance at the man sitting next to him. He didn't need to look again to know that Theo was still a wreck. The fear and anguish radiating off of him were enough to tell, seeping into Kai more with every passing second.

Nicholas was in surgery. The car accident had been bad. *Really* bad. The other driver had been texting, had blown through a stoplight, t-boning Nicholas' vehicle on the driver's side. They'd had to cut him out of the car. Nicholas hadn't been awake, and Theo had only seen him for a few moments before he'd been rushed into surgery.

"I'm going to get some water, want some?" Kai kept his voice soft, but it was still enough to startle Theo. The waiting room had been crowded when they'd been ushered into it a half hour earlier. They'd taken the only two seats available, had sat together in silence.

Theo looked up at him, eyes wide behind his glasses. His pale skin was still drained of all color, had been since the moment Kai had met him outside of the stadium. He pushed his disheveled hair back from his face, tugging at the sleeves of his polyester team jacket as he nodded at Kai.

"Yeah," he finally said. He sounded so distant, eyes unfocused even as they tried to meet Kai's. "Yeah, thanks."

Kai walked down the hall to the vending machine. When he returned to the waiting room, two bottles of water in hand, it became apparent that many of the others who had been milling about the room when he and Theo had arrived had disappeared. The waiting room was empty save for a couple on the opposite side and Theo.

He decided to return to the same seat when he saw the way Theo was cradling his head in his hands, elbows braced on his knees, shoulders slumped in defeat. It felt wrong to sit further away. Theo had been his friend once. Somehow, this time, Kai had ended up being the steady one. The one holding it together.

Kai sat back down slowly, giving Theo a moment before tapping him on the arm. When he finally looked up, his eyes were watery and red. He took the proffered water bottle, nodding in thanks, and the two of them returned to their uneasy silence.

It was cold in the waiting room, cold in the entire hospital. Kai still wore the button up he'd put on that morning, and the thin material wasn't enough to keep a chill from sinking in. He fought the urge to pull his legs up into the chair, to curl into himself.

He watched Theo drink his water slowly, hand shaking slightly as he brought the bottle to his lips. The same question that had run through his mind a thousand times since he'd ended their last call flashed in his head again.

Why had Theo called him? Why had he wanted Kai here with him?

Kai hadn't asked. It had seemed so unimportant initially, when every thought had only been for whether or not Nicholas would be okay. Something they still didn't have a definitive answer to. His life wasn't in danger, but Theo had described just how bad the injuries had looked. Bruises marring so much of Nicholas' skin, blood staining his torn clothes. And now... well, now Kai really just felt like it didn't matter why Theo had asked him to come. Because Kai wanted to be there, in that cold waiting room, fluorescent lights flickering above them.

He needed to be there.

"Did you let anyone else know?" Kai asked softly. Theo's distant gaze focused a bit as he thought for several moments.

"No," he finally said, shaking his head. "Coach said he would tell the team. I didn't... I just saw your name on my call history, I couldn't think straight. I probably should... Ori..."

Kai pulled out his phone, typing quickly. "I'll let him know."

"Thanks."

Kai shrugged as he typed out another message. "You don't have to keep thanking me." He sent several more texts to mutual friends, attention focused wholly on the task. When he finally clicked his phone off and looked up, Theo was watching him intently.

"I wasn't sure if you would come," he said. Kai wanted to squirm under the attention. "But I saw your name on my phone and all I could think was that he would want you to be here."

The words made something wrench in Kai's chest.

"I'm glad you called," he murmured. Theo's considering gaze continued to bore into him.

"I should apologize," Theo said, voice quiet as he finally looked away. "For the things I said to you."

Kai stilled.

You were friends more than anything.

A relationship that was always going to end anyway.

The words had plagued Kai, had run through his head over the last several days more times than he could count. But as he heard them in his mind once again, all of the sting seemed to be gone. They no longer felt so sharp, no longer pierced down to the deepest parts of him.

No, now that Kai had been faced with the idea of truly never seeing Nicholas again... it all felt so small. So insignificant.

"You don't need to apologize," Kai said. He still felt nervous talking to Theo, but managed to keep it from sounding through in his words.

"I do," Theo replied quickly. He sucked in a deep, shaky breath. "I shouldn't have called you like that. I'm sorry for all of the things I said. You set a boundary with Nicholas, and I crossed it. You have every right to hate me, and you're here anyway. You're a better friend than I ever was, and I'm sorry for hurting you. For ever hurting you. So again, thank you."

Kai could feel his cheeks heating. He was embarrassed by the words and didn't know why. Theo's attention on him like this, his apology and the clear gratitude, it felt like too much. Kai didn't know how to respond other than a whispered, "Thank you."

"He was so mad at me," Theo continued. His voice had turned shaky, sounded too full in the small, quiet room. "When he found out I called you, when I told him what I said. He's never been that angry with me before. The last few days have been so tense because of it, because of *me* and now..."

He cut off, choking on the words. Kai held his breath as Theo slumped forward, shoulders shaking as he sniffled, fighting back a sob with a fist pressed to his mouth, eyes squeezed shut.

Kai never knew what to do with crying people. It always made him feel awkward, to see so much emotion expressed.

It made him feel inadequate, ill-prepared to handle it.

"He's going to be okay," he finally said, stretching out a hand in an attempt at comfort, stiffly patting Theo on the back.

"I know," Theo said, wiping at the fresh tears spilling down his cheeks. "But I only got to see him for a few seconds before they took him back. He looked so broken. He didn't look like *Nicholas*. And all I could think of was what if it had been worse. What if our last days together were spent fighting."

The words landed uncomfortably on Kai. Tugged at a part of him that felt a similar regret. A regret for how things had been left for so long between himself and Nicholas, yes. But also for that morning. For how Kai had left Atticus with hateful words and a detached goodbye.

He also couldn't help but see the depth of Theo's grief. When Kai had received the call, when he'd rushed to the hospital, he had been terrified. All of the feelings of loss that he'd let simmer for the last year, all of the anger and pain, all of it fell away at the idea of Nicholas' life being in danger. Kai had only felt terror, a mirror to Theo's own at how things had been left between them.

But the grief he saw there on Theo's face? The agony lacing his posture, crumpling him under its pressure? Kai's own fear paled in comparison. It was clear as a full moon on a cloudless night that the thought of losing Nicholas was more than Theo could handle.

Kai had been able to shut Nicholas out for a year. He had been miserable the entire time, but he had survived. He had found purpose in other things. His job, his friends. It suddenly all seemed so uncomplicated. Kai had been grieving the loss of their relationship, the loss of the life he'd wanted with his whole heart, but he had managed. In the end, he had been okay.

The devastation bleeding out of Theo at even the thought of losing Nicholas... Kai's own pain just couldn't compare. Nicholas was something Theo couldn't fathom living without.

Kai had chosen to live without him.

He had chosen to never respond to Nicholas. Had chosen to shut him out completely. Had shoved away the friendship they'd had for so long. And he knew, *he knew*, that he had every right to do that. Kai knew that friendships didn't always survive.

But he had never really given their's a fighting chance, had he? He knew that they could never go back to what they had been before their relationship. That magical childhood friendship, cursed by nostalgia and beautiful memories. They could never have that again. But Kai had never even given Nicholas, or even himself, a chance to see if they could have anything at all after the end. If they could function around one another, rather than being the cracks that severed their friend group down the middle. Kai had loved Nicholas, but apparently hadn't loved him enough to accept having less of him.

Theo seemed to be getting himself back under control, settling once again into the tense, waiting silence they'd grown used to. It was Kai's turn to fall apart.

Soft, silent tears slipped past his lashes. He lost all care for propriety as he pulled his legs into the chair, wrapping his arms tight around his knees, making himself as small as possible.

He had always only blamed Nicholas for the loss of their relationship. And it was true, Nicholas had been the one to end things between them romantically. But he had wanted to talk. He had wanted to keep Kai in his life. And Kai was the one who had refused to even try.

But that was normal, wasn't it? People didn't stay friends

after messy breakups. And it was unreasonable for Nicholas to ever think that was possible. But closure... closure was a different story. And suddenly, Kai realized that closure was something that was missing from his narrative. Something that Nicholas had offered up, but he himself had refused to entertain.

"He's going to be okay." Theo echoed Kai's words in a whisper, but there was confidence there. A surety that Nicholas *would* be fine, that he would make it through the other side of this. That he would still be there in their lives.

It wasn't long before a doctor entered the room, summoning Theo. Kai watched as his old friend walked stiffly across the room, stepping into the hallway with the doctor to speak privately. Kai's heartbeat seemed so loud, nearly painful in his chest as he waited for Theo to return.

When he finally did walk back into the room, Kai could tell from his expression, before he spoke even a single word, that Nicholas was going to be just fine.

"He's out of surgery," Theo said. The smile lighting his face was beautiful, an expression Kai had rarely seen on him. "Everything went well. His shoulder is pretty messed up. Multiple fractures, they had to put pins in. And he suffered a concussion. But he's going to be okay."

Theo pulled off his glasses, wiping at his eyes once again as he stood before Kai.

"When can we see him?" The question felt so small. His voice sounded distant even to his own ears. What if Nicholas didn't want to see him?

Now that Kai wanted to be there, wanted to see with his own eyes that his childhood friend was okay, what if it was too late?

"The doctor said I can go ahead and go back to his room. He's starting to wake up," Theo said. A long, heavy pause weighed between them. Kai felt as though he were teetering on a cliff's edge. Theo watched him intently before something in his gaze softened.

"I can text you," he continued. "Let you know when he's ready for you to come in, if that's okay?"

Kai nodded, a fresh sting building in his eyes. "Yeah. That would be good."

Theo watched him before turning to leave the cold waiting room. He paused in the doorway.

"He'll be really happy that you're here. I'm happy you're here."

The words settled on Kai slowly as Theo finally left. They sank into his skin, warming every part of him.

Kai's grip on his knees relaxed even as a slight nervousness sparked inside him. He took a deep breath, holding it in until his chest burned, releasing it slowly through his nose. Kai sat silently as he waited to finally have a conversation with Nicholas that was long overdue.

Nicholas slept soundly in the hospital bed. The blood had been cleaned away from his skin, but bruises still peppered his face. His hair though? Just as wild as ever, untamed even by life-threatening ordeals and the most determined of nurses.

Kai played on his phone, curled up in a chair in the corner of the small room. Theo sat next to the bed. He'd sent Kai a message, letting him know that Nicholas was falling back asleep but that Kai was welcome to come sit with him.

It was warmer in the room. Less of the oppressive chill that had been blanketing Kai for the hours that he'd been there, soaking into his bones.

He still wished he had something warmer to wear.

A quick glance showed that neither of the men across the

room had moved since he'd last looked up. Kai had been sitting there for almost an hour, and the entire time he had been watching. Observing. Noticing small things.

The way Theo leaned slightly in his chair, as though his body were drawn by some invisible force toward the man lying injured in the bed. The way one hand held his phone, scrolling mindlessly, while the other always remained touching Nicholas in some way. Fingers trailing lightly along his arm, down across his open palm, back up again. Every so often Kai would catch Theo watching Nicholas, phone held forgotten, something soft written across his features.

Kai hadn't truly spoken to Nicholas in a year, and Theo couldn't go five seconds without touching him, seeing him. Reassuring himself that Nicholas was there, alive and breathing.

It made something in Kai's stomach wriggle. Uncomfortable, but not for the reasons he would have expected. No, as he examined the feeling, as he watched Theo display just how much he cared for Nicholas, Kai found himself unsettled by the fact that he hadn't expected it. He had convinced himself for so long that no one could love Nicholas the way he had.

And maybe that was true. Maybe that would always be true. But that just meant that Theo's love for the man was different. And, much to Kai's surprise, it felt right.

He was less bothered by that thought than he had ever been.

The rasp of a blanket shifting pulled Kai out of his head. He looked up from his phone to see Nicholas moving, his body turned slightly toward Theo as he groggily tried to sit up. Theo was up in a heartbeat, whispering a soft, "Be careful," letting out a sharp *tsk* when Nicholas ignored the warning. Once Theo had helped him into a more upright position, carefully arranging the pillow behind his back, he tapped Nicholas' unharmed shoulder gently and nodded in Kai's direction.

Kai felt as if the world slowed down, as though gravity might lose its hold on him. His limbs felt light, detached, while his insides seemed ready to revolt. Nicholas met his gaze. It took him a moment to register the situation. To understand what he was seeing.

One of the broken pieces in Kai, one of the shattered bits that had cracked so permanently on that night a year earlier, snapped back into place as Nicholas smiled his cheshire grin.

"Kai!"

His voice was hoarse. It sounded as broken as he looked, but there was still something so familiar there, in the way he said Kai's name. A comfort that Kai hadn't felt in a long time.

"Nicky." Kai's own voice came out as hardly more than a whisper, the nickname falling from his lips like an impulse. The other man's eyes went wide, his gaze turning a little watery.

"I'm going to go get some coffee," Theo said, voice quiet but more steady than Kai had heard it since they'd left the stadium. He leaned down, brushing his lips over Nicholas' cheek, a hand squeezing the back of his neck lightly. Nicholas' smile faded into something more tender as he leaned into the touches, his eyes slipping closed. He reached out, squeezing Theo's hand before he pulled away to leave the room.

Suddenly, it was just the two of them. Alone again after so much time had passed. Kai felt as though a part of him had been transported back to that last night they'd been together. He was curled up in the chair the same way he had been curled in on himself on their couch.

"I-," Nicholas began, choking on the word. He looked down at his hand, the one that lay unbandaged in his lap. Kai watched his fingers tighten into a fist, as if maybe the motion could steady him. Nicholas looked back up, meeting Kai's stare. "I'm really glad you're here."

Kai didn't know what to say. He'd had hours to come up with something, anything to say when Nicholas woke. He still felt just as lost for words as he had a year ago. He settled on a small nod.

"Theo told me he called you first," Nicholas continued. Kai was desperate to look away, to focus his eyes on anything else in the room, but found it impossible not to return Nicholas' gaze. Like they were locked in this together until it was all finally over. "He was surprised you even answered the phone. Thank you for being here with him."

Another small nod, apparently all the response Kai was capable of giving. But it seemed to be enough for Nicholas, emboldening him to keep going.

"I know he already apologized," Nicholas said, his brow furrowing over one blackened eye. "About calling you the other day. But I'm sorry too."

A weight settled over the room. Kai felt it acutely, something heavy pressing down on him, holding him in place. Keeping him from running away.

Nicholas' eyes were still so beautiful, a hazel-grey that Kai had lost himself in so many times. Sharp, knowing, sometimes teasing. They had never had trouble meeting each other's gaze.

It was almost the same now. Almost. The eyes Kai had been avoiding for so long met his without hesitation, and he found a twisted comfort in looking back. A simplicity threaded between them, tying them together in a way that Kai had thought long-severed.

The thread was frayed though, and would be forevermore.

"I'm sorry for all of it, Kai." Nicholas was watching him intently, waiting for any sign that he needed to stop, needed to slow down. A part of Kai thought that maybe the timing was all wrong, that maybe Nicholas didn't need to be having this conversation when he'd been close to dying just hours earlier. Or maybe that meant there was no better time to say the things he was finally saying.

"I hurt you," he continued. Kai held his breath. "I hurt you so much and there was nothing I could do to fix it. Nothing I can do now to take it back. Nothing I can do to get back the time we lost, the time I gave up."

And there it was again, the same familiar pressure, filling Kai from the inside out, threatening to burst him wide open while holding him silent. Words, any words at all, felt so far out of reach, his mind spinning too fast for him to catch on to any single thought.

It was the same as before. Nicholas, good and strong, always willing to talk things out. Kai, incapable of matching him, no matter if he wanted to. It was a physical response that he would do anything to leave behind, anything to break free from.

One shaking breath, then another.

Kai remembered how Atticus had looked at him that morning. It felt so far away now, something that had happened in a different lifetime. Atticus, words and eyes pleading for Kai to stay, for Kai to just *talk* to him.

Kai wished he had.

"I never gave us a chance to say anything," Kai said softly, the words too big and oh so painful to push out. But once they had left him... something shifted. A weight slipping away, through a door that had long seemed locked closed. Impulse had him tangling his fingers together as he lowered his legs from the chair, settling his feet on the floor to further ground himself. Nicholas shook his head.

"It's not exactly abnormal for someone to cut an ex out of their life. You had every right to never speak to me again. You still do."

That jabbed at him. It still hurt, that loss. The idea that Nicholas wasn't a part of his life anymore, that they both knew it would most likely always be that way between them. But even more so, it confused him.

Was he going to let Nicholas back in? Kai felt as if his entire perspective had shifted in those few seconds he'd spent on the phone with Theo before rushing to the hospital. He could have lost Nicholas in a wholly different way, in a way they truly never could have come back from. But that didn't make the hurt disappear. That didn't change the fact that Nicholas had upended Kai's entire life in a way that left him irreparably shattered.

"I thought about you every day," Nicholas said softly, pulling Kai back to their conversation. "I knew what I was doing when I ended things, but a part of me had hoped that we could still be friends. I never let go of that hope."

Kai could see it there, in those beautiful, sad eyes. The hope that maybe there was still a chance. It brought back words that Kai had stored away, had kept as a hidden treasure in the back of his mind.

You're a part of me, of who I am. You're there in every decision I make. You're my best friend, just because we're together less doesn't mean I'll ever forget about you.

Words spoken by a young boy that Kai had already loved with his whole heart. Words that had haunted him over their years apart, when they'd rang so untrue.

And there was the crux of the issue. For Kai, it had never been about friendship. For so, so long, it had been about something... not more. Something else entirely.

The same realization that had been buffeting him for the last year poked at him again. Nicholas had never loved Kai as much as Kai had loved him. For some reason, it stung less this time. A slight discomfort, so different from the rending ache that had torn him to shreds for so long.

It hurt less, so much so that Kai couldn't help but wonder if what Nicholas was asking for really was so impossible. Even still, the pain *had* been real. So real that Kai hadn't thought himself strong enough to recover. So real that it had trapped him in a cage, the key hidden with the one person he'd least wanted to see. Kai felt like he was fighting a war within himself. His hand clenched into fists.

"You hurt me." The things he had held in for so long finally spilled from his lips, and oh, their release was a freedom Kai hadn't known he desperately needed. "You took everything from me. Our whole life disappeared, and I had to watch you move on, with our *friend*, as though it meant nothing."

Nicholas finally looked away, as if he couldn't handle the weight of Kai's stare, the weight of his words. He took a steadying breath before looking back. "I know."

"I'm still so angry," Kai continued. He was letting it all loose, a train speeding off the tracks, barreling through every wall he had constructed to hide himself away. The words that had always eluded him fell freely from his lips, and Kai felt unshackled in a way he never had before. "It still hurts so much, and the worst part is that I..."

A lump rose in Kai's throat, forcing him to pause. He swallowed dryly, clenching his jaw and sucking in a sharp breath through his nose before he could continue.

"The worst part is that I miss you. I can't stop missing you. I've tried and I've tried but I just can't do it. I miss how easy things seemed, even though I know they weren't, not for a long time. I miss the routine, I miss always knowing what to expect. I miss our group. It was always just the four of us against the world, but you shattered that. You and Theo both did."

Kai felt wetness on his cheeks, mirroring the silent tears he watched fall from Nicholas' eyes. But it was good, it was *right*. The cage Kai had finally freed himself from slammed shut behind him, and he would be damned if he ever let himself be caught by it again.

"It can't be the same, Nicky," he finally continued. "It can never be the same."

Because sometimes things ended. Sometimes they found their conclusion, natural or not. And that didn't take away the beauty of what they were, what they had been at their brightest times. It only served to make them all the more special, even if they only lasted for a brief moment. Even if losing them hurt like nothing else.

Kai's chest felt tight, his words threatening to hide from him again as he came down from the high of his little speech. He wiped at his eyes, forcing down a sob. "It won't be the same. It can't be." For more reasons than his oldest friend was even aware of.

Nicholas shook his head, and Kai could see resignation in his eyes, a flame finally flickering out. But there was something else there, something that mirrored the newfound calm that was building within Kai.

Closure. Closure that had been long overdue for both of them.

Soft, tear-stained laughter pulled Kai's attention back up. He looked to see Nicholas smiling gently, a familiar, teasing tilt to his lips.

"Maybe I should have gotten into a life-threatening ordeal sooner," Nicholas said. "It finally forced us to talk."

"Don't say that," Kai mumbled, even as appreciation bloomed in him at the word *us*. Nicholas had always been willing to talk, had always been willing to find the closure they had so desperately needed. Kai had been the only one holding them back from finding this precious relief. "For what it's worth, I'm glad you're okay."

Kai's phone screen lit up in his lap a moment later, and he

stared at it for several long heartbeats.

"Kai?"

A tentative worry laced Nicholas' voice, but Kai couldn't force his attention away from the message displayed on his screen.

Atticus: I heard about nicholas. Let me know if there's anything I can do. Sorry for this morning.

It wasn't the short, choppy sort of text Atticus usually conversed with. Reading the words, Kai pictured a puppy slinking back after being scolded. It made something squeeze tight in his chest.

"Are you okay?"

Kai finally looked up. He didn't know what all was written across his face, but whatever it was had Nicholas raising his brows.

"It's nothing," Kai said, locking his phone screen. That nothing was swirling inside him, a thousand different thoughts and feelings mixing together, washing through Kai faster than he could keep up with.

"Uh huh," Nicholas said, smirking, falling back into the persona Kai had known so well with ease. They sat in silence for several heartbeats. Kai's eyes flicked toward his phone again, pulling a chuckle from across the room.

"Do you need to respond to it?"

Kai frowned. "It can wait."

"Hmmm." Nichols looked away, his gaze falling on the seat that Theo had been occupying. "Is it Mills?"

The name shot through Kai like an arrow. His silence must have been answer enough.

"You two looked good together at the party," Nicholas continued, fixing Kai with a steady stare. "He obviously cares about you a lot."

"Just because I don't want you to die, that doesn't mean I want to talk to you about…" Kai floundered, waving his hands helplessly. Were they doing this, really? They hadn't spoken, not really, in a year, and Nicholas wanted to talk to him about Atticus?

"Are you guys…" Nicholas let the question trail off.

Kai frowned. "I don't know what we are." The words were true. Kai had no idea what he was to Atticus, what he wanted to be to Atticus. It was the question that had haunted him for days, the question that had led to their fight that morning. "Right now I don't think we're anything."

And maybe all of the terrible things that had happened that day were finally coming to a head, or maybe it was just leftover tears from his conversation with Nicholas, but Kai felt a tingling in his nose as his vision began to blur. He blinked hard, willing himself not to cry again.

"I think you should respond to him," Nicholas said softly.

Kai leveled him with a hard stare, barely kept himself from slinging a harsh retort. Nicholas shrugged his uninjured shoulder.

"I'm probably overstepping," he continued. "But you've never been all that good at talking about the hard stuff. You're a whole lot better at running away from it all." A pause, and Kai could feel a final punch coming. "Could you go a year without talking to him?"

A simmering annoyance washed over Kai. Nicholas wasn't being fair. The situation was far from the same as their own, and he'd even said earlier that Kai had been well within his rights to cut Nicholas out of his life for so long. And Kai hadn't *asked* for his opinion. They were nowhere near ready to go back to the easy friendship they'd shared in the past. It felt like too much too suddenly, and a loud, burning part of Kai wanted to shut down the conversation, to tell Nicholas that he had, indeed, overstepped.

But the question echoed in his head like an unending, rhythmic beat. Could he go that long without speaking to Atticus?

The answer was so obvious. Since the night they'd met, since they'd first developed a friendship, Kai had talked to Atticus every day. It wasn't always about the important stuff. More often than not it was to see if the other man was up for playing some game online together. An easy camaraderie that had been like a steady thread woven into the last six months of his life.

And now, after spending a week with Atticus, after waking up to see him smiling every morning in the kitchen, after watching sleepy eyes crinkle with a goodnight at the end of every day, after all of the moments in between...

The thought of going any longer without speaking to Atticus made Kai feel as though his entire world were being ripped away.

The churning in his gut was so similar to how he'd felt a year prior, when Nicholas had left and the only future Kai had ever seen had disappeared.

What if it was happening again? What if Kai had fucked it all up, had pushed Atticus away only to lose him for good? To lose whatever possible future was out there for them?

"I can't," Kai whispered, the words falling from him unbidden. They were true. Kai couldn't fathom the idea of cutting Atticus out the way he had done with Nicholas.

"Then don't," Nicholas said, shrugging again.

"It's not that simple." But wasn't it? Julian's words from earlier echoed through him.

Atticus is not going to move on from you. Not after one hard day.

Was he right? They had said such awful things to one another. Atticus had said he was going to move on, as if Kai had missed his chance. What if he put himself out there, tried to fix it, and lost it all anyway?

A moment from the game flashed across his vision, blocking out all else, halting his spiraling thoughts. Atticus at the end line, readying for a serve. Their eyes had met for the briefest of moments, but Kai's heart had nearly stopped when Atticus had seen him sitting in the stands. Those pretty blue eyes had gone wide, sparkling under the bright gym lights. His smile had been tentative, questioning, maybe even a little fearful. But it had been just for Kai, and it had been one of the most stunning things he had ever seen.

Kai clicked his phone on, pulling up the message again. He reread the words, over and over until they were a permanent image seared into his mind. Maybe this was the first step. Maybe Atticus had already taken it, and was offering a hand, waiting for Kai to grab on.

"I need to respond," Kai said, his voice steadier than he felt. Nicholas smiled at him, his expression soft, understanding held in his gaze. Kai could feel his own face pinch as he thought hard about what to say. His fingers typed out each word slowly.

Kai: Thanks. He's going to be okay. I'm going to stay at the hospital until some of his test results come back
Kai: I'm sorry too. Can we talk after all of this?

Anxiety coursed through Kai as he pressed send for each message. A shaky breath escaped him and he dropped his phone into his lap, staring at it wide-eyed.

He'd done his part. Put himself out there, asked for what he wanted. Because it *was* what he wanted, wasn't it? Even if Kai didn't know yet exactly where he wanted it all to go, didn't know how to say what it was he was feeling toward the other man, he did know that he wasn't willing to lose him. He knew with a certainty that whatever hard stuff came with the conversation he'd just asked for, it would be worth it if he could keep Atticus in his life.

Kai nearly jumped out of his seat as an immediate response buzzed in his lap.

Atticus: Of course :) take all the time you need, I'll be waiting

It was late when Kai got home. Hospitals were always draining, even without all the extra emotional labor piled on top. He only stopped to brush his teeth before dragging himself to his bedroom.

Changing into pajamas was an arduous task. Sleep tugged at him, his eyelids too heavy to hold open as he pulled clothes out of his dresser, pausing when a particular item caught his eye.

Kai pulled out his old high school team hoodie, worn and faded red fabric with his name emblazoned in black letters across the back. It had been tainted by memories of playing with Nicholas, of always having the boy he loved ready for one of his sets, and Kai hadn't been able to bring himself to wear it for so long. But now, looking at... now it just seemed like any other hoodie.

He slipped it on, pulling on a matching pair of sweatpants before crawling into his bed. Kai burrowed under the covers, curling in on himself and letting the warmth of being home soak into his bones, lulling him closer and closer to sleep. He pulled his hands into the sleeves of the hoodie, fingers curling into the cuffs, just like how he'd longed to do all day.

It wasn't quite right though. The fabric wasn't as soft, the fit not as large as the one Atticus had given him.

Kai's last thought before falling asleep was that he would need to remember to ask Atticus if he could have his hoodie back.

6 Months Ago

Atticus shifted back and forth, bouncing from one foot to the other as he waited. He couldn't seem to keep still.

Was he nervous?

He didn't *get* nervous. Not for dates. But why did he feel like his insides might float right out of him?

Atticus checked his phone for what was probably the thousandth time, stepping closer to the building. No new notifications, and only two minutes had passed since he'd last looked. He exhaled slowly, breath puffing visibly before him in the chill night air.

Not only did Atticus not get nervous for dates, but he was also *never* early for them. Except this time he had been. Half an hour early, to be precise.

Maybe it was because he had no clue what they were going to do? Well, he sort of had an idea, since he'd been standing and waiting outside of what was clearly an arcade-slash-laser tag center. Atticus had triple checked the address. He was at the right place.

He didn't mind giving up control. He just wasn't usually asked to. But when his date had sent him a text with nothing more than *I'll take care of the plans*, it had made Atticus feel a little giddy. A little more excited than he normally felt for a first date.

He forced himself to put his phone away, swearing that he wouldn't look at it again. There were only a couple minutes left until their agreed upon meeting time anyway. Atticus slipped his hands into his coat pockets, glancing around at his surroundings, looking for a face he'd only ever seen on a screen.

People passed by, barely sparing him a glance as they went about their night. A few walked right by him, entering the arcade. Atticus wondered if any of them were also on a first date. If they, too, had butterflies in their stomachs and silly smiles trying to spread across their faces. Was he the only one feeling such nervous anticipation?

Maybe Atticus was so anxious because he kept thinking about it as a *first* date. He didn't really do second dates. Not for a long time. He'd had a sort of thing going with his teammate, Orion Harper, but that had been more of a friends-with-benefits situation, no feelings attached. Just how he liked it. Atticus wasn't really made for the long haul kind of relationships. It was more fun to live in the moment, to have a taste, to always be ready to see what else the world had to offer.

But this time... he really was already looking forward to a second date. Which was silly, because the first one hadn't happened yet. They hadn't even met in person. Atticus thought that he was probably being a little ridiculous, but he also thought that he probably didn't care.

A flash of a familiar hairstyle, black with teal ends, caught his eye as he continued to scan the sidewalk. Those butterflies in his stomach seemed to go into overdrive. Atticus could feel a flush building on his cheeks and hoped desperately that the cold would be a good enough excuse for it. A pair of wide amber-gold eyes met his own.

NotYourKitten- *no*, Kai, Kai Reid, Atticus needed to stop thinking of him by his gamer tag- looked gorgeous. An oversized, simple gray hoodie, big enough to show off the sharp points of his collarbone. Fitted black joggers that had Atticus wishing the hoodie was a little smaller and didn't fall quite so far past his waist. Kai had told him to dress in something comfy, but Atticus was pretty sure he didn't look *that* good in athletic wear. His own joggers and t-shirt outfit suddenly felt inadequate.

A small smile played on Kai's lips as he approached. His two-toned hair was pulled back, tied into a messy bun at the nape of his neck, shorter strands escaping to frame his face.

"Uh," Atticus began. "Hi Kai." He grinned to mask the horrifying embarrassment of his eloquent greeting.

Kai stopped before him, standing just far enough to be out of reach, but close enough that Atticus could see that his cheeks were also a little pink. Good, so the cold *would* hide his mortification.

"Hey," Kai said with a smirk. Atticus felt so awkward. He'd been looking forward to this date for two weeks, but he felt lost at how to proceed. Should they shake hands? A hug? Why was he flailing, Atticus *never* flailed on dates. He was charming, he knew how to talk to people. Why did this feel so different, so much more significant?

"Nice to finally meet you," was all he could settle on, a crooked grin pulling at his cheeks. Kai watched him, gaze steady and scrutinizing, that small smirk still playing on his lips. It made Atticus want to squirm. He looked down, biting his lip before continuing. "So, laser tag?"

"Yeah," Kai said. "Come on."

Atticus followed him in. They walked close, arms not quite brushing with every step.

"Do you always bring your dates here?" Atticus asked. Kai looked up, considering him for a moment.

"No," he finally said, pulling out his wallet to pay for their game. "But you seem fun."

Atticus could no longer fight back his full grin. He liked that, the fact that Kai already thought he was fun. They'd never officially met in person, had only talked through text or while they played games together, after Ori had introduced them. And there was that one time Atticus had literally run into Kai at a house party. That was it, the whole extent of their relationship. But somehow he'd already done enough to show Kai a side of himself that he really enjoyed. It felt important, like a step in the right direction toward getting that second date.

"Not really great for talking though," Atticus teased as they picked out their gear. "How're we gonna get to know each other while we do this?"

Kai rolled his eyes, but his expression was still light. "Is that not what we've been doing the last few weeks?"

"Well, yeah, but how am I going to charm you if I'm running around a dark room shooting at you?"

Kai's eyes narrowed, looking at Atticus in a way that made something low in his belly start to burn. "Guess you just have to figure something out."

Atticus watched as Kai strapped on his vest and carefully picked up his infrared gun. He glanced around before putting a hand on Atticus' chest and pushing him back a couple of steps.

"Other team," Kai said simply.

"Aww! C'mon," Atticus cried, flinging his arms in the air. "Don't you wanna see how well we work together?"

Kai rested his gun on his shoulder and *fuck* it was really hot. He gestured toward the rest of the players getting ready.

"Wouldn't really be fair if we're both on the same team."

Atticus looked around. Kai had a point. They did seem to be the only adults playing this round. He sighed dramatically, earning another eye roll from the other man. Atticus kind of liked trying to pull those out of him. Felt like something he might want to make a habit of.

"Fine," he said, pouting. "But I'm gonna rally the troops and we'll kick your team's ass."

"You can try," Kai said with a wink- *a wink*- before turning away to listen to the instructor.

Kai was right. This was going to be *fun*.

A bead of sweat dripped down the side of Atticus' face as he crouched low in the shadows. He was posted up in a small, boxy space under a landing, his gaze trained out of a small, cut-out window.

He was maybe taking the game a little too serious.

Before the timer had finished counting down for them to begin, Atticus had indeed rallied the children surrounding him. It hadn't taken much, they were all excited to play, and Atticus' enthusiasm had only fed that fire, kicked it up into a frenzied blaze. In seconds, he had them hanging from his every word, astonished stares fixed on him as though he were leading them into the greatest battle of their lives. He outlined a quick strategy, handed out assignments, gave an impassioned speech, and sent the little monsters off. They had scattered into the dark with a war cry, and Atticus couldn't help but join in.

He knew Kai had been watching, had been paying attention. He'd seen the affectionate smile he was failing to hide.

Atticus had found his place quickly, had stationed himself in the little box that he barely had room to stand up straight in. And then, over the course of several minutes, he began to snipe Kai's teammates, picking them off one-by-one. Youthful cries of frustration sounded off with each hit, but none of the kids could seem to figure out where the shots were coming from.

There was a problem though. Atticus shifted slightly, giving himself a better view of the playing field. So far, he'd only seen the children.

Where was Kai?

Something pressed against the back of his vest.

"Gotcha," Kai whispered in his ear, his breath brushing lightly across Atticus' cheek, sending a shiver down his spine. Atticus heard the click of the trigger just before his vest lit up with a hit.

Atticus leaned back so that he was pressed against the other man's chest, turning his head so that he could see the face next to his own.

"You ruined my hiding spot," he said with a grin.

"You're picking on little kids." Kai smirked, his words teasing and light. Atticus couldn't help but let his eyes fall to the soft pink lips so close to his own.

"Am not," he responded indignantly. "They're warriors. Pretty sure I just saw one of 'em mourning a fallen comrade." He looked down at the side of his gun, noting how long before he could shoot again. "I'm still down for another thirty seconds. Need to figure out a new strategy."

Kai tilted his own weapon to the side. "Mine's reloading."

They were so close, both crouched low in the dark, seemingly hidden away from the rest of the world. All of the awkwardness that Atticus had felt between them when Kai had arrived seemed to melt away. Atticus let out a shaky breath as Kai slipped a hand around one of his vest straps, tugging him closer.

Atticus' heart tripped as Kai moved to whisper in his ear once more. "What was that about kicking my team's ass?"

"Well," Atticus whispered, breathing against Kai's skin. "Maybe a kiss would help boost morale?"

Kai pinned him with those pretty eyes. He leaned close, a

small smile playing across his lips. They were a hair's breadth apart when Atticus' vest lit up again with another hit. He looked down to see Kai's gun pressed to his chest plate.

"Time's up," Kai said, something ravenous in his gaze as he pulled back. He patted Atticus' cheek softly. "Not in front of the children."

It took Atticus several moments to gather himself, to recover from the almost-kiss. He watched Kai's retreating figure, felt laughter bubble up in his chest.

"They're warriors!" The laugh he heard as Kai disappeared around a corner was worth losing the game for.

They ate ramen for dinner at a small place near the arcade, walking close enough that their arms brushed together every so often. Atticus wanted to reach out, to grab Kai's hand. Would that be too much? They *had* almost kissed. Surely hand holding was on the table after that, right?

But Kai kept his hands nestled in the front pocket of his hoodie, and Atticus thought it might be weird if he just reached in there to grab one. So he settled for walking close enough to bump Kai with his shoulder whenever he said something amusing.

Kai was *very* amusing. Atticus had already known that, just from the short conversations they'd shared over the last few weeks. He'd even known it from watching Kai's streams. A sharp wit, scathing retorts. But in person, it felt different. There was something soft beneath Kai's dispassionate outer layer. Something endearing.

Atticus' crush had tripled in size over the course of the night. He'd known he liked Kai, *a lot*, but getting to really interact with him made it all feel more real, more exciting and deep-seated.

The way Kai seemed amused by Atticus' teasing, trying

and failing to hide the smiles and laughter that Atticus was pulling from him. The way he would light up, just a little, when they talked about a game they were both excited for. The way he talked about Ori and their longtime friendship with a fondness that Atticus could relate to as they discussed his teammates. The way he continually teased Atticus for his laser-tag loss, his eyes sparkling as he finally agreed to a future rematch.

Dinner slipped by faster than Atticus was ready for. It felt like no time at all had passed before they were bickering over who would take care of the bill. Atticus stood from their table and simply held it in the air.

"Why are all of you tall people like this?" Kai asked, trying and failing to reach Atticus' hand. They were standing close, and suddenly Atticus felt as though the air in the room had grown thin. He looked down at Kai, frozen in place and acutely aware of the few other patrons seated close by. Atticus lowered his arm, leaning in close. Kai didn't step back, holding his ground as he continued to watch Atticus with those wide, whiskey-bright eyes.

"How about this," Atticus said. His words came out a little breathy. "I'll let you pay if you agree to come back to my place."

Kai was quiet for a long moment, and Atticus thought he could almost see the overworked gears turning in that pretty head.

"Okay," he finally responded, voice laced with a heat that set Atticus' blood scorching through his veins. "Deal."

Hands pressed against Atticus' shoulders, pinning him against the back of the couch. He breathed in sharply before lips met his own.

Kai was in his lap, kissing him like it was what he was meant for. The hands on Atticus' shoulders slid downward, ghosting over his chest and pulling a low moan from deep in his throat. Kai grinned against his mouth.

Atticus could hardly think straight, every movement from the man above him capturing his attention wholly. He pressed up into the kiss, tasting Kai, drinking him in. Kai's hands settled at his waist, fingers digging in hard. Atticus broke away from their kiss, moving to press his lips along Kai's jaw, down the side of his neck, teasing with his teeth in a way that had the other man sucking in a sharp breath.

When Atticus reached the crook of Kai's neck, sucking hard on the skin, Kai's hips rocked against him and Atticus saw stars. He bit down hard around the skin he had just been abusing. Kai dropped his head to Atticus' shoulder, releasing a breathy moan. He moved his hips again, and Atticus bit harder, unable to pull away.

His hands ran along the thighs bracketing his waist. Kai's joggers were like a second skin, and Atticus could feel every shift of muscle as Kai continued to move against him, grinding down on Atticus' cock. His hands tugged at Kai's waist, pulled him closer as their mouths crashed back together. The kiss was sloppy, hurried and wet and fierce.

Atticus moved a hand to cradle the back of Kai's neck, tangling his fingers in the soft hair that was coming loose from his bun. A small sound escaped Kai at the motion, giving Atticus an idea that he ran with. He tangled his fingers in deeper before giving Kai's hair a good *pull*.

A cry escaped Kai, his fingers tightening on Atticus' hips hard enough to bruise. Atticus pressed a light kiss to the hollow of his throat, grinding himself up against Kai's ass. His free hand snuck under Kai's hoodie, trailing along burning skin, brushing along his ribs, teasing a hard nipple.

He released his grip on Kai's hair. Kai looked down at him

with a gaze so molten Atticus thought he might catch fire.

"Want to move to the bedroom?" He ground his hips up again, pressing hard against Kai's ass, a cheeky grin tugging at his lips. "I can't stop thinking about how you might feel around me."

Kai didn't answer right away, only continued to stare down at him. Atticus could feel Kai's hard dick pressed against his stomach, knew that he was just as affected in that moment. Kai finally looked away, brow furrowing slightly, those turning gears of his mind on full display once again.

"Everything okay?" Atticus asked, freezing. "We don't have to if you don't want to."

"It's not that," Kai said. He sounded distracted, but not upset, and Atticus' nerves settled a bit.

"Or...," Atticus continued. An image had popped into his head. Kai's confident hands pressing him down into the mattress as he moved behind Atticus. *Inside of him.* "We could do it the other way 'round. I'm not picky."

Kai's face tilted to the side, his expression shifting into something considering. "I just... I haven't bottomed since..." He trailed off, shaking his head. "It doesn't matter. Are you sure?"

Atticus nodded. Vigorously. It suddenly didn't matter that this was something he himself had never actually done before. He'd always taken the same role in the bedroom, and his partners had been more than happy to oblige.

"Just go easy on me, yeah?" Atticus said, silly grin still plastered on his face. Kai leaned forward, pressing their lips together once again. His tongue slipped into Atticus' mouth, tasting him until Atticus thought he might just die from the fire building between them. Kai pulled away, nipping sharply at Atticus' bottom lip before he sat back.

"Yeah," he said, amber eyes gleaming in the low light of the room, cheeks flushed and chest heaving. He was smiling, soft and teasing, his expression more open than it had been all evening. "Let's go to the bedroom."

Atticus stood up in one quick movement, lifting Kai with him. Legs wrapped around his waist, arms loose around his shoulders. Kai leaned in, kissing along Atticus' jaw as they made their way toward the bedroom.

The moment Atticus sat Kai down on the bed he felt hands begin to pull gently at his clothes. Atticus helped by shucking away his shirt, tossing it across the room mindlessly. Kai's fingers played at the waistband of Atticus' pants, tugging his underwear down with them.

Atticus didn't really care that he was mostly naked and Kai was still fully clothed. He crawled onto the bed in nothing but his socks, pushing Kai back until he caged him in. Atticus looked down in the low light of the bedroom.

Kai was raking his eyes over every part of Atticus, lighting a trail of sparks along his body. Slender fingers brushed along his tattoos, up his arm, across his shoulder. Kai ran a hand down Atticus' stomach, causing him to flinch a little.

"That tickles," he said with a frown, grabbing one of Kai's wrists and pinning it to the bed. Kai only let out a short hum before moving his free hand lower, wrapping it around Atticus' cock, knocking the breath out of him. Atticus curved his body, trembling as Kai began to work him steadily. He leaned down, capturing Kai's lips, breathless sounds escaping between them.

Atticus released his grip on Kai's wrist as heat began to coil low inside his gut, as he began to lose all sense of reality. He'd intended to get his hand back into Kai's hair, to tangle his fingers in the soft strands. Kai, though, had other plans. He released his grip on Atticus, using both hands to push him, heaving them over until Atticus was on his back and Kai was seated on his thighs. Atticus leaned up, pulling Kai into another fiery kiss as he worked to divest him off that damn hoodie.

Once it had been tossed to the floor with the majority of his own clothes, Atticus paused to take in the man in his lap. Kai's hair was a mess, mussed from their activities and mostly fallen from its tie, hanging just past his shoulders, the teal ends brushing along his collarbone. Atticus twirled a bit of it in his fingers, gripping Kai's waist with his other hand.

"You're really pretty," he said. Kai's eyes went wide, a blush immediately spreading across his cheeks. Atticus grinned. "I bet it keeps people from seeing your claws right away."

Something caught fire in the eyes staring back at him, molten amber shining as Kai surged forward, crashing into Atticus. Teeth and tongues, biting and bruising, they pressed against one another, skin to skin. Atticus felt as though every point of contact was sending off sparks, searing him. Kai's hands slipped between them, returning to Atticus' cock, continuing what he'd started earlier.

Atticus was panting against him in moments, clutching tight, his hips bucking up into the touch. Lightning coursed through him, blazing under his skin. Atticus cried out as he came, spilling between them.

He flopped back, noting the mess he'd made all over the both of them. "Gonna have to get you out of these now," he said breathlessly, tugging at the fabric of Kai's cum-soaked pants. Kai tilted his head, eyes flicking over Atticus' body. He leaned forward, and Atticus watched with a little bit of awe as Kai pressed a soft kiss to his abdomen, tongue flicking out to taste the cum spilled there. He moved lower then, ghosting his lips along the length of Atticus' cock, ventured lower still.

And then Kai was there, tongue pressed to Atticus' hole, teasing along the rim. The breath whooshed out of Atticus' lungs as he squeezed his eyes shut, loosing himself in the sensations. Kai's movements grew more sure, more pressing, and Atticus had to hold himself back from pushing into the feel of that warm tongue that was pressing, licking, *worshiping* him.

Careful fingers ran along Atticus' stomach, gathering up a bit of the mess before slipping lower. Kai stopped whatever magical things he was doing with his mouth.

They held each other's gaze, a cord tethering them together, not allowing either to break away. Atticus felt a wet pressure, Kai's finger, at his hole.

"Is this okay?" Kai waited patiently for an answer. Atticus nodded, swallowing thickly. It wasn't like he'd never been fingered. Sometimes that was just the fun thing to do. But more than that? He had only ever topped during sex. A slight bit of nervousness finally began to grab him, to shiver along his insides.

Atticus let out a sharp breath as Kai's finger worked him before finally pressing in gently. His head fell back against the pillow as Kai used his free hand to rub soft circles along his thigh. The touch was gentle, soothing, and it helped him to relax as Kai continued to work him open.

By the time Kai had three slim fingers in him, Atticus couldn't stop the moans that fell from his lips. His back arched as Kai pushed in deep, as he brushed lightly against just the right spot.

"Look at you," Kai whispered. Atticus thought that he sounded a little wrecked himself, but it was hard to focus when Kai was touching him like that. Long, careful fingers spreading him open, pumping into him. "Can you turn over?"

The question broke through Atticus' haze. The softness of the words, the tenderness with which Kai was handling him, it wasn't what Atticus had expected. He had seen glimpses of something feral, something sharp and possessive, something that turned Atticus to putty in his hands. But the way Kai handled him now, with such gentle care, it made something new and bright swell in Atticus' chest. He smiled as Kai pulled his fingers out, turning over so that his face was down in the pillow.

"Stuff's in the nightstand," Atticus mumbled, voice muffled as he kept his face hidden.

Kai didn't move for several long moments, and Atticus could feel his face heating from the way he was spread prone on the bed.

He shivered as a light touch traced along the backs of his thighs. Kai's hand brushed over the swell of his ass, along the base of his spine, the touch worshipping and delicate.

"*Fuck*," Kai breathed. Atticus felt a compliment somewhere in the word, and couldn't help the tentative smile that spread across his face. He heard a shuffle, felt the bed dip as Kai finally, *finally* took off his pants. He watched Kai lean forward, hair falling around his face as he reached into the nightstand. It felt like an eternity wrapped into a few heartbeats before Kai was pressed up against him once again.

"Ready?" Kai asked, voice soft but sure.

"Yeah," Atticus responded, "Yes." He couldn't help but wiggle his hips, drawing a chuckle from the man behind him.

Kai entered him slowly, carefully. Atticus groaned at the sensation, and the way he felt so full, in more ways than one. Every shift pushed Kai into him deeper, and every caress of the other man's skin against his own sang through him, dancing along his veins. By the time Kai was seated fully inside of him, Atticus' breaths were coming quicker. When Kai let out a low sound deep in his throat, something swelled in Atticus' chest. He felt as though he might burst at any moment, might shatter into a million sparks, and he couldn't think of a better way to go.

Atticus pressed back into Kai, his body seeking more, begging for *more*. Soft strands of hair tickled his skin as Kai curled around him, hands bracing Atticus' hips as soft kisses were trailed down his spine. Atticus rocked his hips back again, giving Kai permission to move, to please fucking *move*.

A sharp gasp knocked loose from his lungs at Kai's first thrust into him. It was unlike anything Atticus had ever felt before. His hands buried into his pillow, clutching so tight his knuckles burned as Kai thrust into him again, somehow hitting even deeper.

Atticus reveled in the heavy breaths he could hear coming from the man above him, the soft sounds escaping Kai, the way his hands held Atticus so steady. Kai rocked into Atticus again and again, both of them seeking more more *more*. Atticus' cock was half-hard again, aching for touch.

"Try to sit up," Kai said, something bossy in his voice that made Atticus' cock twitch and intensified the heat burning low in his gut. Atticus did as he was told, pushing himself up with Kai still inside of him. Arms that were stronger than they looked wrapped around him, pulling him back until he was pressed against Kai's chest. Kai rocked up into him, tearing a groan from Atticus.

Kai was so much smaller than him, so slight pressed against Atticus' toned and muscled back, but his presence enveloped Atticus. The way those arms held him, hands splayed across his stomach and chest. The way Kai pressed a cheek to his back, hot, harsh breaths ghosting across his skin and sending shivers down his spine.

Atticus felt as though he could let go of everything, felt as though Kai were giving him exactly what he needed. That bright feeling in his chest swelled even more as Kai continued to thrust up into him, slow and steady. It grew and grew, overtaking every other thought.

He groaned again as Kai wrapped a hand around his cock once more, his other hand clutching at Atticus' chest to the point of bruising. The strokes of his fingers matched the pace of every thrust, and Atticus could finally feel himself approaching the edge a second time. Kai's breaths were becoming more and more unsteady against him, his hips beginning to lose their rhythm.

Atticus cried out as he came again, less forcefully than the first time, spilling onto the bed as he relaxed backward. Kai continued to work him through the aftershocks of his orgasm before letting out a cry of his own. His face pressed into the crook of Atticus' neck as he bucked up into him, moaning through his own orgasm.

Leaning forward so that Kai wouldn't have to bear his weight, Atticus braced himself with his arms. He felt a little shaky, a haze blanketing his mind. Kai pulled out of him, and Atticus immediately missed the sensation. The fullness he had felt… he'd liked it more than he'd expected. Liked it a *lot* actually.

Maybe he would need to do some shopping online later, find something to replicate that feeling himself. Just in case there wasn't going to be a second date.

Atticus flopped to the side, narrowly missing the mess he'd made on the bed. He watched Kai tie off the condom before throwing it away, watched him pull the tie out of his tangled hair. Atticus was thoroughly spent, but seeing Kai run slender fingers through his long hair, seeing the slight flush still spread across his face and chest, it made something in Atticus continue to burn. His insides felt light, like he could maybe float away at any moment. He really didn't like how far away Kai was.

Shifting so that he could rip the soiled blanket off the bed and toss it to the side, Atticus scooted across the mattress, grabbing Kai's waist and pulling him down onto the bed.

"I need to clean up," Kai protested as Atticus pulled him against his chest. "You do too."

Atticus latched onto him. "I'll just wash the sheets

tomorrow." He glanced down at their tangled legs and laughed. Kai had also failed to remove all of his clothes. "Weirdo," Atticus said as he kicked their socked feet together.

"I get cold," Kai huffed. Atticus yanked the top sheet over them before wrapping his arms around the smaller man. Kai curled into him like a cat seeking warmth.

"That was fun," Atticus whispered. "Next time I want you to boss me around more."

Kai chuckled, but Atticus didn't miss the way he tensed a little at the words. "We'll see." A long pause. Atticus thought that a *next time* might not be a sure thing. Kai's face nestled into his chest a little more. "It was fun."

That gave Atticus a small amount of hope. Because, as they lay there, curled together and drifting closer and closer to sleep, Atticus realized he needed that hope. Otherwise he was in trouble.

The light spreading in him, filling his chest with a fizzy, aching, wonderful sensation... it was something new. Something Atticus had never felt before.

He'd known he was falling hard for Kai even before they'd met in person. The way they could joke with one another over texts, the fun they had paying games, everything new he continued to learn about Kai. His interests, his endeavors. The way he would go quiet, thinking too hard about a question posed. The way, sometimes, brilliant laughter would escape him, a sound that was so bright and happy.

But seeing Kai in person, watching him and touching him... Atticus felt ruined. The way those amber eyes would widen if he were embarrassed, or narrow if he were annoyed, but still always glowed with a soft, sparkling light. The way he seemed to actually find Atticus amusing, even if he rolled his eyes a lot. Atticus loved when he rolled his eyes.

The way Kai had held him so steady, had been so careful not to push Atticus toward something he didn't want. The way he had trusted Atticus to speak up if it became too much. The glimpses of something more feral that he had shown, a side of Kai that Atticus was desperate to pull to the surface.

Atticus had already been falling hard and fast. As Kai's breaths against his skin evened out with sleep, as the other man went limp in his arms, curled close, Atticus realized something he didn't really want to admit, even to himself.

It seemed as though, maybe, it had only taken one night for him to begin to fall in love.

16

Present Day

Julian's phone: This is Ori :D:D:D
Ori: Have you heard anything about Nicholas this morning?

Kai: Theo just said that his dr is supposed to come in soon, he'll probably be discharged today.

Ori: GOOD :D:D:D how did yesterday go?

Kai: Fine.

Ori: People usually only say fine like that when things aren't actually fine...

Kai: No, it really was fine. We talked.

Ori: Think things will be better now? For you?

Kai: Maybe. Yeah. Probably. It's weird, but I guess I'm starting to feel okay about it.
Kai: Fucking closure, apparently it's as great as people say it is.

Ori: What about Atticus?
Ori: Sorry I missed your call yesterday, I think I lost my phone

Kai: It's ok, Julian was weirdly helpful

Ori: :D:D:D
Ori: He is great :D
Ori: Don't avoid my question :D

Kai: I haven't really talked to him yet.

Ori: But you ARE going to talk??

Kai: Yes…

Ori: You don't need to be nervous! I talked to him yesterday and he still loves you!!!!
Ori: Julian said I probably wasn't supposed to tell you that
Ori: D:

Kai: Was he still upset?

Ori: Yeah
Ori: Sad upset not mad upset

Kai: I need to go apologize to him.

Ori: You both do
Ori: But then it will all be ok and you can finally be boyfriends :D:D:D

Kai: We'll see.
Kai: I'm still scared Ori. I didn't plan for any of this.

Ori: Sometimes the scary stuff is worth it though
Ori: You've already gotten through all the worst parts
Ori: You did that all by yourself
Ori: But now you've got attie to help you get through this part
Ori: And it won't be as scary because he's not scared of anything :D
Ori: Well actually I think he's scared right now but you can fix that easy
Ori: You've got this kai :D:D

Kai: Thanks Ori, I hope you're right.

Kai sat against his headboard, knees pulled up to his chest, hands tangled in the sleeves of his hoodie. The sun had only just begun to peak through his blinds, settling soft stripes of light across his bedroom.

It was far too early for him to be awake. He had never been an early riser, had always been one to stay up all night instead. But one week with Atticus had him falling asleep earlier than usual, and he woke without an alarm right alongside the rising sun.

Kai tugged at one of his sleeves, getting a better grip on it. His knuckles burned from how hard he gripped the fabric. His heart was beating steady and loud in his chest, a thumping rhythm to accompany the train of his thoughts.

One day, one night, and it felt as though everything had changed.

Just like that night a year prior, Kai felt as though he were waking up to a whole new life. The white-knuckled grip on his shirt mirrored the way he had tried to cling to the past, a desperate fear of what the future might hold.

Only this time… he didn't quite feel as desperate. He wasn't held by that same fear, no longer felt it hovering over him waiting to strike.

It was funny how quickly things could come into focus. How events could fall into place, a puzzle that he'd only had to stand back and watch take form. Clarity washed over him like fresh rain, clearing out the fog and leaving the sun shining through the droplets.

Atticus had accused Kai of still being hung up on Nicholas. If their fight had happened just a week earlier, Kai would have agreed with him. But in that moment, when the two of them had been flinging words back and forth that neither of them meant, Kai hadn't been thinking of Nicholas at all.

Maybe it had been the awful phone call with Theo. Maybe that had been when Kai had finally begun to let go. But he didn't think so.

Kai thought that maybe he had begun to let go six months earlier. On a night when he'd felt more like himself than he had in so long. On a night when he'd begun to see himself as someone who could still *be*. Someone who could exist outside of his painful, sharp parts. Someone who could exist along with them.

He could still see Atticus' face from that night so clearly.

Bleach-blonde hair windblown across his forehead, nose and cheeks a little pink from the cold and maybe something more. A smile that lit his sky blue eyes the moment they picked Kai out of the crowd.

Atticus had been a constant in his life since that moment. And with the closure that Kai had gained the prior evening, finally, *finally* having the conversation with Nicholas that he should have had the night things had ended between them, Kai felt like the final puzzle piece had fallen into place. He felt washed clean in the rain. All of the broken parts were still there, still threatening to stab and slice at a moment's notice. But he could see them all clearly, could see the way they were ready and waiting to be stitched back together.

One night, and everything had changed once again.

Kai's gut churned. It was still *terrifying*. He knew what he wanted, what he needed to do. But he knew that he was standing at another crossroads. It was so much easier to just sit down and curl up, to hide from ever making a decision, from ever moving forward. But as he looked at the road, he knew what he was going to choose the moment he'd screwed his courage up enough. The path wasn't dark and unknowable like last time. It was bright, and he wouldn't be taking it alone.

The sun had yet to rise fully, the sky a dark cobalt fading into the most brilliant orange as Kai grabbed the package he'd ordered two days earlier, when Atticus' attention had been too caught up in the end of *Trigun* to notice what he was doing, and left his house.

Theo: He's being discharged later today

Kai: Good, I'm glad.
Kai: Maybe we can get lunch next time Ori's in town.

Theo: That would be great. Thanks, again Kai.

"You miss him, don't you?"

Atticus watched the kitten flick her tail at his question, her eyes wide and knowing and possibly staring into his soul. She sat crouched at the edge of the kitchen countertop. He reached out a hand tentatively, running it along her soft fur, smiling as she leaned up into his touch.

She hadn't been acting quite the same. Atticus had found her several times in Kai's room over the last twenty-four hours. Kai's room. He should probably stop thinking about it as that.

He felt a now-familiar twisting in his chest, and forced himself to remember the conversation he'd had with Ori the day before. Forced himself to remember that Kai was his friend, regardless of anything else.

It was strange to think about how all it had taken was one night, months ago, for Atticus' whole world to turn on its head. One night with Kai, and he'd seen so clearly what he wanted. Had seen a life he had never really considered for himself before.

Kai made him want to be *more*. Made him want to be steady. He had pulled at Atticus' softer side, ripped away his masks. Atticus' life was better for knowing him, even as just a friend.

The soft chime of the dryer finishing its cycle sounded out through the house. Atticus noted it absent-mindedly. He would need to fold the clothes before they wrinkled. He sort of dreaded it, knowing that his old Cats hoodie was mixed into the load.

He hadn't been able to help himself the night before,

slipping the hoodie over his head in lieu of one of the t-shirts he normally slept in if he wore any sort of shirt to bed. It was just a bit too small, but he hadn't cared as he'd crawled into bed. Surrounded by Kai's scent, he'd fallen asleep.

Unfortunately, Atticus ran hot at night. He woke that morning drenched in sweat. It had been unavoidable then. He'd had to wash the hoodie. His caveman brain was still sad about it, knowing it would just smell like fresh laundry when he folded it later, knowing that it would no longer have that distinctly *Kai* smell.

Kai would definitely roll his eyes if he knew Atticus had been sniffing his clothes.

Atticus chuckled at the thought as he walked over to the cabinet to grab a coffee mug, wishing the scene were playing out right then.

He knew Ori had said to just give Kai time. And Atticus agreed, he agreed that he needed to just let Kai do things at his own pace, especially considering everything that was happening with Nicholas.

But Atticus wanted to apologize. Properly, not in a text message. That didn't count.

He paused at the open cabinet, concentrating hard on his mug options. He hesitated, wanting to take the maroon one. The one Kai had gotten for him. It felt wrong. They should be using the mugs together. He settled on an old, chipped one that Sammie had brought him from the brewery.

Maybe he should just go over to Kai's. He could grab them some breakfast, since Atticus knew Kai didn't like to cook and figured that his kitchen was probably empty anyway after a week of being away from home. Yeah, Atticus could grab them something to eat, and they could talk.

He could apologize. Could tell Kai that he could have all the time he needed. Because Atticus was pretty sure that, except for his moment of panic the morning before, he would wait the rest of his life if that's what Kai needed him to do.

Atticus thought through his plan a few more times as he downed his coffee, could feel the tight grip on his chest twisting into something that didn't feel quite as bad. Something more like excitement.

He rinsed his coffee mug out, double-checked that the kitten still had plenty of water in her bowl, and headed toward his front door. The sun was shining in fully through his windows, setting a golden light across the room that warmed his skin, warmed him all the way to the bone.

Maybe he should text Kai first? Of course, then he would risk being told not to come, but it was probably the right thing to do. Atticus pulled out his phone as he slipped his shoes on, typing out a quick message one-handed as he yanked the door open.

He looked up to see Kai standing on his front porch.

They stared at each other for several seconds, and Atticus was sure the whole world could hear his heart pounding in his chest.

"Attie," Kai said. His voice was soft, quiet as the morning, amber eyes still wide with surprise that the door had been yanked open before he could even knock. Atticus watched him suck in a shaky breath, and felt as though time itself were holding still right along with him. Kai took a small step forward. "I-"

Atticus reached out, unable to stop from pulling Kai into his arms. Kai squeaked, his words cut off as he was pressed tight to Atticus' chest. His nose stung something fierce as his emotions tried to get the better of him, and Atticus pressed his lips softly to the top of Kai's head.

"I'm sorry," he said, his breath ruffling Kai's hair. "I didn't mean any of it."

Kai melted against him a bit, and Atticus felt arms snake around his waist. He fought the urge to pump his fist in the air as Kai hugged him back.

"I'm sorry, too," Kai said, his words muffled against Atticus' chest. Atticus knew that he should at least loosen his grip some before he crushed the other man. It took everything he had, his body and mind screaming for him to never let go, not again.

But he did. Atticus did let go, his arms unlatching from Kai's smaller frame just enough that he could pull back. Just enough to give him whatever space he needed.

And Kai did pull back. It tugged at Atticus' gut, made him feel as though everything he wanted could slip away on the morning breeze.

Kai pulled back, but he didn't let go. His hands gripped the sides of Atticus' t-shirt, held on fiercely. Atticus wasn't sure that he was even aware he was doing it.

"I shouldn't have left yesterday," Kai continued, looking up into Atticus' face, his gaze unblinking. Atticus could see some of his own fear mirrored there, and he wanted nothing more than to wipe it away. He kept silent though, allowing Kai to continue.

"I should have stayed," Kai said, the words spilling out of him in a way that was so unlike his usual, controlled way of speaking. "We should have talked about it, I should have talked about it. You were upset, and I knew you were upset, but I just wanted it to go away. I'm sorry."

Atticus seemed to have fully lost control of his body as his hand reached out, tucking a few stray strands of hair behind Kai's ear. Letting his fingers brush against soft skin, sending sparks up his own arm.

"I shouldn't have pushed you," he said. He took a deep breath, looking away for only a second to steady himself. "I told you I loved you, and then immediately put pressure on you to accept that. After saying you could take whatever time you needed. Kai," he paused, a smile tugging at his lips. "If you want to take the next twenty years to figure out what we are, I can wait for twenty years to pass. I was lying when I said I'd move on, and we both know it. But that doesn't mean you owe me anything. I can love you in whatever way you need, but I promise I'll never stop."

Atticus felt the hands at his sides grip his shirt tighter, watched as Kai went completely still. It was as though the gears that were always, *always* turning in that beautiful mind finally slowed and came to a quiet halt.

"Attie." The way Kai said his name, like it was something sacred and precious, it nearly brought him to his knees. "I-"

The slow squeak of the front door interrupted him, pulling their attention down to the ground.

The kitten bolted off the porch.

"Shit!" Atticus yelled, taking off at a run after her. She was a fast little fucker, flying down the side of the road before turning off into a neighbor's yard.

Atticus could hear Kai running close behind, their footfalls pounding hard against the pavement, as he lost sight of her.

Kai was out of breath from running. They had only been searching for a few minutes, but worry was beginning to cloud past the adrenaline rush he'd felt when they'd both taken off after the kitten. He came to a halt on the side of the road, hands on his knees as he sucked in lungful after lungful of air.

"She's gone," Atticus said, his voice shaky. Kai looked up to see panic written across his face, his eyes scanning the surrounding yards frantically as his hands raked through his hair. "What if she's gone?"

This was a side of Atticus that Kai had only seen once. The morning before, when he'd come into the kitchen looking so terrified, as if he'd known something was about to go wrong. As if he'd known, when he woke up alone, that Kai was going to disappear from his life.

"Hey," Kai said softly, placing a hand gently against Atticus' cheek. Sky blue eyes finally focused on him. "We'll find her. It'll be okay."

Kai knew she'd be back, by dinnertime at the latest. She knew who fed her, and she'd get bored with her little adventure when hunger started to poke at her. But the desperation on Atticus' face made Kai feel sick, and he didn't want to wait until dinnertime for it to disappear. He would do anything to make that look go away. Which is what he should have done yesterday, when he'd seen the hurt clear as day on Atticus' face.

He raised his other hand, cupping Atticus' cheeks, forcing him to focus. "You keep looking around here. I'm going back to the house to grab some treats and a toy. Maybe we can lure her out with those. Okay?"

Atticus nodded, one hand coming up to grip Kai's wrist. "Okay, yeah. Call me if you see her."

"I will," Kai said, hesitating for a moment, soaking up the warmth of Atticus' skin under his palms before turning away to jog back toward the house. They were several blocks away at this point, but it didn't take Kai long to get back.

He laughed when he was finally close enough to see the front porch. A loud, shaky, unburdened laugh that ripped out of him.

The kitten was sitting in front of the door, tail flicking back and forth as she watched Kai approach. The little shit had come right back. It seemed as though neither of them could stay away for long.

He scooped her up, holding her tight against his chest as he pulled out his phone. The relief in Atticus' voice as Kai told him to come back home was palpable, and his soft laugh coming across the line sent shivers skating along Kai's skin.

Kai took the kitten back into the house, checking over her to make sure she hadn't injured herself while out on her little romp through the neighborhood. He sat at the counter, on his usual barstool, feeling at home for the first time in the last twenty-four hours. The kitten looked up at him from his lap, blinking slowly as he pulled the item he'd ordered out of his pocket. He buckled the collar around her neck right as Atticus burst through the front door.

Atticus was still breathing heavy, had seemingly run all the way back, as he approached them.

"I'm gonna give her to Sammie if she interrupts us one more time," he said. "See if she likes it in her boring apartment. Sammie won't spoil her, that's for sure. She's a dog person." The words were teasing, laced with relief that Kai could see clear on Atticus' face.

"What's this?" Atticus asked, long fingers brushing the bright red collar she now wore around her neck. It was a nice one, leather, sturdy and durable. Sleek. Kai couldn't help that he had expensive taste. Atticus' fingers found the metal tag attached to the collar.

"Vash the Stampede..." His voice trailed off as his eyes went wide and met Kai's. Kai couldn't help but smirk at him. Atticus threw his hands in the air. "'No boy names' you said! So picky, every time I threw out a name!"

His voice was loud and filled with laughter, and it made Kai feel lighter than he had in a long time. A smile finally tugged at his lips, and he shrugged.

"It suits her," Kai said. Atticus watched him with glee in his eyes. "Our little feline typhoon." Kai paused, felt his cheeks warm before he could get the next part out. "And it was the first anime we finished together."

Atticus' head tilted, consideration and something more filling his expression. "Hang on," he said, leaving the room.

Kai sat frozen at the counter. The words he had almost said on the porch still burned in his throat, still begged for release. He heard something slam shut just before Atticus came back into the room holding a maroon bundle. The kitten- Vash, *finally* she had a name- jumped out of Kai's lap as Atticus approached, shaking out the bundle he held before pushing it down over Kai's head.

"Wait!" Kai yelped, struggling against Atticus' ambush. A laugh escaped him as he realized what was happening and gave up on fighting back. He straightened out his gamertag-branded t-shirt under the hoodie before popping his arms and head out through the proper holes.

"That's better," Atticus said, leaning back to take in his handiwork. Kai looked down at the Cats hoodie he now wore.

"Why's it so warm?"

"I had to wash it," Atticus said, waving a hand, though his cheeks were tinted a soft pink. "Don't worry about it."

Kai let the fabric warm him, let the feeling seep into his skin, wrap around all of the parts of him he'd thought too sharp and too angry and too sad to ever feel this way again. To feel content. To feel held safe. To feel so wholly loved.

"Attie," he said, eyes still downcast as he inhaled sharply. He had to admit it out loud. He had to admit it to himself. Kai tangled his fingers into the cuffs of his hoodie before looking back up. "I love you."

He watched Atticus' face transform, disbelief shifting into utter joy. His smile was bright, brighter than the sun shining in through the windows. A light that had been there for Kai, always shining in on his darkest parts.

Kai sucked in a breath as Atticus closed the distance between them, as their lips crashed together. Atticus' hands brushed along his jaw, tangled in his hair as Kai melted into the kiss. He gripped the front of Atticus' shirt, pulling him closer so that the other man stood between his legs.

"Does this mean you're done thinking?" Atticus asked, smiling against Kai's lips. Kai hummed.

"Probably not," he said, "I'm never done thinking."

"We'll see about that," Atticus murmured, running his hands down Kai's arms as he kissed him again.

Atticus was right. For once, Kai did allow himself to stop thinking. As Atticus' hands roved over him, everything from the last year fell away. All of the sadness and anger and hurt slid from his skin with every burning touch, every soft movement of lips against his own. Kai tugged Atticus closer, holding on, finally reaching out to grab onto the lifeline that had been held out to him for so long.

Kai felt as though moving on was finally possible. The fear he'd held toward where life would go, the fear of the unknown and unexpected, it all felt so much smaller with Atticus' arms around him.

He wrapped his legs around Atticus' waist, held on tight as the countertop dug into his back. Kai slipped his hands up under Atticus' shirt, ghosting his fingers across warm skin. A small sound escaped from low in Atticus' throat, and satisfaction coursed through Kai.

A scraping sound met his ears. Both men froze.

Atticus sighed, his breath hot against Kai's cheeks as he pressed their foreheads together. The sound of a coffee mug shattering on the wood floor rang out, mixing perfectly with their laughter.

Julian: congratulations shithead, i knew you could do it

Atticus: Thanks fuckface!!!
Atticus: Really tho, couldn't have done it without you and

Ori :)

Julian: sure you could have, just would have taken you another year n a half
Julian: probably

Atticus: …
Atticus: Probably

Sammie: Do you have something to tell me?

Atticus: Oh yeah i need another one of those shitty mugs from the brewery

Sammie: What happened to the last one I gave you???

Atticus: Broke

Sammie: That's the fourth one I'm not giving you another one for free

Atticus: I've always told everyone you don't actually love me, knew I was right

Sammie: Fuck you
Sammie: Now spill

Atticus: Kai lovesss meeeeee :D
Atticus: Wait how did you know something happened??

Sammie: Ivy told me

Atticus: How does Ivy know? It's only been
Atticus: 27 minutes???

Sammie: She said Kai told Ori who told the entire Cats group chat

Atticus: WTF
Atticus: I FORGOT I HAD THEM MUTED
Atticus: *Screenshot*

Sammie: Damn
Sammie: 184 messages
Sammie: Love this for you

Atticus: I hate all of you
Atticus: I'm going to turn my phone off and go make out with my new boyfriend

Sammie: Gross.
Sammie: Before you do that though
Sammie: I'm happy for you attie

Atticus: Thanks :) I'm really happy
Atticus: You could be happy like this too
Atticus: I think you should talk to Kieran

Sammie: I know. It's scary. What if it goes bad?

Atticus: Then we'll just deal with it, like we've always done. I've got your back sammie

Atticus: Always have always will

Atticus: Love you

Sammie: Thanks. Love you too. Now go have fun with your new boyfriend.

Atticus: We're gonna get freaky :D

Sammie: I'm gonna block your number

6 Months Later

Keys jingling in the lock of his front door pulled Atticus from sleep. He'd covered a shift at the brewery after Sammie had called him desperate for help, and by the time he'd come home, showered, and shoveled some leftovers into his face, his eyes had been drooping and his limbs had felt heavy as lead. He'd flopped down on the couch, fallen asleep to the comforting vibrations of Vash purring on his chest.

Atticus lifted his head, barely coming awake as Kai opened the door. A burst of cold air slipped in with the other man, a shock against the bare skin of Atticus' torso. He hadn't even managed to get fully dressed after his shower, opting to nap in nothing but a pair of gym shorts.

"Hey," Kai said, his voice soft as he kicked off his shoes by the door, unwrapping himself from his many layers. It wasn't even that cold out, but Atticus had come to learn that Kai had zero tolerance for any temperatures below sixty degrees Fahrenheit. A thick outer coat, mittens shoved into the pocket. A cozy, knitted beanie. An old red scarf. Unwrapped himself just like a present. Atticus grinned wide.

"Hey," he said. "How was the flight?"

"Long," Kai grumbled, turning toward Atticus and revealing the sweatshirt he'd been wearing underneath all his winter gear. It was an old one that he'd pilfered from Atticus' closet a few weeks prior, branded with his high school team's mascot. More and more of Atticus' clothes had been disappearing, only to show up on his boyfriend a short time later.

It made Atticus insane, seeing Kai in his clothes. They were always too big, always hung off of his smaller frame, hiding Kai in a way that made Atticus want to tear them away and reveal what was beneath. He'd never been patient when it came to unwrapping presents.

Kai trudged across the dark room. The sun had gone down while Atticus was napping, and the only light left came from a lamp in the far corner. Atticus reached out as Kai closed the distance between them, latching on to his thigh the moment he was close enough.

"Shoo," Kai muttered, pushing Vash off of Atticus' bare chest. "My turn."

Their kitten wasn't much of a kitten anymore. She'd grown considerably, her body long and lithe. Her eyes hadn't changed though, still that same searing gold, just a shade off from Kai's. She narrowed them at him as she leapt away.

Kai sighed deeply as he lowered himself onto the couch, curling up against Atticus' chest as though he were a cat himself. Atticus wrapped his arms around Kai, holding him tight, letting his warmth seep into him.

"I heard from Theo on the way here," Kai said, his words a light rumble against Atticus' chest. "He started a group chat with me and Ori."

"Oh yeah?"

Kai nodded. "He told us he's going to propose. Said he's been planning to for a while."

Atticus twirled a lock of his boyfriend's two-toned hair around his finger, the ends still the same soft pink that they had been for a while now, and chuckled. "Was he getting your permission?"

"I think so, in a way," Kai said with a shrug. "I think he was waiting for me." He left the second half of the thought unspoken, but Atticus knew. Theo had been waiting, *hoping*, that in some way, even if it was small, their little friend group could mend the rift that had cracked between them.

"I think he'll be happy to have you be a part of it all," he said softly. Kai only hummed in response, and Atticus wondered if he was beginning to fall asleep.

He was proud of Kai. It had been hard, watching the man he loved struggle to have any sort of relationship with the people that had hurt him. But Kai had tried. Really tried. Closure had done wonders for him, bringing out a more carefree side of Kai that made Atticus' heart trip with affection. And Atticus thought that he was better off for it. He'd seen firsthand how letting go of the anger and bitterness had lit something within Kai that had been close to dying out.

Worry over Kai's feelings for his ex had also ceased long ago. Atticus heard the words *I love you* fall from Kai's lips every day, felt that love in every touch, saw it in every expression. Kai had let go of the things that had held him back for so long, and Atticus got to be the one standing next to him while he'd done it.

"I'm glad you're back," he said, smiling against the top of Kai's head. Kai only let out a soft sound of agreement. It had been a week since they'd seen one another, a business trip taking Kai to New York. "Did you stop at home first?"

"Came straight here," Kai mumbled. Atticus clicked his tongue.

"Interesting," he mused. "It's almost as if you don't even need that place anymore."

Silence from the man curled on top of him.

"It's almost as if everything would be easier if you, oh I don't know, moved in here."

He felt a sharp pinch on his side and flinched away from

the touch, laughing.

They'd had similar variants of the same conversation countless times at this point. When Atticus had first asked Kai about moving in, Kai had responded exactly how he'd expected. He had asked for time to think about it.

And Atticus *was* giving him time to think about it. But he'd found that just because he was giving Kai time didn't mean he had to keep his mouth shut. In fact, Kai didn't really seem to mind at all if Atticus kept bringing the subject up. Almost as if he knew it was just Atticus' way of keeping himself from getting too worried about it. As long as Kai wasn't flat out saying *no*, that was a good sign, right?

"I'm just saying, half your stuff is here anyway, and Vash doesn't act the same when you're not around, and you really *are* here most of the ti-"

Kai silenced him with a kiss.

It was searing, possessive and harsh, making up for all the days they'd just spent apart. Atticus moaned softly, the sound pulling from his chest as Kai licked into his mouth before tugging his lower lip between his teeth and biting down. Atticus' hands found Kai's hips, slipping under the waistband of his sweatpants, fingers digging into the soft flesh there as pain lanced through his lip.

Kai's nails dug into his shoulders, clawed at the skin there as he moved lower, kissing and nipping along Atticus' jaw, down his neck, across his chest.

"You're just trying *ah-*," Atticus gasped out, cutting off with a choked sound as Kai's teeth bit down on his nipple. He sucked in a harsh breath as Kai kept going, his mouth trailing lower and lower down Atticus' body. "You're just trying to distract me."

Kai glanced up, meeting Atticus' gaze. The look in his eyes was heated, something predatory that made fire coil low in Atticus. "Is it working?" Kai asked, punctuating the question by pressing his palm to the bulge in Atticus' shorts. He squeezed, and Atticus threw his head back against the arm of the couch, another gasp ripping from his chest.

"Yeah," he panted. "It's working." He wasn't thinking about the question he'd asked Kai, not anymore. Atticus wasn't thinking about anything at all, his focus entirely captured by every place where Kai brushed and burned against his skin.

Kai tugged at the band of Atticus' shorts, pulling them down as he lifted his hips. Atticus' dick sprang free, already half hard, and Kai leapt on him. Atticus saw stars as Kai licked at the tip, sucking it into his mouth before pulling away, running his tongue down the length slowly.

Atticus' chest heaved with every breath, the air tearing from his lungs, searing his throat as Kai sucked at the base of his cock. It was painful, a twisted sort of pleasure, and something blazed in his mind knowing Kai was marking him somewhere only the two of them would ever see.

By the time Kai moved back up, taking the head into his mouth once again, Atticus had begun to lose control. His hips bucked of their own volition. Kai's hands moved to press him down, fingertips digging into his hip bones.

"Don't move," he said, his voice low and commanding. His breath ghosted across the tip of Atticus' cock, sending a shiver through him as Kai pinned him with a wide, feral stare. "Be good, and maybe we can talk about it when I'm done."

The bossy tone that Atticus loved best, the side of Kai that only he got to see, the voice only he got to hear. He fought to hold still, to keep his hips from rutting up again. It took every ounce of his slipping concentration. Kai's touch on his hips turned soft, his fingers trailing gentle lines down Atticus' thighs.

"Good," he said, voice velvety, almost a purr. "Just like

that."

Atticus breathed hard through his nose as Kai returned his attention to his cock. "Fuck," he muttered as Kai took him in deep with one swift motion. The whole scene was filthy, something out of his dreams. Kai, backlit by the low light of the lamp, the bobbing of his head slow, so agonizingly slow, hair falling out of the tie he'd pulled it back with, framing Atticus' cock before it disappeared into his mouth again and again. The wet heat of Kai's lips around him was too much, and Atticus' thighs began to tremble as he fought to keep himself still.

He clawed at the couch, desperate for anything to grab onto, anything to tether him to the moment. A hand wrapped around his wrist. Kai brought Atticus' fingers to his hair, and despite the way all coherent thoughts had emptied from his mind, Atticus knew instinctively what to do.

His fingers tangled into Kai's hair, gripping hard, pulling a moan out of him that vibrated through Atticus' cock and brought him dangerously close to the edge. His head banged back against the couch arm again, his grip on Kai's hair tightening even more. A hand wrapped around the base of his cock, smearing the spit and pre-cum that was leaking past Kai's lips.

Wet fingers trailed past his balls, pressing against his entrance. Kai pulled away, lifting his face to hover over Atticus' red and aching cock.

"Look at you," he said, a small, sharp smile tilting up the corners of his wet lips. Atticus' dick twitched as their eyes met, as Kai's gaze burned all the way to his core. "Falling apart so fast."

"Kai," Atticus gasped out. He was close, so close, desperate for release. "*Please.*"

Kai's smile widened for a fraction of a second, a flash of teeth, before he took Atticus back into his mouth, sinking down onto his cock until Atticus could feel himself hit the back of Kai's throat. At the same moment, the two fingers that had been working his entrance open plunged into him. Kai knew exactly where to press, hitting the spot that had Atticus' vision flaring white in one fluid motion.

Atticus spilled down Kai's throat, a cry tearing from him as his back arched. Kai held his hips down with one hand, grip bruising, as he continued to rub his fingers against Atticus' prostate, working him to the point of overstimulation. Atticus moaned Kai' name, again and again, until it became a prayer falling from his lips.

Kai finally pulled off of him, a choked gasp leaving Atticus as his boyfriend moved back up his body. Atticus watched in awe as Kai came closer, his cheeks flushed and lips swollen, eyes gleaming in the low light. Kai pressed a thumb to Atticus' bottom lip, tilting his chin until Atticus' panting breaths fanned out hot between their faces.

Lips pressed to his own, and Atticus tugged Kai closer. Kai's mouth opened, Atticus' own cum spilling past his lips, and Atticus groaned as the bitterness filled his mouth, mixed with the taste of Kai, overwhelming his senses. Their tongues met, Kai pressing into him, making sure Atticus drank in every last drop of himself. The kiss turned rough, bruising, before Kai finally pulled away.

"So good for me," he said, voice low and a little raspy. He brushed his thumb across Atticus' cheek, expression considering, that small, feral smile still playing on his lips. "Okay."

Atticus cocked his head to the side. "Okay?"

Kai nodded, nuzzling his face into the crook of Atticus' neck. "I'll move in."

Atticus flipped them over, grinning wide as he perched on top of the smaller man. Kai was trying and failing to hide his own wide smile, and seeing it sent heat coursing low in

Atticus once again despite the fact that he'd just received the best blow job of his life and was so thoroughly spent.

Kai had finally, *finally* agreed to move in with him. Atticus couldn't keep the dumb smile off of his face as he rocked his hips, grinding his ass down on Kai's still-clothed cock, pulling a wrecked laugh from him.

"We need to celebrate!" Atticus rocked his hips again, reveling in the way Kai looked up at him, eyes raking up and down Atticus' body.

"Is that not what we already did?" Kai asked, voice catching as Atticus continued to grind against him, hands wandering up under his sweatshirt.

"Doesn't count," Atticus said simply. "I didn't know you were gonna say yes this time. Gotta celebrate proper now."

Kai laughed, the sound of it light and full of cheer and if Atticus never heard another sound in his life, well, that would be okay. Because hearing Kai so happy, seeing him let go in a way that he really only did for Atticus, it made something in his chest swell so large he thought he might pop like a balloon.

"Okay," Kai said, reaching up to tug Atticus down, pressing their lips together lightly. "Let's celebrate then."

Heat flared back to life in Atticus, coiling low in his abdomen as Kai kissed him, as he pictured the way he was about to look while Atticus rode him. Things were just starting to heat up once again when they both heard a sound that had them breaking apart, eyes wide.

"No," Atticus said breathlessly.

They heard it again.

Mrrrow.

The small meow came from outside, barely audible. Vash had walked over to the back door, her head tilted to the side knowingly.

"*No*," Atticus said again. He couldn't believe it.

Kai moved suddenly, pushing Atticus' bulk off before scampering across the house, his socked feet sliding across the wood floors as he hurried to stop and pull the back door open.

Atticus was fully naked, and it was chilly outside, but he followed anyway, popping his head through the doorway.

It was already too late. Every protestation, every reason he could think of to *not* take in another one died on his lips.

Kai stood on the back patio, a tiny black kitten curled in his arms. The look on his face as he stroked the wispy fur told Atticus that the decision was already made.

"Come on," he said. "Bring it in."

Kai smiled wide, and Atticus couldn't help but grin back at him.

Acknowledgements

Let's get mushy for a minute.

Angy, I mean it when I say I couldn't have written this book without you. Our magical DMs are truly the only way my brain knows how to plot out anything now, so you are very much stuck with me forever. Thank you so much for pushing me to start writing fanfic, for being a huge part of the reason I picked up writing again and finally, *finally* stuck with it, for matching my freak and tolerating all of the unhinged questions I ask about spicy scenes. And thank you so much for being there for the hard parts of all of this, for helping me to stay in love with the fandoms that brought us together in the first place. I promise I'll write chapter two of that Tsukihina fic soon, I PROMISE.

Will, thank you so much for letting me do this. For sticking by me while I took our lives in a direction that I don't think either of us were expecting. Thank you for reading my silly kissing books when I know you'd rather be reading Airframe for the fiftieth time. Thank you for being the constant in my world when so many others haven't stuck around. I love you and our fun little life we have together, and I so very much appreciate your support while I'm finally doing the thing I've wanted to do for so long.

Chels, you are the person who sent me down this road.

You helped me see what a good friendship could feel like, and you led me to so much happiness. So you are also stuck with me forever, the Kageyama to my Hinata, the Luffy to my Usopp, the Vash to my Wolfwood (but with a happier ending for us, of course).

Jonlyn, Erica, and Tay, just… wow. I couldn't have done this without your steadfast support and the community that we have built together at A Novel Romance. You all have made my love of books and love stories feel more valid than ever, and I don't know if I ever would have been brave enough to publish this book without the three of you cheering me on and making me feel accepted for who I am. And, of course, I can't forget our Bella Boy, the best bookstore cat in the world.

Jordan and Camden, you two have cheered me on from the very start of this publishing journey and I will forever be thankful that we found each other. Thank you so much for cheering me on, for finding so many typos, for all the reminders that Attie's jersey is, in fact, maroon and not green.

Thank you so much to Alistair Reeves for bringing my boys to life with your stunning art, I never imagined that I would get a cover so perfect for this book. You went above and beyond, and I'm endlessly grateful to you for making that part of my publishing journey so easy and fun, and for delivering a cover that I still cry over. You captured Attie, Kai, and Vash (the Feline Typhoon) perfectly.

Thank you to Zoë for having such amazing taste in books and for helping me with edits. Cait and Candice, you're both amazing and the most sincere people I've ever met, thank you for always sticking around even when I forget to check my DMs, and for being there for me exactly when I needed you the most. Caitlynne, Rosie, Rainy, Irina, you are all incredible and I'm so glad I get to still have you all in my life. Thank you for being just as crazy about fandom as me, for always encouraging me to keep shrimping, and for simping with me over 2D characters. And a massive thank you is due to Susan Dennard, whose incredible writing advice has taught me so much over the last decade, and whose books have inspired me for just as long.

To all the amazing AO3 users who read my fics and pushed me to keep going, who made me feel like maybe I had a knack for this writing thing, thank you so much for your encouragement and for sharing my works with others. And thank you to Haruichi Furudate, who made me fall in love with volleyball and who led me to find the fun in writing again.

And to the incredible A Novel Romance community- you are the reason I'm getting to do this. You are the reason I'm starting off my author career stronger than I ever thought I could. Thank you so much for accepting me, for giving me the safe space that I needed, and for letting me sling books at you.

About the Author

Katie is a bookseller who loves all things romance. When she isn't writing or slinging books, she is definitely taking in copious amounts of fanfiction with an energy drink in hand. She lives in Kentucky with her husband and their hoard of pets.

www.ingramcontent.com/pod-product-compliance
Lightning Source LLC
Chambersburg PA
CBHW030244120726
47903CB00005B/1605